Heartless
MONSTER
USA TODAY BESTSELLING AUTHOR
RACHEL LEIGH

For the badass reader reading this.

"We stopped looking for the monsters under our bed once we realized they're inside of us."
-Charles Darwin

BLURB

A Dark and Sexy, Enemies-to-Lovers, Step-Sibling Romance from USA Today and International Bestselling Author, Rachel Leigh.

Rome Cromwell isn't just football royalty in our town. He's a heartless monster out for revenge, and I'm the ordinary girl with his target on her back.

One year ago my knight in shining armor stepped out of the fog and rescued me.
With a simple thank you and an "I owe you one", I was on my way.
Little did I know, that was only the start of our deranged story.
Now our parents are married and we're living under the same roof.
My new step-brother presents himself as a masked villain with strikingly good looks and a hypnotic appeal.
Girls want him.
His friends want to be him.
But I only want to run from him.
I see beneath his cracked facade into the heart of the beast.
Rome blames me for the fight that left his football career in shambles.
And he hasn't forgotten I'm in his debt.
Now his claws are digging in so deep, I fear I won't survive.
It's not long before I realize,
Rome no longer wants to save me.
He only wants to own me.
To break me.
Piece by piece by piece.

DEAR READERS

I'm so excited for you to read Heartless Monster. Rome and Elodie are chaotic, intense, and angsty AF. While their story is one of love, they face many obstacles, some more depraved than others. With that said, if you have any trigger warnings, you should know that this story has some dark elements, such as assault, kidnapping, bullying, and dubious consent. Your mental health matters, so please be mindful while reading.

I hope you enjoy Heartless Monster. I welcome you to share your spoiler-free thoughts in my Facebook Reader's Group, Rachel Leigh's Ramblers. If you share on social media at all, a tag would be appreciated so I can thank you!

xo Rachel

PLAYLIST
CLICK HERE TO LISTEN
https://spoti.fi/3ThJtbr

Nightmare by From Ashes to New
Darkside by Bring Me The Horizon
Jaded by Spiritbox
Vampire by Olivia Rodrigo
The Kill by Thirty Seconds to Mars
Unnecessary Violence by Nessa Barrett
Shimmer by Fuel
I love You by Billie Eilish
Dark Void by Asking Alexandria
Push by Matchbox Twenty
Take Me Back to Eden by Sleep Token
Last Resort-Reimagined by Falling in Reverse
Like A Villain by Bad Omens
Shame On Me by Catch Your Breath
This is How Villains are Made by Madalen Duke
Psycho by Asking Alexandria

CHECK OUT THE: PINTEREST BOARD
https://pin.it/4UQTaFDdz

PROLOGUE

ELODIE

My feet don't stop moving as I travel through the park in a town I've been in for less than twenty-four hours. It's dark and clouds cover the sky, preventing any light from shining through as I try to figure out where I am. The scent of rain still lingers in the air and I suppress a shiver.

It's hard enough to maintain my footing as I slip on the wet leaves beneath me. Branches overhead drip with leftover raindrops from the storm that just ended. Thunder is still in the distance, so I pick up my pace, glancing around to see if anything looks familiar. But no, it's just more fucking trees because my dumb ass thought taking a shortcut in a town I don't know, in the middle of the night, was a genius idea.

"You are such a moron, Elodie," I grumble under my breath, cursing myself for being so damn stupid.

I'm lost. Of course I am. Of course this would happen to me. To make matters worse, my cell service sucks in this damn town. At least I've got my flashlight on my phone to lead me toward the light coming from the lampposts ahead.

"Come with me, Elodie," I mock my sixteen-year-old sister. "It'll be so fun, Elodie."

Ugh! It was not fun. In fact, it was tortuous.

I stop walking, do a quick one-eighty, and when I'm back to facing the direction I was headed, I move again, this time faster.

Yep. I'm lost.

With no idea where I'm at or where I'm going, I raise my phone above my head, searching for a bar. But there's still nothing. Defeated, I let my hand fall to my side with a heavy sigh.

Going to that stupid party was the worst decision I've made all year. Who goes to a party full of people they don't know in a town they've never been to?

Me. That's who. Elodie Astor—book smart, but socially stupid.

In my defense, it was Brogan's grand idea. My sister is all-in when it comes to anything social. Bonus points if it involves boys. She begged me to go. Promised to stay by my side. Then, ditched me the second she caught the eye of some jock whose name she didn't even know.

Brogan and I are polar opposites. She's an extrovert by nature —cheerleader, life of the party. Whereas I'm more introverted— class president, honor society.

Although, I did get a small tattoo spontaneously when I was sixteen, and to me, that was pretty damn ballsy. I walked around feeling tough as nails for a week. I laugh about it now because it really wasn't that big of a deal.

Don't get me wrong, I'm not a total prude. There was a guy who piqued my interest tonight. He was a masterpiece in human form. His tousled, yet sexy, dark blond hair fell in front of his bright blue eyes. I could tell from his build he was athletic, even before he mentioned playing football. He was exactly the type of guy I avoided, yet for some reason, I wanted to stand there all night talking to him.

That is, until he stopped talking mid-sentence to make out with some girl who approached us. To make matters worse, she was a cute girl. The type of girl who brings all your own insecurities to the surface.

I'm not talking about a little peck on the lips, either. Those two were ripping into each other's mouths like they were sharing their favorite dessert. It was disgusting, and a little embarrassing to watch.

So, I stood there, tapping the toe of my sandal on the pavement beside the pool while fighting to avoid looking at them.

With his hand resting on her ass, he licked her spit from his lips and proceeded to finish telling me all about his record-breaking pass this season.

I am not the type of girl that sits back while assholes like him do whatever they want, so I just walked away. He got all puffy chested and told me I better not walk away from him when he's talking, so I spun around and stepped into him.

Other people might not stand up to that guy, but I'm not from here, so I never have to see him again, therefore consequences for my actions don't exist.

His eyes lit with a challenge and I happily accepted. The girl that was all over him decided to take a step back, giving me enough space to slowly back him up to the pool's edge. The second he reached for me, I put my knee to his balls and a light shove was all he needed to go falling backward into the pool.

For the brief moment he was under the water, people laughed, but as soon as he could hear them again, *crickets*. I ran out of that place faster than the speed of light.

Now I *do* have to pay the consequences, and it's all for going to that party in the first place.

The truth is, I love socializing for an hour or even two, but then I'm peopled out and ready to go home to climb back into my bubble.

My mom forced me and my two younger sisters to go on this four-hour road trip with her to the town she grew up in, because "it'll be a fun adventure and a great opportunity for me to bond with my girls." Her words, not mine. We're staying at a small hotel not far from the school and I have yet to spend any quality time with my mother and sisters since we arrived.

Mom's a sucker for nostalgia. She kept all her old cheerleader uniforms and let us try them on as kids growing up. I swear that woman would keep a gum wrapper if it was given to her by the right person. The day we arrived, she even had the grand idea of taking us to her old high school to show us around once classes let out for the day.

When we got to the school, my mother used the perfect opportunity to ask if they had a photography room just to see Lake's expression. It was only a couple days ago Lake got caught making out with a boy in the dark room at our high school. The principal called Mom and we've been teasing Lake about it ever since. Mom still treats my youngest sister like she's a baby. She's fifteen years old now. Of course she's kissing boys.

Two years younger than me and Lake's tongue has probably seen more action in a year than mine has my entire life.

I'll be the first to admit, I can be somewhat of a party pooper. I'm the girl who takes drinks from the hands of already drunk people. I cover my tests in class just to make sure no one is cheating off mine. I volunteer my free time at the children's hospital. I'm basically the child every parent dreams to have—except my own.

I can't pity myself too much. My parents are amazing. They've been divorced for over a year now, but they both still show up for me and my sisters when needed.

My dad is my biggest cheerleader and supporter. If it weren't for all the scholarships I've already accumulated, I know he'd financially support any career path I chose. And my mom's proud, too. She just has it in her head that I'm missing out on my youth and trying to grow up too fast.

Not to pat my own back, but my head is on completely straight. I know what I want in life and I refuse to let anything get in my way. My mom keeps telling me I need to start enjoying life more. Though, I don't think getting lost in a park at midnight is what she had in mind.

The lampposts ahead come into view and I sigh in relief, hopeful I can get back to where I started and figure out how to get home from there. I click the flashlight off on my phone to save my battery, all the while my heart hammers in my rib cage. An eerie feeling settles inside me, as if the darkness behind me holds secrets I know I don't want to hear.

When I finally make it out into the light, I find myself in a playground area. Passing by a row of swings, a chill runs down my spine when their chains begin to rattle and squeak as they get caught in a gust of wind. They sway back and forth, almost as if someone is sitting in them and forcing the movement.

When a tiny droplet hits my nose, I squint, looking up at the clouds in disbelief. In a matter of seconds, the sky opens up and rain pours down on me in heavy sheets. In my short time at Willow Creek, I've learned the weather has a mind of its own. One minute, the sun can be shining bright, and the next, we're under a downpour like now.

I throw my hands up in defeat, feeling the weight of the storm on my shoulders. "That all you got, universe?"

I've always appreciated nature and have a deep love for the rain, but I'm not exactly thrilled that it has to happen on a night when I'm walking alone in the dark in a place I've never been before.

I drop my hands and bring my face forward, my lashes attempt to flutter away the moisture. Blinking a few times, I make sure my eyes aren't deceiving me as shadows come into view in the distance. To my surprise, a group of three people enter the park, totally unbothered by the rain.

They're not far enough into the light, so it's hard to tell, but by the sounds of their voices, I'd say most, if not all, are guys.

As they stroll into a beam of light shining down from a lamp-post, I can see clearly that there are three guys, all of whom I'm certain were at the party. Their deep voices echo off the trees and playground equipment around me.

The last thing I want is an altercation with locals, so I make a quick decision and bolt underneath a slide to stay hidden. Rain pelts against the metal in a symphony of pins and clanks and I'm grateful because it masks the sound of my heavy breathing.

The group walks deeper into the park, stopping underneath a small gazebo right beside the slide. Every muscle in my body tenses. One wrong move and they'll find me.

As quick as the rain started, it suddenly stops, leaving a deafening silence that is broken when one of the guys raises his voice.

"Dude, there's no way in hell that girl was leaving the party with you. We're seniors, and she's a fucking sophomore."

"Shut the hell up. That girl would have dropped to her knees if you hadn't got us kicked out of the party."

I can't see their faces, so I have no idea who's talking, but one guy appears pissed while the other two find it humorous.

"She's not even from Willow Creek. Said she was just visiting for a couple days. Move on. You'll probably never see her again."

Sophomore? Not from Willow Creek? Could it be?

No. That's far too much of a coincidence. Then again, this town isn't huge.

"Even better." The guy scoffs. "She might be cool and down to have some fun. Unlike the stuck-up bitches that live in Willow Creek."

I've always been somewhat impetuous, but I've never considered myself to be a complete idiot…until now.

I jump out from under the slide, knocking my shoulder against the ledge. "Are you talking about Brogan?" I rub the ache in my arm, attempting to hide my nervousness.

I need to know if they're talking about my sister, and if they are, I need to know she's okay.

Three pairs of eyes fixate on me and suddenly, the trio isn't as gabby as they were before I came out of hiding. Their gazes are harsh, as if I'm butting into a conversation I have no right to be part of.

They continue to assess me, eyes plodding up and down my

body, and suddenly they seem much more interested as their expressions become sinister. When the taller guy with bright blond hair and piercing emerald eyes smirks, I know I'm in trouble. These are not boys to be messed with, and I'm alone, dangling myself in front of them like a piece of meat.

Blondie's tongue drags across his lower lip and I have to suppress a gag from the way he undresses me with his eyes.

"Well, well, well. Who do we have here?" The blond comes closer, his side brushing against mine as he circles me.

I feel three feet tall and helpless as I stand there, allowing them to drink up my presence. I have no idea who these guys are or what they're capable of. What I do know is that my fear will give them power if they see it.

Straightening my back, I steel my shoulders and lift my chin. "Who's the girl you were talking about?"

"Forget her," another guy chimes in, wearing the same sinister grin as his friend. This one has jet-black hair and eyes so dark I can barely see them. "You're here now. She's just a distant memory."

I cross my arms over my chest, eyes dancing from one guy to the next. "Tell me if the girl you were talking about is Brogan?"

They share a look, shrugging. The blond says, "Hell if I know her name. What I do know is she had sexy curves and big tits that popped out of her pink tee shirt."

Sounds like Brogan. In which case, I'm proud of her for not leaving with these guys. Also a bit surprised because she usually makes terrible decisions for herself.

The blond continues, "She also had a mouth on her." He nudges my shoulder with his. "One I wanted to come all over."

My insides twist in a mix of disgust and terror. I make no attempt to mask my disdain as I snarl at his response. "You're sick," I spit out. "I'd say my sister did herself a favor rejecting you."

A deep, guttural laugh escapes from his lips, sending chills down my spine. My instincts scream at me to run away as fast as I can.

"Sister, huh?" Mischief sparks in the blond's green eyes.

The shorter of the three, with red hair, pats his hand on the dark-haired guy's shoulder. "Come on, guys. Just leave her alone and let's get to the car."

"Fuck off, Miles!" Blondie snaps as he steps even closer to me. With the dark-haired guy at my side and this one in my face, I'm certain if I try to run, they'll snatch me up and keep me in place.

My pulse quickens and I force a smile on my face. "This was fun." I shoot a thumb over my shoulder. "But I really should go."

"You should have never been here in the first place." Blondie scoffs. "The residents of this town aren't too keen on outsiders snooping around."

"There was no snooping." I chuckle nervously. "I'm simply just passing through."

I go to step around him, but as suspected, my wrist is snared. I'm not certain by who, and I don't care. My first instinct is to jerk away, but I fail miserably. I attempt to twist it so that I have the advantage, but I'm too slow and he gains the upper hand.

"Let me go!" I growl, my voice thick with anger and frustration. In seconds, I'm surrounded as the sound of devilish laughter drowns everything out around me.

I shouldn't have tried to take a shortcut. I knew going through the park was a bad idea. But my laziness overpowered my shrewdness, and here I am. Captured by some wannabe thugs who will probably rape me and leave me for dead.

When he tries to pull me close, I shove at his chest, now able to see that it's the blond. "Keep your dirty-ass hands off of me, you disgusting son of a bitch. My sister was an idiot for even talking to your ugly ass."

My eyes go wide when I see him go from playful to downright evil in a split second. His grip on me tightens to the point of pain as he pulls me up against him with his two friends right at my back, leaving me no escape. I'm certain he can feel the thudding of my heart as he grinds his jaw.

His hot breath fans my ear as he whispers, "Your sister might have rejected me, but what she doesn't know is when I want something, I get it." He squeezes my wrist even tighter, causing me to bite my tongue in order to keep from crying out. "And right now, what I want is for you to get on your knees and say you're sorry for running that pretty little mouth of yours."

He's delusional if he really thinks I'm getting on my knees for him. I heard what he said about Brogan. He thinks all he needs to do is snap his fingers and girls will drop for him. I know damn well he's testing his limits right now. If I get on my knees, I've no doubt he'll force more than an apology out of me. I may be terrified of how he'll react when I say no, but I will put up a fight until my dying breath before giving in to him.

I might walk the straight and narrow—might even be considered a goody two-shoes, but what I'm not, is weak. And I'm certainly not a pushover.

I gnash my teeth together, allowing two simple words to spill out. "Fuck you."

My eyes narrow, challenging him. In the blink of an eye he has my hair in his fist as he jerks my head back, breaking my eye contact. "Is that an offer? Because I'll gladly accept."

"I wouldn't fuck you if you were the last man on earth." I try to pull on his grip but it's steadfast. I can see his friends getting a kick out of this from my new angle and I want nothing more than to put them all in their place.

"So cliché," he tsks. "I take you to be that type of girl. Probably come from a rich little family. Bet you drive an Audi. Captain of the cheer team and all that jazz."

"All that jazz?" I laugh glumly. "Sorry, *asshole*, but you're mistaking me for my sister. She drives the Audi."

"Of course she does." He chuckles, looking at his friends as if communicating a secret. "Just another family full of spoiled brats who will live off Mommy and Daddy's money for the rest of their lives."

"You don't know a thing about me or my family." I cock an eyebrow when he finally loosens his grip on my hair. "Don't act like you're any better. Pretty sure Willow Creek was built on rich soil. From what I gather, everyone in this town has money, so don't act like I'm the only one here who was fed with a silver spoon."

"Who said we were from Willow Creek?" Blondie looks at the dark-haired guy. "Damon, are you from Willow Creek?"

Damon shakes his head. "Definitely not, Winton. Thank fuck."

So the blond's name is Winton. At least I have some names to go with these faces. I'll know to walk away if I ever see them again. Not that I will.

Winton looks at the shorter guy. "Miles, are you from Willow Creek?"

Another name. Even better for when I report this.

Miles hesitantly shakes his head no.

I crane my neck in confusion. "Well, if you're not from here, why *are* you here?"

Damon laughs and the sound is harrowing. "This girl has no idea she tripped the line into unchartered territory." He tips his chin. "You're not in Willow Creek anymore, baby. This is Bulldog territory here, and we just kicked the Misfits' scrawny asses on the field tonight."

They start up a barking chant, and as much as I wish it didn't terrify me, it does. All the way down to the bones. These men aren't pretty rich boys who are used to getting their way. They are the scrappy ones who have fought for everything they have and take whatever they can get their hands on. And right now, that's me.

I have no idea who the Misfits are, but I can only assume it's Willow Creek's football team and these guys play for their rival team. And I'm the idiot who crossed the boundary into their town.

The two jerks laugh at my misfortune while their friend stands by idly. He might not be saying anything, but he's an accomplice to their asshole ways; therefore, he's just as guilty.

Winton breaks his grip on my hair and I try to pull away from his hand, but his fingers dig in deeper and I know I'll bruise from this. "Just let me the fuck go so I can get out of this town and never come back."

"Not so fast," Winton growls. "We're not finished with you yet. I want that apology."

I snicker, going lax in his grip so maybe he loosens his hold. "Over my dead fucking body."

His tongue clicks on the roof of his mouth. "That can be arranged." He grabs the V-neck of my dress, his rough hands scraping against my skin while Damon grabs my wrists and pins them behind me. In a swift motion, he tears it in a jagged line, exposing my bare skin from my chest to my waist. Terror grips me as I realize his intentions.

I panic, trying to pull away, my nails digging into his skin as I try to fight them off. But there's nothing I can do. Damon struggles to keep hold of me. When I break from his grip, Winton's hand shoots out, going around my neck in a threat.

"Please don't do this," I try not to let my voice shake, but who am I kidding, I'm terrified and even I know there's no way out now.

"Oh, we're doing this," he chuckles dryly.

"And if you tell anyone," Winton whispers in my ear, a firm hold on my throat while Damon secures my arms again, "you'll live to regret it."

My heart jumps into my throat and the sound of laughter coming from the two of them will forever be ingrained in my memory.

This is it. This is where I get raped and left for dead.

I squeeze my eyes shut, trying to block out the reality around me. A chill runs down my spine and when I feel cold fingers trailing down my bare chest, I force myself to watch. I might be scared, but I plan to fight every second I get. And I can't do that with my eyes closed.

"She's fucking stacked." Winton bites the corner of his lip as he pushes my dress off my shoulders. "I might just fuck these titties and let you guys have the rest."

He drags his fingers upward, peeling up the cup of my bra just to pinch my nipple. I want to cry out, but I refuse to give him anything right now.

I'm frozen, unable to move or make a sound. I'm not even sure if I'm still breathing and at this point, I don't care. To be honest, I'd rather die than face what's in store for me.

"Get on your knees," Winton says, his voice laced with intent. "Lemme slip my dick between those perky breasts."

"Winton, careful." Damon lets go of me. "We could lose a lot for this. Is she really worth it?"

Winton shoves him. "If you don't want in, then stand back with Miles."

I try to turn so I can run but his rough hands grasp my shoulders as he forces me down. My knees buckle under his strength. The damp ground feels cold, dirt clinging to my knees and digging into my skin as I accept my fate. My whole body shakes as Winton fists my hair, yanking me closer while unzipping his pants.

Tears burn the backs of my eyes as I fight to keep some of my dignity. I breathe in through my nose as I clench my jaw shut. If he wants this, he's going to have to fight for it.

"Oh, don't do that, little rabbit." His fingers pinch my jaw forcefully, causing me to open my mouth slightly. He bends in front of me, shoving two fingers between my lips until they hit my gag reflex. This time, I don't fight the tears.

"That's better." Keeping two fingers in my mouth, he stands. "Now keep those teeth away from me and we won't have problems. But if you keep fighting me, I'll knock you the fuck out and do whatever I want with that tight little body of yours."

"Winton," Damon chides. For a brief second I allow myself to hope maybe this won't happen. That's easily squashed when Winton's free hand pets my hair and his eyes dance as if this is just a game. A game he is used to winning.

Winton glares at his friend. "Try to stop me, Damon. See what happens to that leg you need to play running back."

Damon raises his hands, the threat clear.

Bile rises in my throat as I relax my jaw and all hope fades. I have no choice in the matter. I could just bite his dick off, but he has the advantage of being above me.

I begin to hyperventilate as Winton takes a step forward and I think maybe I will just pass out so I don't have to remember any of this.

"Let her go!" The sound of a gravelly voice pierces through the chaos, causing my eyes to shoot wide open.

I cry out in relief and when the guys' attention is stolen and I jump to my feet, ready to flee. Suddenly, Winton grabs my arm before I'm able to run. My dress falls down even farther and I actually sniffle when I realize this guy is all alone.

"I said, let her go," the newcomer repeats himself, this time his voice even thicker, more domineering.

It's hard to see who he is, but he just might be my knight in shining armor. He's wearing a hoodie that's flipped over his downcast head, offering only a shadow of his face. Pushing the sleeves of his hoodie up, I catch sight of a broken pipe in his right hand. The veins in his forearms protrude as he taps the bar to his palm in a slow and threatening motion.

This can't end well. I might be selfish in my way of thinking, but I don't care who gets hurt here, so long as it's not me.

"Get lost before you get your ass kicked," Winton warns.

The newcomer takes two steps forward, his identity still a mystery, though I doubt I'd know him even if I saw his face.

"The only ones who will be getting their asses kicked are the three of you if you don't let the girl go."

"You brought a fucking weapon." Winton actually sounds afraid for the first time tonight. "Hardly seems fair."

"Three on one isn't fair either." The newcomer growls. "Let her go or your face will be meeting this metal pipe."

Suddenly, my wrist is freed. I jump to the left, putting some space between myself and the Neanderthals. I pivot around to face the mystery guy, wanting to run toward him and thank him for saving me. But he isn't done with these guys.

He stands tall, probably six foot, shoulders taut, and there is something oddly familiar about him. "Get the hell outta here."

"I…I don't know where to go," I tell him honestly, pulling the split fabric of my dress together to hide myself.

"Just go back the fucking way you came," he barks.

I turn around, and around, and around. Unsure of which way I came. I'm so fucking screwed right now.

Somewhere between me getting lost in my thoughts to me snapping out of them, the assholes have all huddled around the new guy, exchanging malicious words and threats.

Without warning, the new guy swings the pipe and it meets the back of Winton's skull. The sickening crunch of bones colliding with metal echoes through the air and my stomach lurches.

I gasp at the sight, my hands flying to my mouth. Taking a few small steps backward, I know I need to get out of here. But I'm frozen solid, watching as the new guy tosses down the pipe and barrels toward Winton. He doesn't slow down as he takes him straight to the ground.

The new guy lifts his head, hands wrapped around Blondie's throat, and for a brief moment, I catch a glimpse of his icy blue eyes.

"Go! Now!" I jolt at the sound of his voice, shaken to my core.

I nod repeatedly, feeling like all the air has been forced out of my lungs. "I owe you one," I whisper with bated breath.

I move quickly through the park, passing by familiar scenery, and before long, I'm positive I'm heading in the direction I came.

I'm not sure what would have happened to me if that guy didn't show up tonight. I can't even fathom what those assholes would have done to me.

Unfortunately, I'll never be able to repay him. I'm out of here in a couple days and I'll never see him again.

There is one thing I can do to help him, though. I reach into the small pocket of my ripped dress and pull out my phone. I've always heard I don't need service to make an emergency call, and it's time to test that theory.

My fingers shake uncontrollably as I tap out 911 on the keypad. With the phone pressed to my ear, I steal multiple nervous glances over my shoulder.

When it rings, I feel immediate relief.

A dispatcher comes on the line and I tell her that there is a guy getting assaulted by three males in the park outside of Willow Creek, and the names I got—Winton, Damon, and Miles.

I opt out of sharing my information or requesting a callback because the last thing I want is my name tied to this call. She assures me a trooper is on the way and I hang up, thankful he'll have backup soon.

I suppose not all knights in shining armor ride in on horses.

Some show up as a psychotic misfit cloaked in black with no name.

At least, that's how mine presented himself.

CHAPTER 1

ELODIE

One Year Later

"Why is he staring at me like that?" I whisper to Brogan, who's standing to my right. I glance between Rome, my soon-to-be stepbrother, and the slew of guests seated in front of us. My fingers grip tightly to the fresh bouquet I'm holding, the stems slick with my nervous sweat.

"I don't know," Brogan responds quietly. "It's sort of creepy though."

For someone who once hit on me, he sure does have daggers for me now. I shouldn't be too surprised considering I pushed him in a pool in front of all his classmates. I haven't seen or talked to Rome since that party last year. Until yesterday, that is.

Imagine my surprise when my mother introduced me to the boys who will be my new stepbrothers, and I realized I actually crushed on one of them for a nanosecond.

I haven't told anyone about what happened after that party when I got lost. No one knows what those three guys did to me because the threat Winton made still lingers in my mind. He said I'd live to regret it if I told anyone. I've never been a gambler, and when it comes to my future, I don't take chances. The second I heard we were moving to Willow Creek, I knew I had to keep a tight lid on it.

That night changed me. The dark of the night is no longer my friend, and my trust in people is almost nonexistent.

Lake steals a glance at Rome, now noticing the scathing glare he's pinned me with. "Maybe it's the dress. You do look stunning in it." Her eyebrow arches. "I take that back. That's definitely not a flirtatious stare. He looks like he wants to kill you."

"He doesn't want to kill her," Brogan retorts. "He's probably just upset about the wedding, much like we all are."

"I'm not upset," Lake says. "Mom seems happy and that makes me happy."

"Oh, you youthful little thing," Brogan teases. "You have so much to learn."

"Guys," I stammer. "He's still staring at me." I turn slightly to my right, throwing off the whole formation of our row as we wait for our mom to walk down the aisle. I glance slightly over my shoulder, and sure as shit, he's still looking at me. He must really take rejection hard because I blew him off that night once he started making out with some chick. Sure, I might have made a scene and pushed him in the pool, but it's been an entire year. "What the hell is his deal?"

"Elodie!" Lake spits. "You can't say hell in a church."

"You just said hell," Brogan teases.

Lake's shoulders slump. "Great. Now we've all said hell."

"Hello," I interrupt with a huff. "Psycho to the left. Still staring."

"Maybe there's more to it," Brogan says. "His brothers seem pretty chill right now. Maybe Rome is having a harder time than they are with this arrangement. That doesn't make him crazy."

"Yeah." I wince. "Maybe you're right. But it's weird. I can't believe Mom's doing this to us. Why him? Why *them*?"

We literally met our future stepdad, Grant, and his sons yesterday—the day we moved into their house. Now here I am, standing in a church full of strangers, wearing an aqua satin dress—Mom's favorite color—holding a bouquet of white lilies while waiting for my mom and Grant to get married.

Mom said the timing of everything was due to the school year beginning next week and she didn't want us to transfer mid-semester. Apparently Grant was her high school sweetheart when she attended Willow Creek High, and after graduation, they went their separate ways and lost touch. My sisters and I had no idea Mom was even seeing him, and I'm certain Grant's sons weren't aware of him dating either. The least they could have done is slowly ease us into the situation, but nonetheless, here we are.

Next week Mom begins her new job as the district attorney for the county. Before Lake was born, my mom was a high-profile attorney and her excitement for being back in a courtroom is enough for anyone to cheer on her dreams.

Up until my parents' divorce, Mom had the cushion of my dad's money at her fingertips. I don't fault her for wanting her independence, but I don't see the reasoning for her rushing into marriage again.

The entire situation blows my mind. It's not normal—*we're* no longer normal. Growing up, we were always the family that had it all together. Now we've become people I don't even recognize.

Mom is about to become Celia Cromwell. Just thinking about her name change makes me want to vomit. No one has stopped to think about how this affects me and my sisters—or even the Cromwell boys. It's only been a year and a half since they lost their mom, and their dad is already marrying someone new—someone they don't even know.

Fortunately, I still have both my parents, even if I don't see my dad as often as I'd like. He's now six hours away. If we're lucky, we'll get to see him on holidays. That's assuming he's not traveling the world with his new girlfriend.

My parents have a very odd relationship. They're divorced, yet somehow they managed to remain friends. I'm pretty sure it's all a show for us girls, but he was still invited to the wedding, nonetheless. Dad said he couldn't make it because he'd be in Maui for the weekend, but I'm almost positive Daria, the new girlfriend, talked him out of coming. She's probably the one who booked the vacation—with his money, of course.

I met Daria once, and I don't like her. She's flashy and loud and says things like *oh, doll*, and *that sounds marvelous*. Everything that comes out of her mouth is followed by a squeaky cackle. Then again, she's only twenty-four, so my expectations for her maturity level aren't very high.

"They're laughing at us," Lake whispers, her eyes downcast.

"Who?" I seethe, but I don't even have to ask. I can see exactly who she's talking about. The Cromwell boys—Rome and his fraternal twin brother, Wilder, along with Callan, who is Brogan's age, and Sayer who's only fourteen. Sayer doesn't seem to be partaking in their antics, but I've got my eyes on him, too. From what I can see, all those boys are going to be trouble.

It doesn't help that they're all good-looking. Scratch that, they're the epitome of perfection on the outside, but by the way they're acting right now, I'm beginning to think they have hearts of stone.

I narrow my gaze at Rome, making him aware that I know he's over there cracking jokes about us. I've never been very good at sweeping things under the rug. I hold grudges tighter than I'm holding this bouquet, and that says a lot, considering I just snapped two of the stems in half.

The instrumental wedding march begins and I peel my eyes off him, knowing he's still watching me. I'm not a bit surprised Mom chose this music to walk down the aisle. She's always been very traditional. From our sit-down dinners as a family to doing chores, even when we had a housekeeper to do them for us.

Family togetherness is important, as is not having children that grow up to be entitled adults.

I really can't complain about my childhood. I had a good

upbringing with parents who love me. It's the present that's raging an inferno of anger inside me.

As upset as I am, I'll admit, Mom is a vision of perfection in her ivory wedding gown. Her flared dress is simple but elegant with off-the-shoulder straps and a dipped V at the front. She's stunning as she glides down the aisle gracefully.

As she reaches the arch where her groom is standing, her gaze flickers from me to my sisters, and her eyes light up. I'm not thrilled about what's taking place, but ready or not, this is happening, and I will support her in any way I can.

After Mom and Grant share their vows, and their first kiss, I look back at Rome, catching his stare again. I hold tight to it, challenging him.

I want my mom and my sisters to be happy, but I refuse to let it be at the expense of my own happiness.

You wanna start some shit, Rome Cromwell? Bring it on. I showed you who I was once before, I'll happily do it again.

CHAPTER 2
ELODIE

One Week Later

"Unbelievable," I grumble as Brogan and I step into the foyer and are immediately hit with the sound of *the boys* hollering from the family room downstairs.

The boys being my new stepbrothers, along with their idiot friends, whose names I don't know because I really don't care. Okay, I would know their names if I saw their faces because Willow Creek isn't exactly huge, but I don't know them by the sound of their loud backchat. If I had to guess, it's probably Aiden and Luke. They're the two friends I see at the house most often.

"Get used to it, girl," Brogan chirps. "This *is* our life now."

"Ugh. Don't remind me." I rub my temples aggressively, making my way to the kitchen.

"Stop stressing so much. New brothers means new brothers' friends, and I'd gladly stare at one friend in particular all day, every day."

"Stop calling them our brothers. It literally makes me sick. As for their friends, don't," I stammer, "just...don't."

"Whaaat?" Brogan drags out the word, pouting like she's

innocent. "Wilder and Rome's friends are fucking hot. Don't even pretend you haven't noticed."

It's true. A couple of them are easy on the eyes, but they're exactly like Rome, and Rome is the worst of the worst. One week of living with him and my world has already flipped upside down.

I steal a glance at Brogan as we walk in the kitchen, immediately noticing the way she's staring off in la-la land while biting the corner of her lip.

My head shakes in disapproval, needing to make myself perfectly clear. "Some of those guys might be hot, but they all sit right below Rome on the asshole ladder."

"Maybe I wanna sit right below one of them on that ladder, because then I'd be looking right up at the sexy asshole... literally."

"Brogan!" I smack her shoulder playfully. "They're all cold-hearted jocks, just like Rome."

She laughs. "You're such a drama queen."

"Am not," I huff defensively, now leaning against the kitchen counter. "It's just...you're my little sister, Bro, and I don't want you to get your heart broken."

The sound of the guys' masculine voices ring louder now that they're directly below us. This is a three-story house with eight bedrooms and five bathrooms. We should not be able to hear them.

Brogan's eyebrows furrow as she locks eyes with me, her lips pressed tightly together. She sees the anger radiating from me. I can't stand being in this house, surrounded by those boys—Rome in particular.

"Lighten up, El. Mayhem is to be expected when high school boys are involved."

"They're just so damn immature. And Rome has been awful to me. You've seen it." She just doesn't know the extent of it.

"I have. But I also notice that you haven't really given him a chance to be anything but awful. You're constantly on the defensive. This isn't easy for any of us, but we all have to make the best of it. You included." Turning away from me, she grabs two bottles of water out of the fridge, passing me one.

She's probably right. Brogan is always so positive and happy. Lately I've been even more of a downer than normal. I don't like change. I had my entire life planned out less than a year ago, and moving to Willow Creek was not part of that plan.

"Well, I have to study tonight," I tell her. "And if they think I'm going to listen to their antics all night, they're in for a rude awakening."

"Study?" Brogan chuckles before sipping her water. "Elodie. Tomorrow is the first day of the school year. What in God's name do you have to study for?"

I'm not surprised that she's surprised. Brogan doesn't understand me. No one does.

"Advancing my studies is a beneficial approach to starting off the school year. To put it simply, I like to be one step ahead."

Brogan shakes her head as a bout of laughter climbs up her throat. "You really are a visitor from another planet."

The sudden thudding coming from the basement has my eyebrows caving in and I find myself clenching the bottle of water so tightly, I'm surprised the top hasn't popped off. "How are you not pissed about all of this? Do you hear them?" I pound my foot on the floor, hoping they'll hear my frustration. "Shut up, down there!"

Brogan puts a hand on my shoulder and I inhale deeply, calming myself down as I untwist the top of my water. "Keep the beast inside, Elodie. Do not let it out."

I like to think I do a good job at remaining calm in stressful situations, but ever since our mom told us she was marrying Grant, my anger has gotten the best of me.

I shake her hand off my shoulder, my mind flashing back to the day my life was flipped upside down.

Mom took my sisters and I shopping for the entire day. We had the time of our lives buying anything our hearts desired.

Then, at the end of the day, she brought us to a quiet restaurant —which I now know was because she knew we wouldn't make a scene, or so she thought. Her exact words were, "I met up with an old *friend* on our trip to Willow Creek last year and we've been dating. We're getting married...soon."

The beast Brogan speaks of was unleashed in that elegant restaurant. I sprang to my feet so fast I knocked over my chair, sending it crashing into the table behind us, which spilled the drinks of its occupants. If that wasn't enough, I yelled at my mom and swore I would never forgive her if she married Grant.

I have—forgiven her, that is. But I'm still furious about the entire situation. We had a life in Bakersfield. My sisters and I have never lived elsewhere. My best friend, Maggie, is there. Not to mention, my boyfriend of eight months, who I'm pretty sure dumped me because "long distance relationships aren't really his thing."

Ever since that day last year where I found myself on my knees in the dark at the hands of a monster, I hate when others take any of my control away, and my mother took every bit of it away when she forced us to move in with this family.

"Ahhh," Rome gushes mockingly as he walks into the kitchen. His hands over his heart and a smirk on his face. "I thought I heard voices up here. If it isn't my delightful little sister...and you." His eyes shoot to mine. "I thought maybe that was you stomping on the floor. Always making your presence known, aren't you, Elodie?"

My gaze flicks upward, my body temperature rising as I gulp down the water and try to refrain from throwing my drink at him. "Please give me a warning before you enter the room I'm in, Rome. I'll be sure not to take a drink of water at the risk of choking on it when I see your face."

"I can't help it," Rome sings as he purposely bumps my side, making his way to the refrigerator. "I guess my face just has that effect on the ladies." He snares a half-gallon of chocolate milk and squeezes the top, opening the carton. "Besides, it really wouldn't break my heart if you did choke to death."

I cringe at the sight of him drinking straight from the jug. "You're disgusting."

His tongue drags across his lower lip, licking up the excess milk, and my stomach curls.

Brogan claps her hands together as if this is amusing in some way. "Oh, brotherly love at its best."

"Don't call him that," I snap at her. "Rome is *not* our brother. Neither are Wilder and Callan. Sayer, I'll claim because he's sweet." I sneer at Rome, making sure he's paying close attention as I say, "The rest of them are *nothing* to us."

"Geez, El," Brogan gripes. "I was kidding. Calm down." With her water in hand, she flips her long dark blonde hair over her shoulder and walks out of the kitchen, leaving me alone with Rome.

It's no secret Rome and I don't get along. Ever since we've moved into *his* house, he's been a thorn in my side. He hasn't even given me a chance; therefore, he doesn't get one either. For some reason, his wrath is all aimed at me while Brogan and Lake get a different side of him. It's like he can't move past that moment when I shoved him in the pool thinking I'd never see him again.

There's always a cocky remark to everything I do or say, and when I ask him what his problem with me is, he either ends the conversation or says I'm his problem. I can only assume he's pissed I didn't give him what he wanted at the party, or he's upset about our parents getting married and us all moving into the home he's lived in since he was born. I'm just not sure why I'm to blame for any of that. I don't like this situation any more than he does.

When I look at him and see him standing there, watching me like he's waiting for me to say something just so he can respond with cruelty, I plant my hands on my hips and stare back at him. "You can go now."

"Actually." He pushes himself up on the center island, making himself comfortable as he takes a seat. "This is my kitchen. You may go. After all, that's all you're good for, isn't it? Running away."

I shake my head in slow subtle motions while all the blood in my body rushes to my head. "I'm not going anywhere. So get used to it."

"That's a shame," he grumbles under his breath. But I hear him. I hear every damn sound he makes.

Keep your eye on the future, Elodie. This is just a phase that will pass. This time next year, you'll be pre-law at Stanford University and nowhere near this new family Mom has thrown us into.

Rome snatches an apple from the fruit basket beside him and digs his front teeth into it. Chewing, he watches me. "I must know," he begins, pointing his bitten apple at me. "Do you make it a habit to go out wearing just a bra and underwear, Freckles?"

Rage rushes through me, ready to burst through my veins. Not at the nickname. It's not original at all, and he's not the first person to call me that due to the freckles on my nose. It's his offensive words that piss me off.

I inhale deeply, roll my lips together, and plaster a fake smile on my face as I reach around him on the counter. The granite feels nice and cold against my chest after the intense workout Brogan and I just did at the gym. With my hand in the basket, I look up at him.

"I'm sorry, does my outfit offend you?" I pull out a banana and straighten my back, glowering at him as I peel back the skin. Sinking my teeth into it, I put emphasis on my mouth that his eyes are now watching.

"Not the least bit." He jumps down in front of me and leans close, his breath a whisper in my ear. "If it's a slutty look you were going for, I'd say you nailed it. Tell your nipples I said hello."

He pushes the fruit into my mouth until I nearly choke, but I'm not showing him a sign of weakness. The entire banana fills my mouth until I bite it from the peel, chewing and swallowing while his eyes never leave my lips.

"You've got something," he says, lifting a hand to my cheek, "right here."

He swipes at my lips and we both still for a moment, frozen under each other's gaze. Then he tries to force his fingers into my mouth and I push him back. He laughs as he turns away, clearly having gotten the reaction he was hoping for.

I fight back the memories of another man doing the same thing to me without my consent. My hands tremble as Rome walks away, having no idea what he did.

"Ugh," I growl, chucking the banana peel at his back as he walks out of the kitchen. "I hate you, Rome Cromwell!"

By the sound of his thudding feet on the stairs, I assume he's already going back down with the guys, but I still hear him loud and clear as he shouts back, "Hate you more, Freckles."

CHAPTER 3

ROME

"Hurry your ass up." I pound my fist on the bathroom door, annoyed as fuck right now.

The fact that I'm now sharing a bathroom with Wilder is proof they shouldn't be here. None of this was supposed to happen.

After Mom passed away, Dad swore he had no intention of ever getting married again. I suppose when he said it, he probably didn't. I understand that he has to continue to live his life, but did it really have to be her? My new stepmother comes with baggage that doesn't mesh with ours.

The two younger ones are decent. Brogan is a grade younger than Wilder and me—and Elodie. She seems pretty chill and down for a good time. She's on the varsity cheer team and seems to fit in well with all the other uppity, bubbly cheerleaders. She's the only one of the Astor girls with blonde hair, but they've all got the same matching green eyes.

Lake is a sophomore who prefers to hang out in the dark room my dad had set up for her in one of the storage closets in the basement. She's got the darkest hair of the three—it's almost black—with a streak of purple in the front. She's always got a camera in her hand and more times than not, she's got artwork scribbled on her arms. She's sort of weird, but I don't give her too much shit.

Elodie, though—she's insufferable. Being under this roof with her for the last week has been agonizing. It feels like the walls are slowly closing in and she's the one pushing them, so I push back at her.

The second my dad introduced us to these girls, life as I knew it was over. I couldn't believe my eyes when I saw Elodie. Of all the people in this fucking world, why the hell did my dad have to marry *her* mom?

I knock harder on the door, trying to overpower the sound of running water and Wilder singing "The Kill" by 30 Seconds to Mars at the top of his lungs.

Growing even more impatient, I shout, "Hey! I need in there." I turn the doorknob, and I'm not surprised it's locked, but that doesn't stop me from shaking it while pounding my fist on the door. "I'm gonna be late for school, moron. Let me in so I can brush my damn teeth and take a piss!"

We have five fucking bathrooms in this house. It shouldn't be this hard to take a piss before school.

"You're welcome to use mine and Brogan's bathroom if you need to." The voice comes from behind me, and I spin around to see Lake.

"No, he can't. Brogan is in there," I hear Elodie holler from down the hall. *See. Insufferable.*

"Thanks, Lake. But Wilder should be just about finished." I clench my jaw, trying not to snap at her just because Elodie decided to speak.

She shrugs. "Suit yourself." I watch as she walks down the hall toward the stairs, only for Elodie to step out in her shadow.

The sunlight streaming from the balcony doors at the end of the hall highlights the small freckles dotted on her nose. Her long brunette hair clings to the towel wrapped around her body, leaving wet patches from the dripping water.

I narrow my gaze as she crosses her arms over her chest and

leans into the doorframe, scrunching her wet hair with a towel—my towel.

I set my jaw and growl, "Enjoying *my* bathroom?"

Her hand drops, still holding the towel. "Very much so. However, it has this weird smell to it. Like someone tried to hide the smell of piss and ass with Tom Ford cologne." Her mouth tugs up in a grin and I wanna rip her fucking lips off. "But don't worry, I'll have it smelling like roses in no time."

She tosses the towel at me, hitting me in the fucking face. I despairingly shake my head as all the blood rushes to my cheeks. "Bitch," I mutter under my breath as she turns up her nose and goes back into her room.

I bring the towel closer to my face and I draw in an extra deep breath. She smells far too sweet for a girl so evil. There was a minute where I was attracted to her last year, but that was quickly squashed when she decided to embarrass me in front of the entire school. Not that anyone said anything, they wouldn't dare. But I think Elodie needs to be made an example of for what happens when you mess with Rome Cromwell.

Celia, my new stepmom, pokes her head up the stairs and I immediately drop the damp towel to the floor.

"Everything okay up here?" Celia asks, her tone soft and motherly-like. "I heard shouting and banging."

If I wasn't already pissed, I am now. Dad doesn't even come up here. This is our lair—mine and my brothers'. What the hell is up with these women thinking they can tread on our territory?

I roll my lips together, thankful as fuck when the bathroom door flies open. A waft of steam rolls out and it's taking everything in me not to grab Wilder by the throat and toss him into the hall. But I need to get the hell away from my new stepmother before she sees the monster unleash inside me.

"Ask your oldest daughter," I tell her, before walking into the fogged-up bathroom. I kick the door closed, even though Wilder is still inside.

"Seriously, man?" I huff. "Get the fuck out so I can get ready for school."

He's standing over the sink, his toothbrush hanging from his mouth while foam forms around his lips as he speaks.

"Chill out. It's the first day. Just pretend you don't know where you're going."

"We're seniors, dipshit. Everyone knows we have been in that school for three years. Of course I know where I'm going."

My eyes travel to his phone perched on a tissue box. "Seriously," I huff. "Is this what's taking you so damn long? You're making a fucking social media video of you brushing your damn teeth?" I grab his phone and end the recording, then shove it to his chest. "Out! Now!"

Wilder is one of those guys who can make a video of just about anything as long as he's in it, and the girls will follow. And he does. He records himself doing the dumbest shit and posts it on SnapTok for his *followers.* I'm beginning to think he's obsessed. Though he would say it's because it makes his followers happy.

"Jesus," Wilder mumbles. "Ever since you got cut from the team, you've been a real asshole."

He rinses his toothbrush and drops it in the holder before grabbing a towel hanging on the wall. Hastily, he wipes his mouth then carelessly tosses it back in place before opening the door with his phone in his hand.

I, being the helpful brother I am, assist him with exiting by shoving him out. "I wasn't fucking cut!" I slam the door closed, my entire body trembling with rage.

My hands press to the cold marble vanity and I drop my head, eyes pinched shut while I try to breathe.

This time last year, I had it all. The world was sitting in the palm of my hand. I was the starting quarterback on the varsity team, holding the record in the state for the most passes in a single season. I was getting offers from schools all over the country, while waiting for one in particular.

That offer finally came, and within a week, I had signed the contract. Six weeks later, it was rescinded. I lost everything because of one fucking night. One night. One bad choice, and just like that, it was gone.

I wasn't cut from the football team, but I was benched for half the season, and there's only one person to blame—Elodie Astor.

"You going to practice tonight?" one of my two closest friends, Aiden, asks as he claps a hand on my shoulder.

I reach into my backpack and pull out my Chromebook before tossing my bag inside my locker. "Yeah, I'll be there."

I might not be starting the season on the field, but I'm not giving up just yet. This is my team, and that's my turf.

"Sweet." He drops his hand and leans his back against the locker beside mine. "So, how are the new sisters?"

My eyes roll, palms immediately producing sweat as I close my locker. "It's tortuous, man. I don't know how you do it with three girls in your house, but I'm barely surviving in mine."

"It's a big change. Give it time. Things will get easier." He shrugs like my father marrying someone so fast and flipping my world upside down is just a normal day.

My head rolls, cracking the tension in my neck. "If one more person tells me to give it more time, I'm gonna fucking snap."

"Speak of the devils," Aiden says, and I follow his gaze to see Brogan and Elodie coming down the hall toward us. Their eyes dance from the papers in their hands to the row of lockers.

Brogan says something, which I assume is her saying she's found her locker because she smiles briefly at Elodie and goes to the junior rows across from ours.

Elodie keeps on coming toward us and each step has my heart thumping faster and faster.

No. No. No. Keep walking. Don't you dare come near us.

But the universe is not on my side when she stops directly in front of Aiden. Her eyebrows lift to her forehead and she pretends I'm not even standing there as she speaks to him.

"I'm sorry, but I think that's my locker behind you." Her voice drips with sentimental charm. Elodie wants everyone to adore her, but I see through the charade. Her eyes are cold and calculating, betraying the true nature behind her innocent act.

Aiden waggles his brows before stepping aside. "Have at it, baby."

She smiles at him and the idiot can't tell it's fake.

My eyes snap to Aiden's, warning him not to fall for her honeyed games. There's no way in hell I'm letting this bitch play my best friend with that fake smile and those fluttering lashes.

"Demand a switch," I tell her, tone forthright.

Finally, she acknowledges that I'm standing right fucking here.

"Excuse me?"

"You heard me. Demand a switch. I already have to see your face every day in my house. I refuse to look at it between every fucking class."

"Then don't look." She flashes me a cocksure grin. "Pretend I'm not here, just like I plan to do with you."

I clench my hands as I watch her put in the combination to open the door. "No! It's not good enough." My fist slams into her locker. "I need you out of my fucking sight, Elodie."

She's a constant reminder of everything that went wrong in my life. Not to mention, she moved into my house like it was always hers to begin with. There's no respect. No boundaries. She does whatever the hell she wants and she gets away with it even when I threaten her.

Not this time. Not with *me*. She might not believe I'll follow through with my warnings, but she is toeing a dangerous line today.

Whether she knows it or not, Elodie is about to meet the heartless monster that lives inside me. And I have no plans on holding him back from taking exactly what he wants.

"How about you switch?" She chuckles sarcastically as she twists the last of the combination. "I'm not going anywhere."

As soon as the locker door pops open, I plant my open palm on it and push it closed.

Chin down, I glower at her, waiting for her reaction.

"What are you doing?" she asks, playing dumb.

"Yeah, man, what point are you trying to make here?" Aiden asks. When I meet his gaze, he slinks into the background.

I keep my hand in place as she twists out the combination again, but when she tries to pull the door open, I hold firm, keeping it closed.

"Rome!" She scoffs. "Let me in my locker!"

"I don't want you here," I tell her truthfully. One thing I've noticed about Elodie in the past few days is she hates when someone else makes a decision for her. She wants control at all times, and I plan to slowly strip that from her until she feels as much pain as I have over the past year.

Her hand drops from the lock and she turns to face me, causing my chest to flutter.

"And I don't want to be here. But you know what? I am! I'm stuck here, Rome. So can we please try and make the best of it?" Her eyes plead with mine, but it's too late. I lost all urge to protect her a year ago.

Aiden points a finger back and forth between the two of us. "Are you two still talking about the locker, because I get the feeling there's something more to this."

"Yes!" I blurt out at the same time as she says, "No!"

"I'm not moving my locker." Elodie sighs, as if I am the one causing her trouble in this situation and not the other way around. "I'm done trying to accommodate everyone else." She looks at Aiden as if he's her friend, on her side. "I'll try again later when Rome isn't behaving like such a child."

She pulls her messenger bag tighter to her shoulder and spins around, walking away.

"What the hell, dude?" I huff, shoving him. "Why are you being so nice to her?"

Aiden lifts his shoulder, eyes wide. "She seems pretty chill. And you're acting like this is all her fault when we both know the person you should really be pissed at is yourself, or your dad."

"That's what she wants you to think. She's not *chill*. She's the reason my life has gone to shit." Aiden doesn't know the truth about that night, and I have no plans to tell him. Now that the girl who destroyed me is living in Willow Creek—in my house— I plan to use it to my advantage, but I need to get some of this aggression out before I explode.

"Eh," Aiden tsks. "You are sort of behaving like a child. Just suck it up and get through the school year."

My teeth grind out a harrowing sound, cutting him off as I punch my fist to her locker door.

Pain shoots from my knuckles up to my forearm. I shake my hand, forcing away the sensation as I grit out, "You're either on my side or hers, but you don't get to be on both."

With that, I walk away, nursing my sore hand. I don't know what I'm going to do with Elodie Astor, but one way or another, she's going to feel the same pain I've lived with for the past twelve months.

Even if it breaks her.

CHAPTER 4
ELODIE

I was feeling pretty good about my schedule, up until this point. I slid through my first couple classes without having a single one with Rome, but now every time the bell rings, there he is. Walking through the doors with his boy gang of football players, laughing his ass off without a care in the world.

Why would he be anything but happy? This is the school he attended his whole life. These are his classmates. This is his town. His team.

So why am I so bitter about his joy?

I'll tell you why…

I've been carrying around a bag full of books at my new school all day because Rome guards his locker—and mine—during the five-minute break between classes. I've avoided confrontation and just walked right past him like it didn't bother me one bit. Kill him with kindness, right?

I mean, who the hell does this guy think he is bullying me like this? There is no reason, that I know of, for Rome to hate me *this* much. Bitter would be understandable after I rejected and embarrassed him, but taunting me like this is absolutely ridiculous. Is this why everyone here bows to him? Because he tortures them into submission?

I guess there's only one thing left to do. I have to try and have a civil conversation with him because I refuse to live each day tiptoeing around this new town.

I'm a stellar student with a 4.6 GPA. I won't allow Rome, or anyone else, to distract me from my goals. If my grades drop, I could lose not only my scholarships, but also my acceptance to Stanford.

With all the supplies I need for my American lit class laid out perfectly in front of me—two mechanical pencils filled with lead, a notebook for taking notes, and a folder for any papers our teacher might hand out—I place my arms on the table and take a deep breath. Meditation is supposed to help calm your nerves, and I have found that a minute or two of breathing and letting my mind go blank helps me start fresh with each new class.

When I zone back in, I notice a few students with their laptops and Chromebooks out. This class doesn't require the use of them, as stated in the online syllabus I found on the school website. Instead, we'll be getting good old-fashioned textbooks, and the classic novel, *A Tale of Two Cities*. It just so happens I've read it twice. I happen to prefer the tactile experience of flipping through pages, versus swiping on a screen.

There's an awful dread knowing Rome is in here, but I'm determined to make the best of the situation.

The boisterous sound of him and his idiot friends rings closer and closer, but I don't dare give them the satisfaction of a glance. I'll admit, Rome has been living under my skin for the past few days, but that all changes now.

I straighten my back, lift my chin, and prepare myself for better days ahead. Rome Cromwell can stand in my shadow and play his games all he wants. I'm moving forward.

Our teacher, Mrs. Jenkins, steps in front of the class, and the whispers and hoots coming from the male students tell me they knew exactly what to expect from her. She looks young. Mid-to-late twenties, maybe. She's also gorgeous. Sleek onyx hair that stretches to her mid-back and bright blue eyes that look like they're glowing.

Out of nowhere, I'm snapped from my trance when I feel the thud of something against the back of my head. It's not hard, and it didn't hurt, but it was definitely noticeable. And by the sound of laughter coming from behind me, it was also intentional.

I turn in my chair, my fingers gripping the backside, to find Rome with his head down in his arms while his body shakes with uncontrollable laughter. His friend, Luke, is sitting beside him with his hand over his mouth, sputtering into his palm as he tries to fight the urge to combust. Then there is Wilder on his left, who is biting back a smile, refusing to make eye contact with me.

Everyone in the back row knows one of those three boys just threw something at me. Some are whispering, others are wide-eyed in surprise, and of course, there are the immature ones who are cackling right along with the kings of the class. Yet, no one says a word.

I dig my fingers into my hair, feeling the sticky mess of what I can only assume is gum. My body flushes with humiliation. My fingers tremble as I stretch the sticky substance, attempting to pull it out of my hair. Tears prick the corners of my eyes and a ball of fire lodges in my throat.

I wince in complete embarrassment. "Seriously?" My eyes move from Rome, to Luke, then to Wilder as my head shakes in disgust with these guys. A flash of remorse passes over Wilder's features, but he still can't look me in the eye, so his wordless apology falls short, and it's certainly not accepted.

I push the legs of my chair back and get to my feet as I ball the small piece of gum in my fingers, knowing there is still more on the back of my head. "Excuse me," I say to the girl beside me as I suck in my stomach and maneuver my way behind the row of chairs.

"What's going on back there?" Mrs. Jenkins asks as she makes her way toward the middle row where I'm sitting.

I hold up the ball of gum, showing her proof of what just happened. "Rome Cromwell and his friends threw gum in my hair."

Someone in the class—a girl—coughs out the word, "Narc," and my eyes quickly snap around the room, wondering why she would insult me with name-calling. If any girl in here were in my shoes, they'd do the same thing. Those boys threw gum at me and they deserve to be punished.

Mrs. Jenkins lifts a brow, pinning Rome with an authoritative glare. "Is that true, Rome?"

Rome sticks a pencil in his mouth, biting down like it's a toothpick as he sinks into his seat comfortably. "Wasn't me."

Mrs. Jenkins looks at the other boys while I hold Rome's scathing glare.

No one fesses up, and when I think Mrs. Jenkins is just going to let it slide without the boys reaping any consequences, Rome pipes up, "Pretty sure I saw Brady Newton throw it at her."

My eyebrows pinch together as I follow Rome's cynical smirk to, who I can only assume is, Brady Newtown. He's on the other side of the room, sitting straight with his hands clasped in front of him on the table. He's got tight blond curls with a pair of bright blue sunglasses sitting on the top of his head with a Hawaiian button-up shirt. He looks like he's ready to go on vacation somewhere tropical, versus sitting in an American lit class.

Brady lifts his eyebrows and clears his throat. "I did it." He looks at me and I immediately shake my head, urging him not to take the blame for something he didn't do. "I'm sorry I threw gum at you."

I shake my head at Brady for going along with this shitshow. "That is a pathetic excuse for a lie." I gesture to Rome acting like the king of the world. "Rome is clearly bullying him into confessing. I know it wasn't Brady. The trajectory…"

"Trajectory?" Rome's deep, booming laughter fills the class-room, and half of the students join in. "Sit down, new girl. You're embarrassing yourself." He shifts in his seat, his features morphing into that charismatic grin he wears so well. One that I'm sure wins everyone else over. But I see the insincerity behind his smile. Rome's charm doesn't sway me one bit.

"Ma'am," he says to Mrs. Jenkins, "Brady and I are cool. So how she thinks I'm," he air quotes, "'bullying' him, is beyond me."

I glower at him, shaking my head in slow movements. *I'm onto you, asshole.*

I raise my hand coyly before speaking out of turn. "Mrs. Jenkins. If I may, I'd like to recant my outburst. Turns out, it's my fault." I chuckle before running my fingers through the back of my gummy hair. "Silly me. You see, Rome is my new stepbrother who I just moved in with. Last night, I borrowed his pillow, and he must've fallen asleep with gum in his mouth before I took it and it must have rolled out with his drool."

A few snickers ring out around the room, encouraging me to keep going.

"I know it's disgusting, but Rome drools a lot when he sleeps. It's probably a medical condition and really not his fault." I flash Rome a devilish smirk as his jaw tics in response. "I guess I rolled onto his chewed gum while I was sleeping. I apologize for disrupting the class."

I expect a few giggles or laughs when I finish my rant, but instead, the class grows eerily quiet. His pull on these students is literally sickening.

"You're sure about that?" Mrs. Jenkins asks warily, eyeing Rome.

I nod slowly, feeling the heat radiate from my cheeks as they flush a bright shade of red.

"Very well." She gestures her hand toward my seat. "Please, sit down and we'll continue."

The sound of rustling papers and whispers fill the room as I awkwardly make my way behind the students in my row and back to my chair.

I sit down, stealing one last glance over my shoulder, only to find Rome fuming, and the other assholes sputtering laughter. Rome growls and slaps Luke in the chest and Luke immediately goes blank-faced.

I knew Rome was going to give me a hard time in school, considering how he treats me at home, but I had no idea he would act so quickly and so cruelly.

Mrs. Jenkins opens the classroom up for discussion on the topic of American literature and what that word means to us. Normally I'd be the first to raise my hand. Not this time. I've drawn enough attention to myself and I'd rather become invisible in my seat. If only that were possible.

Every couple minutes, I hear someone laugh or make a noise and my eyes immediately scan the room wondering where the sound is coming from and if the jokes are about me. Each time, my gaze ends on Rome and the smirk on his face tells me he's the instigator.

When the bell rings, I exhale a bout of pent-up air, feeling as if I've held my breath the entirety of class. The sound of chairs scraping against the linoleum fills the air as students rush out while Mrs. Jenkins is still giving us our assignment to read chapters one and two in our textbooks, which I've already done.

I move slowly along with a couple other students, one being Brady. It isn't until he's walking toward the front of the class that I pick up my pace to catch up with him.

"Brady," I say loudly, stealing his attention. He pivots around to face me, looking shocked. "Can I talk to you for a minute?"

"I'd like a word with the two of you as well," Mrs. Jenkins says as the last of the students leave the room. "If you don't mind."

Brady doesn't say anything. He just stands there as if he knows speaking about Rome will put a target on his back.

"Would either of you like to tell me what really happened

today?" Her tone is authoritative and I sense she knows I was lying about the gum.

I could tell her it wasn't really my fault, or Brady's. But I'm not sure it would make a difference. Rome is a leader at Willow Creek High and he'd likely find a way to weasel himself out of any trouble he might get in.

One glance at Brady and I can see the sweat beading around his hairline, proof that he'd rather avoid this conversation altogether.

"Brady didn't do anything," I tell Mrs. Jenkins. "That's really all I can say on the matter."

"I know you're new here, Elodie, but I am well aware of how Rome Cromwell operates, as I'm sure Brady is as well." She looks at Brady who silently fidgets with the cover of his textbook. "I want you both to know this is a safe space and you don't have to cover for him. Bullying is not accepted in my class."

Brady shoots a thumb over his shoulder. "Yeah, I gotta go before I'm late for my next class."

I clear my throat as I watch Brady take slow steps backward toward the door. I worry that Rome has something on him for a minute with just how fast he was willing to take the blame. Maybe if he just told us the truth we could help him. But he's not ready, and I honestly don't think I am either.

"Wait up," I tell Brady before shifting my eyes to Mrs. Jenkins. "I should go, too. I'm excited for class. American literature is one of my favorite subjects."

"I'm glad, Elodie. Welcome to Willow Creek. I promise there is more good than bad here. You'll see."

I nod in response, pressing my lips into a tight smile. "Thank you."

Brady and I leave class together, and before we part ways, I say, "I'm sorry he did that to you."

"No sweat," he says, lifting a smile on his face as he drops his sunglasses down over his eyes. He's much livelier outside the classroom, and his carefree attitude sets my nerves at ease. "I'm used to it. It's me that should be sorry for you. You have to live with that fuckwad. See ya around, new girl."

He leaves down the hall and I stand there watching, thinking as he walks away.

It's true that Rome is a monster. He acts like he's a god around here, lording his power over the weak and making them fall at his feet for stupid bullshit. Hell, it's only been a day and I can already see the chokehold he has.

I sigh, turning to go to my next class as I try to think about what to do with my new stepbrother. My only hope is we can learn to coexist, and maybe with time, I'll see proof that he actually has a heart.

CHAPTER 5

ROME

"DUDE." Luke buzzes as he pulls open his gym locker. "Did you see the look on Elodie's face in class? The bitch almost burned your ass, Rome."

"But she didn't." I scoff. "No one fucking burns me. I'm the king of this fucking school. I do what I want, when I want."

Luke drops his bag of gear on the bench and with a chuckle he says, "Yeah, everything except playing ball."

Fury courses through my veins, igniting a burning ball of rage in my chest. With the sweep of an arm, I send Luke's gym bag flying to the floor. "What the hell did you just say?" My voice shakes with anger as he smiles smugly, trying to downplay the situation. As if he didn't just outright insult me in front of the whole team.

The room falls silent and all eyes turn toward us. Tension hangs heavy in the air, everyone waiting for a fight to break out between Luke and me—best friends since grade school.

Luke snickers like this is some sort of joke. "I'm just messing with you, Rome. Chill out."

He goes to pick up his bag, but I stomp it back down. A subtle growl climbs up my throat. "I don't think you are. Say it, Luke. What the hell is on your mind?"

I look around at the crowd circling us. "Anyone else have anything to say about me not playing?" I raise my voice and pat my hands to my chest. "Give it to me! Let's fucking hear it!"

No one says a damn thing. I shake my head as these idiots cower. "That's what I thought." Pushing my way through them, I head toward the open doors to the field. On my way out, I pass by another row of lockers and slam one of the open doors. It ricochets, popping back open like it's laughing in my face. Before I'm even out of the locker room, the whispers begin.

I know what they're all saying. He did this to himself. He fucked up and he's the reason he's on the bench the first four games. He's also the reason UCLA rescinded their offer.

What they don't know is, I didn't do this to myself. She did this. And if it's the last thing I do, I will make her pay.

"Dinner's ready," Celia calls out from the bottom of the stairs.

I'm not sure who this lady thinks she is coming in here and rearranging our lives. Not only is she forcing sit-down dinners, she also demoted Tina, our housekeeper, to part-time, only coming in once every two weeks to clean. She even had the audacity to tell Tina not to clean our rooms anymore because that should be our responsibility. *What the actual fuck?*

A knock at my bedroom door has me sighing heavily. "What do you want?"

Wilder opens the door, without permission to enter, and pops his head in. "You coming down?"

"Fuck that," I grumble. "I'll get something later."

"It's lasagna," he sings. "Your favorite."

"No," I correct him. "My favorite was Mom's lasagna. I'm not eating that woman's shitty-ass meals."

Wilder steps into the room and closes the door behind him. I turn to my side, giving him my back. "If you're gonna try and lecture me, you can turn around and walk right back out."

"Not a lecture," he says. The mattress dips under his weight as he settles down at the edge of the bed. He slaps my ankle and I kick him. "Just give them a chance. They're not that bad, Rome."

"Nope." I pop the P. "They're strangers living in our house and I refuse to make them feel welcome. Especially the woman who's trying to replace our mother."

"You're acting like a spoiled brat."

I tsk. "Well, you can blame Mom and Dad for that."

"They raised me, too, brother, and I still know how to show some respect." I can hear the disappointment in his tone. I'm not sure why Wilder thinks he needs to father me all the time, but it's getting old. He's the same age as me, born on the same day, and while we may look different, we're pretty much the exact same. He just hides his emotions better than I do.

I toss onto my back so I can see him. "They're sucking you in, aren't they? You're falling for their witchery?"

"I'm not sucked into, or falling for, anything. This is the first time I've seen Dad happy since Mom died. Don't you want him to be happy?"

I pinch the bridge of my nose, knowing he's right. Ever since Mom died, he walked around with this gray cloud over his head. Now, it's as if all he sees is sunshine when Celia is in the room. I just wish it didn't have to be the mother of the girl who ruined me.

"Of course." I huff out in a single breath. "Just not with her."

"What has Celia done to make you think she's trying to replace Mom?"

Here we go. Here comes the lecture.

"My problem isn't Celia. It's her daughters. One in particular." I eye him, daring him to push me on this. He has no idea what she did, what she's responsible for. Maybe I should tell him now. Surely it would have him on my side.

I can't do that, though. There is power in being the only one that knows the hell she raised her first night in Willow

Creek last year. I just haven't figured out how to wield it quite yet.

"Lemme guess. Elodie?"

"She's poison, Wilder. The worst of the worst."

He laughs, nudging me on the bed. "She's not that bad."

"You don't know her like I do." I sit up and push him away. I might be acting like a child, but I just need some space to breathe right now. I need to forget who is in my house, touching my things, eating my food, and showering in my fucking bathroom.

"I know enough. She's book smart and sweet. Had you not given her the typical Rome welcome, you two could have been friends." He acts like he's disappointed in me for treating her like shit. It's only because he doesn't know.

My nostrils flare as I try to be as polite as possible, failing miserably when the words pass through my lips. "That bitch will never be my friend."

"Are you sure this isn't really about school and Coach putting you on the—"

"Don't!" I snap. "Don't even fucking go there." My teeth grind as I try to get a grip on the monster inside, rearing its ugly head.

Wilder throws his hands up defensively as he stands, knowing this is a conversation I refuse to have. "All right. Too soon. Just know that, eventually, you have to talk about it."

"There's nothing to talk about." I look away, training my eyes on the television.

"Gotcha. Well, I'll be downstairs eating a delicious warm meal with our delightful new family. Soft pasta. Mmm. Marinara and cheese with garlic bread on the side."

"Yeah. You enjoy that." I pull the pillow out from behind me and toss it at him as he exits my room. The fucker closes the door just in time to dodge the pillow and it falls to the floor.

CHAPTER 6
ROME

SKIPPING dinner wasn't smart on my part. My stubbornness overpowered my hunger and now here I am at midnight, cooking a frozen pizza while everyone else in the house sleeps.

I shove the pizza in the oven before the preheat timer even goes off because I'm impatient as fuck, then I head downstairs to the family room to watch the Broncos game I recorded earlier. I had every intention of watching it with Wilder and Callan after they had dinner, but the dipshits invited the girls down here to hang with them. No way in hell would I choose to hang out somewhere *she* is, so I went to the gym instead.

Our family room is spacious and I probably could have gone without having to look at her face. Knowing she's near, though, instantly makes my skin crawl. It's comparable to the sensation of a thousand tiny insects climbing all over me. Possibly worse.

Above the gas fireplace is a seventy-five-inch flat screen with a sectional pointed at it. There's also a full bathroom down here, as well as Sayer's new room. I fought Dad hard on letting me have the room in the basement, but for some reason, he thinks if Wilder or I had it, we'd sneak chicks in and raid the bar. Not that we don't do that already. Now, Elodie has my old bedroom and bathroom. Lake is in Sayer's old room, and she and Brogan are sharing his old bathroom. It's a fucked-up situation I'm not happy about.

In the far corner down here, we've got a built-in bar. On the other side of the room, there's a pool table and foosball. Neither get much use anymore, but before my mom passed away, we'd have family game nights down here and pool was always my game of choice.

Our house has become the hangout spot for all our friends, and that's what this space is for. We play video games, watch football, Netflix and *chill*.

I drop down on the couch and recline, kicking my feet up as I grab the remote. My head rests back for a second while the television powers on and I close my eyes. It's been a long fucking day.

The next thing I know, the sound of a smoke detector is ringing in my ears. My eyes pop wide open as the blaring sound continues.

"What the hell is that?" I grumble, and without hesitation, I leap to my feet and hurry to the stairs, not stopping until I'm pushing open the door at the top.

I step up into the hallway, my nostrils immediately assaulted with the stench of something burning.

Is the house on fire? Is someone cooking?

Fuck! My pizza.

As quick as the sound hits my ears, it stops. I hurry down the hall into the kitchen, only to find Elodie fanning a towel over her head beneath the smoke detector.

"Jesus, Rome." Elodie scoffs, wearing a black mitten while tossing down a pan of burnt pizza on the stove. "Don't tell me this is your doing?"

"Fuck my life," I grumble as I walk right past her to my pizza. It's now a blackened disk, sitting on top of a scorched pan. A thin trail of smoke curls from it, and there's a faint sizzling sound.

Elodie tosses the towel on the center island with a hefty sigh. "You're welcome for saving your ass."

I flash her a condescending look and tsk. "I didn't ask for your help."

If she really thinks I'm going to thank her, then she's lost her damn mind. I grab the pan with the pizza on it, ready to toss it in the sink to cool off, and it burns the fuck out of my hand. I drop it back down, causing the metal to collide with the stove in a loud thud.

"Dammit!" I quickly turn the cold water on in the island sink, running my hand under it.

Laying her elbow on the countertop, she slowly pulls the oven mitt off with a pleased look on her face. "I'm not going to pretend you didn't deserve that."

"Ya know what, Elodie. I really don't give a shit what you think."

When I turn my head slowly, I notice she's wearing only a baby pink nightgown with no bra underneath. *Fuck.* My cock twitches at the way her puckered nipples threaten to cut through the fabric.

She notices my stare and quickly crosses her arms over chest. The sound of disappointment mixed with a heavy breath of air escapes her. "That's so typical of you to not thank someone for saving you." She grimaces tightly as she lowers her hand to put the oven mitt back in the drawer. "Can't say I'm surprised."

My lips flatten as I reach over and push the drawer closed with her hand still inside.

"What the hell, Rome!" She lets out a shrill cry as I hold her fingers hostage. "Stop it, or you're gonna break my fingers!"

I remain stoic, my expression unreadable. "Say sorry," I tell her calmly. "And maybe I'll let you walk away with your bones intact." My tone is full of menace and hate, reflecting exactly what I feel right now.

Her eyebrows pinch together tightly as my threat hangs heavy in the air. "For what?" She huffs out a shaky breath. "Standing up to you? Pulling your burnt pizza out of the oven and fanning away the smoke from the alarm before you woke up the entire house?"

I'm not talking about right now, I'm talking about a year ago. I need her to fucking apologize because just thinking about what she did has my blood boiling. It was the deepest betrayal that she could have ever carried out. My jaw tightens as I try to keep my temper in check, not allowing the drawer to snap her fingers just yet.

I shake my head. "None of that. You know exactly what I'm talking about."

"If this is about class today, you started the bullshit. It took me almost an hour to get all that gum out of my hair after school." She pulls on her hand, but I don't let up. When she sees the evil behind my eyes, she actually flinches, looking afraid for the first time since she moved in here.

The gum shit was pretty hilarious. A good show to start the day off right. But this isn't about that either.

"I'm not talking about today, or even yesterday." My voice rises a few octaves. "I'm talking about how you ruined my fucking life."

"You really are insane!" She attempts to pry the drawer open with her free hand, digging her other fingers into it while she uses all her strength. When she fails, she digs her nails into my arm, trying to pull my hand off hers.

Her breaths become heavy as she tries to free her hand to no avail. "You're obviously as upset about our parents getting married as I am. But that's not my fault. Trust me, I don't want to be here either." Finally she gives up and pulls her claws out of my skin. Her shoulders slump in defeat and she drops her head. "Just let me go back to bed."

In a swift motion, I yank her hand out of the drawer by the wrist in a vise she can't break free from, and I pin it to the counter behind her. The sting on my arm is a reminder that she just left a band of scratches, and it only fuels the fire inside me.

"Ouch!" She seethes. "You're hurting me!" Tears well up in her eyes and even though she's afraid, I can see she's not ready to let them fall for me. So I push even further.

"Good," I spit, my face a mere inch from hers. "I want it to hurt. Your cries are a sweet symphony to my ears. I want to be the reason for every tear that falls down your pretty little face. You fucked my life up, and now I plan to return the favor."

"Why?" she screams. "Tell me why, Rome! Why do you hate me so much?"

She wriggles to free herself while I open my mouth to speak, but before the words can come out, another voice overpowers mine.

"What the hell is going on in here?"

I look at the entryway and see my dad standing there with a heavy brow. Quickly, I let Elodie go and she rubs her wrist that my fingers were just wrapped around.

"I burnt a pizza," I tell him honestly, leaving out everything that came after the fact.

"I can see that." He walks toward us, fanning away the lingering smoke in the air. "It's almost one o'clock in the morning. Why in God's name are you cooking pizza at this hour when you have school in the morning?"

"It's not a big deal, Dad." I blow out a laugh, trying to lighten the mood. "I was at the gym and missed dinner and just got hungry."

Elodie stands there innocently, hiding her arm behind her back where I no doubt just left a mark. She's quiet with her eyes downcast as if she's waiting for permission to leave the room.

"Were you part of this?" Dad asks her, and she lifts her wide eyes.

"I just heard the smoke alarm and hurried down here before it woke anyone up. Apparently I didn't get to it soon enough. I'm sorry."

Could she be any more of a kiss ass? I look at my dad,

wondering if he's really buying into her sweet act. By the way his features soften, it's obvious he is.

"I appreciate that, Elodie. But the smoke alarm isn't what woke me. It was my son's shouting." His eyes glide to mine. "Care to explain what that was about?"

"Sure." I shrug my shoulders nonchalantly while raising my arm. "Elodie scratched me."

Let's see whose side he's on now.

Elodie's eyes widen in shock. "Are you serious? I scratched you because you shut my hand in a drawer."

It's obvious by her reaction that she isn't called out for her bullshit often. Unlucky for her, I have every intention of doing just that.

"You deserved it," I tell her point-blankly.

"Oh, *grow* up," she grumbles with a heavy eye roll.

"Elodie," Dad says, "why don't you go back to bed while Rome and I have a little talk?"

She nods with a pressed smile on her face. "Good night, Grant."

I take in a deep breath, fingers drawing around my mouth. *Fucking great.* I'm gonna get a lecture from my dad while perfect little Elodie walks away scot-fucking-free. Typical.

Once Elodie is out of sight, Dad's face contorts in a furious scowl. "What in God's name is going on with you?" I can practically feel the rumble of his deep roar.

You brought four females into our house only a year after we lost Mom. One of those bitches destroyed my life. And you're treating her like she's a saint. That's what's going on with me.

But I don't say that. Instead, I blink slowly, shoulders lifting and falling carelessly. "Nothing." Downplaying the situation is the best approach. If he even has to ask what's going on with me, then he has no business knowing how I truly feel.

"Coach Ivers was at the board meeting tonight. He said you and Luke got into an argument before practice today." He crosses his arms, signaling to me that he plans to have more than just a quick chat.

Fucking great. Here we go. There's no privacy in this small-ass town.

I sweep my hand through the air with a sigh. "It was nothing, Dad."

"Luke's your best friend. It had to be something. Whatever's going on, you gotta let it out, son. Holding it in—"

"Nothing is going on!" I nearly shout. "I'm fine. Everything is fine. Now go back to bed with your new wife and enjoy your happy fucking life." I storm past him, leaving the kitchen a mess, my entire body trembling with anger.

The sound of heavy feet slapping against the hardwood rings in my ears. "Not so fast." Dad huffs, grabbing me by the shoulder from behind. "Since when did you think it's acceptable to speak to me with that tone?"

He's right. It's not acceptable. I've never lashed out at my dad like that before. Lately, my emotions have been getting the best of me. I know him and my brothers see it. Why don't they understand why I'm hurting? Why aren't they just as upset?

Dad played ball at UCLA and it was always my plan to play there, too. Wilder might not have gotten the offers I did because he isn't as stellar on the field, but he's got the brains and a career path he's headed down. Without ball, I've got nothing. I *am* nothing.

It's not their fault, though. Not Wilder's, Luke's, or my dad's.

She's the only one to blame.

I drop my head down, unable to even look him in the eye out of sheer shame and regret. "I'm sorry, Dad. There's just been a lot of changes and I'm trying to adjust the best I can."

He comes around to face me, hand still on my shoulder. "Look at me, son."

I slowly lift my eyes to his, feeling the sting of his pitiful gaze. That's what he feels toward me right now—pity. I'm the fuckup child who lost it all.

"Football isn't the only opportunity in life. You've still got a bright future ahead of you."

Do I, though? I'm not smart. I barely slide by, keeping my grades just where they need to be to stay on the team. I'm not even sure if UCLA still wants me. We've appealed to the board in hopes of them holding true to their acceptance, even without my contract or scholarship, to play ball there. The decision is still undecided.

"I know," I tell him, desperate for this conversation to end.

"I tell you what," he begins. "Let's have that talk tomorrow. Sit down, map out your new plan for the future…just in case."

Just in case they rescind my acceptance and I've got no offers from any other schools? He doesn't wanna say it, but I know what he's thinking.

I shake my head no, just like last time, and the time before that. "Not yet," I tell him. "I'm not ready."

His hand drops from my shoulder and he taps his wrist. "Time is ticking, Rome. Graduation will be here before you know it, so you better get ready."

I rub my temples, closing my eyes for a second. "Yeah. Maybe next week."

I begin toward the staircase, stopping when he says, "Be nice to Elodie. She's a good girl, Rome."

My chest inflates with air, nostrils flaring as cruel words sit on the tip of my tongue. But I hold them in because her time is coming. Soon, everyone will know Elodie isn't the good girl she wants the world to believe she is.

CHAPTER 7
ELODIE

THAT'S WEIRD. I really thought I'd be carrying all my books today, just like yesterday. Rome wouldn't let me anywhere near my locker, so I just stayed away from it to avoid confrontation.

My eyebrows rest high on my forehead as I look left, then right. I spin around in search of Rome, but he's nowhere in sight. No Rome. No Luke. No Aiden. With my head held high, feeling like this is the start of better days ahead, I walk to my locker.

I twist out the combination and lift the lever, then pull the door open with my sore hand. I still can't believe Rome shut my hand in a drawer. Only a psycho would do something so cruel.

As soon as my door pops open, a sweet scent wafts out, and I find it odd but the second I look inside, I can see where the fruity smell is coming from. My heart drops, beating rapidly as it sinks further and further into my stomach. And when the laughter all around me begins, my cheeks catch fire.

Inside my locker are dozens—no, hundreds—of multicolored wads of gum stuck to every surface. Layers upon layers plastered on every inch of the metal interior. The shelves, the inside of the door, the walls.

My eyes land on a note hung by the largest wad of them all. I yank the note down, ripping the top piece that remains under the gum.

Then, I read it…

> Go back to wherever you came from. You're not
> wanted here.

The harsh words pierce my heart like a sharp blade. How can Rome be so heartless? My eyes fill with angry tears as I keep my face hidden from the crowd watching me. They're probably waiting to see me cry so they can laugh more.

I won't give them the reaction they so desperately crave. Swallowing hard, I suck up a few sniffles with my face inside the locker. When my tears are dry, I hang my bag inside as if the gum doesn't even faze me. Unzipping my backpack, I pull out my books for my first class, then close the locker and spin around, head still held high.

With a fake smile lifting my lips, I offer up a casual *hey* and *hello* to the nosey assholes I pass by. Until I get to Rome.

He's curled over, busting at the seams with laughter.

I stop directly in front of him, hugging my books to my black cardigan sweater. "Real cute, Rome. Thanks for infesting my locker with the saliva of Willow Creek's finest. You're truly a class act. Bravo."

"Hey, Freckles," Rome sputters between laughs. "How did the gum cross the hall?"

"Grow the hell up." I shake my head in annoyance as I walk past, not willing to give him another second of my time.

But as I'm leaving, I hear him holler, "It stuck to your shoe."

Every student in the hall cracks up laughing at his dumb joke. I act like I didn't hear what he said, but when I turn down another hall and I'm away from the noise, I kick up my white Converse shoe and see a piece of purple gum covered in debris stuck to it, hanging off the edge.

"Dammit!" I let out a frustrated sigh as I drop my foot and

keep moving. Each step has my shoe clinging to the floor. With someone's chewed gum stuck to it, I take a sharp turn into the girls' bathroom.

Walking over to the sink, I set my books down on the floor with a thud. My face heats as I quickly peel off my shoe, my no-show sock barely holding on just like my sanity. Grabbing a handful of paper towels from the dispenser, I proceed to pull off a big chunk of the gum.

Gross. I toss it into the open trash can beside me.

My hands shake as I continue cleaning up, and I have to pause to take a breath. I knew Rome hated me, and I thought I was prepared to deal with that. It's easy to tell someone to just ignore bullying, but when you know it's going to be your life, day in and day out, for a year, it hits differently.

Today it's gum. But what about tomorrow? Or the next day?

My breaths come in short spurts and I make eye contact with myself in the mirror. This is not going to be me. Not here. If I do break down, it will be in my bed at home. No one can see this getting to me here.

With new resolve, I grab more paper towels, this time two feet worth, and I dampen them under the running water.

"So disgusting," I mutter under my breath as I vigorously scrub at the sticky residue. After a few minutes of determined effort, I think I've got it all.

Of course, now I'm late for class.

I shut off the water, snatch my books off the floor, and haul ass out of the bathroom. As I'm weaving through the maze of an exit, my body collides with another.

"Watch it, Gumby!" The tall blonde seethes as she stands there with her nose stuck in the air, eyes peering down at me. She's a good three inches taller than me with a perfect frame. Long legs stretch out from her jean miniskirt and her cleavage peeks from her low-hung white tee shirt. Her skin is flawless, her eyes glowing blue.

It takes me a second to register where I've seen her before, but it all clicks pretty quickly. She's the girl from the party. The one Rome was sucking face with in the midst of hitting on me. I can tell by her nasal voice she's the same girl who coughed out 'narc' when I told on Rome and his friends for throwing gum in my hair. Hence, the nickname she seems to have plagued with me—Gumby. It's fitting, I suppose, but also childish on her part. It's easy to assume she's on Rome's side. I mean, who in this school isn't?

I step around her, but I'm stopped by her shrill voice. "I'm Abby, by the way."

"It's nice to meet you, Abby." It's a lie, but it's better than telling her the truth—that I don't care who she is. "I'm Elodie. *Not* Gumby."

"So, you live with the Cromwell boys, huh?" When I look at her, I can immediately see that she's not asking a question, rather fishing for information.

"I do," I tell her, though she already knows.

"I see." She nods in slow, subtle movements while examining her nails, freshly coated in bright pink gel. "Well," she begins, eyes now on mine. They're stern and serious as she says, "If you think for a second you've got a chance with Rome, or Wilder… you don't. So…"

"I don't think that at all." I laugh, though there is no humor in the sound that escapes me. "Rome and Wilder are my step-brothers. And even if they weren't, I don't go for guys that are complete assholes."

"Good." She plasters a fake smile on her face. "Because Rome doesn't date…like, anyone. He's a fuckboy. And right now, he's mine. So, fair warning, you'll probably see me around at night."

I wanna laugh so hard right now. This poor girl. She's bragging about being used by Rome for sex. She actually thinks that makes her special.

"In that case, I'll see you around…but only at night, that is." I shake my head in disbelief as I leave.

For some reason that conversation cheers me up a bit. I might have to deal with Rome and his taunting, but I will never have to spread my legs for him, only to be thrown out the next morning like trash.

It's quiet out in the hall now, practically empty, aside from a couple stragglers who are in no hurry to get to where they need to be. But I'm in a hurry. Which is obvious by the way I'm practically running down the hall, my long brunette hair blowing behind me. I need to get away before Abby has anything more to say. At this point, I'm already late for class, so once there's a good distance between myself and the restroom, I slow to a steady walk.

So, Rome is a fuckboy? I'm not surprised. And Abby is definitely someone I could see Rome falling for, and vice versa. They're both attractive and confident. She's probably the head cheerleader, and he's the quarterback. They're a match made in heaven, if you ask me.

I wonder how long they've been fuck buddies. Or if their relationship could be heading somewhere. Abby says Rome doesn't date, but if he's keeping her around, he must have some feelings for her.

Ugh. Stop thinking about them, Elodie. Stop thinking about *him*.

I pick up my pace, getting to class eight minutes late. The teacher waves me to the back and I shrink in my seat as fast as I can, hating that I'm already making a spectacle of myself in this school. For someone who doesn't like to stand out, I'm sure doing a lot of that lately.

"He's an asshole," the girl next to me whispers while looking straight ahead and listening to the teacher's lecture.

I turn to look at her with questioning eyes. I'm not sure I've seen her before. She's got chin-length caramel hair that matches the color of mine. She's a petite little thing, wearing an army green turtleneck sweater dress with a band of silver bracelets on her sleeve.

"Excuse me?" I say to her in a hushed tone.

"Rome. He's an asshole." She looks at me, eyebrows raised.

"I think it's cool that you're not letting him bring you down. Keep your chin up and show him he's not getting to you. He hates that."

"I'll keep that in mind," I tell her with a low giggle. "I'm Elodie, by the way."

She offers me her hand, a wide smile on her face. "Julia."

"It's nice to meet you, Julia."

"Same to you. Brady told me all about you. Said you actually stood up to Rome and called him out in class. I'm just sad I had to miss it. I've been waiting my whole life for someone to do that." Leaning back in my chair, I'm thankful I was late for a moment because now I'm stuck at the back of the class with someone at this school that doesn't bow to my stupid stepbrother.

"You know Rome well?" I ask her, noticing the way she tenses up when she says his name.

She rolls her eyes. "Everyone knows Rome. And Wilder. And even Callan. As for knowing them, well, thankfully not. I've had the typical Rome Cromwell experience that most girls in this school have had."

I tilt my head to the side, frowning sympathetically. "I'm sorry to hear that."

"Eh." She presses her lips together into a thin line, then sighs. "It is what it is."

The teacher tells us to pair up and I turn to Julia just as she turns to me excitedly. "Hey! You should have lunch with me and Brady today. We can fill you in on all the dos and don'ts when it comes to the Cromwell boys."

"Sure." I beam. "I'd love to."

I think I've just made my first friend in Willow Creek.

"So," Julia begins as she takes a bite of her ham sandwich, speaking as she chews. "Rome and Wilder might be twins, but they are very different. Not just their looks, but also their person-alities." I take a big bite of my own sandwich and nod along, already knowing this from having lived with them.

Rome is chaos through and through, whereas Wilder is calmer and more organized.

"Both hot, though." Brady waggles his brows. "Did I just say that out loud?" He shrugs his shoulders, then returns to poking at his salad.

I chuckle. "I've definitely noticed that Rome is more intense than Wilder. But I don't trust either of them."

"Good," Julia says. "Because neither of them can be trusted. In fact, I hate all football players because they abuse their power."

She leans in close, eyes wandering around the room before saying, "Rome and I dated for like a nanosecond in eighth grade and—"

"You went on a date," Brady interrupts. "One date. One time."

"Wait a minute." I raise my hand up. "I thought Rome didn't date."

Brady shakes his head and mouths, "He doesn't. They didn't date."

Julia balls a fist and punches him in the shoulder. "Shut up and let me tell my story."

He laughs and resumes eating, and Julia takes that as her cue to continue. "*Anyways*, Rome and I dated for…a night. When the date was over, we kissed. It was my first kiss, and we all know how those first kisses make us feel. I was certain I was on the verge of falling in love."

Her face sours, and it already has me wanting to punch Rome in the face for whatever he did to her.

"Well, the next day I told a couple people. I wasn't bragging." Brady scoffs at her remark, and she continues, "Okay, maybe I was. But I was excited. Then your jackass of a stepbrother denied the whole thing, saying I was making it all up and that I was strangely obsessed with him."

Julia sets her sandwich down in defeat. I'm not much of a comforter, but I reach out and cover her hand with mine for just a second. Getting a girl's hopes up is bad enough, but embarrassing her and making her look desperate, now that's downright evil.

Julia clears her throat and shakes her head like nothing happened. "I've been trying ever since to get my reputation back to what it was. *That's* how much of a pull that asshole has in this school. I'm warning you now, Elodie. It's great you're standing up to him, you might be the only one that will ever be able to do that. But you need to watch your back."

I shake my head in disbelief, feeling a bit worried for myself. If Rome could ruin her reputation over a kiss, I can't even begin to imagine what he's going to do to me.

We finish eating and head to the second half of our classes with plans to go to the football game on Friday night.

CHAPTER 8

ELODIE

LUCKY FOR ME, the rest of the school day was surprisingly uneventful, aside from the growing wads of gum on the outside of my locker. It seems the entire school has decided to partake in Rome's antics. I'm not sure why the staff is letting this slide, but I can only assume they haven't noticed yet.

Regardless, I continued to go to my locker, even with the sound of giggles and whispers around me, opening the door to swap out my books like nothing was happening. Each time, Rome watched as if he was waiting for a reaction from me, but I failed to give it to him.

Which is probably why he's walking steadfastly down the hall behind me, trying to catch up to my brisk pace.

I'm immediately hit with the scent of his intoxicating cologne. Someone this cruel shouldn't smell that good.

"What do you want?" I grumble when he meets my side.

"You really think you're fooling everyone, don't you?" His voice is laced with intent, and I know he's getting desperate for that rise I refuse to give him. "No one believes you're the innocent girl you want them to think you are."

"Fooling everyone?" I chuckle as I keep walking toward the exit doors where students are huddled. "I don't even think about any of you, Rome. Unlike you, who seems to be putting a lot of thought into me lately. As for what everyone else thinks of me, I really don't care."

I move faster, though he keeps up, walking in step at my side.

Rome glares at me with a smoldering rage. I can practically feel the steam rolling from his flared nostrils. "The only reason I think about you is because I want to destroy you."

"By getting the whole school to put gum in my locker? Ouch, Rome." I slap a hand over my heart and laugh mockingly. "That hurt. You win. Consider me destroyed."

"Fucking bitch!" He seethes, taking me by surprise as he snares my wrist and jerks me backward.

Instead of expressing my bemusement and giving him any kind of reaction he could be looking for, I keep a blank face.

Suddenly, I'm pushed through a door into a room with dim lighting. My back collides with a row of lockers, my head thudding against them. It isn't until I look around that it hits me where we are. The boys' locker room. There's no one else in sight, but I can hear the distant voices of guys talking.

As I struggle against him, Rome's hand clamps over my mouth and his other holds tightly to my wrist against the locker. "Get off me!" I sputter incoherently into his palm. My fingers curl into a fist and I try to pull away, but his grip tightens in response.

"Don't fight me, and don't you dare scream," he grits out. "It'll only make things worse for you in the long run."

The look he levels me with is foreign, more sinister than I've ever seen before. For the first time in all my encounters with Rome, I'm actually scared of him and what he might do.

Tears prick at the corners of my eyes and I pinch them closed to try and hold them in. "What do you want from me?" I whisper as his hand moves away from my mouth.

Memories of last year when I was assaulted flash in my mind

and my heart races. Sometimes I can still feel that guy's cold fingers against my chest and wrapped around my arm.

I open my eyes just in time to see Rome's jaw clench as he looks me up and down. It's not sexual, more like he is trying to see just how far he wants to take this.

"I'm done playing games, Freckles. You cost me my life, now I want yours in return."

I wave my hands in the air, beyond confused as to what he's talking about. "What does that even mean?"

Before I can blink, he's in my face, baring his teeth. I flinch back, startled by the sudden change in him. Rome has a beast hiding under his skin, and I think I just woke it up.

"I want your compliance," he spits. "You will do what I say, when I say to do it. Your future is in *my* hands now. No decision will be made on your part without going through me first, understood?"

"What?" I huff. "No. Not a chance. My future is my own."

He pulls my wrist away from the locker, only to slam it back against it harder, causing my body to tremble at his outburst.

"You owe me, Elodie."

Owe him? What the hell is he even talking about?

He can't seriously think I'm going to obey like his little pet. Rome has no idea who he's up against waging a war with me. I'm a strong, independent woman who stands up for herself. There's no way in hell I'll bow to this man.

"I don't owe you shit, Rome."

He chuckles darkly, the kind of laugh I remember all too well from that night a year ago. He has no intention of letting this go, letting *me* go. "You belong to me now, Elodie. You do what I want, or I'll make damn sure Stanford is nothing but a distant memory."

His words hit me like a punch to the gut, stealing my breath away. All of the anger and frustration that had my hands curling into fists swiftly turns into anxiety, making them tremble.

"How...how do you know about Stanford?" I haven't told

anyone yet. Not even my mom. I was waiting to tell my family after things settled down from our big move and the wedding. My acceptance letter has been hiding in a folder next to my journal, along with over a dozen other acceptance letters from colleges around the US. "Did you go through my things?"

A smug grin tugs at the corners of his lips. "I know a lot more than you think I do. With that said," his pitch rises, "you will keep no secrets from me from here on out. You think I didn't notice your new friends? They have secrets too, and my mouth might slip if you try to hide things from me."

I scoff, hoping he's bluffing because I might be a loner most of the time, but even I want friends that Rome can't destroy. "You're kidding? You expect me to tell you my secrets just so you can use them against me? You really are delusional."

He squeezes my sore wrist tighter, and I'm sure I'll be wearing his fingerprints as a bracelet for the next couple days, especially after last night. "You either tell me, or I'll find out on my own. And if I don't like what I hear, you'll be punished."

"Punished?" I blurt out in an exasperated breath. "You're insane, Rome." I try to tug my wrist again, and I'm about two seconds away from spitting in this psycho's face if he doesn't let me go.

"Rome," I hear a familiar voice holler from somewhere in the locker room—Luke's voice. "Is that you?"

Rome's voice drops to a whisper as his mouth ghosts my ear. "You heard me right. This isn't a joke, Elodie. This is *my* school. I have more pull than you could ever imagine. It'll be in your best interest not to cross me because the students of Willow Creek High will eat you alive if you do."

Luke appears from around the corner and Rome drops my hand. I stand here frozen, unable to even look at either of them out of shame and humiliation.

"Practice is starting," Luke says, a look of confusion on his face. "Let's go, man."

Rome pats a hand to my cheek, smirking. "Remember what I said, Freckles."

"Quit calling me that," I shout as he gives me his back and walks away.

I watch as they leave, and when Luke flashes me a glance over his shoulder while murmuring to Rome, I quickly turn away, not willing to let him see the tears that are now falling down my face.

Rome already knows he won this round. I will just have to try harder next time. I have no idea how I "ruined his life," but I will make damn sure he doesn't ruin mine.

CHAPTER 9
ROME

I'M on the bench in the locker room, waiting while the guys suit up for tonight's game. I've got my jersey on, but no equipment, no compression pants, no knee pads. Just a pair of black warm-ups, high-top Air Force Ones, and my teal-and-black Willow Creek Misfits jersey.

"It won't be the same without you tonight," Aiden says as he pulls his shoulder pads over his head.

"It is what it is," I tell him, knowing there's nothing I can do about it. As much as I want to pitch a fit about being on the bench and not playing with the team I've been with since I was a kid, I'm keeping my cool.

One game down, three more to go, then I'll be back out there. I've been going through phases, thinking it doesn't matter that I'm missing these games to feeling like I can't wait to come alive on the field again.

But what's the point when I'm not playing for scouts anymore? No one is watching and waiting for me to come play for them after high school. Now it's just about my love of the sport, and the more I watch my team from the sidelines, the less connected I feel to the game. There are moments when I wonder if I really loved football as much as I thought I did, or if I just loved the control I had on the field. I feel powerless without the ball.

I know they all look at me like I'm a fuckup. I'm the one who beat that fucker with an old pipe. What they don't know is why I did it. It wasn't for *me*. They also don't know why I got caught. That was all because of *her*.

"Ready, man?" Luke asks with a clap to my shoulder.

I nod and drag my ass off the bench, only to go sit on another one outside under the Friday night lights.

There was a time when I'd walk out these doors to the field and the crowd would chant my name. But no one cheered for me louder than my mom. Her voice could overpower the hundreds of people in the stands, and I always heard her.

I could easily save myself the embarrassment of even showing up tonight, but I'm not giving up just yet. I look at the blue skies and see the sun setting low behind the clouds. I can only hope I'm making my mom proud in one way or another. At least I'm here, facing the consequences of my actions.

I don't dwell on her often, and it's not because she doesn't cross my mind. It's definitely not because I'm never reminded of her. In fact, everything reminds me of her. She appears in my thoughts every minute of every day. I just push the thoughts away because I'm not ready to face the truth that I'm never going to feel the warmth of her hugs again. I'll never hear her voice tell me to keep going when I'm at my lowest. I always tell myself I'll allow my heart and mind to grieve her absence tomorrow. So today I'm not going to miss her. Maybe tomorrow I will.

"Huddle up," Wilder curls his fingers, calling us to circle around him.

It sucks that I feel like an outcast. Like I don't even belong here anymore. I know it's what everyone is thinking. I was replaced by my brother as quarterback and he's kicking ass. It's his time to shine and I can't deny the bitter mix of envy and pride in my chest. Wilder has always been a stellar running back and I always believed he would finally get the recognition he deserved one day. I just never imagined it would be by taking my spot as QB.

Wilder wouldn't even accept the position until he talked to me about it. It was sprung on me out of nowhere and to say I was fucking shocked would be an understatement. I assumed Gage, my backup, would fill in. After all, that's what his role on the team is. I'm still not sure what the fuck Coach was thinking when he made the call.

On a whim, I told Wilder it was cool—no hard feelings. But at the first game last Friday, when I heard the crowd chanting his name over mine, it felt like a fucking knife was stabbed into my back. Not just by him, but everyone—Elodie included. Her role in my downfall is more than she could ever imagine.

I hang back a few feet, listening as Wilder pumps the team up for the game. It's impossible not to feel his energy as he grabs Luke by the mask on his helmet and growls, "Let's crush those Panthers!"

"Hell yeah," Luke booms back, grabbing the shell of Wilder's helmet with both hands. The team joins in on the excitement, pumping each other up.

I lazily make my way off the field while they get into formation. Meeting Coach on the sideline, I stand beside him with arms crossed tightly over my chest as the first play begins.

"You're almost there, Rome," Coach assures me, reading the pitiful expression on my face.

"Yeah," I respond softly. "Almost."

I haven't asked Coach what happens when I return. When I watch Wilder out there, I feel a pang of guilt that I'll be taking the spotlight away from him when he just got it. I'm not sure I've ever seen him happier than he is when he's out there making passes.

That's my position, though. It's my team, too. In a couple weeks, Wilder is going to feel what I felt when the game was ripped away from me. He'll still get to play, though. So it's not all that bad.

The first two quarters go by quickly without incident and we're up 28-7. There were a few moments when I found myself smiling as Wilder dominated the field. His passes were powerful, his footwork swift. There's no doubt he was meant for this position. My brother's a good guy—a great guy. He deserves this. I just wish I did, too.

Halftime rolls around and I find myself not caring about the game or what I'm missing for once. The stadium comes alive with energy as we hold the lead. But that's not what I'm focused on. It's the dozen cheerleaders surrounding me that have my attention.

Wilder might have stolen the field and most of the school's attention tonight, but these girls have always been mine. It's how I've controlled the school for so long—that and the secrets I collect from students.

Ana's father donates lots of money to the school and hates when she's upset, so if I ever need anything, she knows how to work her father's magic.

Abby is the resident mean girl, so if I need girls to fall in line, she is my go-to.

Brogan is new to the squad, but I'm sure she will fall in line like the rest of them. Maybe I can even use her against her sister if Elodie won't do as she's fucking told.

"We're so sad you're not out there, Rome," Ana pouts. "You're the true MVP."

"You sure are," Abby says, slithering up to me. Her arms bracket my neck and her fingers intertwine behind my head. "You know where else you're the true MVP?" I peer down at her, eyebrow cocked, and she whispers with hot breath on my ear, "Between my legs."

"All right, Rome." The cheer coach scoffs. "Back to your team. You're distracting my girls."

Abby frowns before kissing my cheek. "I'll see you at the party tonight, lover."

Fuck me. I should've known this girl would get too attached if

I didn't just keep things to a one-night hookup. In my defense, she can suck dick like it's nobody's business.

Her hands drop and I walk away with a semi in my pants. I wiggle my pelvis trying to adjust myself without being obvious because just the thought of that mouth does things to me. But the idea of being attached to Abby makes me want to gag.

The game continues, and when we're down to the last minute, it's all tied up.

We have a first down with thirty seconds to go.

This is getting intense. I'm watching with trained focus, my heart fucking pounding.

Then, Luke fumbles the ball.

I stomp my foot to the ground, my nerves shot. "Damn it. Come on, boys!"

Fifteen seconds left.

My fingers draw around my mouth and I hold my breath on the next pass while the announcer screams in our ears.

"Misfits' Wilder Cromwell takes the snap from Carver and hurls the ball to receiver Luke Aarons. It wasn't long ago that Wilder was catching those passes from his brother, Rome Cromwell. Those boys sure have some fire in their arms." I grit my teeth, not even able to look at the field right now, or anyone for that matter. "What a pass! And Aarons has got it! He's going…and he's in!" the announcer roars. "Marking another victorious *touchdown*. And the Misfits win the game."

The stands go wild, but my ears pick out a distinct voice in the roaring crowd.

I spin around, looking in the bleachers, and I see Elodie. Her hands are in the air and she's jumping up and down along with everyone else, celebrating the Misfits' win. Her eyes are on the cheerleaders, mainly Brogan. To her left are Brady Newton and some chick whose name I don't remember, though I'm almost positive I've had a past encounter with her. No surprise there. On her right are my dad, Celia, and Sayer. Callan's likely in the student section with the junior varsity team.

Elodie and I lock eyes as she cups her hands around her mouth and screams, "Way to go, Wilder!"

Something snaps inside me.

She's staring right fucking at me, as if she was intentionally trying to hurt me with her words. Little does she know, it doesn't hurt. It only feeds the brewing storm inside me. It solidifies that everything I am doing is justified. She's an evil fucking bitch who's going to get exactly what she deserves.

But she's not solely responsible for the searing rage I'm feeling.

Everyone carries on around me and I'm standing here frozen solid to the ground, watching the picture-perfect family cheering on my brother—*only* my brother.

It's as if my mom was just plucked out from between them and Celia was set down in her place.

Elodie continues to purposefully cheer on Wilder and I know it's to get a rise out of me. My dad must have opened his big fucking mouth and told her I was suspended for half the season. Fucking great. Now she's got ammo to piss me off even more. I'm watching intently as she turns around to grab something off the bleachers, and my heart stills.

On the back of her Misfits football hoodie is *my* last name— *Cromwell.*

Just like the one my mom used to wear to all our games.

Dad wouldn't give her my mom's hoodie. No fucking way.

When Elodie turns back around, her phone raised in her hand snapping pictures, I hear her shout, "We're so proud of you, Wilder!" She looks at me again, and the fury inside me grows tenfold.

She flashes me a crooked smile, completely unaware of the impact of her actions. I clench my fists, my own smile growing on my face as I think about all the ways I'm going to tear that girl to shreds.

Her first mistake was crossing me. Her second was putting on *my* mom's shirt.

"And that's a wrap! Another victory for the Misfits. Quarterback Rome Cromwell has carried his team to the state championship. Even as a sophomore, the boy is a beast. I think we're all pretty excited to see what he does for the Misfits in the future."

The announcer's words continue to fill the stands, and my heart races as I stand on the field, helmet in hand, surrounded by my teammates. At this moment, I'm a star. I'm fueled by the energy of the crowd chanting my name. Adrenaline surges through me, and nothing can compare to this feeling. This might just be football, but I feel larger than life right now.

I look out at the crowd and see my mom. "Way to go, Cromwell boys," she beams victoriously with her hands in the air.

Grinning from ear to ear, her dimples deepen and her eyes sparkle with pure joy. I can't help but mirror her smile, feeling the warmth of her excitement radiating through me.

We exit the field and Wilder and I are immediately surrounded by our parents, Sayer, and Callan.

Dad pats me on the back and congratulates me, while Mom pulls me in for a hug.

Her arms wrap around me tightly. "I love you, son. I couldn't be prouder of you."

Mom's my biggest cheerleader, and I can't imagine doing this without her support.

"I love you, too, Mom."

A ball of hot lava lodges in my throat as I shake away the memory. Peeling my eyes away from Elodie, I haphazardly look around the field in search of a distraction. That's when I see Wilder getting the recognition he deserves.

He's being hoisted in the air like the champ he is. I should be happy for him, but this—on top of all the emotions already swimming through me—is just too much. So, I sprint off the field, leaving my team, and my brother, behind me.

CHAPTER 10
ELODIE

I'M WATCHING Rome as he stares at me with a worried crease on his forehead. He snaps out of whatever daze he was in and hurriedly looks away. His eyes sweep the football field, landing on Wilder being lifted in the air triumphantly by his teammates. I watch as his eyes flick with envy. Suddenly, he sprints toward the school, leaving everyone behind.

Something is definitely wrong, and I get the feeling this isn't just about his brother being in the spotlight.

It's possible his sour attitude has something to do with the reason he didn't play tonight. I asked Grant about it, but his response was short. Just said Rome had to sit this one out. I didn't press because it's not my business. But I can't help but feel responsible in some way.

Perhaps the gum incident caused this and that teacher didn't just drop it. Could that be what he meant by me ruining his life?

I know I was taunting him by cheering on Wilder, and I shouldn't care that something seemed to break inside him when he looked at me. He's been a dick ever since I moved in. Hell, he's been a dick since I met him at that party and he made out with Abby mid-conversation with me.

So why am I pushing through the sea of people in the

bleachers and jogging down the metal stairs to chase after him? I haven't the slightest idea. But something inside me is saying I need to help him. No one else is.

No one else seemed to have noticed the way his eyes fell the moment he walked onto the field, or the tension in his shoulders every time Wilder threw the ball. But I did. At first I thought it was just jealousy, but he looked at his brother like he was genuinely happy for him.

That's when something made sense to me. Rome doesn't play just to be the best, he plays because it lets him out of the cage he traps his emotions in until they break free. The field must be where he opens the door for them willingly. Maybe that's why he's been such a jerk to me. He hasn't gotten to play and needs a punching bag.

Moving quickly, I keep a safe distance between us, and when I see him enter the back doors to the gym, I follow.

Just before the doors close, I slip through the crack quietly, not ready to make my presence known. I need to get a feel for his temperament first.

"Fuck!" I hear him shout, his voice echoing off the four walls in the empty gym.

I stop walking, unsure what the hell I'm even doing. But I have a heart, unlike Rome, and I'm empathetic to the sadness I saw in his eyes.

He definitely needs a minute to cool down, so I hang back, watching as he slams his palm against the door to what I assume is the boys' locker room. He enters, and I pace back and forth, rubbing my temples.

I really should leave. Rome's issues are not my business.

Yet, once again, I'm making a stupid decision and walking to the door that just closed behind him.

Pulling it open, slowly, I hold tightly to it, making sure it doesn't make a noise when it shuts. On the toes of my shoes, I walk quietly, taking care not to make a single sound as I creep around a row of lockers.

The second I see him, I jolt backward, pressing my back to the wall. He didn't see me, thankfully.

I inch out slightly, just enough to steal a peek. His head is hung low and his palms are pressed against the metal doors of two lockers in front of him. Could this be about his mom? These games can't be easy on him or his brothers. This is their first year without her. The empath in me aches for him. I can't stand Rome, but seeing someone hurt who comes off so strong and confident is heartbreaking.

Suddenly, my phone beeps, breaking the silence in the room and, undoubtedly, giving me up. Sure enough, Rome's eyes lock with mine, and my entire body flushes with heat, my pulse skyrocketing. Without a second thought, I haul ass out of the locker room the same way I came in.

You'd think a killer was coming for me with how fast I'm moving. A hefty growl comes from across the gym, followed by the thud of heavy footsteps.

My heart rate excels, my feet move in longer strides, and when I'm in the center of the gym, I glance over my shoulder to find Rome stalking toward me, the scowl on his face heavy.

When I realize he's not slowing down, I turn in his direction, so I'm not taken by surprise when he grabs me…again. "I was just leaving," I tell him, hoping he won't make a big deal out of this. But his only response is fuming breaths of anger. I take a step backward, but as suspected, he grabs me by the forearm.

"Hey," I snap as I'm pulled toward a closed door. I'm not sure where it leads since this is my first time stepping into the gym, but I think I'm about to find out. "Is this how you treat someone who just came to make sure you were okay?"

"Make sure I was okay?" He laughs condescendingly. "Once again, I didn't ask for your help, and I certainly don't want it." With my arm still clutched in his iron grip, he turns the handle of the door and shoves me inside. I'm getting really damn tired of being manhandled by this asshole.

A motion light comes on just before he enters and kicks the

door closed behind him. I look around, noticing we're in a storage room. There are jump ropes hanging from hooks, basketballs in bins, footballs in crates, and shelves filled with a variety of things ranging from arm weights to small orange cones.

Before I can even get a word out, Rome's hands suddenly grab the edge of my sweatshirt. Confused, I look down and watch as he aggressively pulls the fabric up, taking my tee shirt underneath with it. With the hem of both shirts snug around my breasts, I narrow my eyes at Rome, noticing the way he's looking at the small dandelion tattoo on my waist.

I've always loved dandelions. *Some see a weed; I see a wish.*

The tattoo was spontaneous and reckless, considering I allowed a complete stranger in an abandoned warehouse to do it. My best friend, Maggie, convinced me it was safe, and the artist was skilled. It was the first time I ever took a risk, but I'm happy with how it turned out.

I wince as Rome's fingers graze over the skin of my stomach, a trail of goosebumps waking in their path.

Rome's heavy gaze bores into mine, and I swear I'm staring into the eyes of Satan himself. Then, in a swift motion, he jerks the sweatshirt up farther.

"What the hell!" I grumble into the detergent-infused fabric as he moves it past my face. My hands shoot up instinctively as the layers are peeled off my body.

My cheeks flush with heat and I quickly cross my arms over my chest, trying to cover my bra and exposed cleavage with my hands.

"Why the hell are you doing this?" I question, feeling two feet tall and vulnerable. I'm not one to cower, but I'm not a fan of being stripped randomly. I'm not one of the pretty girls Rome is used to seeing without clothes on, and I have no desire for him to cut me down even more than I already do myself.

Rome balls the sweatshirt in his trembling hand, seething. "If I ever see you wear this hoodie again, mark my fucking words, you *will* pay."

He's mad about the sweatshirt? Because it says Cromwell on the back? "Look," I begin, "I wasn't too keen on wearing your last name either, but—"

"This isn't about my last name!" he shouts as he slams the shirt to the cement floor like it's a football and he just scored a touchdown. My body jolts backward at his outburst and my back hits a row of shelves behind me. Chills run down my spine when I notice his fists balled tightly, as if he wants to pound them into me. "You have no fucking right!" His voice is loud and laced with malice.

I'm not sure when I lost all modesty, but I no longer care about my tits being seen by Rome. My hands are now stretched behind me, slapping around on the shelves as I search for something to hit him with if he starts getting physical.

Suddenly, I hear the creak of the doors in the gym, and the sounds of voices ring nearby.

Rome immediately slaps a hand over my mouth, his jersey flush with my bare skin as he grits, "Don't you dare make a sound."

I swallow hard, my stomach twisting in tight knots. I know he can feel the rapid beating of my heart with his chest pressed to mine. Not to mention, my entire body is shaking. Tears prick in the corners of my eyes, but I blink hard, hoping my eyes will just swallow them up because if Rome sees me cry, he'll enjoy torturing me even more.

The voices travel farther and farther away until they are nonexistent.

Rome's hand moves from my mouth downward. His fingers skim over my cleavage and I draw in a shaky breath.

He keeps going until he stops at my tattoo. His thumb grazes over the dandelion on my skin, and he takes a step back to look down at it. "I have to say, Freckles, I'm pretty fucking surprised at this. Thought for sure you were a square."

I don't respond because I'm too caught up in the moment,

trying to wrap my head around what's going on. Nothing good can come from being this close to Rome.

More voices draw near and Rome puts his finger over my mouth. "Shhh," he whispers, and the next thing I know, he's popping the button on my jeans.

Warmth spreads like fire through me. I don't say anything. I'm too stunned to process what is happening, let alone form a complete sentence.

The worst part of all this is the way my body reacts to his touch. The tingling sensation between my legs, followed by the feeling of dampness in my panties, is like nothing I've ever felt before. I just hate that it's happening because of him.

No one has ever touched me like this before, and yet for some insane reason, my body decides to come alive under the brush of my enemy's fingers.

I'm not fully inexperienced. A friend of mine got me this small rose-shaped toy that vibrates against my clit and I've used that a handful of times, but I always get nervous, thinking someone is going to walk in and catch me. It's probably been a good four months since I've even pulled it out.

I'm a virgin—in every way possible.

It's sad, really. I'm not saving myself for marriage or anything. I've just never allowed any guys to go that far. Ethan was my first real boyfriend, and we dated for eight months before I moved, and the most he's ever done is squeeze my breasts above my shirt. Apparently Ethan needed a break to decide what *he* wants out of this relationship. I'm not sure where we stand at this point in time, but it's been long enough for him to decide if he wants me or not, so I'd say I'm off the hook there.

Ethan is the complete opposite of Rome. Ethan is the square Rome speaks of. In fact, he was appalled at my tattoo. Thought it was careless because one day I'd regret it. Maybe I will, but it'll be my regret, not his.

Rome's breath fans against my neck and my elbows balance me on the shelf pressing into my back.

Oh my God!

I shiver when Rome's fingers dip below the waistband of my jeans, teasing. I find myself sucking in my stomach that is coated in tiny goosebumps, just to try and give him better access.

What am I doing right now?

The tingling sensation intensifies and I'm a total idiot for just standing here and allowing this. My mind says run, but my body says stay and just keep my damn mouth shut because this feeling is something I never knew I wanted.

As his hand moves down into my pants, his hot breath on my skin again, my stomach tightens nervously. But when his fingers reach between my legs, my traitorous body betrays me and I widen my stance.

"Rome," I whimper, dragging my tongue across my dry lips. "You shouldn't…"

"Oh, yes. I should." His voice is gruff and unfamiliar. His eyes drink in the way I'm breathing. For a moment, I could swear Rome has a soul, because right now, I'm staring directly at it. It's the most beautiful sea of blue I've ever seen, and I want to dive into the water, never to come up for air.

Instinctively, I reach out and grab his free hand gently. I'm not sure why I do it. Maybe to stop him. Maybe just to touch him. But whatever my plan, it fails as he lifts it over my head and pins my hand to the shelf behind me.

I meet his gaze, the coldness in his eyes I'm so used to is still there, it's just covered with something new. Lust, maybe?

For the first time since I met Rome, I don't want to fight with him, and I can't bring myself to stop him.

His fingertips continue to graze over my sensitive clit and I wince in response. I shouldn't want this. It shouldn't feel this good. And the small dimple at the corner of his curled lip tells me he's pleased with the way my body is responding to him.

The tip of his middle finger dips inside my dripping center and my heart prepares to flee from my chest.

"Damn, Freckles. You are tight as fuck. Seems you've been keeping another secret."

If he's referring to my virginity, it's not a secret. I just never told him because it's none of his damn business.

He pushes in deep, sending a jolt of slicing pain through my core. My body bucks upward as he continues to drive his finger in and out of me as if he wants to hurt me and make me feel good at the same time.

I reach out and grab him again, this time by the shoulder blade, squeezing. I'm not sure why, but his expression suddenly morphs into something dark and forbidding. I can see the muscles in his jaw clenching as he grinds his teeth. It's a chilling sound that drowns out my labored breathing.

As if he's punishing me for reasons I can't fathom, he aggressively adds a second finger. I gasp at the discomfort, but it's quickly replaced with pleasure when he hits a spot that makes the pain worthwhile.

His body aligns tightly with mine and I feel the hardness of his arousal pressing against my thigh. A rush of desire floods through my core, knowing I gave him that erection.

I wiggle my bound wrist, desperate to be free from his grip so I can squeeze something—anything to alleviate some of the pressure building inside my body.

Holy shit. What is happening to me?

Sounds I've never made before slip between my lips, airy and audible. My cheeks flush pink because I hate that he's making my body react this way.

"Rome," I try again, still unsure what it is that I want. One thing's for sure, I want whatever feeling comes next.

My head falls back slightly, my mouth agape as I moan in pleasure. Just when I'm on the edge, about to fall into that water I'm sure I'll never want to resurface from, Rome slides his fingers out of me. Suddenly, I'm left feeling empty, unfinished, and like the biggest idiot in the world. My pussy feels like it has its own heartbeat. It desperately needs to be touched—filled. "What are you doing?" I ask him, my voice dripping with equal parts anger and need.

He removes his hands from my jeans and takes a step back. Holding up his index and middle fingers, a sly smirk lifts his lips. My eyes widen when I realize they're the same two fingers that were just pumping feverishly inside me.

Without missing a beat, he drags his tongue down his digits, licking my arousal.

"Mmm," he mutters. "Virgins really do taste better."

I gulp. Unsure of whether I'm turned on or disgusted right now.

How does he even know for sure I'm a virgin? Is that something a guy knows just from fingering a girl? Either way, I don't validate or invalidate his thinking. Instead, I bend down and snatch up the sweatshirt I was wearing.

"What the fuck are you doing?" he snaps as he jerks the sweatshirt from my hands, pulling my shirt out from inside it. "I took this off you for a reason."

I'm stunned. Unsure what the hell is happening. "I thought..."

He tosses my shirt back at me and I catch it against my chest, using it as a shield to hide my breasts now that my brain is back online and Rome doesn't look like he wants to murder me with his bare hands.

"You thought wrong." He holds the sweatshirt in the air, the veins in his hands protruding as he squeezes it. "This is my mom's and you have no fucking right wearing it."

My eyes go wide. "I'm...I...I'm sorry, Rome. I had no idea."

"Like hell you didn't." His jaw feathers, and that anger I was afraid of morphs his features once more.

"It's true," I tell him, trying like hell to prevent that side of him from coming back while we are locked in a small space together. "Sayer gave it to me before we left the house. I told him I didn't have any Misfits apparel to wear to the game and he went to his room and got it."

His shoulders slump slightly and relief floods my veins when I see he believes me. Rome brings the sweatshirt to his chest as if he's trying to hold tight to his mother with just that lifeline. I get it now, the anger, the sadness. And I threw it all in his face when I cheered for his brother like an idiot just to try to prove a point. And for what? To hurt him more than he already is?

That's not me. Rome might have some anger issues he needs to deal with, but I don't have to stoop to his level just because he picked on me. I can be the bigger person here so that he can grieve however he needs to.

"I really am sorry," I tell him again, this time not talking about the jersey, but I don't know if he realizes that.

He drops his hand to his side, still gripping the sweatshirt, and narrows his eyes. "Prove it."

"Prove I'm sorry? Aren't my words enough?" *Really?* Rome has this way of making me feel bad for him, just to say something stupid and affirm my resentment toward him.

"Not even close. Come to the party tonight, and maybe I'll forgive you."

If I thought my heart was beating fast when he was fingering me, that doesn't hold a candle to the lashing it's giving my chest right now. Brady and Julia mentioned something about a party earlier and I shut down the conversation before they could tell me where it was. The last time I went to a party in Willow Creek, bad things happened.

I take a minute to study him. He's not angry, doesn't look like he's planning anything particularly evil. But this uneasy feeling settles in my gut.

"I can't," I tell him. "I have homework."

"I see." He nods slowly, his lips pressed tight. "Then I guess you're not really sorry."

Wow. Gaslight much?

I have no idea why Rome wants me to go to this party. He doesn't even like me. I certainly can't stand him. Even more so now that he carried me to the brink of an orgasm and literally left me hanging high and dry. I should have known better. I really am a glutton for punishment.

And here I am, about to make another terrible choice for myself.

"Fine," I blurt out. "I'll go to your stupid party. But don't expect me to have fun."

His eyes light with mischief, only confirming my unease.

"Oh, I know you won't have fun, Freckles. Which is exactly why I want you to go." He turns around and pulls the door open. Thankfully, I don't hear any of the guys around as Rome slips out, giving me one last glance.

I quickly zip up my pants and put my shirt back on, feeling frazzled as hell as I watch him leave.

After a couple minutes of collecting my thoughts and mentally beating the shit out of myself for allowing things to go as far as they did, I forgive myself. Because I'm certain after this party tonight, I'll have a new reason to want to kick my own ass.

CHAPTER 11
ELODIE

"C\ome with me, B\rogan." I steeple my fingers, holding my hands together. "Please. I'm begging you. I barely know Brady and Julia and it would make me feel so much better having someone at the party who I can hide behind if needed."

The second I got home, I ran to my sister's room. Regret had been gnawing at me the entire ride and I knew I would need backup if I wanted to make sure I actually showed up to this party. I'm sure if I blew it off, Rome would find a way to "punish" me. While I pride myself on being an independent person, who makes her own life choices, I also would really like to avoid dealing with more gum in the future.

She sighs overdramatically, then says, "I guess I can go."

My eyebrows hit my forehead. "Really?" I didn't think it would be that easy. Then again, asking Brogan to party is a lot like asking a monkey to eat a banana.

"Sure." She shrugs as she sits at her vanity, sweeping the blush brush back and forth on her high cheekbone. "But you owe me one."

Her words take me back to the party, and the fight, that happened last year. I think about my hero often since moving to

Willow Creek. I'm still not sure who he is, but I hope one day I find out because I owe him one, too.

"You name it," I tell her, feeling hopeful about the night now that she's coming.

"Let me get you ready." Brogan lives for giving basic girls like me makeovers, so I should have seen that coming.

"Fine," I drag the word out. "But be kind, please."

"Always. Besides, I planned to go to the party anyway." She strokes her other cheekbone, grinning at me in the mirror. "I just wanted to fuck with you for a bit."

I grab the brush out of her hand and pull her head back, then I swipe the brush across her forehead. "You suck."

We both burst out in laughter as she takes the brush back from me. I look at her in the mirror as she drags her fingers across the streak of shimmery pink on her forehead. "Well, now I'm really not going."

"Screw you." I chuckle. "You're going and you're not leaving my side."

Knowing I'll have my sister there makes me feel at ease. She might be a year younger than me, but her social skills are way better than mine. Plus, Rome is less intense around everyone else. He says I'm the one who's pretending, when really he's the one who puts on a show for my family.

Brogan plucks a tissue from the box on her vanity and gracefully glides it across the blush on her forehead. "If I remember right, you're the one who left me last time we went to a party in Willow Creek."

I frown. "I did do that, but with good reason. You told me to." She knew I was over it when I walked away from Rome as demanded I come back and, what? Watch him make out with a random chick?

"You're right." She nods slowly. "But in my defense, I was a *little* bit tipsy that night."

I raise my eyebrows. "Mmmhmm. But not too tipsy to hang

out with Willow Creek's rival football team." Specifically, the three guys whose faces I will never forget.

"You know I'm a sucker for hot guys. Good, bad. Asshole, straitlaced. I like them all."

"Oh, I know you do. I just hope they're not there tonight. I don't even understand why they were at that party last year if they're such big rivals."

Brogan knows about what happened that night, to an extent. I couldn't bring myself to relive all of the events by telling her about the assault. What's done is done and as long as I don't see Damon, Miles, or Winton again, I'll be okay.

I haven't seen any of those three guys since that night last year. I don't even know if they got in any trouble when the cops showed up. I haven't asked, and I really don't want to. I'm all about putting the past behind me and moving forward. Chances are, if I see them tonight, I'll pretend like I've never met them before. They've probably forgotten all about me anyways.

"They likely went to start shit with the Misfits' team," Brogan says confidently. "And like you said, they got kicked out. The motives of men are impossible to understand, so it's best to not even try."

I wish I could live life as carefree as my sister. She knows who she is and owns it. I know who I am; I just want to be the one that gets through high school so she can start following her dreams.

"You're probably right." I sigh as I lean against the doorframe. "I'm sure they've learned their lesson and we won't see them again."

I'm sure Winton hasn't forgotten getting hit with a metal pipe, so hopefully that was enough to keep them all away.

"Don't hold your breath on that," Brogan says, crushing my hope as she pushes out the stool in front of her vanity and gets up. "We will see them again, no doubt. Ravencrest isn't that far away, and like you said, they're rivals."

She walks over to her bed and strips out of her cheer uniform, then tosses it on her bubble gum pink comforter.

Eyeing the teal-and-black uniform has me thinking about my encounter with Abby yesterday.

"What do you think of Abby?" I ask, out of nowhere.

Brogan goes to her walk-in closet and disappears inside. "Abby Bower? She's all right. Sort of stuck-up. Why did you ask?"

"No reason," I tell her, although it's a lie. I'm not about starting unnecessary drama. If I tell Brogan the things she said, she'll go straight to Abby in my defense. Brogan and I look out for each other like that.

Brogan pops her head out of the closet. "You sure? Because if she did something—"

"No, no." I assure her as I pick up a tube of mascara off of her vanity. "It's nothing like that. She just mentioned that she and Rome have a thing, and that we might see her around here at night. That's all."

She disappears back into her closet and raises her voice. "I'm not surprised. Rome holds the attention of most of the school. I don't know Abby well, but she definitely loves to be noticed."

"Like someone else I know."

"Hey." She huffs. "It's true. I like getting attention from guys. But I'd prefer the attention of just one. I just don't know who that *one* is yet. I have to get my feelers out there."

She walks out of the closet looking like a supermodel in a black satin halter dress that accentuates her hourglass frame, barely covering her ass. She spins around and I take in the open back with a single braid of fabric going up her spine. "Damn, Bro. You look hot."

She bats her lashes. "Why, thank you."

Just seeing her makes me feel miniscule and basic. I could never pull off a dress like that. I'm not petite like Brogan. I don't consider myself big, but I've got a thicker waist with more in-depth curves. Though, I do have nice legs and boobs that Brogan says she'd kill for.

Brogan joins me beside the vanity and grabs my hand. "Your turn." She takes the mascara from my hand and tosses it on her vanity before dragging me out of her room. "I'm thinking that cute black baby doll dress would be perfect."

I scrunch my nose. "The one I wore to our great-gran's funeral last summer?"

"Oh yeah. Scratch that. I'll just have to have a look-see." She pushes me toward my door with determination. I have a love-hate relationship with being Brogan's Barbie doll. On one hand, she always makes me look hot. On the other, I never feel like myself in what she dresses me in.

"You do realize I'm fully capable of picking out my own clothes?"

"Of course you are. It's just…"

"Just what?" I ask as I'm shoved into my room.

"We're going to pretend the party last year didn't happen." Brogan exhales, looking sad. "So, this is basically our debut party in Willow Creek. I just think…"

She trails off in a way I don't see her do often. I place my hand on hers. "Think what?"

Coming back to herself, her expression lights up. "We need to go big."

I remember that night so clearly, I doubt I'd ever forget. I was wearing a solid white tiered dress with puffy sleeves that rested about two inches above my knees. It was paired with a very cute pair of strappy Birkenstock sandals.

"I looked cute as hell at the party last year." It makes me depressed to think about how that night ended. How my dress was destroyed. How covered in mud my sandals were. The stains on my knees that I scrubbed for hours from falling in the leaves too many times to count while I waited to hear footsteps behind me.

Footsteps that never came. Thanks to my hero.

"You always look cute as hell," Brogan says as she heads to my closet. "But tonight, we're not going for cute. We're going for fucking hot."

I scratch my head, knowing I won't win this battle. I love my sister to death, but she is one persistent beotch.

"All right." I throw my hands in the air, letting them fall as I drop down on my bed. "Go have your look-see. But I want options."

She claps her hands together excitedly. "Then options you shall get."

Brogan and I compromise on a long-sleeved black smock dress. I haven't worn it in a couple years, so it's shorter than I'd like. She said that's what holds its appeal along with my boosted cleavage that peeks out of the top. Fighting me on my shoes is a battle she knows she won't win, so she didn't even fight me on that. The finishing touch is a pair of black open-toed midsummer sandals with straps that hug my ankles.

I checked the weather this morning, like I do every day when I wake up, and it looks like clear skies with a high of sixty-five tonight, so I should be okay without a sweater.

After begging—on her knees, I might add—I agreed to let Brogan do my makeup. We go back into her room and I hesitantly sit down on her vanity stool.

"Just subtle, Brogan. I mean it."

Brogan's favorite pastime is doing mine and Lake's makeup. I won't deny that she's really damn good at it, but she adds on a lot more layers than what I prefer. I wear makeup daily, but Mom always says, "The best way to wear makeup is to make it look like you're not wearing any." So that's what I do.

Brogan makes a throaty sound and cranes her neck. "Subtle is my middle name, sis."

I cover my mouth and cough out the word, "Bullshit."

Brogan presses her chin to my shoulder and looks at my reflection in the mirror as she drags her fingers around my hairline, bunching my hair. "Have I ever lied to you?"

"No," I say truthfully. "At least, not that I know of."

Brogan and I tell each other pretty much everything. There are some details of my life I leave out, if I think it's necessary. Such as the drama with Rome and Abby. I'm just not at a point where I feel like I need to share anything about that. It's mostly out of worry for Brogan. She's a new junior and Abby's an established senior with a big following at Willow Creek High. The last thing I want is for her to confront Abby and risk her name getting dragged through the mud.

I made the decision pretty quickly not to tell Brogan, or anyone else, about the way those guys groped me last year. It wasn't just because of the threat, but I know my mom would try to pursue legal action. At that time, I didn't plan to ever return to Willow Creek. I was fortunate enough to make it back in the hotel without Mom or Lake noticing my destroyed dress. I quickly changed, and the next day, I threw the dress in the large dumpster on the side of the hotel.

I also have zero intentions of telling Brogan about what happened in that storage room today. Do I feel guilty about not telling her? On so many levels. But more so, I feel ashamed. Rome is our new stepbrother. What would she think of me? Rome and I didn't even kiss—not that I would have wanted that. But he did put his fingers inside me. Now that I'm thinking about it, I feel dirty *and* ashamed. If I could go back and knee him in the balls before his hand went down my pants, I would.

After a few minutes of dabs and strokes on my face, and some curls in my long brown hair, Brogan takes a step back, grinning from ear to ear. "Girl, you are going to give the guys a run for their money tonight."

"If only," I mumble. For once I'd like to grab the attention of a guy who isn't Rome. But something tells me he's definitely going to be in my path tonight. He wanted me to go to this party for a reason, and I can't even begin to imagine what that reason is.

CHAPTER 12

ELODIE

WITH MY ARM locked around Brogan's, we walk down the paved driveway from where I parked on the side of the road. I decided to drive my car because I'm sure Brogan will have a couple drinks. We made a promise that when one of us wants to go, so does the other.

I still don't know whose grand estate this is, and I haven't bothered to ask. I could tell from my first night here last year that all the residents of Willow Creek are extremely wealthy, but I'd guess someone very important lives at this house.

"Greedy" by Tate McRae blasts through the speakers, and I feel the bass through the ground as we get closer to the house. The loud chatter and laughter are barely even audible over the blaring music.

As we approach the house, the smell of burning wood fills my nostrils. The front door is wide open with people coming in and out, drinks in hand.

There are people scattered everywhere—out front, around the fire, coming up the driveway, and going down. I'm not sure I've ever been part of a crowd so big. I've been to a few parties, but none of them were this lit. Then again, Bakersfield is much smaller than Willow Creek. Even so, the party last year was half this size.

Sensing my unease, Brogan asks, "How ya doing?" She squeezes my arm, doing an excellent job of making sure I'm comfortable. It's one of the reasons I wanted her here with me.

"Good, actually." I smile, meaning the words I say. "This should be fun." Seeing how many people are here sets my nerves at ease a bit because it means no one is going to give a damn about little ol' me.

"Hell yes! It's going to be fun!" Her voice booms over the music as she raises her free hand in the air. "It's Friday night, baby!"

Brogan does not give a flying fuck who hears her, what anyone thinks of her, or what anyone has to say about her. I admire that so much. She seriously is who I want to be when I grow up. It's funny considering she's only seventeen and I'm older than her, but it's the truth.

I spot Julia walking toward us, her hand slicing through the air as she waves. "You made it!" She looks freaking adorable in her baggy jean overalls and cut-off white shirt underneath. She's only about five feet tall with a short bob cut and bangs. She sort of reminds me of Velma from *Scooby-Doo*, but with much more appeal.

Brady is running up behind her while holding two cups, one in each hand. He's sporting another Hawaiian button-up shirt—this one mint green with palm trees on it—and a pair of tight-as-hell skinny jeans. "Slow down, wench," he hollers to Julia, trying to balance the cups without spilling them.

"Oh God," Brogan mumbles. "I don't know who these crazy people are, but if we just keep walking, maybe they'll pass by us."

I chuckle as I unwrap my arm from hers. "Stop it. Those are my friends."

"You have friends?"

"I met them at school. They're a lot of fun."

"Yeah." She pauses for a beat. "I can see that."

Picking up my pace, I meet Julia and Brady halfway, mostly to save Brady from spilling those drinks all over himself. But also because I'm pretty excited to see them. I knew they'd be here, but I have to admit, I was a little nervous I might not find them in the crowd.

"I see how it is." I hear Brogan grumble from behind me. "So you have friends now and I'm just chopped liver."

"For you, my dear." Brady passes me a drink, warranting a side-eye glare from Julia.

"Hey," Julia hisses at Brady. "Where's my drink?"

I laugh. "You can have it." I put my fingers on the cup and move it toward Julia while it's still in Brady's hand.

Instead of taking that one, Julia snatches the other cup from him. "That's okay. I'll just drink his." She smirks at him over the rim of the cup as she takes a drink.

"Thank you," I tell Brady as I accept his offer. I bring the cup about an inch from my nose, and my suspicions of it being alcohol are confirmed when the smell of diluted ethanol rolls up my nostrils. With no intention of drinking it, I hold the cup anyway. It makes me feel like less of a goody two-shoes, and it also eliminates the need for anyone else to try and give me a drink.

Julia throws an arm around my shoulders, still holding the cup that's sloshing liquid. I crane my neck, trying to make sure it's not spilling on me. "We are so happy you're here." She beams excitedly, the stench of vodka on her breath.

Brogan joins us and I slither slowly out of Julia's hold on me. "Guys, this is my sister, Brogan."

"Welcome to *mi casa*," Brady says, taking me by surprise as he offers a hand to Brogan. "The fire is warm. The drinks are cold. And the music is dance-worthy."

Brogan accepts his handshake. "Thanks for having us."

"Wait a minute," I cut in. "This is *your* party, as in your house?"

"My party—my parents' house. But don't worry. They're out of town until sometime next week, working on some campaign bullshit."

Brady Newton. It all clicks. *Senator Newton.* Brady's dad is the damn state senator. I'm not sure why I'm surprised, but I am.

I don't get it. If Brady throws these immaculate parties, then why is Rome so cruel to him? Better yet, why would Brady allow Rome to come to his house after the way he treated him?

There is so much to learn about these people and this lifestyle I've been thrust into.

"Shall we?" Julia says, motioning to the house.

We all walk together and join the party. There are people inside, outside, and I think I even saw someone trying to climb on the roof from an upper balcony, but I can't be certain. Perhaps they were looking for a window.

It looks like the entire junior and senior classes are here, and even students from the surrounding schools. The party is insane. Drinks are flowing, bass is thumping through my body, and it looks like an all-around good time.

The house looks even bigger as I stand in front of it. Like, three times the size of Grant's house. Everything is pristine and white—the house, the marble stairs leading up to it, the shutters. Two large pillars frame the entrance and in the center of the freshly cut front lawn, a water fountain glows with colorful lights.

"Who wants to go out back by the fire?" Brady asks, pointing from Julia, to me, to Brogan.

"Actually," Brogan says, "I'm gonna go chat with a couple girls on the cheer team." Her eyes move to mine. "You good?"

I nod. "Yeah, I'm fine."

We made a deal to stay together, but I actually feel pretty at ease here, especially knowing it's Brady's house and not some stranger's.

"I'll meet you both back there," Julia tells us before heading toward the house.

"Looks like it's just me and you," Brady says, locking his arm around mine. "This way." He gestures toward the side of the house and we're met with a cobblestone path.

We get out back and I'm surprised to see there are even more people back here than out front. Through the crowd, I see a contained fire on a brick patio. Orange flames dance around and smoke billows toward the sky. I discreetly discard my drink and watch as a guy jumps through the fire and I hold my breath, certain he's going to fall in. But when he lands on the other side, laughing his ass off, I exhale a sigh of relief.

There's a huge underground pool and a few girls sit on the ledge with their feet in the water. Beside it is a hot tub that's packed. I'm not sure another body could squeeze in if they tried.

"This is crazy," I tell Brady, my face showing my surprise. "I've never been to a party like this."

"What can I say? We know how to party in Willow Creek." He grins, clearly proud of what he's accomplished here. I watch him for a second, surveying the crowd, and I find that I really do like Brady. Not to date, but he just makes me feel comfortable in every sense of the word. As if we were once good friends in another life.

Then I see him.

The one person I really didn't want to see tonight, but knew I would. Standing on the other side of the fire is Rome, making out with Abby. His hands are resting on her ass that's barely covered in her bright pink dress. I wanna throw up right here and now. It was only hours ago he was tasting my arousal on the tongue that's inside her mouth.

Before I'm able to look away, his eyes land on mine, peering over her shoulder. There's a sudden shift in his demeanor. His eyes widen, and he takes a step back. I watch as he whispers something in her ear then dismisses her with a pat on her ass.

"Great," I mumble under my breath as he approaches us. I notice Brady stiffening, and it makes me question what secrets Rome was talking about earlier.

I watch behind him as Abby scowls in my direction, or maybe she's scowling at me. Either way, she is *pissed*.

Rome is putting a target on my back right now and he doesn't even realize it.

"Damn, Freckles." Rome's eyes skim up and down my body as he steps directly in front of me. "You clean up nice."

I shiver under his gaze, pretending like I didn't hear anything he said.

"Newton," Rome chirps as he claps a hand on Brady's shoulder. "Why don't you be a good host and go fetch me a beer?"

My jaw drops open. "Seriously, Rome? What the hell is the matter with you?"

A mischievous glint sparks in Rome's eyes as he narrows them at Brady, challenging him to object.

"It's all good, Elodie," Brady says, as if there is nothing wrong with Rome making him *fetch a beer*.

I exhale heavily, annoyed as hell with the way Rome treats Brady. But I'm even more annoyed that Brady allows it.

Once Brady is out of hearing range, I shove Rome. "You're a real asshole, you know that?"

"Hey, at least I don't deny it. What you see is what you get. Unlike some people I know."

I huff airily. "I'm out of here." I sidestep him, making my way onto the patio by the fire. Out of nowhere, my foot lands on a slimy banana peel and I go sideways. My arms fly out, ready to soften the impact when I hit the ground. But before I do, I'm grabbed by the waist by someone behind me, saving me from the humiliation of a public fall.

Once I'm steadied on my feet, I spin around and see that it's Rome who caught me, his hands still on my waist. "You're welcome," he says with a cocksure expression on his face.

I step out of his hold, opting to use a few words from his vocabulary. "I didn't ask for your help." I echo the words he used when I saved him from burning down the house.

I am grateful, don't get me wrong. But I won't let Rome know that. This guy's ego is already too big for his head. A simple thank you might make it explode.

He nods slowly. "Oh, I see how it is. Someone saves you and suddenly they're the fool?"

"Nope," I say confidently. "The only fool is you. You made me come to this party thinking I'd have a terrible time, and aside from my almost-fall, I'm actually enjoying myself."

My words trail off when Rome jerks me by the arm, pulling me away from the crowd.

The next thing I know, my spine is slammed into the side of the house and I'm staring back into the eyes of Satan—the same ones that bore into mine in the storage closet earlier today.

"Jesus Christ," I bellow. "You want a *thank you* for catching me, then thank you." Rome really has no chill.

"You think this is about me catching you? It's not!" he shouts. I glance around and suddenly realize no one would be able to hear me over the music if something were to happen. "This just adds to the number of times I've saved your ungrateful ass. You wanna know why I didn't play in the game tonight? It's because I was benched for half the season…because of you."

My eyes go wide in shock, my jaw practically on the ground as I stare at Rome, waiting for him to tell me he's fucking with me. But he doesn't. In fact, he shows no sign that this is a joke. There is no way he got put on the sidelines for half the season for throwing gum in my hair.

"Well shit, Freckles. Cat got your fucking tongue? You don't even give a damn, do you?"

"I do…I do care, Rome. I don't understand, though. How can I be to blame for you being benched?" My voice cracks as I speak, an immense amount of guilt heavy on my chest for reasons unbeknownst to me.

"I'm suspended from playing because of the nice little assault charge on my record. Because *some rat* decided to call the cops on me last year—Ravencrest fucking cops."

No!

My mind goes blank as I stare at Rome. A flood of memories from a year ago come rushing back to me. Those icy blue eyes, his voice as he told me to run. I've thought about the guy who saved me for so long, and here he is—standing right in front of me.

And the rat he's referring to is *me*. I called the cops—but not on Rome. I called them so he could have backup because those guys were ganging up on him.

This explains so much. The constant jabs, the pranks, the threats. Him thinking I owe him my life. Rome truly does hate me, because he blames me for his suspension and I have no doubt that charge caused a lot of other things to happen in his life over the past year.

"I'm so sorry. I had no idea…"

I reach out and touch his forearm, but he jumps back. His head shakes in utter disappointment. "You ruined everything. I lost my offer to play ball in college. No one wants me now. My whole future went up in flames because of that impulsive fucking phone call." He clenches his fists as some of his hair falls in his face, and I see it all now.

The knife just keeps digging deeper into my chest. He lost so much and it's all my fault.

"Rome," I whisper, trying again as I reach for him.

"Don't fucking touch me!" He backsteps before dragging his fingers through his hair and walking back toward the front of the house.

When Rome said I ruined his life, he meant it.

Tears blur my vision as I watch him walk away, his shoulders hunched and his hands shoved into his pants pockets. Rome saved me from those guys last year, and when I thought I was helping him, I was actually digging the grave for his future as a football player.

Brady walks up to Rome and hands him a cup. In a violent motion, Rome smacks the red cup out of Brady's hand. It flies through the air, beer spilling in its wake before the cup hits the ground.

Brady's eyes are wide with caution as he comes toward me, my back still flush against the side of his house. "What the hell is his problem?"

It's not my place to share Rome's troubles, so I just shrug my shoulders. "It's Rome. Everything is a problem to him."

I know I should leave Rome alone and give him time to calm down, but the agonizing ache in my chest tells me I need to go after him and try to fix this. Explain to him that I didn't have ill intentions when I called the police. Maybe then he'll forgive me and let me off the hook he's hung me on.

"Actually," I say as I jump away from the house, taking small steps toward the front as I speak. "I forgot to tell Rome something important. I'll meet you out back, okay?"

His eyebrows nearly hit his forehead. "You're sure it's a good idea to go after him when he's in a mood?"

"I live with the jerk. I can handle him." Before Brady can say anything to stop me, I jog out front. My eyes scour every face in search of Rome and after a minute of looking, I find him. Stopping for a second, I watch as he walks up the stairs to the front door. A couple people try to talk to him—stop him—but he brushes them off and keeps moving forward with his head down.

I pick up my pace and hurry up the stairs and through the front door, only to be submerged in what looks like a mosh pit at a heavy metal concert. A crowd is gathered at the entrance. Some trying to enter, others trying to leave. The musky scent of sweat fills my senses and when I look up, I see why. Right beside me is a guy who is at least six and half feet tall with his hands in the air holding a large cooler. "Out of the way, assholes," I hear him say as he makes his way through the door.

I'm at a standstill, waiting for people to move, because no matter how hard I push, someone pushes back harder.

Feeling defeated, I'm about to turn around when I see Rome

going up a winding staircase. I cup my hands around my mouth and shout, "Rome!" But my effort is futile as my small voice is swallowed up by the riotous sounds around me.

"For the love of God. Let me through," I whisper-yell. Then, giving it all I've got, I lunge forward, breaking through the wall of bodies. Once I'm away from the entrance, I'm happy to see there is breathing room.

While there are a lot of people inside the house, it appears most are outside—aside from the two dozen at the door.

I look up and see Rome walking past the open banister upstairs, heading left. I follow him with my eyes, watching as he enters a room.

I hurry to the stairs, going up two at a time. The hallway is as long as the house with around seven different doors up here, and at the end of the hall is another staircase. I move quickly to the room Rome entered and once I'm there, I pause for a second in front of it. Without thinking, because I know I'll talk myself out of this, I knock gently.

"Rome," I say softly. "Are you in there?"

When there's no response, I turn the handle, and to my surprise, it opens. I step into a very large bedroom, closing the door behind me. It's pretty basic, so I take it to be a guest room.

There's a stream of light coming from a cracked open door on the far side of the room that catches my eye. I tiptoe toward it, my heart thumping at warp speed in my chest. "Rome," I say again, this time my voice nearly a whisper. Maybe I don't really want him to hear me. Maybe part of me knows this is a terrible idea.

Yet, here I am, gently inching the door open just enough to poke my head inside.

I see him standing with his palm pressed to the marble sink, his eyes down. Pushing the door open farther, I step inside, rubbing my slick palms together.

"Rome," I say one more time, this time loud enough for him to hear me.

His head shoots up and he eyes me through the reflection in the mirror. "What the fuck?" he snaps, spinning around quickly. He jabs a stern finger in the air, pointed at the door. "Get the fuck out!"

The way his icy blue eyes are glazed over with animosity makes my insides shiver. I quickly close the distance between us and propel forward. Not allowing him to get the upper hand, I immediately reach out and grab his arm, feeling the tension in his muscles. I'm taking a risk here, but I need him to hear me out. "I didn't mean for you to get hurt in the process, Rome!"

The veins in his arm protrude and he uses his free hand to grab me by the throat. "Do you have a fucking death wish, Freckles?"

Cold fingertips dig into the skin of my neck, cutting off my air supply. Then in a swift motion, he pushes me into the wall with his hands on my shoulders.

I gulp, drawing in a few bumpy breaths. "Let me fix this." I feel the words claw their way up my throat, hot tears welling in the corners of my eyes. "Please!"

He's in my face, his jaw ticking with fury. He plants his hands on either side of my head, caging me in. "You wanna fix this?"

I nod rapidly, sucking in another deep breath. "Yes, I really do."

His features suddenly shift from someone terrifying to a person intrigued. His mouth tugs up in a sly grin, his voice thick and raspy. "Then get on your knees and fix it."

My heart jumps into my throat. How can he even be suggesting this? He saved me from this exact situation and now he thinks I will just give it to him. Not to mention, we're practically related.

He's my stepbrother, for fuck's sake.

I feel like I've been transfixed back to that park a year ago and I'm staring at a complete stranger who wants to use and abuse my body.

My eyebrows pinch together tightly. "You can't be serious?"

"I'm dead serious." He leans in and his fingers painfully pinch my chin. "You want to fix this, then make me forget how brutally you fucked up my life."

My head shakes no and he tightens his grip. "That's not going to fix anything."

"I beg to differ." He stands to his full height, towering over me and trapping me between him and the wall at my back. "I'm gonna fuck your mouth and you're gonna let me. If you don't, I'll tell the whole student body you're the one who potentially cost their team the season by having their star player benched."

The threats just keep coming and coming. No matter what I do, I can't win. Rome quite literally has me wrapped around his finger.

I have to be strong. It's the only way I'm going to survive this next year.

Without another word, Rome puts his hand on the top of my head and pushes forcefully. I drop to my knees, my body trembling.

The sound of his zipper coming down is deafening, but it's nothing compared to the boom of his pants dropping to his ankles.

I look up to see him fisting his cock in his hand. It's girthy and long and I'm suddenly terrified. Still gripping himself, he presses his soft head against my lips.

"I can't," I tell him, my voice shaking even more than my hands, which is really saying something.

"You can, and you will. You say you're sorry, then prove it."

He said the same thing when I realized I was wearing his mom's sweatshirt. How far do I have to go to prove my apologies are authentic?

"I've never done this before," I tell him honestly. He grins widely. Rome looks at me like I'm a toy he wants to break, and he has no idea how many cracks this is already causing.

"Oh, Freckles. By the time I'm done with you, you'll be sucking dick like a hooker."

I can't breathe. My chest is rising and falling, but it doesn't feel like air is actually entering my lungs, or expelling from them. I try to tell myself this isn't the same thing as what Winton did to me. I could shove Rome back and refuse, but I don't want to face the consequences of that. I don't want to risk my new friends being on his war path. And I don't want him to sabotage my future.

If this is what will make him believe I really am sorry, then I have to do it.

Feeling dizzy and unsure of what the hell I'm doing, I circle my tongue around his swollen head, allowing him to guide himself inside my mouth. I keep my hands at my sides, my fists balled in tight knots.

I can do this. It's no longer just about earning Rome's forgiveness. Now my reputation in Willow Creek is at stake. I have no doubt when Rome sets his sights on destroying someone, he follows through. So I have to make sure this is the best damn blow job of his life.

With his hand on the back of my head, he inches me forward while guiding his cock into my mouth. I open wide, taking care not to bite him, though the thought crossed my mind.

Bite him and run. That'll teach him not to blackmail people.

But I don't. I remain still as Rome moves his hips back and forth, watching the tight seal of my lips around his shaft.

My cheeks hollow as I suck him deeper into my mouth and the groan he lets out has heat racing to my core. The tip of his dick grazes the back of my throat and I feel a shiver run through his body.

Rome flattens his palm on my head, rolling his hips to my sucking motions. I focus on the scent of his cologne that wafts in and out of my nostrils—it's earthy and crisp and allows me to step out of this moment. I imagine myself walking through a forest in the rain, feeling the small droplets of water hit my nose.

I'm snapped back to reality when Rome lets out a guttural growl. Something strange happens inside me. I begin to revel in the control I have over his pleasure. I can make this good for him and maybe that will be enough. I don't exactly know what I'm doing, but I've watched porn, so I try to do what those girls do.

My tongue dances along the length of him, taking in every inch and swirling around the head with each stroke. His legs shake and my hands reach out to grab them as I bob my head without him having to force me. Both of his hands slam into the wall behind me as he sucks in a breath.

Suddenly, he pushes himself farther into my mouth. I gag. The corners of my eyes sting from hot tears. But they're not tears of sadness. It's a bodily reaction from his forceful thrust.

As I push up on my knees to get a better angle, I can feel the wetness between my legs. I want someone to make me feel as good as I am making Rome feel right now.

I'm not sure when I went from being an independent woman to someone on their knees for a man as an apology. Or when I went from being uninterested in sex to horny as fuck. But Rome ignited something in me in the storage room and whatever it was, it can't be undone until I feel the ultimate high I'm carrying him to.

Rome moves his hand from the back of my head and puts two fingers beneath my chin, forcing it up. "Watch me, Freckles. I wanna see those eyes when I come in your mouth."

His husky voice makes my eyes become hooded as I stare up at him. He really is beautiful in every way. The veins in his arm bulge as I bring him to the edge.

I can do this. We're almost there.

I want to surprise him; I want to be more than what he thinks he sees right now. So, before he can stop me, I reach between his legs and grab his balls, massaging them. He gasps as he leverages himself on the wall with his free hand.

"Fuck!" The head of his cock pulsates against my tongue and his features morph into a lustful daze.

I hold my breath, prepared for what comes next. Hot cum shoots onto my waiting tongue as my eyes stay on his.

Instead of swallowing right away, I let the salty, bitter liquid pool. It isn't until he pulls away that I take it all down in one gulp. We stay there for a minute, frozen. The ache between my legs is throbbing and I want nothing more than a release as powerful as the one I just gave him. For the first time since I've known Rome, he isn't looking at me like someone he hates.

I don't know what this look is, exactly, but I don't dislike it. Just when I'm about to say something I would regret tomorrow, Rome shatters the bubble of peace we were in.

He pats his hand to my cheek, condescendingly. "See, that wasn't so bad, was it?"

I wipe the back of my hand across my mouth, my heart racing at warp speed while my own tingles of desire shoot through my core.

My stomach churns with a mixture of Rome's cum and my own regret. I have to stop allowing myself to get into these situations. Rome and I cannot be alone together anymore. I may be strong, but being on Rome's bad side isn't something either of us will survive.

"Are we even now?" I ask him softly, hoping this is the end.

Once he's got his pants pulled back up, he crouches down in front of me, his hot breath on my face. He drags his thumb across my lower lip. "Not even close. You said you owed me one last year, and as long as you're living in my house, I'll be collecting."

I swallow hard. "It doesn't have to be this way. We can find a way so this year is not so awful, Rome."

He chuckles, and the relaxed man I witnessed just a moment ago is gone as his eyes darken on me. "Don't you get it, Freckles? Have you not heard a damn word I've said? You destroyed my fucking life."

"I didn't mean for you to get in trouble." I try not to raise my voice but sometimes talking to Rome is like speaking to a child who refuses to listen. "I swear! If you'll just tell me what happened, maybe—"

He fists my hair and yanks my head back as he crowds me. "I'll tell you everything, Freckles. I saved you. You ruined me. The end. But if you keep this up and do exactly what I say, maybe I won't ruin your life in return."

With that, he lets go of me, gets to his feet, and walks out the bathroom door. I'm left on my knees with his cum stained on my tongue and a pit of regret hollowing out my stomach.

CHAPTER 13
ELODIE

AFTER A FEW MINUTES of wallowing in self-pity, I force myself up and head downstairs. I'm grateful to see Julia almost immediately. Though, I'm not exactly thrilled to see she's chatting it up with Abby. I suppose I shouldn't be surprised, considering they attend school together. Just because I'm new doesn't mean everyone else is. There's a sense of loneliness that comes with being thrust into a class of people who grew up together. By the way Brogan has garnered a crowd around her, I don't think she feels that same loneliness as me.

"Hey, girls," I say when I reach Julia and Abby.

Julia looks at me, and I can immediately tell she's not excited to be standing here with Abby. It's reaffirmed when she mouths the words, "Help me."

I chuckle a little and I'm about to say something to her along the lines of, *Can I talk to you for a sec?* when Abby inserts herself between us. She throws an arm around Julia, who is a whole half foot shorter than her. Abby seems a little too happy I've interrupted their conversation.

"I'm so glad you're here, Elodie. We were just talking about you."

I grin at Julia in anticipation. "Is that so?"

Any conversation with Abby about me has to be interesting. I can already tell Abby doesn't like me. I don't know her at all, but I don't like the vibe I get in her presence.

Julia rolls her eyes and I can tell she's bored and ready to get the hell out of here.

But Abby, not so much. It almost feels like a trap. As if she was using Julia for information, or to bait me. I refuse to think too much into it because I don't care what Abby, or anyone else, thinks about me.

"We were wondering where you've been all this time. Then we saw you walk down the stairs. I mean, you don't even know anyone here. So…" Abby smacks her glossy lips. "Who were you with?"

"You're right. I was upstairs. I had a headache, so I found a bed to lie down in." It's a lie, but there's no way in hell I'm telling her, or anyone else, the truth—that I just had my step-brother's big fat dick in my mouth.

Now that I think about it, it's a little exciting having this secret and knowing that Abby has no idea what happened between Rome and me today—twice.

"Alone?" Abby asks, pressing for details.

"Like you said, I don't know anyone here, so is there a reason to think I was with someone, *Abby*?" My tone drips with sarcasm and if she doesn't pick up on it then that's her problem.

"Good point." Her tone shifts rapidly, giving me whiplash. "Let me grab us all a drink so we can cheers to Elodie's arrival in Willow Creek." She moves a finger between Julia and me. "Don't go anywhere."

The second Abby slips away, I grab Julia's arm. "Run?"

She laughs. "I thought you'd never ask."

It's just my luck that the second we turn around, I walk smack-dab into Luke Aarons. "In a hurry?" he asks in his sexy masculine voice.

Why do all the good-looking guys have to be jerks? It's not fair.

"Actually, yes," I say.

But at the same time, Julia says, "No."

My expression morphs into puzzlement. "Julia," I grit out while nodding my head to the left. "Let's go."

A smug grin spreads across her lips. "What's the hurry?"

I exhale tiringly, now fully aware that Julia has a crush on Luke. Are all the girls in this school brainwashed by the football players? All of them but me?

My shoulders slump in defeat when Abby approaches us with a girl I've never seen at her side. She's adorable with a pair of plastic frames that are far too big for her face, and side swept bangs that attempt to hide a forehead full of pimples. Abby passes me a drink, then Julia. She turns to the girl and takes the cup she's holding. "Thanks, Jenna. You're a doll."

She used her to carry her drink? What a fucking bitch!

"Actually, Jenna," I blurt out. "You're welcome to stay with us." I push my drink toward her. "You can have mine. I'm not drinking tonight."

A smile raises Jenna's cheekbones. "Really?" I nod in response and she reaches for the drink, but Abby snatches it from my hand.

"Of course you're not," Abby sputters. "Rome mentioned you were a bit...prudish."

"Prudish?" I repeat. "Rome said that?"

I think Abby is full of shit. But even if what she's saying is true, I don't care what Rome thinks or says about me. Yet, for some reason that comment almost hurts worse than me being pushed to my knees just five minutes ago.

"Mmmhmm." Abby brings her own drink to her mouth, nodding as she sips.

"Fuck Rome. He doesn't know a thing about me." I snatch my drink from her hand and waste no time tipping it back and sucking down all the contents.

How's that for prudish? Or how about how I just gave him a blow job upstairs. Or let him finger me after the game? I wonder if he'll tell her that. I can guarantee after tonight, he'll be calling me many names, but prudish won't be one of them.

Maybe for once in my life I don't have to be the good girl. Maybe, just this one time, I can let loose and enjoy life without overthinking.

Feeling pissed off, I say, "Jenna, let's go get you that drink." I leave Julia and Luke talking and pass by Abby with a smirk. I would love to stick my tongue out at her and flip her drink up just so I can see her face when it spills down her ugly pink dress. It's not really ugly, but I'm going to convince myself it is because her soul is fucking horrid.

Before we even make it to the kitchen, where drinks are being poured left and right, the alcohol I drank begins to take hold. My body feels as light as a feather, my chest warm and fuzzy inside.

"I don't know what was in the cup," I tell Jenna. "But it was strong." Then it hits me, I haven't even introduced myself. "I'm Elodie, by the way."

She pushes her glasses up and smiles widely, showing off a full set of metal braces. "I know who you are. You're Rome's new stepsister, right?"

I grumble, "Don't remind me."

She laughs lightly, but it's more out of pity. "If you just stay out of his way, you'll be fine."

Easier said than done. It seems lately, I'm always in Rome's way. And if I'm not, he inserts himself in my path.

Some guy Jenna knows offers us each a shot of caramel-colored liquor and I pass. Whatever I just had is hitting me like a ton of rocks. Julia joins us, and I stay with them while they both take a shot.

Julia slams the small glass on the counter and her mouth draws back. "Damn, that was spicy."

Within a matter of minutes, I'm feeling more alive than I've ever been. Even when I went to parties with Brogan, I never drank. That drink is likely the largest I have ever consumed and the most I've ever drank in one night.

"Juliaaaa," I mumble, throwing an arm around her shoulder and allowing the weight of my body to hang on hers. "Please don't tell me you like Luke Aarons."

"Like him, no? Do I want him to do dirty things to me? Hell yes. I would cut off my left tit just to feel that man's arms wrapped around my naked body."

"Oh my God, Julia." I crack up laughing. "You are baaaad."

Jenna and Julia fill their cups, and I realize I haven't seen Brogan in a while. I'm scouring the kitchen when "Wild Ones" by Jessie Murph and Jelly Roll blasts through the air, stopping me in my tracks. "We have to dance!" I scream over the music and the loud noises surrounding me.

Julia and Jenna shake their heads no, but my body starts moving to the beat, and before I know what's happening, I'm being lifted onto the center island in the kitchen.

Not giving a damn who's watching, I let myself go and sway my limber body to the music. A crowd gathers around me and I feel like the star of the show. I've never had attention like this. People are chanting my name. Hands are raised, trying to give me drinks, but I don't accept them. I just let my head roll back and my body moves effortlessly. I feel amazing right now for someone who's only had one drink. It'll wear off by the time I need to drive, so I'm good. Even though I know I'll regret all this tomorrow, I'm living for tonight.

My mind is anywhere but at this party when I suddenly feel cold fingers run up my leg. Something snaps inside me. It's dark and foreboding and a reminder of why I don't trust people.

Tension infiltrates my body, and I stop dancing, remembering what it felt like to be touched when I didn't want to be. I imagine them being Winton's grimy fingers, prodding around on my body when I begged him to stop. In an instant, I swing my foot forward, kicking someone wearing a football jersey right in the face.

Not letting him ruin my night, I keep on dancing. Tomorrow I can be Elodie Astor. Tonight I just want to be free.

CHAPTER 14

ROME

AFTER I LEFT Elodie in the bathroom, Abby was waiting for me outside the bedroom door. Imagine my surprise when I saw her standing there looking all pissy like I was doing something wrong by being behind a closed door. She asked who else was in there, and I told her it's none of her damn business. Then, she begged me to leave with her and go back to her place. I politely declined in the best way I know how and left her upstairs to dry her pitiful tears.

I've been outside for the last half hour. I keep expecting to see Elodie, but when she doesn't appear, I decide to go back in the house.

Now that Elodie knows the hell she raised that night, it's time to find out how far she'll go for forgiveness.

She didn't wanna suck me off, that was obvious. I'm actually surprised she didn't put up a fight after everything I've done to her. Or at the very least, made me finish what I started after the game.

I made her feel so fucking good earlier. She was creaming all over my fingers as I carried her to the brink of her orgasm and left her there. She's probably been thinking about it all day. I could tell when I fingered her that I'm the first to ever enter her. She was tight as fuck. I'd love more than anything to slip my dick inside her and claim that cunt as mine.

In due time, I will. The feeling I got knowing she's never been touched is indescribable.

A sense of possessiveness took over my mind in the storage closet. Just the thought of someone else taking my place between her legs has my blood boiling. Knowing I'm the first guy she's ever sucked off only made it that much better.

She was incredible too. When she began to take control, it was like my body craved every bit of her. For a solid minute I just watched, utterly transfixed on what she was doing as she learned how to swallow my cock.

I want to destroy Elodie for what she did to me, but I have a feeling she's going to be my demise in the process.

With a cold drink in my hand, I use the French doors off the deck that are supposed to be off-limits. Brady says that foot traffic from too many doors is messy, but I've never been one to follow rules. Besides, this place is fucking trashed as it is. I can almost guarantee once the party clears, it will take no more than two hours for him to have the house spotless with his hired help.

As soon as I step through the door into the kitchen, I see her dancing like a fucking idiot on the kitchen counter. Something's not right. This is *not* Elodie. She would never.

She's wearing a dress, so naturally guys are gaping at her from below. Squeezing the cup in my hand, beer foams out of it and I crush it in my fist, feeling slivers of the plastic dig into my skin.

"Elodie!" I shout over the loud music and chatter coming from every direction. "Elodie!" It's no use, she either can't hear me, or she's too fucked up to even care. It's been, like, twenty minutes. How could she get this trashed in twenty minutes?

Fuck. This is Elodie. I would put money on the fact that she's never really had alcohol before and she got her hands on some jungle juice shit.

I'm pushing my way through the crowd when I see Gage, Misfits' backup QB, with his hand on her legs. His fingers creep upward and I move faster, ready to knock his fucking teeth out.

Before I make it to Elodie, she takes notice of Gage touching her. Her body freezes, her slitted eyes down on him. For a second I think she's just going to yell at him or tell him to back off. But in one powerful movement, she lifts her leg and kicks him square in the face, sending him reeling backward. Everyone around her gasps and cheers, but she pays no attention to the crowd. She's in her own little world right now.

Not missing a beat, she keeps on dancing, and I see the fire in her eyes. It's burning as bright as it did the night she pushed me in the pool. Elodie's got guts, I'll give her that.

I'm not sure if I should be proud of her right now, or pissed that she put herself in this position. I finally reach her when I catch Abby out of the corner of my eye. She's tucked away in the corner with her phone raised. Bypassing Elodie, I let her do her thing for a moment longer.

Creeping up to Abby's side and without a word, I snatch her phone from her hand. "What the hell are you doing?"

I look at the video still recording while Abby laughs her ass off like this is the highlight of her night. "This is epic, Rome. I mean, look at her making a fool of herself. I couldn't resist."

Ignoring everything she says, I stop the recording and quickly text it to myself, then I delete the text log between Abby and me and the video from her phone, leaving no proof that it existed.

I shove her phone into her chest. "The only one who looks like a fool is you."

Her eyes go wide and she stomps her high heel to the marble floor like a child. "Rome!" she hollers. "Are you seriously taking her side?" When I ignore her, she shouts louder. "Rome!"

I make my way back to the center island and nudge some gawking asshole out of the way. He huffs in response but doesn't say a word because he knows better.

Then, Luke slithers his way past me, a wide grin on his face, and his eyes dead set on Elodie. "Why don't you come down and dance like that on my lap, baby?"

No the fuck he didn't.

I ball my fist and bring it straight to his shoulder. "What the hell are you doing?"

"She's fucking toast, man. Let me have her."

I roll my neck, breaking up the tension before shoving my palms to his chest, sending him crashing into a few bodies behind him.

"What the fuck, Cromwell!"

I just shake my head at him, teeth grinding.

I walk behind the counter and reach up, grabbing Elodie by the waist. I then slowly lower her feet to the floor. "Fun's over, Freckles."

"Hey," she mumbles. "I was dancing." Her words slur and the stench of liquor rolls off her breath.

She sways to the left, then to the right, but I steady her with my hands still on her waist. "I'm taking you home."

In an instant, she spins around to face me with a smoldering glare. "Like hell you are. I'm staying here with my friends."

Aiden appears out of nowhere and I'm curious if he's been watching this shitshow too. "Let her stay, man. She's having fun."

I glower at him, my jaw set. Since when are *my* best friends suddenly so interested in my stepsister?

Aiden tosses his hands in the air and doesn't argue. "Does she need a ride?" he asks, so sure that I'll actually pass her over to him and let him drive her home.

"No, she doesn't need a ride," I stammer. "I've got her. Now fucking go."

I'm not sure why I'm so annoyed right now but something about my boys watching Elodie dance on the counter rubs me the wrong way. The fact that everyone was watching her, looking up at her panties, touching her legs, sends a raging inferno inside me.

"Rome," Elodie chokes out. "I don't feel so good."

Jesus Christ. "Okay, come with me." I lead her through the back doors in the kitchen, while everyone we pass by assesses us.

"You taking off, Cromwell?" I hear someone say in the distance. I just nod, getting a few pats on the back and a couple *see ya laters.* Pretty sure I even heard someone say something along the lines of, *He really does get all the ladies, even the ones who live in his house.*

The second we hit the deck, Elodie runs to the side and begins vomiting profusely over it. A couple stragglers follow us out the door, and it isn't until I'm crossing the deck to Elodie that I realize one of them is Abby.

Music and laughter from the yard below ring in my ears, and at this point, I'm just ready to fucking leave. I came here to have a good time, maybe fuck with Elodie a bit, but now that she's inebriated, it's not even fun. I did get my dick sucked, so it's a typical Willow Creek party.

I train my eyes on anything but Abby, since I prefer her to think I don't even notice she's there, but she speaks anyways. "Why are you helping her, Rome? You said yourself, she's a stuck-up bitch who thinks she does no wrong."

Not exactly what I said, but close. Shows how well Abby pays attention. I'm pretty sure my words were just, *Elodie is a bitch.* And I stand by that. Me helping her right now has nothing to do with my hatred toward her. It's simply a matter of getting her out of here before someone takes advantage of her and I'm forced to choke the life out of them with my bare hands. In which case, I'd go to prison and I'd probably blame Elodie for that, too, because she doesn't know how to control her-fucking-self.

"You ready?" I ask dryly at Elodie's side.

She lifts her head for a moment, her fingers wrapped around the ledge of the deck. Then she opens her mouth and throws up some more.

I turn around, putting my back to the railing with my hands held to it behind me.

Abby takes slow steps forward until she's directly in front of me, her hands on my sides. "Come on, Rome. Just forget about her and leave with me."

I look past her and see Gage in the yard with an ice pack on his eye. I should feel sorry for the fucker, but I don't. If anything, I wanna blacken the other eye just to teach him a lesson. Elodie is off-limits, to him and everybody else. And they are about to find that out very soon.

"Rome," Abby says again, and I'm getting really tired of hearing my name come out of her mouth.

"What?!" I huff. "What the fuck do you want, Abby?"

Her hands drop from my sides and she takes a step back. "Wow. So that's how it's gonna be?"

I throw my hands up. "How's what gonna be? We're not a couple, Abby! Hell, I don't even think we're friends. So please tell me what the hell you want from me."

Her head shakes as she drags her tongue across her pouty lip. "Nothing. I want nothing from you. Go home with your drunk stepsister, who you hate, and have a nice fucking life."

"Finally," I grumble, watching her walk back toward the wide-open French doors.

I spin back around to Elodie, who's leaning onto the deck railing with her hands hanging over it. "Come on, Freckles." I take her by the waist again, trying to steady her on her feet, but when her body goes slack, I realize she's not even awake. "Elodie," I say, shaking her a little to try and wake her up.

It's no use, so I lift her up and throw her over my shoulder, hoping like hell she doesn't vomit down my back. "You get sick on me or my car, you're cleaning up the damn mess." She can't hear me, but I mean every word I say. I'm not dealing with that shit. I don't even wanna deal with her drunk ass right now.

I'm carrying Elodie down the stairs to the backyard when I hear someone holler my name. "Rome!"

I glance over my shoulder and see Brogan hurrying toward us. "Is she okay?" She messes with Elodie's hair, flipping it out of her face. "Oh, El. You poor thing."

"She's fine. Just drunk off her ass."

I keep going down, stopping when Brogan asks, "How the hell did this happen off one drink?"

I stop walking. "One drink?"

"Yeah. Her friend Julia said she only had one, that she knows of, and the next thing she knew, Elodie was dancing on the kitchen countertop. I know my sister is a lightweight, but she's not a child. She should be able to handle *a* drink."

Elodie is getting heavy as hell on my shoulder, so I keep going down, and when we make it to the bottom, I reposition her. "I'll find out what the hell happened. Right now, I just need to get her home and in bed."

"I'm coming with you."

"Fine," I tell her. "Where's her car keys? I'll leave mine here."

"She left them in the car inside her glove box." Brogan steps to my side to follow me and I look around.

"Gage," I holler when I spot him by the fire. "Get your ass over here."

With an ice pack still pressed to his eye, he walks briskly toward me. "Look, Rome. I didn't mean no harm—"

"Shut the fuck up," I snap at him, not giving a damn what he has to say.

"I'm just saying. It was the heat of the moment and she looked so hot..." His words trail off when he realizes he's only digging himself deeper by talking.

"Just quit talking and go find Brady. Tell him I'm leaving my car here tonight and I'll pick it up in the morning."

He nods. "Yeah. Sure. Anything I can do to help."

I snarl at him, remembering the way his fingers slid up her dress like they were moving with intent, and it's taking everything in me not to hand Elodie off to her sister and kick his fucking ass.

Brogan leads the way to Elodie's car and pulls open the back door for me so I can lay Elodie down. She hops in the passenger seat while I get Elodie somewhat buckled up. I round the car to the driver's side, stopping in my tracks when I notice the front tire is completely flat. "What the fuck?" I walk back around the car, checking all the tires, noticing they're all flat.

"What's wrong?" I hear Brogan ask as she opens her door back up.

"The tires are fucking flat."

Brogan gets out and starts walking around with me, observing the rims practically sitting on the ground. "Oh my God. They weren't like this when we drove here."

"No shit," I tell her. "You wouldn't have made it here if they were. This happened here. And it was definitely on purpose."

"Who would do this to Elodie? She's so sweet to everyone."

I keep my lips sealed, not willing to cut Elodie down to her sister by telling her why she isn't this sweet girl everyone thinks she is. Even if her intentions were pure with all the dumb shit she's pulled, she still doesn't stop to think about her actions and how they're going to affect the people around her. However, this shit is uncalled for.

"I don't know," I tell her. "But I sure as hell plan to find out."

I walk around the car a couple more times to see if there was anything left behind that might give me an idea who did this. After crouching down to eye level, I notice the tires have all been slashed.

Naturally, one person comes to mind. Abby definitely has the motivation because of her jealousy of Elodie. She doesn't like that she lives with me, even though it's because our parents are married. And she thinks I put too much of my energy into Elodie, even though it's only negative energy. But just because she didn't like Elodie, doesn't mean she'd go as far as to slash her tires. Whoever did this used a sharp knife, and I can't imagine Abby carrying one around with her to use at an opportune time. I don't think it was her, but she's not off the hook until I know for sure.

Once we get Elodie moved to my car and relay the message that it's Elodie's car that will be staying here, I get the girls home.

Pulling into the paved driveway, I move all the way to the front before hitting the garage door button to the four-stall garage. As of right now, myself, my dad, Wilder, and Celia park inside, but I wouldn't be surprised if Dad makes Wilder and I give up our spaces for the girls. Callan already got booted for Celia since he's the youngest driver in the house.

Just thinking about how these women have rearranged our lives makes me want to break shit. I brush it off for now because I know it won't last forever. This time next year, I'll be graduating, and even if I don't know where I'm going, I'm getting the hell outta here.

I pull into the garage and tell Brogan to head in through the door to the walkout basement after assuring her I've got Elodie. Brogan knows I don't have a soft spot for her older sister, but after promising her I won't drop her on her head, she walks around out back.

Not that I'm opposed to breaking a promise to Brogan.

I sit there for a few minutes, thinking about the events of the night. Wondering why the hell it irked me so much when I saw those guys gawking at Elodie the way they were. I've never been the jealous type when it comes to girls. Every girl I've fucked around with, I've passed along to my boys. There's just something I can't put my finger on that makes me feel insane when it comes to Elodie. I don't want her, but I don't want anyone else to have her either.

I shoot a quick text to Brady, putting him in charge of finding out what the fuck happened to Elodie's tires.

> Me: Someone slashed Elodie's tires in front of your house. I need you to find out who it was.

His response is immediate because he knows the repercussions if he leaves me waiting.

> Brady: Fucking A. I shut off the security system, but I'm on it. And don't worry about the tires. I'll take care of them first thing in the morning then have her car delivered to your house.

I don't know exactly how it happened, but Brady has a soft spot for Elodie. He isn't usually one to make friends, but I think Elodie standing up for him made him take notice. He's not interested in women, though, so that helps keep my monster at bay while we figure this shit out.

> Me: Let me know the minute you hear anything. And I need you to ask around and find out exactly how much Elodie had to drink tonight. She acts like she drank a whole pint of liquor and I'm certain she didn't.

He texts back.

> Brady: You got it.

I know I should thank him, but I'm actually the one doing Brady a favor, and he knows it. So anything he can do to help me out only digs himself out of the debt he's accumulated on my behalf.

I'm pretty good at collecting secrets and using them to my

advantage. It's one of the many reasons the students at Willow Creek High worship me—because they have to. Along with a few adults, such as our high school history teacher, Mr. Boyd, who had porn magazines in his desk. And our pool guy who I caught stealing a pair of Celia's wet bikini bottoms that were drying on the patio. Fucking sicko.

I find my power in the dark corners of other people's lives. We all have skeletons, some just hide them from me better than others.

Elodie makes a few groaning sounds in the back and I use it as my cue to get her out. Throwing up in her car would have been one thing, but if she gets sick in mine, she's cleaning that shit up tonight. I don't care how fucked up she is.

I get out of the car and pull open the back door. Elodie is still passed the fuck out. When I reach for her, I notice she's drenched in sweat. Running my fingers through her wet hair, I push it off her forehead, grateful to see that she's breathing normally. Aside from her nostrils flaring, she makes the softest snoring sound. It's kinda cute, actually.

I scoop her into my arms, cradling her like a baby, then I kick the car door closed. Opting to use the back doors, I make my way around the house and bring her into the basement. Brogan must've gone up to bed already because it's pitch dark and there's not a sound to be heard.

At risk of my dad or Celia waking up and seeing how drunk Elodie is, I lay her on the couch and cover her with a beige sofa blanket my mom knitted when she was ill. Normally I wouldn't let her touch this, but right now it feels different.

"How'd you get like this, Freckles?" I whisper, crouched down in front of where she's lying.

It's heavy on my mind. Wondering how she got so drunk off one drink. It doesn't make any sense. I can only guess that someone slipped her something. The question is, who? If that is the case, it was likely the same person who slashed her tires.

I know Elodie's got a side to her that others don't see, but no one else should know that. As far as the residents of Willow Creek are concerned, Elodie is a fucking saint.

No one but me should be fucking with her.

A text comes through on my phone, so I stand up and pull it out from the front pocket of my jeans, hoping Brady found something.

Abby: I forgive you.

For fuck's sake. Why won't this bitch take a hint? I don't want her. Never have. Never will. She's always in my face, trying to make out as if she wants everyone to see. When I push her away, she just comes back for more. Doesn't she realize she's a temporary distraction when I have nothing else to do?

I don't even bother texting her back. Instead, I scroll up to the video I sent myself from her phone.

Moving toward the other end of the couch, I plop down next to Elodie's feet. Feeling slightly humane, I take her shoes off and toss them on the floor. The faint outline of dirt around her purple toes is proof she had a good time tonight. The wheezing snores with each breath she takes is a sign it was a little too much fun.

I hit play on the video, watching as the whole dancing situation transpired.

This is definitely going to be beneficial for me, but unfortunately for Abby, it no longer exists because I deleted it from her phone.

There's something about the way Elodie moves so carelessly that has me entranced as I watch her. It's a complete one-eighty from the girl I live with. There's a mischievous spark in her eyes as she throws caution to the wind. Her long brown hair falls back as she closes her eyes and lets the music take control of her body. She's completely unbothered by any stares or judgment as she dances without inhibitions.

I want to know that girl.

I'm still watching when Gage appears on the screen. I lean

forward, my elbows resting on my knees as I clutch my phone in both hands. My eyes trail him as he approaches the counter with a gaping smile on his face.

My vision turns red, my hands gripping my phone so tightly I'm surprised it hasn't cracked yet. An urge to go back to that party and unleash the beast inside me is stronger than ever. Not just on Gage, but on Luke, too. Maybe even Aiden if he pushes me far enough. All three of those guys either had eyes or hands on Elodie tonight and, for some reason, it pisses me the fuck off.

But when Elodie swings her foot back, bringing it forward onto Gage's face, I realize I don't have to. Elodie is a force that no one in this town saw coming, not even me. When she pushed me into that pool, something changed inside me. A lot of people look at Elodie like she is a sweet little flower, when she's really a bee that is prepared to sting.

I rewatch the part where Gage gets kicked about a dozen times, and by the final time, I'm laughing my ass off.

Another text comes through to my phone and I close out of the video, saving it for later because it's going to be of use to me.

> Brady: No word on the tires. Might have just been a random act by some drunk fuck. As for how much Elodie had to drink, I gave her one when she first arrived but I'm positive she didn't even drink it. Rumor has it, Jenna Marshall gave her one as well. After that, she went from sober to shit-faced in like 5 minutes. Seems a little sus if you ask me. I'll let you know if I hear anything more.

Jenna Marshall? Who the fuck is that? Ohhhh. Right. That smart chick who let me copy her history test last year. They're friends? I shouldn't be surprised. Elodie seems to befriend all the outcasts.

I fucking knew it. It seems someone wants to hurt Elodie. Someone other than me. After watching this video, I'm more than certain it's Abby.

Unfortunately, Abby isn't going to have that opportunity, but thanks to her I will.

I type out a quick text, then rest my head back on the couch, already wishing it were morning so I can see the look on Freckle's face once she realizes what she's done.

CHAPTER 15

ELODIE

I WAKE up disoriented with pain slicing through my head. My mouth is dry and I can barely keep my eyes open. I'm not sure how long I was sleeping, but it doesn't feel like nearly long enough.

Once I manage to lift my eyelids and get a look around, I realize I'm not in my bed. Panic hits me immediately as I shoot up on the couch.

Why the hell am I in the basement?

I take a deep breath, trying to remember what happened last night, but everything's a blur. I backtrack to my last memories of the night.

I found out Rome was the mystery guy who saved me last year.

Dammit. I wish that was just a really bad dream. But nonetheless, it's true. Rome hates me because I called the cops and he got arrested, costing him his offer to play college football and forcing him to be benched for half the season.

He was pissed at me, naturally so, and I went after him when he walked into a bedroom upstairs at Brady's house.

Then I gave him a blow job. My cheeks flush just thinking about it. I also wish that was part of a really bad dream.

After that, I went back downstairs and hung out for a bit, then I had one drink. That drink hit me *hard.*

That's all I remember. It must have been some potent booze in that cup, either that, or I just have an extremely abnormal intolerance for alcohol.

I just hope I didn't do anything stupid.

As I get up from the couch, my legs stretched out, I hear a thud and look down to see my phone on the floor. I bend down and pick it up, noticing a text message from Rome. We've never texted one another before. Grant gave me all the boys' numbers in case I ever needed to reach them, and I guess he gave them our numbers as well.

Nervously, I swipe it open and read four simple but spine-chilling words…

> Evil Stepbrother: I own you now.

That's when I notice a video above the text. Without hesitation, I tap play.

No. No. No!

My mind goes blank, my body completely numb aside from the continuous pounding in my head.

This can't be happening. This isn't real. There's no way in hell I would get on top of a counter in front of all those people and dance. Holy fuck! I'm practically flashing everyone around me.

But there I am. Dancing to my heart's content. Moving like no one is watching and acting like I don't care about anything.

How did this happen, and why can't I remember any of it?

With a shaky hand, I type out a text to Rome and hit send.

> Me: Who recorded this? And who else has seen it?

There's so much more I want to ask, but those two questions

are most important right now. This video *cannot* get out. My life will be over.

But that's exactly what Rome wants. He wants to destroy my future the same way I destroyed his.

Even if no one else has seen the video, that doesn't mean this is the only one. Someone else could have recorded me up there. *Everyone* could have recorded me up there.

This is bad. This is really fucking bad.

My hands won't stop shaking as I hold my phone out in front of me, waiting impatiently for Rome to respond. I'm not ready to go upstairs yet. It's Saturday morning and I know my mom is here. By the scent of bacon and toast, I'm certain everyone is in the kitchen.

The next thing I know, the door to the basement opens and the sound of footsteps thudding down the stairs rings in my ear.

I lift my head slightly, turning my eyes in the direction of Rome coming off the steps.

"Good morning, Freckles. Sleep well?"

I jump to my feet, regretting it instantly when all the blood rushes to my head. I cringe, putting a hand over my forehead while trying to hide my ailments. "Don't good morning me, asshole!" I hold my phone up, showing him the video. "What the hell is this?"

He points a finger at my phone, grinning. "That's you dancing like a little whore with a slew of guys looking up your dress."

Oh my God. What in the world have I done?

Feeling dizzy, I sit back down on the couch. It feels like an elephant is sitting on my chest and his trunk just keeps smacking me in my head over and over again.

I shake my head in disappointment with myself. "Why didn't anyone stop me from doing that? Where were my people when all this was taking place?"

Granted, I don't have many, but I do have a couple friends,

and siblings who should have pulled me down and slapped some sense into me.

"Depends on which people you're referring to because half the party was probably watching you."

"Stop." I hold my hand up while palming my face with the other one, pain slicing through me while I try to process this. "Please stop. I can't hear anymore. It's too humiliating."

"Humiliating." He exhales audibly. "Let me tell you what's humiliating." I lift my eyes to see him standing tall in front of me, his fists balled at his sides. "Getting an offer to play ball at the same school your father, and your grandfather, attended then having it ripped away in a split second."

"Rome, I said I'm—"

"I'm not finished," he stammers. Unlocking his fists, he stretches his fingers, only to clench them tighter. "Being the star quarterback who everyone expected to carry the team to state, then being benched for half the season."

When he steps forward, his knees hitting mine, I sink into the couch, cowering away from him. Not because I'm scared, but because the guilt is agonizing. The way Rome looks at me, it's as if he wants to kill me. And now, realizing what I've done to him after he tried to help me, I might just let him.

"Rome," I say softly, only to be interrupted again.

"Shut up!" he shouts, shaking me to the core as his muscular body vibrates with pure rage over me. "Don't fucking talk to me about humiliation. I've lived it. I *am* living it!"

He crouches down until we're eye level and he pinches my chin with his fingers, pulling me forward. "But don't you worry, Freckles. I have every intention of getting my revenge. That video is proof that I own you in every way, shape, and form." His fingers loosen to slide down my throat, making me swallow.

"You fuck up again, it *will* go viral. Your days of dancing on fucking countertops are done. And if I hear the word 'no' come out of your mouth when I tell you to do something," his hand flexes against my throat, fingers curling around it in clear warning as he whispers in my face, "I'll personally email it to the admissions office at Stanford."

I'm speechless. Utterly lost for words because there is nothing I can say to make this go away. I can't take back what I did and I can't save Rome from what happened after. So, I sit here, a shriveled-up mess while Rome spits threats at me.

As long as that video exists, I'm powerless. Not to mention, Rome said he'd tell the whole school that I called the cops on him that night, and they'll surely turn against me. I have no choice but to fall in line now.

I'm not one to cower, but if he turned the school against me, I have no doubt half of the students would go out of their way to make sure Stanford was just a distant memory for me. One wrong move, and the future I mapped out for myself will be derailed.

"What do you want from me?" I whisper just loud enough for him to hear me. I shiver at the thought of what his response will be, but I have to prepare myself.

He leans closer, his breath fanning my face. "Everything." His fingers squeeze around my throat until tears burn my eyes.

I gulp, unsure what he means, but knowing Rome, it can't be good. His eyes watch me carefully before he lets go and places his arms on either side of me, trapping me like a caged animal.

"I want your mind, your body, and your soul. Once I've secured that, I want you to fix the damage you've done. I don't care how you do it, but get it done."

Goosebumps erupt over my body in fear and maybe even because of something else I refuse to acknowledge. I can give Rome my body. I don't want to, but it's his for the taking if that's what keeps that video out of the public eye. My mind is already consumed with thoughts of him because he's made sure of it. My soul will be crushed without Stanford. But there is no way I can fix the damage I've done.

"That's impossible, Rome. I'm nobody. How am I supposed to fix this?"

"You're the key witness that was missing when my case went to trial. You're a smart girl, Freckles." He bops my nose and I wanna grab his hand and bite it. "I'm sure you'll figure it out. After all, you want to go into law. Prove to me that I should let you have that chance by finding a way to fix what *you* broke."

He's right. I am a key witness. A thought pops into my head and I jolt forward, forcing Rome to inch back. "I think I have an idea," I tell him.

My mom! She's the district attorney. She wasn't when this case was handled, but she is now. I've been studying for pre-law since I was a sophomore and one thing I know is the district attorney can do just about anything when it comes to cases in his or her county. There has to be some way she can help.

"Good. Just get it done." He stands again and peers down at me. "Now, go take a shower, you smell like bad choices. Once you finish breakfast, we're going for a ride."

"A ride where?"

"You'll see." Rome walks back up the stairs, leaving me with my thoughts. I think back to a textbook I read about key witnesses and how they can affect the sentencing. My headache subsides slightly when I finally feel a bit of hope that I can turn this situation around. Surely my mom will help. But before I talk to her, I need to figure out exactly what transpired that night.

Standing, I make my way upstairs on shaky legs and vow to never drink again. I have no idea what was in that cup, but the way I feel now was not worth the five minutes that my brain quieted down.

I grab a piece of greasy bacon on my way through the kitchen and eat it on my walk to my bedroom. I was lucky enough to avoid my mom and Grant so far this morning. And there were only a few laughs about my night from Brogan and Lake.

I just jabbed my middle finger in the air and ignored them, trying not to get pissy with Brogan for not trying to stop what happened. I know I am responsible for my own actions, and I drank when I'm a known lightweight. I just can't help but wonder where she was if she wasn't out there where everyone could see me dancing on the damn counter.

After a quick shower, I feel a little bit better, but my head still feels like it's been inflated with air. At least I've washed off the bad choices, as Rome called them. Man, he can be such an ass. I know I fucked up, but in my defense, I had no idea one drink would mess me up *that* bad.

Opting for comfort today, I'm sporting a pair of black sweats and an oversized gray hoodie as I search the house for Wilder. Sayer said he was doing something outside that he didn't know how to explain.

I finally find him in the backyard, recording himself doing some crazy-ass dance, and suddenly Sayer makes more sense. I don't ask any questions because I'm pretty sure it's for his social media. I also don't want to embarrass him because I need him to give me some clarity.

"Wilder." I tap him on the shoulder as his fingers move around on the screen. His head shoots up and he spins around. "Hey, can I talk to you for a minute?"

"Damn, Elodie." He winces, his eyebrows pinching as he takes me in. "You look like shit."

I comb my fingers through my hair. "I know. Rough night."

And I thought Rome was the asshole.

He tries not to smile, but I notice the way his lips crack. "So I've heard."

"Let's all just forget about last night." My cheeks heat up and I would love nothing more than to just sink six feet into the ground. "Anyway, I was hoping I could ask you some questions about Rome."

His eyebrows shoot to his forehead. "I dunno, Elodie. Rome's my brother and—"

"Nothing too personal. I promise." I look up, squinting a bit with the force of the sun as my head pounds harder.

Wilder shrugs, sliding his phone in his pocket and giving me his full attention. "I guess you can ask, and I'll decide if it's worth being under his wrath by answering."

I nod toward the patio table and chairs. "Mind if we sit?"

He agrees and we each make our way to a seat. The sun is on full blast today, so the shade from the umbrella helps ease some of the sweat already forming on my back. Once we're sitting down, I take a deep breath and say, "I need you to tell me about the night Rome got in that fight last year."

Wilder drags his fingers through his brunette hair as he looks away. It's clear he doesn't want to talk about this. But eventually, he lets out a long breath as he faces me. "You know he'll be out for blood if he knows we're even having this conversation."

I nod. "I think I might be able to help him, but I need a few more details. Can you tell me exactly what happened?"

He goes silent for a second, likely contemplating the consequences of telling me, but to my surprise, he does anyway.

"According to Rome, and his statement to the police, he followed some girl he was simping on who pushed his ass in the pool. When he found her, he saw she was being harassed by some of the Bulldog team in Ravencrest Park."

My mind flashes back to what he must have seen. I wonder how long he let it go on for, how long he watched Winton. The ghost of Winton's fingers around my throat threatens to make me gag, but I hold it back as I listen to Wilder.

"After hanging back for a minute, things got intense, so he jumped in and defended her. That's when he was ambushed by three guys." Wilder closes his eyes, the pain he feels for his brother clear as day. I want so badly to fix this, not just for Rome, but all of them. I can't imagine what it felt like to see their brother go through all of this, especially right after losing their mother.

"His only defense to fend them off was a broken pipe he had."

I remember my reaction when I saw him holding that pipe. It felt like he actually had a chance, and for the first time since I saw the intent in Winton's eyes, I believed I was going to be okay.

"Anyways, he said shit hit the fan and he cracked Winton Brooks over the head with the pipe. Apparently, the cops showed up shortly after that and Rome was arrested. He mentioned helping some girl, but he had no idea who she was."

Well, he sure as hell knows who I am now.

"So, what happened next?" I need to know everything. How he got caught. What happened with his dad. If he had to serve any time.

"Winton was taken to the hospital with a compound skull fracture and Rome was charged with battery after Winton told them what went down, claiming he wasn't trying to hurt the girl, only trying to help her find her way home, which seemed like a load of bullshit."

I clench my jaw over that. Knowing Winton was able to use me in any way against Rome makes the blood in my veins turn to lava. I wasn't planning on coming out against Winton; I just wanted to ignore it. But I can't sit back and do nothing anymore.

Wilder sits forward, folding his hands together. "Our dad was able to get the charges dropped to assault and Rome had to do community service and probation with a hefty fine."

Wilder cringes and I hate to know that there's more. "About a week into community service, UCLA caught wind of the charges and they rescinded their offer for him to play ball there. We're still waiting to see if they pull back his whole acceptance."

"Jesus." I sigh heavily. "Why didn't anyone tell me any of this?"

Wilder cranes his neck, looking at me with confusion on his face. "Why do you care?"

"I...I just wish I could have helped in some way. That's all."

"He wouldn't have let you anyways. Rome clammed the fuck up the minute he was arrested. He was pretty wasted that night and parts of the incident are still patchy to him. Not to mention, Winton got in a few good hits in the brawl as well. Rome had a minor concussion when they put him in the back of the police car."

"Was Winton charged with anything?"

This time Wilder's face flushes red with anger. "No." He closes his eyes as if to try and gain his composure. "Aside from being suspended from his football team this season, he didn't get jack shit. The court felt that his upbringing and the fact that he was left with a bunch of medical bills was enough of a punishment for him since he was from the less fortunate side of town."

This right here is why I want to be a lawyer. So shit like this stops happening.

I could tell Rome was drinking that night, but I didn't know him, so I had no way of knowing he was wasted. From his behavior, I just assumed he was an ass—which he is. But his behavior makes more sense now that I know his mother passed away six months prior and he was playing his first season without her there. I'm not excusing his behavior and he deserved to be pushed into the pool for the way he treated me. But he didn't deserve what came after.

"I think there's something I can do to help Rome," I tell him. "But I can't do it alone."

Wilder shakes his head, a look of sympathy on his face. "That's nice and all, Elodie. But it's done. Rome has already been sentenced by the court."

I lick my dry lips before saying, "But that was before the girl he rescued moved into town."

He straightens his back and leans forward, elbows pressed to the patio table. "What are you saying?"

"I'm saying the girl he rescued from those scumbag Bulldogs was me, and I'm ready to tell my side of the story."

As much as I don't want to relive what happened that night, I'll do it if it means clearing Rome's name, getting his future back, and saving my own ass in the process.

Wilder draws his fingers around his mouth, eyes wide in surprise. "Are you serious?"

I nod, biting the corner of my lip.

"Damn, Elodie." He chuckles "Does Rome know?"

I laugh. "He's known longer than I have."

"I...I don't even know what to say." He sinks back into the chair, his legs spread wide beneath the table. A realization hits him and a grin spreads across his face. "So, you're the girl who pushed him into the pool?"

I scratch the back of my neck, before saying, "Guilty."

I'm surprised when he reaches across the table with his hand raised for a high five. I feel like a snake for hitting his hand back, but I do it with a little giggle. Before Wilder even asks, I need him to know something.

"When I called the cops that night, I didn't do it with the intention of Rome getting in trouble. I really was just trying to help him. I left after that and didn't return to Willow Creek until two weeks ago. If I had known—"

Wilder holds up a hand. "You don't need to explain your-self to me, Elodie. I know how Rome is. I'm just glad I finally know why he's been behaving like such a prick lately. I mean, he was in a pissy mood ever since the arrest, but when school started back up, it intensified. Now I know it had nothing to do with school or football. He's giving you alotta shit, isn't he?"

"Honestly, that's an understatement. But don't worry, I can handle Rome." *I hope.*

"I don't doubt that for a second. Just prepare yourself, his words and actions can cut deep."

Don't I know it.

Wilder's phone chirps and he picks it up off the table, steals a glance at it, then lays it back down. "You said you think your witness statement can help. So, what's your plan?"

"I need to talk to my mom. I'm certain once I do, she'll be able to file a motion for a new trial with the new evidence I'll bring to light."

Wilder's eyes sparkle, and I can't help but feel like maybe

this whole moving here thing isn't going to be the end of the world. "Damn, girl. Look at you talking in courtroom lingo."

"What can I say, I have a passion for the legal system and seeking justice where it's deserved." My headache has faded to the background as my mind starts to clear and my plan becomes more and more solid.

"Spoken like the daughter of a district attorney." Wilder winks.

"More like a future pre-law student." It's the first time I've told anyone that I'm actually going pre-law. To this day, Rome is still the only one who knows I've been accepted to, not only my dream school, but many other prestigious universities.

His hands go up before landing on his knees. "What can I do to help?"

"Actually," I drawl. "I was hoping you'd go with me to Ravencrest Park to see if there is anything I can remember that I might have suppressed. Anything that can help Rome before I give my statement. I haven't been back there since that night last year, and I could really use the support, and backup, if needed."

Just thinking about going back to that park sends a rush of anxiety through my body. My palms get clammy, my heart races. There's no way I can go alone.

"Treading into Bulldog territory and potentially raising some hell? Count me in."

"We will not be raising hell. With any luck, we won't see any of those assholes."

I'm not sure how I'd react to seeing Winton, Damon, or Miles again. The weeks that followed my stroll into the park were filled with panic attacks, restlessness, and sleepless nights. There was a dull ache in the pit of my stomach, knowing I would never get to tell my story about the hell they put me through. They might not have actually assaulted my body, but they violated me, and the internal wounds they caused are just now scabbing over. I just hope going back to that park and giving my statement doesn't reopen them completely.

The sliding door to the walkout basement opens and Rome appears. I tap my foot nervously, hoping Wilder will give me an answer before we're interrupted.

"I've got practice after school on Monday, but we could go after?" He tracks Rome as he gets closer.

I breathe in a sigh of relief. "That's perfect. Thank you, Wilder."

"You betcha." He taps his fingers to the table before getting up. "I need to finish this video before I head to the gym. We'll talk soon."

I watch as he walks away, then my eyes find Rome in the middle of the yard. He curls his fingers at me and hollers with a stern voice, "Let's go."

CHAPTER 16

ROME

WITH MY CAR pulled in front of the house, I wait for Elodie, drumming my fingers against the steering wheel to the beat of "Like a Villain" by Bad Omens.

She walks out in a pair of sweatpants and a crossbody purse hanging over her tee shirt. She's got her hair in a high ponytail behind a pair of plastic-framed sunglasses perched on the top of her head.

That's not what has my attention, though, as she makes her way to me like the obedient puppy I asked her to be. Her eyes lack the sparkle they normally hold and she looks paler than normal. I can tell just by the way she's carrying herself today, with her shoulders slumped forward and no pep in her step, she's not feeling too hot.

Normally, I'd say she deserves it. She drank the booze and had the fun and now she has to reap the consequences. But I'd bet my life that booze didn't do that to her. And if Elodie would have known that one drink would have stripped her of her control, there is no way she would have drank it.

Elodie pulls open the passenger side door and sinks into the seat. Before she closes the door, she drops her sunglasses over her eyes. "Where are we going?"

Even her voice is different. There's no enthusiasm or zest for life. Who is usually a chipper and sassy girl is now someone who looks completely defeated. I suppose I can take credit for that.

"You'll see," I tell her as I shift the car into drive and press my foot to the gas pedal.

As if she just had an epiphany while passing by her car, Elodie shoots up in her seat. "Who the hell drove my car home last night? Please don't tell me I drove."

"You didn't. And it wasn't brought home last night. Brady drove it here this morning."

Around eight o'clock, I got a text that he had dropped it off. I was pretty surprised to see that all four tires were replaced. He must really know some people to have pulled that off on a Saturday morning.

Elodie pushes her sunglasses back on her head and I can see clearly now that her eyes are still glossed over. "So who drove *me* home?"

"Yours truly." I smirk. "You're welcome."

She sinks back into the seat and mumbles a very quiet, "Thank you."

I'm actually surprised she thanked me at all, considering the way I've treated her. Thought for sure she'd say something smart-ass like, "I didn't ask for your help."

"We didn't..." She pauses, moving her finger between us. "Ya know?"

I know what she's asking, but the depraved side of me wants to humiliate her and make her say the words. I love to watch her squirm, and maybe it will bring some of that spark that I love to play with back into her today. "Didn't what?"

The color slowly returns to her cheeks. "We didn't do anything, did we?"

I bite my lip and look her up and down. "Do anything, like what?" My eyes return to the road, only after I watch her jaw drop.

She shakes her head, looking away from me and resting her head on the window. "Never mind."

"Come on, Freckles. Just ask the damn question. Did we, what?"

There's a strange feeling that starts to take hold of me. Almost something like sadness or regret when I look at Elodie. This is a woman who fights not just for herself, but for those around her, always.

Seeing her without that drive actually bothers me more than I thought it would. I have no real intention of ruining her life by sending that video to Stanford. I just want her to fall in line. But if this is what that looks like, then I'm not so sure I want it.

I stare at the road ahead and decide to give it one last go. If this doesn't get her attention, then maybe Elodie isn't the girl I thought she was. Maybe I've already broken my new toy.

"It's Brady you should thank. He replaced all your tires that someone slashed last night."

The casualness in my tone unnerves Elodie. She jerks her seat belt forward and turns in the seat to face me. "What?!"

That's my girl. Well, not *my* girl. But whatever.

I shrug my shoulders, fighting hard not to smile. For some reason, I love seeing her face when she's taken by surprise. I love it even more when she's pissed off and the tips of her ears turn red.

"Please tell me you're joking, Rome?" It's fair for her not to believe me. I thought about keeping it from her while I did my own little investigation. However, I realized that's just stupid because if there is someone out there after her, and she has no damn clue, that doesn't help her at all.

"Would I joke about something like that?" I take a turn a little sharper than I should and her body slides into the door.

"Yes. Probably." Her tone is flat and it makes my anger tick up a notch.

"Not this time, Freckles. Someone has it out for you."

She scoffs. "It was you, wasn't it?"

"Yeah." I huff. "You caught me. I carried you away from the party, put your drunk ass in your car, then I slashed your tires just so I would have to carry you back out of your car, into mine, and then drive your passed-out ass home, and put you to bed." Honestly, for someone so book smart, she really isn't that sharp with people.

She rubs her temples aggressively. "I can't handle any more of this. Why would someone slash my damn tires? I've lived in Willow Creek for two weeks. Who would hate me this much?"

I raise my hand slowly, warranting a fist to the shoulder from my sweet stepsister. This time, I actually let out a small laugh, but she doesn't hear it, thankfully.

"If I find out you're behind this, Rome..." She shakes her head as her words trail off.

"Then, what?" I laugh, but the sound is empty of humor. "You'll destroy my future?"

"Why are you so damn cruel and unforgiving?"

I veer off to the side of the road and slam the car into park as I turn my body toward her.

"Am I not allowed to be pissed, Elodie? Do you really think this is something I should just let go? This is my fucking life! Everything I had and worked my ass off for was destroyed because of you. I lost my mom, then my entire future because of you!"

I'm shouting at her now. My hands are shaking as my breaths come in harsh pants. But Elodie surprises me. Instead of shrinking back like she has done ever since she found out the truth, she meets me in the middle, her anger just as alive as my own.

"I get that, Rome. I really do. I messed up!" She throws her hands in the air, wincing from the fast movement. But she pushes on. "If I could go back and not make that call, I would."

"Not make the call?" I shout. "How about not going into that fucking park in the first place? Or how about not pushing me in the pool in front of the entire school. In front of people who respect me and look up to me. You ruined everything that night, and you're still ruining me now!"

She pushes a finger into my chest, just like before. "Don't you dare! I will not apologize for standing up for myself. You were a complete ass to me and you tried to touch me without my permission. I should have slapped you across your damn face, but I went easy on you."

I grab her hand and toss it back at her. "Just remember, Freckles. What goes around, comes around."

"So you want to destroy me in return?" We are no longer yelling, but it feels like the car is about to overheat. Elodie looks and acts like this composed person all the time, no one ever gets to see this side of her. No one but me.

"Yeah. I do. Because you deserve to feel the same way I do." I sit back in my seat and throw the car into drive, signaling to pull back out on the busy street as Elodie stares at me.

"And dragging me down is supposed to fix all your problems?" Her voice is much softer, as if it's a real question.

"At least then I won't be alone."

When she looks at me with pity in her eyes, I know I should elaborate, but I leave it at that. It's really fucking lonely knowing all my friends have their futures mapped out and I don't know what the hell I'm going to do after graduation. I tried to help this girl out, even after she made a fool of me at the party, and in the end, I only fucked myself even more.

It's quiet for a while as I make my way across town, and I'm glad for it. Everyone looks at me with pity. Everyone sees a kid who messed up his life by making one bad choice. The thing is, I'd do it again. I might want to strangle Elodie, but there's something about her that I can't ignore.

"I'm sorry, Rome. I don't know what else to say." She looks at me, then out the window. I refuse to make eye contact because I don't want to see the pity again. I'm so fucking over it. At least if she's angry with me, she doesn't have that look in her eyes.

"Then don't say anything."

Elodie taps the screen on her phone, and when I steal a glance, I see that she's thanking Brady. A couple seconds later, I look again, noticing that he told her he's going to find out who did it. With a heavy breath, she tucks her phone back into her purse and crosses her arms over her chest, glowering out the passenger window.

The rest of the twenty-minute ride is quiet. The tension in the small space is so suffocating I'm forced to roll down my window just to breathe.

When we pull down Dr. Lamont's driveway, I peek at her. Dr. Lamont took care of my mom when she was ill and he made frequent visits to the house. Being a concierge doctor, I knew he'd be able to help me outside of normal business hours.

Brady isn't the only one with connections. My dad might not be the state senator, but as the owner of Cromwell Bank, with institutions all over the United States, he's gained the respect of many.

In 2020, he was named Businessman of the Year by *Time* magazine. He's also been an esteemed member of the city council for the last six years. Needless to say, my dad has connections, too—connections I like to use to my advantage.

"Where are we?" Elodie asks, straightening her back to get a better view of the large brick house with the creek running beside it.

"This is Dr. Lamont's house." I choose not to elaborate and let her sweat it out for a few minutes.

"Why are we going to see a doctor?" she asks, just as we pull up to the home.

I cut the engine and turn to her with a wide grin on my face. "You're getting a blood draw, Freckles."

In an instant, she jerks her sunglasses off, her face even more pale than it was when she got in the car. "Have you lost your damn mind? What do you mean I'm getting a blood draw?"

"It's exactly how it sounds. The doctor inside that house is going to jab a needle into your arm and draw blood." I don't think I will ever get tired of the exasperated look on her face. This is so fun.

"Why the hell are you speaking like this isn't a huge deal!?" She throws her hands in the air, gesturing toward the house like I don't realize where we are. "Why in the world would I allow some strange man to take my blood for no reason?"

I wait until she's done with her little fit before my face turns serious. "How much did you have to drink last night, Elodie?"

Her shoulders rise, and she blinks rapidly. "I... All I remember is one. It hit me hard within just a few minutes. I must have drank more. I just can't remember the other drinks."

"That's because you only had one." I hold up my index finger. "You think one drink did that to you? Not a chance in hell."

"What are you saying?"

I turn my head to the side. "You want to be pre-law. What do you think I'm saying?"

She crosses her arms, clearly refusing to speak. I think Elodie already knows the truth, she's just too afraid to face it.

"I think someone slipped you something in that *one* drink. Then they slashed your tires to make sure you were trapped there, out in the dark and alone."

Her expression drops, eyes wide as she realizes I'm not making this shit up. "Someone drugged me?"

"We won't know for sure until Dr. Lamont draws your blood." I let my voice go soft for her because it's clear the drugs are still messing with her. If her hands shaking are any sign to go by, I'd say it's going to take her at least three days to feel normal again.

"He's a good doctor. Said it'll take a couple days since the lab is closed on the weekends, but if you were drugged, we need to do this now before it's out of your system. He's doing this as a favor to me, and I think you should let him."

I watch as she rests her head back, tears welling in her eyes. I don't know why I'm doing this. If someone wants to mess with

Elodie, I should be glad. But there's this nagging thought in the back of my mind telling me I am the only one who is allowed to mess with her.

I'm actually surprised when she takes off her seat belt and grabs the door handle. "Let's get this over with."

Her defeated posture resumes as we walk up to the entrance, so I place my hand on her back, trying to offer her some support. For some reason, taking care of her right now feels like I've been transported back to taking care of my mom, and I want to do this part right.

We're greeted at the door by Dr. Lamont, and memories of the last time he was at my house surface. It was the morning Mom passed away. She lay in her bed, frail and weak, thanking him for everything he did for her at the end. My brothers and I didn't leave that room all day. After they came and took her body, I lay in her bed and cried for hours.

"Rome?" Dr. Lamont says. I'm still frozen until Elodie nudges my side.

I come back to reality, while wishing I could go back to the day and hug my mom one last time.

Clearing my throat, I stick out my hand. "Sorry. It's good to see you again."

"You as well, Rome." He extends a hand to Elodie after shaking mine. "And it's a pleasure to meet you. I just wish it were under different circumstances." He chuckles lightly. "Though I guess circumstances are rarely good when seeing a doctor."

Elodie shakes his hand with a tight smile. "Thank you for doing this."

Dr. Lamont steps aside and gestures for us to come in.

"Normally I make the house calls, however, Rome mentioned this couldn't wait a minute longer. He's very persuasive."

"That he is," Elodie says, the smile fading from her face the second her eyes lock with mine.

I'm not sure why she's giving me the cold shoulder. We're

here because I'm trying to help her. Well, I'm actually trying to determine who the snake is that drugged a girl at a high school party, but it helps her nonetheless.

Dr. Lamont leads us into his office where he has a medical bag open on a small table. Beside it is a sharps container and a box of gloves.

"Go ahead and have a seat," he instructs Elodie by waving toward a chair next to the table. He prepares the needle and vial, then fastens a rubber tourniquet around her upper arm.

"Rome," Elodie says softly. I lift my eyebrows, questioning her. "I'm scared of needles."

"You have a tattoo. How are you scared of needles?"

Dr. Lamont stands there for a moment, assessing us both to make sure she's ready to do this.

With no choice in the matter, if we wanna know the truth, I go to her side and crouch down. My chest tightens as I reach out and hold her hand. It's small and delicate—a perfect fit in mine. I hate how the look in her eyes reminds me so much of my mother's when she would hold our hand during blood draws.

She takes a deep, shaky breath, and I mirror her, squeezing her hand tighter in reassurance.

"Are you ready?" Dr. Lamont asks her, and she responds with a nod.

"Look at me," I tell her.

As I meet her gaze, my heart races. Her emerald eyes seem to look right through me, but at the same time, I'm looking through hers. She's scared—not just of the needle, but of the uncertainty of her future. Despite our conflicts, it's as if all the resentment and anger washes away and we've found common ground.

Her body shakes slightly as the needle glides into her vein and I place my other hand over the top of hers while rubbing my thumb across her delicate skin. I'm not sure why I do it, but it seems to offer her a sense of calm. She closes her eyes as her grip relaxes and something in my chest shifts.

It's as if I don't want this moment to end. Feeling needed is something I didn't realize I was missing until now. I want to hold on to it.

"All done," Dr. Lamont exclaims. "You did great, Elodie."

He keeps talking, but I don't hear anything he says. I'm stuck in this moment.

Then, Elodie pulls her hand away so fast you'd think she felt a zap of electricity.

Or maybe it was only me who felt it.

I stand up while Dr. Lamont tells me he'll call in a couple days. After I thank him, we leave.

The ride home is quiet. For the first time in a while, I have nothing to say to Elodie. Or maybe I'm worried if I speak, I'll lose all the leverage I've gained because I don't have the energy to be cruel right now.

So instead, we drive in silence, and before long, Elodie's fast asleep.

Every couple minutes, I steal a glance at her, noticing that she's not snoring like she was last night. But her nostrils still flare slightly and a light sheen of sweat builds on her brow. She's got a cute nose, and when the sun hits it just right, her freckles look reddish brown. She looks peaceful—more peaceful than I've ever seen her. I'm partially to blame for that. The girl is so high-strung and defensive. With reason, I suppose.

I want to hate her. I really do. But when I see her like this, in perfect form—so vulnerable—I'm not sure how that's possible.

Once I'm parked in the garage, I turn my car off and pull out my phone to scroll through SnapTok so she can sleep a little longer. Because when she wakes up, she'll be the enemy again. And I'm not ready for that just yet.

CHAPTER 17
ELODIE

ROME HAS BEEN UNUSUALLY quiet the last couple days. Ever since we went to Dr. Lamont's house three days ago, something seems different about him.

A minute ago, I passed by him in the parking lot, and he didn't even say anything cruel. Just side-eyed me and kept talking with Luke and Aiden. I don't dare let my guard down, though, because when I least expect it, I know he'll bite.

"Hey!" I shout, picking up my pace as I approach my open locker. "What the hell are you doing?"

In front of my locker is a guy with tousled light brown hair and honey-colored eyes. However, one of his eyes is marred by an angry bruise that spreads down to his cheek. It's actually sort of gross, and I'm fighting hard not to stare at it.

I can't remember his name, but I know he's on the varsity football team. He's holding a plastic grocery bag and wearing a pair of blue nitrile gloves.

Just when I thought Rome's antics might be coming to an end, I'm reminded that I'm still his enemy, and I'm still indebted to him.

I snatch the bag from my locker's unwanted guest, fuming and ready to put this asshole in his place. "What the hell is this?"

He curls his lip in disgust. "Chewed gum, likely from every student in this school."

"And you're sticking it in my locker?" I shove the bag at him. "Get lost, asshole!"

He rolls his eyes at me, taking the bag away from me. "If you'd give me a minute to speak, I'm actually taking the gum *off* your locker."

"Oh." I take a step back, assessing him. "Why?"

"Orders from Rome Cromwell."

Rome is making this guy take the gum off my locker? That doesn't make any sense. Rome is the one who started this disgusting display.

"Why would he make you do that?" I move to stand beside him as he scrapes another row of chewed gum from around the hooks inside.

Dropping them in the bag, he glances at me. "As an apology, which I owe you." He turns to face me, eyes downcast. "I'm sorry I hit on you at the party and touched your leg while you were dancing."

I fight back a smile because I'm actually flattered. "You hit on me?" I slap a hand over my mouth. "Oh my God! Did Rome give you that black eye?"

"Actually," he pauses for a beat, appearing embarrassed about what he's about to admit, "you did."

My mouth forms an O and I crane my neck. "I did?" I laugh a little, but it's not funny. Well, it sort of is. I gave a varsity football player a black eye.

He points to his marred eye. "The toe of your heavy sandal... straight to the face."

I fold my lips tightly, trying not to laugh. Then I plaster a serious look on my face, shoulders drawn back like the tough beotch I am. "Well, it serves you right. I guess it's safe to assume you learned your lesson then?"

He nods, getting back to work.

I must've kicked him while I was dancing on the counter. I've been trying hard to forget about the video and everything I supposedly did that night, but it's hard when proof just keeps popping up left and right. I really should rewatch it and find out who all was around.

He keeps plucking away, dropping gum into the bag. "For what it's worth, I was wasted and totally deserved it."

Dammit. The softness in me is about to come out. If anyone knows about regret, it's me. Even if I was potentially drugged that night, I should have never drank anyways.

"Don't worry about it," I tell him. "Rome is just…protective." Which baffles me because Rome hates me. This still doesn't make any sense. "Honestly," I continue, "I probably wouldn't have cared if I'd been in the right mind."

His eyes widen. "Really?"

"Yeah. I'm new here and don't know many people. I'm sort of flattered anyone paid attention to me. I'm not usually that girl."

Now that I've admitted that, I'm slightly embarrassed myself. This guy isn't bad-looking, despite the black eye, and he actually seems sort of sweet. We all make mistakes, and he apologized. One thing I support is second chances.

His hand holding the bag drops to his side, and he raises the other. "I'm Gage." I look down at the glove he's wearing and chuckle at the smears of spit on it, knowing I'm not shaking that hand. "Sorry." He laughs as he pulls off the glove. "Let's try that again. I'm Gage and I lose all inhibition when I drink. Maybe we can start over?"

I shake his hand, grinning. "I'd like that."

"How about a movie tonight? *Blackouts* is playing at the cinema downtown."

I'm not sure if Gage is asking me on a date, or just being friendly, but either way, excitement pools in my stomach. "Sure. That sounds nice."

The next thing I know, Rome steps between us and slams my locker door shut. "What the hell is going on here?"

Ignoring Rome, I say, "Gage, do you have extra gloves?"

His eyes move nervously from Rome to me as he reaches into his pants pocket. "Sure. Why?"

I snatch them from his hand, smirking at Rome. "So I can help you." I slide on the glove and begin pulling a big wad of pink gum off the door, but before I can drop it on the bag, I'm jerked by my arm, away from my locker.

Rome sneers. "What the fuck are you doing?"

"What does it look like I'm doing?" I hold up my gloved index finger, showing him the gum stuck to it.

"Are you trying to be cute right now? Because you're not." I don't understand this guy. One minute he is taunting me and making half the school put chewed gum in my locker, then the next he's making someone who touched me without my consent clean it up for me. Now he's angry because I'm cleaning up a mess he made?

"Cute?" I laugh. "I'd hardly call pulling chewed-up gum from my locker cute."

He growls, and for some damn reason, that does things to me. "I don't mean the gum. I'm talking about you and Gage." Possessiveness flares in his eyes and I would smirk if it wouldn't lead to Rome actually flipping his lid.

I see now, Rome. You want me to have to rely only on you. Well, that's not gonna happen.

"What about me and Gage?" I may or may not be taunting him right now.

"Why are you being nice to him? The guy crept his fingers up your leg and if you hadn't stopped him, he probably would have stuck those fingers right inside you while you danced like a cheap stripper."

My eyebrows nearly hit my forehead. "Cheap stripper?"

"I said what I said." He lifts his brows in a challenge.

"Ya know." I shake my head. "For a minute I thought things

took a turn in the right direction for us. But the minute you open your mouth to speak, I remember that you'll always be a complete jackass!" I move my hand toward him then stick the pink wad of gum right on his shirt before spinning around and walking confidently back to my locker.

"You can leave this, Gage." I pull the glove off my hand and drop it in the plastic bag he's holding. "I should get to class. But I'll see you tonight."

Rome's heavy footsteps thud behind me, but I pretend he's not there as he shouts my name.

"Elodie!"

Gage gulps, his eyes on Rome who's approaching us.

"Yeah," he says quietly. "I'll pick you up around seven."

For added emphasis, I press a chaste kiss to Gage's cheek just to piss Rome off. "Can't wait."

Rome's jaw clenches, his fists tight at his sides. "Don't you dare walk away from me when I'm talking to you."

With my head held high, wearing the biggest damn smile I can, I step up to him. "The last time you said that, I pushed you in a pool. Do you really want to do this again?"

He leans in, his mouth so close to my ear, I can hear the grinding of his teeth. "Have you forgotten what I can do to you?"

I'm well aware that Rome can destroy my reputation with the tap of a button. He can even turn everyone against me by telling them I potentially ruined the season for the Misfits by calling the cops and getting their star quarterback arrested. The thing is, I'm so worked up right now, I don't even care.

"Do what you have to do, Rome. While you're stuck in the past, I'm going to live my life."

I go to step around him, but he throws an arm out to stop me. "What part of *I own you* don't you understand?"

I smirk at him, batting my eyelashes like the innocent girl he thinks I pretend to be. "Most people don't want to break what's theirs, Rome. So if you own me, then I suggest you treat me a little better before someone else does." I glance back at Gage. I wouldn't mind if he made me forget my life for a little while.

For once, Rome doesn't have anything to say, so I use this opportunity to yank out of his hold and get to class before he thinks of another way to punish me. And I have no doubt that will happen sooner or later.

CHAPTER 18
ELODIE

As soon as we pull into the empty parking lot at the Ravencrest Park, my heart begins to race. It looks different than the last time I was here—more run-down.

The gazebo made out of wood has graffiti covering the chipped, white paint. The metal slide I hid under that night is rusted out with a few steps missing on the ladder. There's an overflowing trash can with litter lying around it. It's a far cry from the lively place I imagined it was when I first stepped foot in it. But now, seeing it like this, it's a place I never want to enter again, and certainly not in the dead of night.

Thankfully, there is still daylight and I have backup this time; otherwise, I'm not sure I'd be able to do this.

Wilder turns the engine off, and the sound of his keys dangling together startles me. It's as if Winton is here somehow. Like his eyes are boring into me and setting my nerves on edge.

"You okay?" Wilder asks, likely unsure why I look like I'm on the verge of a meltdown. I take a deep breath and try to convince myself that my anxiety is over the lack of control I had that night and not because of fear. I have control now. I can walk away and get in the car where Wilder will take me home the second I want to.

Wilder knows a small bit of what happened that night, but he doesn't know the extent of everything I endured. He doesn't know I still wake up struggling to breathe. He doesn't know that any time I kneel down I have flashbacks to the moment I was pushed to my knees.

"I'm okay," I tell him as my shaky hand reaches for the door handle. "Ready?"

He nods, swinging his door open to step out, while I take a little longer to get out of the car. As soon as my right foot hits the cracked pavement in the parking lot, apprehension stops me from moving my other foot out.

It's silly to feel like this. No harm came from those guys. Sure, they touched me and ripped my clothes and were *about* to do unthinkable things to me, but they didn't. I survived it. I walked away—or ran, rather. Nothing has touched me since that night, except a slew of terrible memories—and Rome—but I'm okay.

"You sure you wanna do this?" Wilder asks, now at the door I'm desperately trying to force myself to climb out of. "There are other ways."

"No," I say, swinging my other foot out. "I'm fine. I need to do this."

This isn't just for Rome; this is for me, too. I haven't gone to therapy for my PTSD, but I have done a lot of research. One of the best ways for a victim to claim back control of being sexually assaulted is revisiting the place of the crime. Some choose to vandalize it, to mark it up so it feels as ugly as they do on the inside. Others will clean it up, even memorialize it as the place where they survived.

But not me. I plan to use this trip as a way to make sure Winton is taken down and never able to hurt another person again.

I stand up and close the door, forcing myself to walk into the park. Wilder is at my side, so I know nothing bad is going to happen. I was warned once about stepping onto Bulldog territory, and I thought I learned my lesson. But coming back here is crucial.

"Anything look familiar?" Wilder asks as my eyes scope out the scenery.

"It's a lot different in the daylight." I glance around, trying to replay the scene in my head. "That night I was here, I only had the light on my phone and the dim lampposts to illuminate everything."

"Yeah." He scoffs, kicking up dirt. "This place is a shithole."

"What are the residents of Ravencrest like?" I ask, genuinely curious if they're all jerks like the ones I had a run-in with.

"Some are all right." Wilder shrugs as he leans against some of the dirty playground equipment, only to stand back up straight and dust himself off.

"But most aren't too fond of us Willow Creek residents because we're more financially stable. Willow Creek has all the appeal Ravencrest doesn't. I don't want to say they're poor, but our towns are night and day in comparison. Not to mention, we're sports rivals. So that only adds to the tension."

"Are they any good?" I ask, curious if money gets the better players or not.

"They do have one hell of a team, I'll give them that."

Looking around, I can see what he means about the lack of appeal. Even the area surrounding the park looks dead and unloved. There's a house in the distance that's missing pieces of siding. The one beside it has a screen door hanging from the hinges and three rusted-out cars in the driveway, one with the hood up.

As I approach the slide where I hid, I already feel like I'm entering a new stage of healing. I crouch down, just like I did that night, and close my eyes, knowing I look crazy, but also aware that this is what I need to do.

I see it all so clearly. Like a movie replaying in my mind. I graze my arm, remembering the way it felt when Winton wrapped his fingers around me.

Drawing in a bumpy breath, I fast-forward to Rome's voice when he told them to let me go.

I try to picture him in my head, that black hoodie and his familiar blue eyes, but all I can focus on is the sound of Winton's threatening voice saying if I tell anyone, I'll live to regret it.

Chills dance down my spine as the words repeat over and over in my head. Because now I have told someone.

If Winton finds out, assuming he hasn't already, he could very well follow through with his threat. I look around, those eyes on me feeling even more intense now that I'm out in the open. I can feel my chest rising and falling rapidly, but I am no longer aware enough to stop it.

My body trembles until I feel the soft touch of Wilder's hand on my back. "You're safe," he assures me. My fear escalates when I realize that bringing Wilder here could put him in danger.

I can do this. I have to do this.

Look past Winton, Elodie. Search for Rome. Winton isn't going to hurt you again.

I pinch my eyes tight, bringing the shadowy figure into the light.

There he is. My knight in shining armor who now has a name. Rome.

A sense of calm washes over me now that he's appeared in my memory.

"I see him," I say out loud, eyes still closed. "He's picking up the pipe." My eyes shoot wide open. "He picked the pipe off the ground," I say again. That's not something I remembered from that night until just now. I assumed that Rome came with it, but he didn't.

"That's helpful," I tell Wilder. "It's proof that Rome didn't come here with malicious intent. He picked up the pipe in self-defense."

"That's great," Wilder exclaims. "When you give your witness statement, tell them that. Because you're right. It does prove he was just defending himself, and you."

I nod my head frantically as I jump up, all those feelings of dread vanishing in an instant. "I'm doing this," I tell Wilder excitedly. "I'm going to my mom and telling her everything so I can save Rome's future and his reputation."

Wilder pulls me in for a hug. It's warm and safe and gives me a whole new perspective on who Wilder is as a person. He's not this cold monster I created in my head. Just because Rome and him are brothers—twins, rather—doesn't mean they hold the same anger in their hearts. For once, I truly believe Rome isn't heartless either. He's just hurt.

As we exit the park, I turn to Wilder, feeling immense gratitude. "Thank you for going with me." My hands are still shaking, but I feel a sense of relief and accomplishment for coming here and facing my fears.

"No problem. I'm glad it was helpful." His smile is warm when he looks at me. When we first moved in with the Cromwells, I really did think it was going to be nothing but torture, but maybe having a brother isn't so bad. Brogan has always been on my side, but having Wilder on my side too makes me feel untouchable.

Not only was today helpful for Rome's case, but in some strange way, coming here was good for my healing process. Looking back, I feel a sense of pride for how hard I fought back against those guys. I'm proud of myself for not cowering immediately, even when I felt so hopeless. It gave Rome time to get to me.

When I walked into that park the first time, last year, I was weak and scared. But I walked away unscathed because of the strength I didn't know I had. And a guy who was willing to put himself in danger for me.

That night changed me—it changed a lot of us. But it also built me into something new. I can only hope that something good comes out of this for Rome. Regardless of my anger toward him, he saved me, and I do owe him one.

We go back to Wilder's car, and once we're inside, I pull out my phone to text my mom and let her know I won't be home for dinner tonight. She responds by asking me if I have a date and adds a winking emoji, causing me to chuckle.

"What's so funny?" Wilder asks, pulling out of the parking space.

"Just my mom. I've got plans to go to a movie tonight and being the nosey person she is, she's asking questions." I pocket my phone and look out the window.

"Movie plans, huh? Like a date?" Wilder glances over at me, studying my reaction.

I scoff. "Not you too?"

Wilder drapes his wrist over the steering wheel and sinks back in the seat once we're on the main road. "Just looking out for my little sister."

"Ugh," I grumble. "Don't call me that. Besides, we're both eighteen."

He lazily looks over at me with all the confidence of a playboy. "Rome and I are a month older than you, so technically, you are our little sister."

Just hearing Wilder refer to me as Rome's sister makes me want to throw up. Siblings don't do what we did. They don't treat each other the way we do.

"I'll claim you as my brother, but claiming Rome is a *big* no."

Wilder chuckles, fixing his gaze back on the road. "He's not as bad as he seems, I swear." He looks at me with a fractured smile on his face. It's sweet that he's defending Rome, but he doesn't know half of what he's done. "He's just had a rough year."

"Rough days and years do not make rough lives. Rome acts as if I'd destroyed his entire future."

"Well," he drawls, pausing briefly. "You sort of did." My eyes pop wide and he holds up a hand. "I'm not saying it was intentional, but that arrest really did fuck things up for him."

"I know," I say softly. "I wish I could just go back and change everything."

I'm staring out the passenger window, looking at the sun that's setting behind dark clouds, and guilt consumes me once again. If I wouldn't have gotten lost in that park, none of this would have happened.

Rome wouldn't hate me. He'd be preparing to go to UCLA to play football. And Stanford would be a sealed deal. Nothing in my life is going to be safe until I repair the damage I've caused. But there is hope now, and that's enough to eliminate a tiny fraction of the unease I've felt for days.

"You never told me who you have plans with tonight," Wilder says, breaking the silence. "Care to elaborate?"

"Not really, but I guess I can tell you." I sigh. "I'm going to the movies with Gage."

Wilder's eyes snap to mine before drifting back to the road. "Gage Hanson?"

"Yeah. Is that a bad thing?" Worry sits heavy in my gut as I watch Wilder's expression.

He rolls his shoulders and taps his fingers on the steering wheel. "I know someone who might consider it a problem."

"Let me guess, Rome?" I say his name like it's a curse because at this point, it is.

"He's not Gage's biggest fan. They had some beef back in middle school and it's been lingering ever since." Middle school was a long time ago. I thought girls were the type to hold grudges, not guys.

"Well, my business isn't Rome's, so he'll just have to deal with it." I cross my arms, sealing the deal in my mind. Since I arrived in Willow Creek, Gage is one of the first people to act interested in me. I am sure as fuck not going to cancel my date just because Rome doesn't like the guy.

That's why he got all puffy chested when I was talking to Gage. It shouldn't make me giddy that Rome might be a little pissed I'm going to the movies with Gage, but for some reason, it does.

CHAPTER 19

ROME

IN THE MIDDLE OF PRACTICE, Coach asked me to meet with him to talk about my return in a couple weeks. I've been on pins and needles ever since, worried he's going to bench me longer because he can do whatever the hell he wants.

He could suspend me the entire season, or let me play now. The ball is in his court. But he said he couldn't allow me to go unpunished, so he decided on taking me out half the season. I fought like hell, but it wasn't enough. However, if he is bringing me in here to tell me I *am* out the rest of the season, I won't leave this room until I change his mind.

"You wanted to see me," I say, grabbing Coach Ivers's attention as I walk through the door to his office.

He lifts his head from the playbook opened in front of him and gestures to the chair in front of his desk with the pencil in his hand. "Have a seat, Rome."

I'm practically holding my breath, ready to pass out as I sit down. I slap my hands to my knees, ready to hear what he has to say.

"I wanted to check in with you. See how things have been." A sympathetic look washes over his features and I finally draw in a breath. "I know this year hasn't been easy for you and your brother."

He's referring to the loss of my mom. Of course it hasn't been easy, but I'm not willing to talk about it with him. Coach treats us boys like we're his own kids. He guides us, checks in on us when we need it, and even reprimands us as he sees fit. He's like a therapist and coach all in one. But the topic of my mom is one everyone knows not to touch.

"Things are good," I tell him, not willing to give him much more of a response.

He leans into the desk, leveling his eyes with mine, and I blink away, feeling like I'm under scrutiny. "Your grades are telling me otherwise, son."

Fuck. I should've known. Preparing myself for *this* conversation, I bite my bottom lip and take another deep, audible breath.

"You're still passing, but they're slipping fast. You've got two and a half weeks to get them where they need to be if you want back on that field."

I nod. "I know. I'm gonna try harder. I can do it."

"I know you can. You wouldn't be sitting here if I didn't think you could. I believe in you, Rome. Now you just need to believe in yourself."

"Thanks, Coach," I say, emotion welling in my throat. It means a lot that he believes in me.

My phone beeps in my front pocket and I put my hand over it to silence the sound out of respect.

He presses his pencil to the playbook. "Go ahead and get that. We're finished here. Go home and read a book or something. Keep your wits about you and stay out of trouble. You're almost there, son."

"I don't know about reading." I chuckle as I stand. "But maybe I'll actually finish my homework tonight."

He smiles. "That's a start."

Once I'm back in the locker room, I pull my phone out of my pocket and read a text from Wilder.

Wilder: I don't want to start shit, but I thought
you should know one of our sisters is heading
to the movies as we speak with Gage Hanson.

I hastily type back a response.

Me: Which one?

I swear on everything, if it's Elodie, I will make Gage wish he were never born.

Wilder: Elodie

"Fuck!" I shout as I ball my fist, pounding it right into the locker. My fingers flex and I instantly regret it, just like every time I punch shit.

She's trying to get under my skin. That has to be it. No way would she be going to the movies with Gage for any other reason. Then again, she doesn't know him like I do. He's not a good guy.

Me: Did she leave already?

Wilder: He picked her up about ten minutes
ago.

God dammit!

I remember the way his fingers glided up her leg with purpose. She handled it that night, but tonight she might allow him to go further. I shouldn't care. I should let Elodie make her own mistakes then pick at the cracks whenever he breaks her.

My jaw tics as the rage inside me simmers, threatening to boil over. I can't let that happen, though. Over my dead fucking body will he lay a finger on her.

I bolt out of the locker room, practically running down the hall before shoving the exit doors open. I don't stop moving until

I'm in the driver's seat of my car. Before I even close the door, I bring the engine to life.

I'm in workout clothes because I chose to lift after practice for a bit, then Coach wanted to talk, so I didn't even think to grab my bag.

Fuck. I should've just gone straight home after practice. Gage was acting all high and mighty at practice, even after I put him in his place and told him to stay away from Elodie. Now I know why.

It's a ten-minute drive to the theater, but I make it in six. As soon as I slam the car in park, I'm out the door, fleeing the car and heading into the building.

Luckily, there are only two movies showing, so it's easy to figure out they're watching *Blackouts* because the only other option is an animated movie that doesn't start again for another half hour.

I get one ticket, a large bucket of popcorn, and a soft drink, then I head in to watch the show.

Just as I enter the room, the lights dim and the previews begin. There aren't many people here, maybe a dozen at most. I'm not surprised, considering it's a Monday night. Even better for me as I search for them. Chances are, he's already trying to swoon her with his hand on her leg or around her shoulders.

Squeezing the popcorn bucket, some of it topples over, landing on the floor. Then, I see the back of her head. On the far side of the room beside the wall in the back row. Fortunately, all the seats next to Elodie are empty.

I inch my way down the row in the nearly empty movie theater, the sticky floor clinging to my shoes. She's so engrossed in what's on the screen that she doesn't even notice me until I plop down beside her, causing the seat to squeak. She turns and looks at me, her eyes narrowing in surprise.

Her mouth drops open as shock consumes her and I toss a handful of popcorn in my mouth while I smirk.

You wanted to play a game, Freckles? You picked the wrong opponent.

She shifts in her seat, her shoulders tense, and I realize she's wearing a dark-colored skirt. One that's far too short for this *date* she's on. Fortunately, she's got a sweater on her lap to hide her skin from this fucking dickwad and everyone else in this room.

Elodie's eyes nearly pop out of their sockets as she sets her jaw. "What in the world are you doing, Rome!?"

I notice Gage straightening his back and leaning forward to get a look at me.

Causally, I hold the bucket of popcorn out to Elodie. "Want some?"

"No, I don't want some," she whisper-yells.

"Suit yourself." I offer some to Gage, who seems to be in a state of shock because he's not saying anything at all. When he doesn't reach his hand in, I shrug my shoulders and return it to my lap.

"Rome!" Elodie snaps. "Why are you here?"

"Shhh." I nod toward the big screen. "Movie's about to start. The beginning is the most important part."

Elodie and Gage exchange a few whispers and when he puts his hand on her leg as they talk, I reach over and peel his filthy fingers off her. "Yeah. That's not happening." I toss his hand back into his own lap.

"Dude," Gage growls, throwing his hands in the air. "Why the fuck are you even here?"

A couple people from a few rows in front of us turn their heads, scowling, before returning to the movie.

I don't humor Gage with a response because his thoughts on this situation don't matter to me one bit. This is about Elodie.

"You are unbelievable," Elodie grits out. "Do you have any idea how embarrassing this is?"

Gage stands up and his seat flips back. Reaching out to Elodie, he says, "Let's just go somewhere else. We can watch a movie at my place."

I laugh humorously as I stand up, too. *Over my dead fucking body.*

Leaning down, my lips brush Elodie's ear. "Don't forget, I own you."

She turns her head slowly, the anger on her face replaced with fear in her eyes. "Don't do this," she says softly so that only I can hear.

"You've given me no choice."

I sit back down and pop a handful of popcorn in my mouth, my eyes trained on the opening credits on the screen.

When I hear Elodie tell Gage that it's fine and she'd like to stay and watch the movie, I smile. Power is a beautiful thing.

"Rome!" she whispers my name again, searching for a way out of this very uncomfortable position I've put her in.

After a minute of staring at me like I'm an alien invading her space, Elodie sinks back into her seat with her arms crossed over her chest. Every so often, a heavy sigh escapes her lips, reminding me that she's pissed.

I keep looking at the screen, but I'm not watching the movie at all. Even when it's halfway through and everyone in the theater gasps, except for the three of us, I'm still not interested.

I'm not even sure why Gage is tolerating this and staying here. He either really likes her, or his mind is set on hooking up with her after.

When I glance over at Elodie, just to make sure they're both keeping their hands to themselves, she turns away quickly.

I wonder how she would have reacted if Gage had crept his hand up her leg in this dark theater. Would she push him away, or would she allow him to go as far as he wanted? I wonder how she'd react if I did.

Curious, I stretch my arm out and rest my hand on her upper thigh. Elodie clears her throat and shifts nervously before grabbing my hand and setting it on the armrest.

I smile. Then I try again, this time taking her hand in mine and squeezing it to show her I'm the one in control here.

She squeezes back harder until my bones are grinding together. It's a reaction I like because it shows how tough she can be. Not that the black eye Gage is sporting isn't proof enough. I hope she'll use that feistiness if he comes on to her again. That is, if I don't get to him first.

Wiggling my fingers free from hers, I put my hand back on her leg, and this time when she tries to pry it off, I squeeze her thigh, relishing the way her meaty flesh separates my fingers.

Fuck. Something about this girl drives me wild and I hate it. She sucks in a sharp breath and that sound alone does things to me.

Placing the popcorn bucket in her lap to hide my hand, I watch as she carefully balances it on her other leg.

She's my damn stepsister. I shouldn't be caressing her leg like this, teasing and moving her skirt up inch by inch as my fingers splay across her flesh.

I definitely shouldn't be ghosting my fingers over her center, only to find her panties damp from arousal.

And I have no business pulling those panties to the side, just to feel the way her arousal coats my skin in an instant.

My nostrils flare when I realize her legs are shaking. But she doesn't close them. In fact, when I tilt my wrist up so I have a better angle to circle her clit, she widens the gap to give me better access.

Elodie shifts upward when I dip the tips of two fingers inside her. Her hand slaps over mine and she turns her head, giving me a look of warning. But she doesn't mean it. Her body is already reacting to me and she knows it.

I smirk back at her, then lace my fingers together and sink them deeper inside her, my knuckles rolling against her slick entrance. As I curl my fingers, her body trembles, and I move my thumb up to rub her clit.

Her mouth falls open again as she struggles with what to do. I can see her brain ticking, trying to push her to stop me. But I also see the arch of her back and the way her eyes are hooded.

Elodie quickly pulls her sweater over my hand to hide the sinful act of her stepbrother fingering her in a movie theater.

Watching her mouth gape, I challenge myself to force a sound out of those beautiful lips. Lips I can't help but picture my dick gliding between.

Her gaze moves back to the movie while she attempts to ignore me. As much as she wants to pretend this isn't happening, it is, and by the time I'm done with her, she's going to be begging for more.

Elodie is still a virgin. My fingers are the only ones that have ever entered her pussy, according to her very detailed journals, but she has yet to feel the intense pleasure of a full-blown orgasm. It's possible she's got herself off, but it's a pale comparison to how I'm about to make her feel.

She should have never come here, let alone with Gage. I made it very clear that she is to run everything by me before she makes plans or decisions, and she keeps failing.

I sink my fingers deeper, hitting the spot that I know is going to make her moan.

She steals her back against the seat, squeezing my wrist until her nails dig into my skin, and I relish the burn. When she lets her fire out, it only makes me hotter.

I promised Elodie she would be punished if she crossed me, and now that she has, her punishment is going to be the best form of humiliation.

My body tingles with anticipation as I imagine the endless ways I'm going to ruin this girl for any other guy. Elodie is my toy to play with, and it's only a matter of time before she succumbs to my every desire. She wanted me to treat my toys better? Well, she's going to get her wish.

I lean into her, pumping my hand steadfastly against her core. "How's that feel, Freckles?" My breath fans across her neck. In the dim light, I see goosebumps pebble across her flesh, making me bite my lip in satisfaction.

Pretend all you want, you're mine.

She turns her head slowly, nostrils flared. "I hate you," she grits between her clenched teeth.

I smile back at her, loving how her hate feels in the palm of my hand.

"How much?" I ask with bated breath, wanting more than anything to shove my hard cock in her tight cunt. I have to adjust myself just thinking about it.

"More…" I move my fingers in a circle before pressing down on that soft spot inside her. "M-more than you will ever know."

And because of that response, I force pressure on her clit, rubbing circles that make her squirm. If she hates me that much, I better make her wrath worthwhile.

Gage stands up and Elodie's shoulders pin to the seat nervously. I keep working my fingers because I don't give a flying fuck if he sees where my hand is. Hell, I almost want him to.

Elodie panics and grabs my hand, pulling it away from her. Slowly, I bring it into my lap as Gage tells her, "Be right back. I have to use the bathroom."

He comes in front of me, then leans down, invading my fucking space. "You think you're clever, asshole, but I don't give two fucks about you or what you're doing. Keep loosening her up for me because I plan to get some later."

My chest heaves as I go to stand, ready to shove him into the seats in front of us, but he dips out before I can even get to my feet.

I'm gonna end that asshole when he least expects it. Now, more than ever, I'm ready to make this girl cry out just so he hears it.

I move my hand back into her lap and she shakes her head. "Don't fight it, Freckles. You know you want it."

"He'll know," she says, tone low. "And I'm not that girl."

What she doesn't realize is, Gage already knows. He knows why I'm here, what I'm doing, and what he *won't* be doing with her tonight. He has a plan and I'm here to derail it because there is no fucking way Elodie is going anywhere with him ever again.

Moving my hand back between her slippery legs, I resume fingering her. "Just admit it. You might not be *that* girl, but you want to be."

A soft moan escapes her parted lips as I increase the intensity of my thrusts, still focusing on her swollen clit.

She's so damn wet. So tight. Fuck. I'd love nothing more than to get on my knees and separate her thighs with my face. I'd drag my tongue up and down her sex, tasting the sweet innocence of her arousal. Once I got her cleaned up real good, I'd slowly glide my cock inside her, claiming her body as mine.

My cock twitches, knowing I'll soon make that desire a reality. Until then, her pleasure alone has to be enough. I push upward until she's practically sitting on my fingers, her body riding up and down against the seat. "Rome," she pants, just as Gage comes back down the aisle. This time, I don't stop. I know she wants me to. She's worried Gage will see. She's worried about what happens next. How her body will react as she comes around my fingers.

Gage finds his seat and Elodie stares straight ahead at the screen as her walls clench and I force more pressure. Gage shoots a look in our direction, but I just smile and nod. He looks at Elodie and she plasters her eyes on the screen, trying to remain motionless. But the second he looks away, my fingers fuck her harder.

"Rome," she says again, breathlessly. But this time, she doesn't dig her nails into my hand to stop me. This time, she adjusts my hand as she sinks down on it, and I watch, shocked and mesmerized all at once. Elodie thrives off of being in control, and normally I want to strip that from her. But dammit. Seeing her take control of her pleasure right now is hotter than sin itself.

Her legs spread wider and she rolls her hips as her head rests back against the seat. Her eyes pinch closed and her mouth falls open.

A rush of adrenaline courses through me when I feel her clench my fingers. Her body tenses up and she cries out, "Rome!"

Gage shoots upward in his seat, and Elodie's eyes pop open, landing on him.

I slowly slide my fingers out of her even as her cunt begs to milk my hand for all it's worth. My work here is done.

My hand moves to her thigh, dragging proof of her orgasm as I stroke her sensitive skin.

"Is everything all right?" Gage asks, and I chuckle. The guy is such a fucking moron. I just gave his date an orgasm and he allowed it.

Pulling my hand away from Elodie, I snatch the popcorn bucket and reach in with her juices still coating my fingers. I grab out a handful, then pass it across Elodie to Gage. "You should try it. This is some good shit."

Elodie gasps, realizing what I've done, as Gage ignores me completely.

I shrug, scooping up more for myself.

Holding eye contact with my stepsister, I toss the popcorn in my mouth, then proceed to lick my sweet and salty fingers.

CHAPTER 20
ELODIE

"WHY ARE YOU STILL HERE?" I grit out at Rome, who is walking on my left side, while Gage is on my right. We exit the theater, stepping into the dark night, and I stop before heading into the parking lot.

"You can go now," I tell him, knowing damn well he's not going to listen. Rome does what he wants, when he wants. And somehow, he always gets away with it.

"Actually," Rome begins, his eyes on Gage as he speaks to me. "My dad texted a couple minutes ago and asked that Elodie and I meet the family at Big John's Pizza for dinner."

He's such a fucking liar!

"Oh," Gage says. "I thought maybe we could spend a little more time together."

Rome grabs my hand, pulling me toward the direction of his car. "You thought wrong. G'night, Gage."

"Remember what I said, Cromwell," Gage hollers as Rome drags me away.

"What does that mean?" I ask Rome, unsure of what Gage meant.

"It means he's a fucking dead man. That's what it means. Now, let's go." The way Rome looks at Gage makes me feel like he isn't joking. However, that thought fades as fast as it comes while Rome continues to haul me toward the car.

"Are you serious right now?" I pull and bend and twist, trying to break free, but it's pointless because Rome isn't letting me go for anything. "Screw this! I'm not leaving with you!"

"Sure you are. Now quit fighting me." His eyes darken while his grip tightens, but I'm not his obedient little toy tonight. I can't believe he did this. It's fucked up and totally unforgivable.

We stop at the passenger side of his car and he pulls the door open for me. "Get in."

"No!" I jerk my hand again and he finally lets me free. Glaring at him, I hold my ground, crossing my arms over my chest.

"Get in the damn car, Freckles." He tries to crowd my space, but Rome no longer intimidates me. If he really wanted to destroy me, he would have done it by now. My face flushes red just thinking about what he did in that theater.

"Get away from me!" I shove his chest, my eyes down because I can't look at Rome right now, or anyone for that matter. I have never been so humiliated in my life. Tears prick the corners of my eyes. "How could you do that to me?"

I'm still yelling as I gain the courage to look at him for an answer. But this is Rome, he takes nothing seriously.

His arms go wide as his lips twist, trying to hide that evil smile. "Stop being so dramatic. It's not that big of a deal."

"Not that big of a deal?" I raise my voice to a near scream. "You showed up on my date." I hold up one finger. "Embarrassed the guy I was with." Another finger. "Touched me where you had *no* business touching me." A third finger. "Then, you cut my first date in months short, all to what? What, Rome? Take me to dinner with our family, which we both know is total bullshit?"

I grab the sides of my head in frustration as I begin to pace, just thinking about how he made me orgasm for my first time in a public place while I was on a date with another guy.

"Not to mention…" My voice trails off because I really don't want to even talk about that part.

"Not to mention, what?" Rome walks closer, closing that gap of safety I tried to put between us.

I hold up a finger, shaking it. "Don't. Don't you dare do that again. You just want me to say it because you like making me feel stupid, don't you? You know damn well what I'm talking about."

"Are you saying you didn't enjoy it?" He lifts an eyebrow in challenge.

The smug expression sets something off inside me, and before I can even think, my hand flies out, smacking hard against his cheek.

Rome stumbles back in shock. He really shouldn't be surprised. He's the one who pushed me to this point.

I shake my hand, feeling the sting of the slap, and when Rome's sly grin only widens, I realize the only thing I did was intrigue him. I'm beginning to think he likes when I snap back. He likes when I lose control.

Before I can blink, he's back in my face again. His hands reach out to grab my wrists and he pins them to my sides, his nose practically touching mine. "Say it, Freckles. Tell me you enjoyed my fingers fucking your wet cunt."

I turn my head slightly, avoiding eye contact out of fear he'll see through my lie. "I *hated* it." I emphasize the word with every drop of anger I have at myself right now because I know that's not true.

The truth is, I loved every second of it. I'd prefer it had not been in a theater while I was on a date with someone else, but the way he made me feel was indescribable. Just thinking about it has me clenching my thighs that are still sticky with the remnants of my arousal.

"You're lying." Rome tips his chin up while eyeing me up and down. "Admit it felt good and we can get the hell outta here."

I cock a brow. "For dinner with our families?"

He's such a bullshitter. The minute he said his dad texted him, I knew he was lying. Rome doesn't want me anywhere near Gage, and I haven't determined if it's because he hates Gage, like Wilder said, or if it has more to do with his possessiveness over me.

Rome tsks. "Gage is a fucking dumbass. He would have stood in that parking lot all night waiting for you to get in his car just so he could bring you somewhere and take advantage of you."

"Gage isn't like that," I tell him, getting defensive of a guy I hardly know. But he was kind to me and never crossed any boundaries. The whole ride to the theater I was on cloud nine because of how charming he was. "He's sweet and attentive."

"You don't know him." I see the vein in Rome's jaw tic as he says that. "Gage has a one-track mind when it comes to the ladies. Ask any girl in Willow Creek. Ask Abby. Hell, ask your friend Julia."

"What do Abby and Julia have to do with any of this?"

I do remember Julia saying she hates all football players because they abuse their power, but I just thought she didn't like jocks. I thought about texting her just to get the inside scoop on Gage but decided against it at the last minute because I'm normally a good judge of character.

"Rumor in the locker room is that Julia threw herself at him while he was dating someone else during sophomore year. He wasn't having it and rejected her, then she got all crazy. Gage made her out to be this obsessed chick and everyone turned against her. But I didn't buy that shit."

"I think you're just jealous." I said what I said and I have no regrets. Rome has proven time and time again he doesn't like when I get attention from other guys.

"I'm jealous?" He laughs. "I saw the look on your face Friday night at the party when Abby threw herself at me. I think you're the one who's jealous."

I try to move my arms so that I can slap him again. Maybe this time some sense will pop into his head with it. "Did I show up on a date you had with another girl? No. If anyone is jealous, it's definitely you."

"I don't date, Freckles. So that would be pretty hard to do." He laughs again. "Besides, why would I be jealous of Gage Hanson? The guy's a dweeb."

"Gage and Julia had a thing. You and Julia had a thing—"

"Hold the fuck up." Rome laughs. "Me and Julia? Not a fucking chance."

I cock an eyebrow. "You sure about that?"

"Julia?" He puts extra emphasis on her name. "No. Just no."

"So you didn't kiss her?"

He stares off, likely sorting through the faces of the many females he's hooked up with. Then he grins, nodding. "You know what? I think I did kiss her once. In eighth fucking grade."

I shrug. "Still a kiss."

He blows out a heavy puff of air. "A very meaningless kiss."

"Still jealous."

He scoffs. "Not even a little bit. Gage Hanson is not a threat to me in the least."

"Oh yeah? How would it make you feel if I left right now and fucked Gage?"

His Adam's apple bobs in his throat as he swallows, malice flashing in his features. "I'd kill him before he got the chance to lay a finger on you."

Yep. Jealous. I can see it now. The way Rome is looking at me, he really does think I belong to him.

Rome can deny it all he wants, but something snaps inside him when he sees other guys talking to me, touching me, even so much as looking at me. Even Brady, although he doesn't make quite as much of a fuss with him.

Rome lets go of me, pushing my arms back and throwing me off-balance for a moment while creating space between us. "I'm warning you, Gage is not a good guy. You gave the fucker a black eye for groping you. That speaks volumes."

"I wasn't in the right state of mind when I kicked him." I mean, Rome's not wrong. I watched the video. However, Gage did one thing Rome has never done. He apologized and owned up to his actions.

"Or maybe," Rome seethes, his eyes getting darker as he reapproaches me slowly, "you just didn't give a flying fuck for once in your perfect little life." He leans into my face, whispering as if it were a secret. "Maybe you stopped trying to please everyone around you for a second and you actually *defended* yourself."

His words cut me deep. Deeper than he will ever know. I think back to the night that everything went wrong. I tried to defend myself. I took the logical step every time. But what I didn't really do was fight. I could have punched Winton in the balls when I was on my knees. I could have done so much more. But I got scared and I surrendered.

Rome will never know how much I regret that. But I can't live in the past, and that moment taught me a lot. It taught me to stand up to those around me that try to take advantage.

So instead of acting like he just stabbed me in the chest, I stand tall.

"I don't try to please everyone around me."

"Oh yeah." He scoffs. "Then why are we still standing here?"

He's got a point. But he's blocking my path. And as much as I believe in standing up for myself, we both know I'm no match for the town's top quarterback. Crossing my arms over my chest, I glare at him.

"Move out of my way and I'll leave." I gesture back to the theater. "I'll go find Gage and we can go get pizza like we planned for our *date*. Ya know, since we're not actually meeting our families. Maybe you could invite *Abby*." The sarcasm in my tone is apparent when I speak her name, and by the way Rome rolls his eyes, it's clear he doesn't give a shit about her. I just can't seem to let that one go, though.

"Fuck Abby and fuck Gage." Rome grabs my arm and jerks me toward the car while he begins walking. "As for you, you're not going anywhere, unless it's in my room, on your knees with my cock in your mouth."

I gasp as he opens the passenger side door and tries to push me in. "You're disgusting." I try to pull away from him. I'll walk home if this is how he thinks the evening is going.

Before I can get even an inch between us, he shoves me against the side of the car, my back thudding on impact and causing me to momentarily lose my breath.

Rome crowds my space as he trails a finger over my cheek. "And you're turned on." He slides his hand down my chest then under my skirt that is probably too short because it's Brogan's.

When his palm presses between my legs, he drags his fingers upward until he's cupping my crotch. "You disobeyed me, Freckles, and your punishment isn't over." He uses his other hand to draw circles around my lips and I freeze, lost in his gaze. "I'm horny as fuck, and you owe me one."

My skin pricks with desire under his touch. My body is betraying me again, responding to his presence with a mixture of anger and longing. It's like every nerve inside me is tuned to his frequency. Electricity crackles between us and if I don't get away from him right now, I'm afraid of what I might allow him to do next. Damn Rome and his power over me.

"Just take me home," I whisper as I turn my head to refrain from looking at his lips. His fingers push against my entrance and I roll my lips together to keep from making a sound.

"Is that really what you want, Freckles?" His voice is raspy and thick, sending a rush of adrenaline through my core.

I nod slowly, wishing I hadn't.

To my surprise, he pulls his hand out from under my skirt and reaches behind me to grab the handle on the passenger door.

He leans in, lifting it up before saying, "Then let's get you home."

The entire ride is quiet. I'm pissed and I'm regretful. I'm desperate and I'm needy. I want him and I hate him. I'm a damn mess.

Rome has somehow made me crave him. Even when I know I shouldn't. He's going to break me, and I don't know if I'll be able to put myself back together in the end.

When we pull into the garage, I'm surprised to see that it's empty. "Where is everyone?" I ask.

"Big John's Pizza."

I gasp, turning in my seat so fast I'm surprised I don't have whiplash. "Wait. For real?"

Rome's knuckles turn white as he grips the steering wheel. "Yeah. The whole family went out for dinner."

"So you weren't lying?" I'm actually surprised. I really thought he was making that up.

"Yes and no." He lets go of the wheel and opens his door, slamming it behind him. I get out to follow. "They really are there, but I told my dad I wouldn't be joining them, and he said you told your mom the same." Rome walks to the door, the tension in his posture evident. I don't know why, but I just want to see it gone for once. Maybe if Rome could relax, I could stop reacting to him.

CHAPTER 21

ELODIE

ONCE WE'RE in the house, the tension between us thickens. Rome turns on a light in the living room, and as I move toward the stairs to go to my room, I feel a hand reach out and grab me.

I spin around to face him, speechless as I wait for him to stay something.

But he doesn't. I watch as his eyes trail down to my mouth and against my better judgment, I watch his too. I can't help it. As hard as I try not to look at him—to want him—there is this magnetic pull between us that I can't resist.

"Where are you running off to?" he asks, his voice raspy and thick.

I gulp. "My room."

Pulling my shoulders back, I take a deep breath when his tongue drags across his bottom lip and he sucks it between his teeth. "Are you trying to get away from me, Freckles?"

"Maybe," I whisper so low I don't know if he can even hear me. His hand pulls me closer and this time, I go willingly.

In the blink of an eye, our mouths crush together. I'm not sure if he made the move, if I did, or if it was a joint effort, but either way, it's electric.

This kiss is powerful, like nothing I've ever felt before. The way our tongues tangle in a messy web of desire leaves me desperate for more.

Rome lets go of my hand to pull me close, his erection pressing into my stomach through our clothes. There is power in knowing what I do to Rome. He may want to hate me, but he can't deny whatever this is.

His hand moves to the back of my head, caging me against him while a moan slips from between my lips. A subtle growl climbs up his throat and I swallow it down.

Tilting my head slightly, I open and close my mouth to his liking. I wish I didn't crave more of him the way I do. I wish he didn't taste so good—like sweet sin with a hint of butter and salt.

My fingers weave through the soft strands of his hair before pulling him closer and taking back some of that control we both desperately seem to crave. His warmth radiates through my entire being, almost as if we've become one.

"Rome," I mutter into his mouth. I'm not sure why I say his name, but there's an unexplainable urgency inside me. Instead of using words to tell him what I want, I reach down between us, feeling the rough denim of his jeans as my fingers wrap around his bulging hardness.

He breaks the kiss, pressing our foreheads together while we breathe deeply. But no amount of time or space is going to change my decision here. I know what Rome wants, and in some fucked-up way, I want it too. Maybe if I let him take this piece of me, he will stop taking everything else.

"You shouldn't do that," he warns, but I don't relent. I keep rubbing him, tormenting both of us further. "Freckles," he growls. "If you don't stop right now, you're gonna regret it."

I close my eyes and sink into the feeling he brings me when we aren't trying to tear out each other's throats. It's dangerous to remove the hate between us because whatever is left is all-consuming.

"Then make me regret it, Rome."

The next thing I know, I'm being hoisted up. My legs wrap around Rome's waist and his mouth moves to my neck, sucking and kissing as he carries me up the stairs with heavy footsteps on the hardwood.

My core throbs against him, desperately seeking friction as he kicks open the door to his room. In no time, I'm surrounded by the scent of him. It's masculine and utterly addicting. His lips move back to mine and my arms pull him tighter as I press my breasts up and arch my back.

Rome sits me on the edge of the bed as he kisses his way down my neck. Carefully, he lifts my shirt and I help, tossing it across his room while his teeth skim my flesh. I'm so wet, I am sure there will be a puddle on his sheets when we are finished. Pulling away, he looks me in the eye. "You should have stopped me when you had the chance, Freckles."

His mouth trails hot kisses along the curve of my cleavage, nibbling and sucking feverishly before moving to the other side. As he fumbles with the clasp of my bra, I arch my back, tingles shooting through me. Once he's got it unhooked, it falls down and I feel his gaze set on my breasts.

"Damn, baby." He lets out a low grumble, sucking his bottom lip between his teeth.

Butterflies flutter though my stomach when he calls me baby. It makes me feel lightheaded and giddy.

He kneels between us, taking one of my nipples in his mouth and sucking it between his teeth. I whimper in response, which he must like because he eagerly works his way to the next one. His hand cups my free breast, pinching my nipple and making me cry out. I swear lightning shot straight to my clit when he did that.

Rome's breathing kicks up with every reaction I give him. He is my first for so many things and he seems to enjoy that as he explores my body in ways it has never been explored before.

With a gentle push, Rome guides me down on the bed, then he stands at the footboard to remove my shoes. His fingers move to the hem of my skirt and he pulls down, taking my panties along with it and leaving me completely naked.

He watches me for a minute and I don't dare move. I have a feeling that if I were to flee, he would love nothing more than to catch me. Slowly, he climbs onto the bed. Leaning over me, his lips brush against mine. "Last chance to run," he whispers.

I draw in a deep breath, and I say nothing. I don't want to give Rome the satisfaction of knowing how badly I want this, but I also don't want him to stop.

His lips softly press to mine, leaving me breathless and dizzy. And when he stands back up, I prop myself up on my elbows, transfixed as he peels his shirt over his head. I drink in every inch of his chiseled form. His tan skin glistens with sweat, accentuating the rigid curves of his abs. *Is this really happening?* Rome is gorgeous. In every way, shape, and form. I want to reach out and trace over every defined muscle on his body while trailing kisses behind my fingers.

I shouldn't want this—not with my new stepbrother, someone who has taunted me and tried to make my life hell. But goddammit, I do want it.

The sound of his zipper coming down echoes in my ears, a reminder of what's about to happen between us. As his pants drop, and his cock springs free, a surge of warmth spreads through my body.

I watch in awe as Rome gives his hard cock a few strokes before he scoops up both my legs and lifts them, crawling between my thighs.

I feel exposed and vulnerable as he stares down at my center. I just shaved yesterday, have been since I started my period when I was fourteen years old. It's also when I started taking birth control to control my heavy cycles. I still can't help but worry that maybe I didn't do a good job cleaning up down there as he scrutinizes every inch of me. Rome is experienced and it makes me feel self-conscious knowing he's been with other experienced girls.

His skilled fingers trail down my stomach, stopping on my clit as he forces pressure. I raise my hips, loving the way he makes me feel.

But when his head moves between my legs, I find myself clenching them together nervously. *Oh my God, he's going to taste me.*

"Relax, Freckles. This'll feel good. I promise." His eyes light up when they look at me this time and I feel myself giving in.

Rolling my lips together, I put my hands over my face in embarrassment. Ever so slowly, Rome parts my legs. His body settles on the bed and I feel his hot breath fanning just over my core.

His tongue trails down my sex, and surprisingly, my heightened nerves settle, replaced with desire and curiosity.

Oh, okay. This is good. Oh God, this is really fucking good.

My breath catches in my throat when his hot tongue laps around my entrance, the tip sliding in, then coming out and licking patterns again. There's still a slight resistance on my end as my legs attempt to envelop his head, trying to hide what's on display for him, but the way he's making me feel is worth it.

His fingers move feverish circles around my clit and an intense sensation spreads through my body. Heat settles in my core, my toes begin to curl when he pushes two fingers into me.

Goosebumps erupt over my skin and I buck my hips up before grabbing a fistful of his hair. "Oh, God," I cry eagerly as I force pressure, pushing his face into me. Rome works his magical fingers inside me, curling them and hitting just the right spot to send me soaring.

I pant and moan as I come undone for my stepbrother. My eyes roll into the back of my head while pleasure ripples through me.

Rome sucks my clit between his teeth, forcing wild sounds from my mouth that I never knew I was capable of making. I never knew this could feel so damn good.

I feel so dizzy and tingly.

He keeps going as I come down from my orgasm. It feels like all the blood in my body has rushed to my hypersensitive core. There's an odd sensation I've never felt before, and I'm forced to pull his head up to stop the zaps of electricity jolting through my body.

Rome lifts his head and licks his wet lips as my legs tremble on either side of him. "Told you it would feel good." The tips of his fingers rub around my soaked sex and I reach down and grab his hand.

"It feels weird. Like too much." Not to mention I have no idea why my legs are shaking like a newborn horse.

"Sensitive?" he asks, and I nod. "It's normal. Just means you had a really good fucking orgasm." He winks, sending butter-flies through my stomach. "You're welcome."

I exhale heavily, shaking my head against the pillow. Of course Rome would expect me to thank him.

Just when I think we're done here, Rome slides up until his body is blanketing mine. I want to say that I hate it, that this is the weirdest feeling in the world, but somehow this feels right.

"My turn," he whispers.

The way his bare skin feels pressed against mine is indescrib-able. I might be crazy in thinking our souls have connected on a new level, but it's the way I feel. Like the past doesn't exist, and the here and now is all that matters.

"Are you on the pill?" he asks, and I nod in response.

My heart pounds in a frenzied tempo as he slides the tip of his cock inside me. It goes in with gentle ease, as if I were molded just to fit him.

There's a tinge of pain, but it's not unbearable. Likely because his fingers have stretched me enough to keep it minimal.

Rome pushes himself up with his forearms pressed into the mattress on either side of me while his face hovers over mine. He leans closer, his warm breath tickling my neck as he grinds his hips against me.

My arms instinctively wrap around his neck as my breasts

graze his chest. I take a deep breath, inhaling him as he continues to work himself deep inside me. His skin is soft and inviting against mine as I pull him even closer.

I clench my teeth as he pushes farther, his body coming down on mine as he finds a new angle. A whimper slips through my slightly parted lips and he lifts his head, his eyes boring into mine. It feels like he's peering into the depths of my soul. Warmth spreads through my body, a feeling of contentment and longing.

"Jesus, Freckles." He grunts on a thrust. "You're tight as fuck."

I'm not sure if that's a good or bad thing, but by the way his breaths are coming in heavy pants, I'd say it feels good.

My breath quickens as I feel him sink deeper, filling me up with his length. I dig my fingertips into his skin, dragging them as he rocks in and out.

"You okay?" he asks. I'm surprised he even cares, but something about Rome right now is gentler than I have ever seen him. Other than that moment when he held my hand while I gave blood, this is the only other time Rome hasn't looked like he wants to take every piece of me and light it on fire.

I nod in response and the next thing I know, his mouth is on mine.

Rome kisses me hard. So hard our teeth clank together and I feel the skin on my bottom lip bust open. The metallic taste of blood seeps onto my tongue, but it doesn't stop what's happening. If anything, it seems to turn him on even more.

He picks up his pace, and the heat between us intensifies. I pull him closer, sweat pooling between our cemented bodies. My hips buck up, matching his rhythm as my entire body trembles with pleasure.

The pungent scent of sex mingles with his intoxicating cologne and it's like a drug I'm inhaling. I can't seem to get enough. Just one taste and I'm addicted…to this, to him, to *us*.

It's a scary thought, but Rome officially has me in the palm of his hand.

My nails dig deeper into his skin, dragging downward as soft moans of pleasure escape him. I wrap my legs around him, pulling him as close as he can be while grinding my clit into his pelvis.

I want more. I need more. Oh, God. "More," I moan, and that's exactly what he gives me.

He fucks me harder and faster. The headboard ricochets against the wall, pounding out a rhythm that echoes our moans and gasps.

Rome growls headily, slamming his pelvis against my center.

He lifts up, breaking our kiss as his eyes watch me.

"Come for me, Freckles. Milk my cock."

Electricity courses through me, and the intensity of this orgasm is like nothing I've ever felt before, and everything I want to feel again.

Thrusting and panting, sweat beads around his hairline and his mouth falls open, mirroring mine as the head of his cock swells inside me. His fingers return to my clit, pinching just when my walls contract around him, doing exactly as he asked.

Not a second later, he comes undone, pulsing inside me until I am sure not another drop could fit. Those ice blue eyes land on mine, and he leans down to kiss me one more time before dropping the weight of his body onto me.

We lie there quietly—for what feels like hours, but it's only been a couple short minutes—before Rome pushes himself up.

He looks down at me again, lust still in his eyes. Yet, when I look closer, I see a look of regret on his face.

Biting his bottom lip, he acts as if he wants to say something, but no words come out of his mouth.

Say it, I beg of him internally. *Tell me what's on your mind.*

He doesn't. Instead, he climbs off me and stands up, instantly breaking the spell he had me under. He sighs heavily before fishing around for something on the floor.

Then my shirt flies through the air, followed by my bra, landing on my chest. "Thanks," I whisper as I hold it close to my body, unsure how I should feel right now. "Hey, Rome," I say and he shoots me a glance. "I don't want to offend you or anything, but you're clean, right?"

"Of course I am. Just got tested last month. Papers are in my top drawer if you wanna see them."

I nod, knowing I don't need to. I believe him.

This was everything I thought it would be, but the emotional aspect is lacking. I always imagined lying in bed, laughing and cuddling after my first time. But Rome isn't like that. I shouldn't even grieve that part of this process because it shouldn't have been expected with him.

With his clothes in hand, Rome heads to the door, his firm round ass on full display. "I'm gonna shower," he says before leaving the room, not even a glance back in my direction.

I scoot up on the bed, my heart breaking, and I don't even know why.

Rome got what he wanted and I have to admit I got something out of it too. For just a few minutes he made me believe he wasn't a heartless monster, only to remind me of the kind of person he really is.

I take my time standing up, weirded out by the stickiness between my thighs as I rush to my bathroom.

As I step under the spray of my shower, I wonder if Rome will just drop me like everyone says he does when he's finished with a girl.

It would be better that way. Even if it breaks my heart.

CHAPTER 22

ELODIE

It's been four days since I went to the movies with Gage, only to leave with Rome and give him something I'll never be able to give again—my virginity.

I'm still feeling the ache between my thighs from his brutal delivery. Rome was gentle at first, which I appreciated, but as things intensified between us, he was violent and unwavering. Yet, I loved every second of it.

What I don't love are the twin bruises on each of my breasts from him sucking so damn hard. Fortunately, no one will ever see those. They will eventually fade, just like the memory of my first time. It has to. Rome is my stepbrother and this can never happen again.

Not that I think Rome would want it to. He's been avoiding me since that day, and I've made no attempt to ask him why.

Rome started this shit between us, and if he wants to talk or yell or fight, then he can take the initiative.

Pushing those thoughts aside, I focus on what needs to be done today. My mom is going to work in a few minutes and I told her I needed to talk to her before she left.

As hurt as I am by Rome's countless cruel actions, I still feel the need to try and help him.

I walk downstairs to find her in the kitchen with a mug of steaming hot coffee in her hand and some papers laid out in front of her.

"Good morning, honey." She takes another sip then sets her mug down beside the papers. "Sleep well?"

I shrug. "Not terrible." The truth is, I haven't been sleeping well. Every time I close my eyes, I see Rome. I lie in bed and dream of him touching me again. It's both a blessing and a curse.

"What was it you wanted to talk about? It sounded important." Her concerned face makes me anxious. My mother cares a lot about me and has always created a safe space for me to tell her if anything happened in my life. I don't want to upset her or make her feel like any of this is her fault.

"It is," I tell her. "Can we sit?"

"Of course." She grabs her coffee and we round the kitchen island to the row of barstools on the other side. "What's going on, Elodie?" I can feel the worry in her tone and it makes me even more nervous for what I'm about to tell her.

"I need to talk to you about what happened when we visited this town a year ago."

"Okay." She places her mug down, turning to me with her undivided attention.

So, I tell her everything. Every sordid detail about that night. I leave absolutely nothing out because if I want this to work in Rome's favor, she needs to know the whole truth.

"Elodie," Mom says with a bite of disappointment in her tone as she strokes my back. "Why didn't you tell me any of this?"

"I was scared. Thought maybe I could just move on and forget it ever happened. Then we moved to Willow Creek and I quickly realized it wasn't just going to go away."

Mom tucks a strand of hair behind my ear, a look of remorse on her face. "I'm so sorry you had to go through that alone. You know you can tell me anything, honey." I nod in response, a pang of anguish in my chest. "Grant told me all about Rome's case and I did look into it to see if there were any discrepancies, but without a witness on his behalf, he was sentenced accordingly with the evidence presented by the defense attorney."

It breaks my heart knowing Rome also had to go through that alone while those three guys created their own narrative of what happened. It was his word against theirs, and in the end, he lost so much.

"So," I say, desperate to hear her tell me she can fix this. "Do you think you can help Rome?"

"Oh, Elodie, as much as I would love to, Rome has already been sentenced. In fact, he's completed his community service, paid his fines, and in a few months, he'll be off probation."

"Probation?" I spit out. Rome never mentioned being on probation still. Why didn't he tell me that?

"Yes," Mom strokes my head again, calming me in the same way she has since I was a little girl. "When Rome was found guilty by the court in February, he was sentenced to one year of probation."

"So that's it?" My voice cracks as defeat washes over me. "Nothing can be done, even now that I'm willing to give a statement as a witness?"

All the hope I've felt since Rome told me he got in trouble is now gone in an instant. That is until my mom's eyes perk up and she says, "Actually, there might be something."

My eyes shoot wide open and a glimmer of hope flickers inside me again. "Really?"

"I can't make any promises." I can see the wheels turning behind her eyes. "Give me a couple days to review his case and look into a few things."

I throw my arms around her, squeezing her while she hugs me back. "Thank you, Mom." I try not to let the tears fall as I hold her tight.

"You're welcome, honey." She pats my back and kisses my cheek. "I have to get to work but try not to worry about this too much. No matter what happens, Rome will eventually forgive you."

I nod, smiling back at her but knowing this isn't only about forgiveness, this is about Rome's future that I stole from him.

Mom leaves for work and I'm already running behind, so I quickly get ready for school. By the time I'm done, everyone has left the house.

Moving fast, I step outside, pulling the door closed behind me. It feels unusually warm for early October, but the dull gray sky and the fresh scent in the air tells me a storm is coming. Reaching into my purse, I pull out my keys and remote start my car before I even get to it. Except, as I approach, something catches my eye on the windshield. I go in front of the car and pluck out the envelope stuck underneath my windshield wiper.

Chills shimmy down my spine as I unfold the flap and pull out a lined paper note.

What goes around for a snitch, comes back like a bitch.

Dread washes over me as I let the note fall slowly to the ground. Not because of what it says, but because of what I see sticking straight out of the front seat in my car.

Cautiously, I go to the driver's side door and pull it open, my hands shaking uncontrollably. My eyes land on a rusted-out pipe that's been stabbed right into the cushion of my seat, dripping with blood.

I gasp and instinctively stumble backward. My feet slip on the slick pavement and I lose my footing, my ass hitting the driveway with a loud thud.

Not a breath leaves my lungs as I sit there for a second, staring at the bloody pipe sticking out of my seat, wondering whose blood that is. It has to be an animal. It can't possibly be human blood. Who the hell would do something so deranged?

There's no way it's the same pipe Rome used to hit Winton that night because the cops would have taken that in for evidence, assuming it was found on the scene. Regardless, it's meant to scare me—a symbol of what happened that night, and the fact that I told someone when I wasn't supposed to.

This has Winton's name all over it.

But what if it's not? What if this is Rome's doing? He could still be punishing me. Just like he said he would. Maybe he's been punishing me all along. It could have been him who drugged me at the party so he could get that video of me dancing on the counter. He could have been the one who slashed my tires just to scare me.

Suddenly, everything feels so fake. I feel so used and I have no idea what's real and what's not. I felt a spark with Rome. As hard as I tried not to, it kept flickering inside me to the point that I allowed it to fully ignite. And now, I'm the one who is going up in flames.

Still in a state of panic, I get to my feet, feeling off-balance and lightheaded. I kick the car door shut with my foot and snatch the note off the ground, now feeling the uneasy threat of eyes on me. He could be out there, watching me this very minute.

With the note in hand, I run back into the house, locking the door behind me. Creeping slowly, I go over to the bay window and peer out. The lights on my car flicker and I jump back before realizing it's because the engine timed out from using my remote start.

I take a deep breath and back away while keeping my eyes glued to my car, afraid that if I stop looking, someone is going to appear and I'll miss them.

Knowing I should call the cops, or even Brogan, or my parents, I hold back because of the note. I read it again…

What goes around for a snitch, comes back like a bitch.

If I tell anyone about this, what will they do next? Rome

wouldn't hurt anyone but me, but Winton, I have no doubt he would go after anyone in his path.

Maybe I should tell my mom to forget about looking into Rome's case. He can finish out his probation and go to whatever school accepts him and live his life. Sure, he won't have football, but at least the rest of us will be unscathed. He'll resent me forever, but I'll deal with it. This sexual thing between us needs to end anyways. He's my stepbrother, for crying out loud.

But that's not the kind of person I am. I can't let what Rome did to save me ruin him. I just have to make sure I am more careful about how I go about all of this.

As for the feelings brewing inside me, they'll go away eventually. I have no business feeling anything other than normal sibling emotions for Rome anyways.

Pulling my phone out of my purse, I go into the kitchen and sit down on a stool at the center island, the sensation of someone watching me still looming.

I send a text to Brogan, letting her know I'm staying home today so she doesn't wonder where I am.

> Me: Hey, Bro. I won't be at school today. Not feeling great. See you when you get home from cheer practice.

She doesn't respond and it's likely because class has already started.

Then I text my mom because I know she'll get a call from the school and immediately worry. I haven't missed a day of school since the start of my junior year when I had a bad case of the flu, and even then, I begged her to let me go.

> Me: Hi, Mom. I started getting bad cramps when I was getting ready for school. Think I'm going to stay home today.

Her response, however, is immediate.

I can't drive my car until I clean up the mess, but just the thought of going out there alone to face it has bile rising in my throat. And with it comes the memory of Rome hitting Winton last year. The sound of metal meeting bone rings heavily in my ears.

I jump off the stool, knowing I need to distract myself before I go crazy. Eventually I'll have to go back out there and clean up the mess before anyone looks in my car. But not right now.

As I take the stairs up to my room, I allow the tears to fall. I should have been allowed to have one night where I went to a party and came home and nothing bad happened.

I go up to my room and curl into a ball under my blankets, wondering when this madness will end.

I think about that night, and everything in between. Digging up the memories of how it felt when Rome first touched me compared to the last time. In my heart, I feel like we've made progress and come so far. But in my head, I know it's just an illusion of what I want to be real.

The truth is, Rome hasn't forgiven me and he never will. He's toying with me, just like he planned to. And I'm a fool for falling for his tricks.

I must have drifted off to sleep because my groggy eyes shoot open when my phone beeps with a text message.

Slapping my hand around on the mattress, I grab it and hold it over my head, seeing that it's a message from Rome.

It's the first time he's initiated contact with me since we had sex, and I can't pretend I'm not anxious to see what he has to say.

His first words to me since I gave him my virginity, and it's a question asking me where I am.

Wow, Rome. You sure have a way with the ladies. No wonder he's slept with so many—he treats them like complete trash after. I bet Abby was the only one to beg for seconds.

I sit up quickly when I see that it's already after noon. I slept for over three hours! I must have needed the sleep. I wipe my groggy eyes, adjusting them to the light shining into my room.

Still certain Rome is the puppet master behind all this, I shoot him back an angry text.

> **Me:** Home in bed. I got my period. Forgive me. I forgot I needed your permission to fucking bleed!

His response is instant, making me think he had his phone out to watch it as he waited for my reply.

> **Evil Stepbrother:** Drop the sarcasm and don't lie to me. Are you with him?

What the hell is he talking about?

> **Me:** With who?

> **Evil Stepbrother:** Gage. I swear to God, Freckles. If you're with that asshole, you'll both live to regret it. He didn't show up today either.

Interesting. In that case, maybe I'll have a little fun of my own.

You wanna fuck with me, Rome Cromwell, I'll fuck with you right back.

> **Me:** Maybe I'm with him right now. What do you plan to do about it?

When he doesn't respond, I drop my phone back down and take a deep breath, relishing the fact that I've got ammo with Rome's jealousy.

Mustering up some courage, I get out of bed and walk over to my window that overlooks the front lawn, including the driveway and my car that's parked in it.

How did we miss someone coming into our yard and breaking into my car? Granted, it probably wasn't locked because I never lock my doors, but still. We have cameras all over out there. I suppose it's possible the ones aimed at the driveway are not pointed in the direction of my car. It just seems like there would be some kind of alert to trespassers.

I sigh, working up the courage I need right now. What's done is done and I can't dwell on the how; I can only try and figure out the why and who.

After staring for a couple minutes, I change into some old sweatpants and a grungy hoodie that Lake got paint stains all over, then I begin my search for a pair of rubber gloves so I can pull that damn pipe out of my seat.

I find a pair in the laundry room inside a mop bucket that the cleaning lady left behind, as well as an industrial dust mask. I already know if I smell even the slightest bit of fresh blood, there's a good possibility I'll either pass out or throw up.

With my gear on, I head outside, but I stop halfway to my car when I see Rome pull into the driveway, coming toward me at warp speed. I jump back out of fear, just before he comes to a sudden stop.

He leaps out of the car, the engine still running and his door left open. Rome shouts as he walks steadfastly toward me with a heavy scowl on his face. "Where the hell is he?"

Stopping, he assesses me, his eyes dragging up and down my body, landing on the mask over my nose and mouth. "What the fuck are you wearing?"

I pull the mask down until it's resting under my chin. "Why aren't you at school?"

"I left. Now tell me where he is so I can beat his ass." He jabs a finger into my chest. "Then I'll take care of you."

When my mind catches up to what's happening, I have to hold back a laugh. I guess I went a little too far trying to get a reaction. I had no idea he'd actually leave school and come home. It's obvious Rome doesn't only get jealous, he gets possessive.

My eyebrows pinch together tightly and I throw up my hands that are covered with large yellow gloves that run all the way to my elbows. "Calm the fuck down," I hiss. "Gage isn't here."

He steps into me, challenging me. "You're lying."

"For Christ's sake, Rome." I shove at his chest with my gloves and he looks equal parts confused and furious. I'm not sure which I prefer. "Why in the world would Gage be here? He hasn't even talked to me since you crashed our date at the movies."

"If I find out you're lying to me..." Rome bites his fist, raging as his face turns red. "I will murder him with my bare hands then make you bury his body in the backyard."

"Look around." I wave my hands through the air. "Do you see his car? Do you see any sign of Gage at all?"

He comes closer to me, leaning in as he draws in a deep breath.

I push him back. "What the hell! Are you sniffing me?"

He lifts one side of his lip in a half smirk that makes me want to take that damn pipe out of my car and hit him over the head with it. "Sex has a very distinct smell, and you're lucky I don't smell it on you."

"Wow," I drawl, shaking my head because this is absolutely ridiculous. "You have officially lost your mind." I step past him, ready to show him that I know what he did to my car. "Thanks for the little note you left. Real cute, Rome. Anything to get a rise out of me, huh?"

"Now you're the one who's lost your mind. I don't write

notes. I text." He scoffs as I approach my car, refusing to believe a single word out of his mouth.

He comes up behind me as I pull open my car door, then I step to the side, holding on to the frame so he can see the remnants of his work. "You're a real asshole, you know that?"

His eyes go wide and he points at the pipe sticking out of my seat. "You think I did that?"

"Don't play dumb. I *know* you did it." He comes closer, but I block his path; he's already done enough damage as it is.

"Elodie," he says my name point-blankly while moving me out of his way, "I didn't fucking do that." Reaching in with his bare hand, Rome yanks the rusted metal out of the seat in one swift motion. He tosses the bloodied pipe onto the pavement and it hits with a vibrating thud.

"Now you're the one who is lying," I say with a shaky breath, worried he is telling the truth.

"You really think I did this?"

I nod, arms now crossed over my chest. "Sure do. Convince me otherwise."

"Umm," he drawls. "How about I'm not a fucking psychopath and I have no reason to pull a childish prank like this."

"This isn't a prank, Rome." I gesture to the blood. "This is a threat." I reach into the pocket of my sweatpants and pull out the note I folded up. Shoving it to his chest, he grabs it.

After reading what it says, worried eyes lift to mine. "I didn't write this, Elodie."

It's rare that he calls me Elodie. Rome *always* calls me Freckles. Which almost makes me think he's taking this seriously and it really wasn't him.

A sense of dread overcomes me. "Tell me the truth. Please," I beg him. "Tell me it was you."

I need it to be him. I *need* it to be him.

He folds the note back up and passes it to me. "Wasn't me."

A hard lump lodges in my throat and I swallow hard as my lips tremble. "Who would do this?"

Rome's nostrils flare, jaw clenched. "I think I know exactly who it is." He walks over and picks up the broken pipe, eyeing it as he says, "And they're gonna wish they'd never stepped foot on my fucking property."

"Rome," I warn. "Don't you dare do anything stupid while you're on probation. You'll—"

He turns so fast, he nearly hits me with the pipe. "How do you know I'm on probation?"

"I…talked to my mom. She told me." His face flushes red as he drops the pipe, only to crowd my space.

"So you're snooping around in my business?"

Like always with him, I begin to yell, "Don't even start that. You went through my shit. Besides, I'm trying to help you!"

"Just get your ass inside the house while I clean up *your* fucking mess again."

There's a pang in my chest, a feeling like my heart has sunk deep into the pit of my stomach. Rome is the master at making me feel like complete shit.

I rip off the gloves and toss them at his feet. "Fine!" I snap back. "Just stay the hell away from me!"

Tears prick the corners of my eyes as I storm back inside, not moving until I'm behind my locked bedroom door. My back hits the wall and I slide down with my head in my hands, doing everything I can not to break right here and now.

Four days ago I felt a shift in my relationship with Rome. I thought the turmoil was over and better days were ahead.

But, once again, Rome has proven that a zebra can't change its stripes, and a misfit can't be trusted.

CHAPTER 23
ELODIE

SINCE I MISSED school and I've got a test coming up in environmental science, I really need to find a quiet place to study. Lake and Brogan have been arguing all evening over Lake borrowing her sweater and spilling juice on it. I'm staying out of it because it's not my business and I have more important things to worry about. Such as this test.

After calling a place in the neighboring city to come get it, my car is currently at the body shop. I told my mom I had to have the seat replaced because it got caught on my backpack and I ripped it. Fortunately she didn't press on the subject. It's going to be at least two days before I can get the new seat put in, so instead of asking one of my delightful siblings if I can borrow their car, I've decided to walk to the public library. There's still daylight for another hour or so and I can just call my mom for a ride when I'm done.

I know it's probably not smart, considering someone is out to get me, but I'm not going to let this asshole scare me off. And I'm certainly not going to achieve less than one hundred percent on my test next week.

After I went up to my room earlier, Rome went back to school. At least, I'm pretty sure that's where he went. He literally pierced my heart and left. Just like he did the night he took my virginity. Just like he always does.

It's fine. I'm fine. It's time to move on from that chapter because I can't keep reaching for something that isn't there. I'll go crazy.

Walking down our quarter-mile-long driveway with my messenger bag flung over my shoulders, I look up at the sky. Dark clouds loom, blocking any hint of sunlight. The weather has been strange today with bouts of rainstorms that come as fast as they go. Hopefully it's over for a while and I don't get stuck walking in a downpour.

Although, that sort of sounds nice. I love the rain and storms and rainbows after the rain. It's proof that nature knows exactly what it's doing.

I wish I knew what I was doing. Lately it feels like I'm running on a hamster wheel, moving but not getting anywhere.

One good thing, I'm not fearful of Rome sharing that video anymore. He makes a lot of threats, but his follow-through is lacking. I wish I felt the same about whoever left that note on my car today, along with the bloody pipe in my seat.

After Rome went back to school, I pulled out the note I found in my locker my first day at Willow Creek High and I compared the writing to see if it was the same, but the one on my car was in block letters, while the other was more of a quick scribble. There were no similarities, but I'm not ruling out that they're the same person.

At this point, it could be anyone. Rome, Gage, Abby, Winton, or even Brady and Julia. I've gotten to know them well, but how well can you really know someone after a couple weeks?

Walking down the street at a leisurely pace, I look at each house, admiring their manicured lawns, expensive cars, security cameras, and gated entrances.

I wonder what their lives are like behind those walls. Do they have secrets? Are they keeping secrets? What are their jobs? What do they do for fun?

When I was little, I used to love watching people—walk, drive, run. I'd create scenarios in my head of what their lives were like and where they were going.

I wonder what the nine-year-old version of myself would guess if she saw me walking down the road right now. She'd probably think she's got it all. A nice home, a loving family, a bright future. And maybe it's true, but what I wouldn't see are the endless thoughts swirling in my brain, and the trauma that put them there. We only see what people show us, after all.

Turning down the street that leads to town, I approach a row of small businesses—a cafe, an insurance company, the post office, and a bookstore.

Willow Creek really is beautiful. A picturesque town that isn't too small, but also not too big. It's a great place to grow up, and someday raise a family. I only hope one day I connect to this place and I'm able to call it home. Right now, it just doesn't seem possible.

I reach the end of the street where the public library is. It's a towering Victorian building—ornate and very old. If the walls inside that library could talk, I bet they'd have so many stories to tell.

I walk up the cement stairs to the large double doors, my fingers wrapping around the wrought iron U-shaped handle. I pull hard, the door much heavier than I imagined.

The minute I step inside, I take a deep breath, inhaling the aroma of old books and paper. If I could pocket a scent forever, it would be the smell of this library.

After roaming through the maze of shelves, trailing my fingers down the spines of books, I find a quiet corner tucked behind a row of non-fiction novels. There's a small table with two empty chairs, and I settle in, silence my phone, and begin studying.

This is the thing I am good at. Tuning out the world and putting my nose in a book. There is comfort in knowledge.

Science doesn't lie, history doesn't change, and math shows you a million ways to get the same result.

Studying is how I breathe. Some people think it's odd that I read over the summer. They might think it's just to get ahead, to be a goody two-shoes or whatever, but that couldn't be further from the truth. I read and study even when I'm outside of the classroom and normal schoolwork because it keeps me grounded.

Somehow, time escapes me, and the next thing I know, I'm being interrupted by a tall lady with curly brown hair and a name tag pinned to her ivory blouse. "Excuse me, dear. The library is closing in five minutes."

I gasp, eyes shooting out one of the windows in the distance. "I'm so sorry," I spit out, slamming my laptop closed and stuffing it in my bag. "I didn't realize what time it was."

She chuckles. "It happens to the best of us."

Once she disappears down one of the aisles, I gather up all my things and stand before pushing my chair in.

A sudden movement in the aisle beside me catches my eye. I whirl around to see where it went, my gaze landing on a faint shadow darting behind one of the shelves. My heart races as I step around the shelf, trying to catch a glimpse of who it might be, but no one is there.

I shake my head as I take a deep breath. It has to be my imagination. It's been a long day with the note and missing school. Now being in this library that's probably hundreds of years old and casting shadows all around with the odd lighting. My thoughts are getting the best of me.

With my bag slung over my shoulder, I head down the row toward the exit. Just as I round the corner, I see the shadowy figure again. Only, it's more than a shadow. It's someone wearing a black hoodie that's flipped up, and a pair of black denim jeans. They move quickly, as if they're playing a game of hide-and-seek.

I pick up my pace, following in their direction. "Hello," I say softly. "Who's there?"

Suddenly, they zip past the end of the row, going left. I spin around and hurry down the row, hoping to catch them at the corner.

There's no way this is a coincidence. Someone was watching me, and now they're fucking with me. If it's Rome, I swear I will punch him in the throat when I catch him.

Nearly tripping over my feet, I move faster, watching as they bolt toward the exit. They are quick, I'll give them that.

"Hey!" I shout as they push through the doors and leave. I thought that maybe if I could catch them in here with a witness, it would give them less of a reason to keep following me. My shoulders slump in defeat, my heart trying to catch up to my heavy breaths.

The librarian appears at the door, a look of concern on her face. "Is everything okay, dear?"

I curl over, pressing my hands to my knees as I calm myself down.

"Are you okay?" she asks again, now at my side.

I straighten my back and nod, still panting. "Did you see the person who ran out of here?"

She looks at the door, then back at me. "No. It's only been you in here for the last fifteen to twenty minutes."

My eyes are wide as I look up at her. "Are you sure?"

"Positive. Every night at a quarter to nine, I walk the entire library to let guests know we will be closing soon. Tonight there was only you." She gestures toward the exit. "I'll see you out and lock the door behind you."

I gulp before saying, "Have a good night."

Hesitantly, I follow her to the exit. She pushes the door open for me and I give her one last look in hopes that she'll memorize my face because if someone is out there waiting for me, she could be the last person to identify me.

"Be safe out there," she says before the door closes and the lock is engaged.

I step out into the dark of night, dread heavy on my shoulders. I stay on the top step as I dig in my bag for my phone, so I can call Brogan or my mom to come pick me up.

Just as I get it in the palm of my hand, I see someone standing across the street under the lamppost. Same black hoodie, same pants, and a black ski mask pulled over their face. Through the eyes of the mask, I'm able to see the glow of their eyes set right on me. They're tall, probably a good five inches taller than me. Based on the build and frame, I'm certain it's a man.

I gasp, my heart pounding against my rib cage. They're just standing there, watching me.

I pull my hand out of my bag, fumbling with my phone as I open up the phone app and tap *Mom*.

My hands shake, my body shivering as it rings, and rings, and rings.

Come on, Mom. Pick up. Pick up!

The mystery man steps off the curb and into the street, coming toward me. I spin around and pound my fist on the library door. "Hello! Let me in!"

When no one comes, I turn back to face the mystery man who is now stopped right in the middle of the road.

This time, I try Brogan. But same thing, straight to voicemail.

Dammit. Where the hell is my family when I need them?

With no other choice, I text Rome, hoping like hell he actually reads my message.

> Me: Please come get me! Hurry! I'm at the library in town. Someone in a ski mask is watching me! I'm scared!

I breathe a sigh of relief when he texts back immediately.

> Evil Stepbrother: On my way!

With my phone still gripped tightly in my hand, I step forward on the step, the toe of my shoes teetering on the edge. Knowing it will take Rome less than five minutes to get here gives me a bit of courage. "What do you want from me?" I shout at the top of my lungs.

Then I see it, something I can't unsee. In his hand, at his side, is a dead rabbit, dripping blood onto the road.

I jump back, my spine crushing against the handle on the library door. Clasping my hands over my mouth, I try not to scream while my limbs shake uncontrollably.

He takes two slow steps forward, leaving a trail of blood. I cast my eyes down, unable to look at that poor rabbit, or the monster who's holding it.

I reach behind me, searching for the handle of the door, and when I've got it, I pull it over and over again while screaming, "Let me in! Please open the door!"

It's no use, no one is opening this door. I expel a pent-up breath, ready to surrender as he reaches the sidewalk, just below the stairs I'm on. "Why are you doing this?" My voice trembles. "Why me?"

The roar of an engine rings in my ears and I follow the sound to see bright headlights approaching in the distance.

A vehicle comes flying down the street, showing no signs of slowing down. I don't move as I pray it's my stepbrother. When it comes closer, I can see that it's Rome's car and I release a shaky breath.

All the fear inside me dissipates knowing he's here, once again, to rescue me.

I look at the person in front of me and watch as he tosses the dead rabbit onto the stairs before sprinting down the sidewalk.

Rome's car whizzes right past the library, following the direction of the black-hooded guy. I jog down the stairs, sticking to the side railing to keep away from the rabbit. As I pass by it, my stomach turns when I get a whiff of the fresh blood.

I gag, slapping a hand over my mouth as bile rises in my

throat. The blood on that pipe in my car must have come from this poor rabbit.

How could someone be so cruel? I'm trying to convince myself this was roadkill he picked up because if I think any differently, I might lose all hope for humanity in this town.

Aside from being cruel, this person is straight-up unhinged.

Hugging myself tightly, I step onto the sidewalk, shivering as I wait for Rome to come back. With any luck, he captured the guy and he's beating the shit out of him right now.

A minute later, after my thoughts got the best of me and I was certain Rome was dead, his car comes creeping down the street.

Oh, now you wanna take your time and drive slow?

I shouldn't complain. If Rome hadn't got here when he did, I could be lying on the steps next to that poor rabbit.

Rome brings the car to a stop, right in front of the library. The passenger window comes down and he hollers, "Get in."

Wasting no time, I hop in the car and roll the window back up. "Oh my God, Rome. I've never been so scared in my life."

My knees are knocking, hands shaking. But a sense of calm washes over me when Rome rests his hand on my lap. I look down, unsure why it's there.

When I look back up, I see his eyes on me. "You're safe now, Freckles."

I shouldn't believe him, but I do. I feel safe when Rome is around.

"Please just tell me you got a look at his face."

"I wish I could say I did." He sighs as his hand tightens around my leg. "But he ran into the woods before I could catch him. I almost got out of the car and chased him on foot, but I doubt I would've got him. He had a pretty good head start."

It doesn't matter right now. One way or another, I'm going to find out who is doing this to me.

I peer down at his hand again, noticing the way his thumb grazes subtly over the fabric of my sweatpants. "Rome," I say quietly before looking at him again. "Thank you for saving me… again."

"No worries. I'll just add it to the list of debts you're accumulating." The smug smile he gives me doesn't make me angry like normal. Instead, I can see the humor dancing in his eyes.

I laugh, even though it's not funny at all because Rome *will* collect.

"I believe you now," I tell him, hating the way it feels to be so wrong. "I know it wasn't you who slashed my tires, left the note, or stuck the pipe in my seat."

"'Bout fucking time." I watch as he drives with one hand, his corded muscles flexing as he takes the turn near our driveway.

"He killed a rabbit, Rome. A poor little rabbit," I whisper as the reality of what just happened begins to settle into my bones.

"Whoever it is, is a fucking freak." His hand grips me tighter, trying to calm my nerves and for some reason, I find comfort in it. That's when it hits me.

Oh my God! "A rabbit," I repeat before shouting, "stop the car!"

Rome slams his foot on the brakes, bringing the car to a screeching halt. "What is it?"

I turn to Rome, my voice too loud for the small car. "That night, last year. Winton called me 'little rabbit'. It's him." Chills break out all over my body as the memory hits me full force. "I know it's him."

He shakes his head, so sure of what he's about to say. "But it's not, Freckles. I thought it was, too, after I saw the pipe in your car. Everything leads to him. But when I got the text from you tonight, I was at Big John's having pizza and Winton was there."

No! That can't be. It has to be Winton. It makes perfect sense now. The pipe, the note, the rabbit.

"But…" My words trail off, because my mind is spinning as I try to figure this out. "He called me little rabbit."

"It has to be a coincidence," he says regretfully. "I do have news, though." My eyes perk up, ready to hear what he has to say. "Dr. Lamont called and the results from your blood work came back." He moves his hand from my leg and opens the glove box, retrieving an envelope before handing it to me.

I open it up, reading the results, and I gasp when I see the word "positive." Beside it is the drug name Rohypnol.

"You were slipped a very potent date rape drug at the party. Dr. Lamont said the full effect can take up to thirty minutes to an hour. It makes sense why you were suddenly so lively, then you got sick and crashed. It also has amnesia properties. It's odorless and flavorless."

I hear the words he's saying, but I can't process them. All I can focus on is the fact that I was drugged.

"Someone slipped me a date rape drug?" Tears form in the corners of my eyes before spilling down my cheeks. "Who would do that to me?"

"Sorry, Freckles." His hand reaches for my cheek, slowly wiping away a tear. "I know it sucks. I'm gonna find out who did this and I'm gonna make them fucking pay."

It feels like a train is sitting on my chest. I can't even think straight, or talk. I sink into the seat, bringing my knees to my chest as I hug my legs. "I wanna go back to Bakersfield. I want to go back to my old life."

I wanna go home.

CHAPTER 24
ROME

THREE DAYS AGO, Elodie said she wants to go home—to her old life, in Bakersfield. I've been making it my mission to ensure that doesn't happen. I don't want her to leave. She still owes me.

Fuck that. It's not about her owing me. As much as I want this to be about me making her pay, it's not that anymore. It's about *her*. She's got me under this spell that I can't get out of. I've never had a girl linger on my mind the way she does.

Even now, at practice, I can't fucking think. I can't concentrate because she's in my head. Last week when I took her virginity, something shifted inside me. Emotions I've never felt before surfaced and they scared the hell out of me. When I looked down at her after I finished, they hit me out of left field.

I tried to say something, but it was like my brain wouldn't connect with my mouth.

I've been avoiding her out of hopes these feelings will go away and she'll get out of my damn head, but she's always there. She's fucking everywhere.

The weight of another body crashes into mine, taking me straight down to the ground. Once I roll onto my back, I see that it's Gage on top of me. "What the fuck!" I snap, feeling the sharpness of the fall in my shoulder.

"Get your head in the game, Cromwell," Coach hollers from the sidelines. "If you can't play in the scrimmages, you don't deserve to play in the games."

"Yeah, Cromwell," Gage mocks. "Get your head in the game."

"Screw you," I grit out, bringing my fist to his shoulder, immediately regretting it because he's wearing fucking shoulder pads. *Every. Damn. Time.* I really gotta stop punching shit.

"Hey now," Gage sings as he stands up, brushing himself off. "Don't be salty. If anyone should be pissed, it's me. You tainted the pussy I was ready to claim."

I grit my teeth as I stand. "If Elodie died with her legs spread open, she still wouldn't fuck you. She has taste, that's why she was in my bed after our movie date Monday. Thanks for the invite."

"You fucking asshole!"

"Get the hell outta here." I sweep my hand through the air. "Don't you have a bench to keep warm?"

He tsks, ripping his helmet off and throwing it to the side, challenging me. "Don't you?"

"You son of a bitch!" I hurl toward him, wrapping my arms around his waist as I take him straight to the ground. "You're fucking dead," I seethe, fist cocked and ready to blow. Before I can bring it down on his face, someone grabs my hand.

"Both of you, on your feet," Coach growls. "Now!"

I push myself up just before Coach grabs the mask on my helmet, dragging me off the field. "Get your ass over here, Hanson!"

Gage and I sulk, shoulders dropped as we're forced off the field by Coach Ivers. Once he lets go of my helmet, I pull it over my head.

"What the hell has gotten into you two?" Coach's face is red hot, spit flying from his mouth. "You're part of a damn team, and when you're on *my* field, you act like it. Now, unless you both want to be out for good, you're gonna behave like teammates, even friends, for a while. And once I'm certain that's what you are, maybe I'll let you play in *my* game."

"What are you saying, Coach?" Gage asks, sweat dripping from his face.

God dammit. This is the last thing I need. I had one more game to go before I was off the bench. Now, thanks to the dipshit running his damn mouth, I'm at risk of being out longer.

Coach looks at me, then Gage, before walking over to the bench and digging in his duffel bag. "I'm saying, you two are gonna spend a little time together." He pulls out a beige braided rope and comes back to us. "Gimme your hand," he orders me, and I do as I'm told. He ties the rope around my wrist, then barks at Gage to stand next to me. By the time he's done, mine and Gage's wrists are bound together. "Let's start with two laps around the track. We'll see how much you hate each other by the time you're done, and we'll go from there."

"Come on, Coach," Gage whines. "You can't be serious?"

"I'm dead serious, boy. Now, get to it."

I look at Gage before wiping the sweat off my forehead with my free hand.

"Well," Coach grumbles. "What the hell are ya waiting for?"

Not wasting any time, I start running and Gage follows suit.

"This isn't over," I tell Gage through gritted teeth. "As far as I'm concerned, you're not even part of this damn team."

"Maybe I would be if you fucking Cromwell boys didn't get everything handed to you on a silver platter." Our paces easily match because despite the fact that I hate the guy, we are used to being on a team together.

I laugh dryly. "We don't get a damn thing handed to us. We work our asses off on that field."

"Oh yeah?" Gage huffs. "Is that why I'm the second-string quarterback and as soon as you got benched your brother took the position? A player who was *already* in the game?"

We make it halfway around the first lap, and sweat is dripping down my body. "Is that what this is about? You're pissed because Coach moved Wilder to QB and not you? Take that shit up with him, not me."

He shakes his head as if I'm missing something. "Forget it. You don't even give a shit. You and Wilder pull the strings and everyone does your little dance."

What the fuck is he even talking about? "You're delusional. We've played on the same team our entire lives. You know damn well how hard we've fought to be where we are."

"Yeah." He chuckles. "And now you're on the bench right beside me."

His words cut deep because I have worked my ass off. Sure, I fucked up and got my ass landed on the bench, but it has nothing to do with the way I play.

"Temporarily," I remind him as we begin our second lap. "Next week I'll be back out there, and you'll still be sitting with all the second strings."

"We'll see about that." Gage jerks the rope, pulling me toward him, but I pull right back. "Go ahead, Rome. Give it your best shot. Take me down and out."

I see what he's doing now. He's trying to get under my skin. He *wants* me to fight his ass because he wants me off the team. "You'd like that, wouldn't you?"

"I just don't think you've got the balls to do it." He tries to jerk again, but this time I'm ready.

I laugh, picking up my pace and pulling him right along with me. He keeps spewing nonsense and threats, but now I just ignore him because it's obvious he wants a reaction out of me.

We finish our second lap, and I'm out of breath by the time we cross the line. I immediately rip the rope off my wrist, letting it hang from Gage's. Practice is over, so everyone else is leaving the field as Coach approaches us.

"Well, boys. Are we buddies now?"

I pat Gage on the back with a big-ass smile on my face. "*Best* buddies," I tell him. "Can't wait to do this again, Gage." I look at Coach before walking off. "See ya at practice tomorrow."

"Sure thing," Gage says, spreading the icing on my lie.

"Whoa, whoa, whoa." Coach curls his fingers, calling me back over. "We aren't finished yet."

My shoulders sag as I walk back over to him.

"Shake on it," Coach orders.

I extend my hand to him and Gage clasps it in a firm shake before releasing it. I let out a heavy sigh, pissed at myself for not realizing what this asshole was doing sooner.

He doesn't give a shit about Elodie. He just wants to crawl between her legs to send me into a rage that'll get me kicked off the team permanently. All so he can have his time on the field.

"Listen up, boys," Coach stammers. "Any more of this BS and it'll be a whole lot worse." He points his finger between the two of us. "Remember, we're a team."

I nod in response, ready to get the hell outta here.

"You can go now," Coach growls, and I don't hesitate to jog back to the locker room.

You wanna fucking go, Gage. Let's fucking go.

As soon as I get inside, I slam the door to one of the open lockers.

"What was that all about?" Luke asks as he dries his damp hair with a towel.

I bite my lip, nostrils flared as I raise a finger. "I'm gonna fucking kill him, man. Once this season is over, he's dead."

"Don't tell me this is about Elodie." He tosses his towel on the bench to lean against a locker. "She ain't worth it, Rome."

I glower at him. "Who said this has anything to do with Elodie?"

"Come on." He claps a hand to my back, but I shrug it off. "I've seen the way you look at her. But even more so, I've seen the way you get when another guy looks at her. She's just a piece of ass, man."

Luke smirks like he normally does when we talk about sharing a girl or passing her around. But that's the thing. Luke can already see Elodie means more than that to me, so he really should have seen this coming.

I roll my neck, cracking it before balling my fist and bringing it straight to his face.

Luke curls over, cupping his nose as blood drips onto the white linoleum. "What the fuck, Cromwell!"

I take a deep breath, feeling the weight of what I just did heavy on my shoulders. But I don't think he gets it, and if I have to spell it out for my best friend, then maybe we aren't as close as I thought.

Leaning down in his face, I make myself crystal clear. "Talk about my stepsister that way again and it will be more than just your nose next time. Got it?"

His brow furrows, so I get closer, the threat more than obvious.

"Okay, okay, man," he grumbles, stepping back.

"Do me a favor and tell Coach you slipped. Don't need him making us do buddy laps at practice tomorrow." Luke glares at me, but I just smile. "Catch ya later, bro."

With that, I book it out of the locker room and straight to my car.

I've gotta go. I need to get the hell out of here.

CHAPTER 25

ROME

I DIDN'T STICK AROUND to see what went down after I punched Luke in the face after practice yesterday. I'm sure Coach knows by now and it's only a matter of time before he calls me into his office and tells me I'm off the team.

For someone who's trying to fix the mistakes they've made, I'm sure as hell doing a terrible job. Each day it feels like something else goes wrong and I dig the hole I've fallen into deeper.

Walking toward the door, so I can head to school, I hear Celia call my name. "Rome. Is that you?"

I drop my head back, sigh, and holler, "Yeah."

The sound of her feet smacking against the hardwood comes closer and closer until she's standing in front of me, briefcase in hand.

"I've got great news." Her eyes light up and I pinch my eyebrows together in response. "I looked into your case after Elodie came to me—"

"Elodie came to you about my case already?" That's news to me. I know I told her she needed to fix the mess she made, and she mentioned her mom helping, but I didn't realize she actually followed through with it until this point.

"She did. She really wants to help, and I think you should let her." She fumbles with the strap on her briefcase before tightening her hand around it. "I know you and Elodie haven't had the easiest time adjusting to the changes in this house, but I can see you've both got big hearts and I hope one day you'll open them up to one another as family."

If she only knew I've buried my fingers, cock, and tongue inside her daughter, she'd be singing a different tune.

Not to mention, Elodie's already ripped my heart open, crawled inside it, and made herself a home there. As hard as I've tried to get her out and stitch up what's left of myself, she won't leave.

That's when I realize I've fallen for her. I've fallen hard. I can't believe I'm even admitting that to myself. I'm not sure how I'll ever admit it out loud, but I feel like if I don't tell her, or someone, I'm going to lose my damn mind.

"Rome," Celia says. "Did you hear me?"

"Sorry, what?" I shake my head and try to ignore the revelation I just had about my damn stepsister.

"Yesterday after school, Elodie gave an official statement of what happened that night. I need to know if you'd like to move forward."

She gave a statement already? Damn. That was fast. "Um. Yeah." I graze my chin, nodding. "Of course."

I still can't believe this is even happening. Elodie might actually pull this off and fix what she broke like she said she would.

"I think that's very smart, and brave of you. With the new evidence brought to light, I think we've got a really good chance here. I've got a meeting this morning with the defense attorney, and with any luck, we'll be filing a motion for a new trial." Celia shuffles around in her purse until she's pulling out her keys. "I'll keep you updated."

"Thanks, Celia," I say, my tone full of gratitude. "I really appreciate what you're doing."

"It's my pleasure, Rome." She smiles at me, placing a hand

on my shoulder the same way my mother once did. "Everyone deserves a second chance."

She's wrong. Not everyone deserves one, and maybe I'm one of those people who don't. But I know someone who does.

I follow Celia out, and she leaves for her meeting while I get in my car to try and make it to class on time, for once.

As soon as I walk through the front doors of the school, I see Elodie. It's like my eyes know exactly where to find her. And as easily as they do, she finds me, too.

Her gaze pierces me. Heat floods through my body as I walk toward her, ready to hear her say something smart-assed so I can poke back. It's what we do. I piss her off, and she pisses me off in return.

I keep moving in her direction, and when I see Gage approach her, I move faster.

What the hell is he up to now?

I watch intently as Gage puts his hand on Elodie's shoulder and I make a mental note to break his fucking fingers. Elodie spins around to face him as he says something that makes her laugh.

Coming up behind Elodie, I put a hand on her waist, but she quickly moves away from my touch. I glower at her, wondering why she suddenly doesn't want me to touch her. She didn't seem to mind a week ago when we were in my bed. Or when I picked her up at the library.

Playing it cool, I look at Gage who's quiet now. "Pretty sure I told you to stay away from Elodie."

He chuckles airily. "Pretty sure I told you to mind your own damn business."

I stroke my chin, looking past him. "Nope. Don't recall that."

He tries to take her hand, but I swat it away. "Then I'm telling you now, mind your own damn business."

I step up to him, nose to nose. "Make me, bench boy."

Elodie gets between us, her arms spread as she pushes us both back. "Both of you, stop it!"

Dropping my scowl, my features soften as I look down at Elodie. "Can I talk to you for a sec?"

She shoots a look at Gage, then back to me. "Yeah, of course."

Without hesitation, I take her hand and pull her away from that dipshit.

"Before you say anything," Elodie begins. "He wasn't hitting on me. He just thanked me for going to the movies with him."

The fact that she thinks he wasn't hitting on her speaks volumes about her character. He was one hundred percent baiting her and kissing her ass.

But that's not what this is about.

"Fuck Gage. This isn't about him." I lace my fingers with hers briefly, and I can't help but notice how they fold together perfectly.

We stop in front of the gym doors, away from the rows of lockers.

Elodie leans against the wall, pulling her hand free. Her arms cross over her chest while her bag hangs from her shoulder. "That's good to know. But what do you need to talk about?"

"I...um." I pinch the bridge of my nose, searching for the right words while avoiding eye contact. Shit like this isn't easy for me. "I wanted to say thanks for talking to your mom and giving your statement."

When I look at Elodie, I see her biting back a smile. She puts her hand behind her ear and leans closer. "I'm sorry. I didn't hear you. Can you repeat that?"

I poke her side and grin. "Just say you're welcome and get to class."

Sincerity washes over her face as she says, "You're welcome."

She goes to walk around me, but I throw my arm out, pulling her back toward me. "Not so fast."

Her shoulders slump and she grumbles, "I should've known."

I peer down at her. "Why'd you step away when I put my hand on your waist in front of Gage?"

"Please don't start on this Gage drama again." She sighs, like I'm the one being dramatic here.

"I just wanna know. Was it because of him, or because of me?" Her face twists in confusion.

"You're my stepbrother, Rome." She looks up and down the hall, dropping her voice to a whisper. "People will talk."

"Fuck them," I spit out. "Do you think I care?"

"Maybe you don't. But I do." Her fingers pick at the hem of her shirt. "It's my first month in Willow Creek and I feel like everyone already hates me. The last thing I need is to hear whispers about how I'm fooling around with my stepbrother."

I cock a brow. "Fooling around? Is that what we're doing?"

It's cute how she blushes and tucks her head between her shoulders like a turtle. "I don't know what we're doing."

"I assumed you were just falling in line and enjoying the ride," I joke. Elodie never falls in line.

"Right," she says with a pained expression. "That's all this is. I'm just obeying my master."

It's obvious I took her by surprise, and probably embarrassed her a little bit in the process. That wasn't my intention. If what's happening between us means more to Elodie than what meets the eye, then I'd like to know. I might feel less crazy for how much it suddenly means to me.

I narrow my eyes. "Is that really all this is to you?"

"Sure." She forces a smile on her face. "And once my mom gets your charges dropped, it'll be over."

The weight of her words hangs heavy on my mind. Elodie is right. Soon there will be no reason for her to *obey* me any longer. I'll be off the bench, and the charges will be dropped. UCLA is still an uncertainty, but as more time passes, I'm starting to realize it's only one of many options.

"Well then," I say. "Guess our time is almost up, huh?"

She nods. "I guess so." Her eyes dart around again, as if she wants to be anywhere but here. Except, we both know that's not true.

"In that case." I grab her hand and pull her close, watching with bated breath as a smile forms on her lips. "Let's make the best of it. Since your car's still at the shop, come somewhere with me after school, then I'll drive us home."

She giggles and narrows her eyes. "Like a date?"

I laugh. "Nooo. Not a date. I'm your stepbrother, you sicko." I poke her side again, this time letting my hand linger there as she shakes her head at me. "I'm fucking with you, Freckles. I just wanna celebrate the potential good news...*with you*."

She squints at me. "What's the catch, Cromwell?"

She doesn't trust me. Naturally so. "No catch," I tell her, squeezing her waist as the bell rings. "Just an evening away from life's noises."

The second bell rings, warning us to get to class. Elodie looks at the ceiling where the sound is coming from. "We should get going before we're late."

I tighten my hold on her waist and bring us together. "So, is that a yes?"

She shrugs her shoulders, grinning. "It has to be. I'm not allowed to tell you no."

Biting the inside of her cheek, she steps past me and heads down the hall. I spin around to watch her walk away, dragging my fingers through my hair and wondering what the fuck this girl is doing to me.

It's when she looks back with that full smile on her lips that I realize she just might be feeling the same way.

CHAPTER 26
ROME

I'M PACING back and forth in front of the exit doors while students rush out, all but one.

Where the hell is she?

Panic begins to set in when I imagine Gage cornering her at her locker, trying to win her over.

Just as I go to walk back through the doors to track her down, and possibly save her from him, I spot her coming down the hall.

I backstep, holding the door open until she comes out the exit. "What took you so long?" I ask in anticipation.

With her eyebrows practically on her forehead, she grips the strap of her bag that's flung over her shoulder. Looking around, it's as if she is taking note of all the people surrounding us. They're not paying us any attention, but Elodie seems oddly nervous as she continues to walk with her eyes fixed on the parking lot.

"Were you waiting for me?" She doesn't even look back at me as she talks, and I try not to let that get on my nerves.

I jog to keep up with her long strides. "We had plans, remember?"

"Don't you have practice?" She *still* won't look up as she walks to my car.

"I'm skipping tonight." Just to prove a point that no one is paying attention to us, I toss my arm over her shoulders.

She turns her head slowly to face me, confusion written all over her face. "You're skipping to hang out with me?"

"Sure. Why not?" I drop my arm to fetch my keys.

Elodie stops walking, doing a quick ninety-degree turn. "What's really going on, Rome? You don't even like me. So why are you being nice all of a sudden and skipping practice to hang out with me?"

Her skepticism is disheartening, though I can't say I blame her. I've been a complete jackass to Elodie. I've bullied her, forced her to do things she didn't want to do, embarrassed her and lied to her. Part of me wonders if she'll ever see the sincerity in my actions now that I don't hate her solely for the air she breathes.

I've never given a girl attention like this. Never cared to. But no girl has ever torn me open and pulled out the raw and real parts inside me the way Elodie has. No one has ever believed in me like she does.

I tuck a strand of hair behind her ear then drag my hand down to her side. "I just wanna be around you."

She bites the inside of her cheek again, an action I'm starting to see a lot when she's thinking hard. "But why?"

I shrug. "I dunno, Elodie. Because I like who I am when I'm with you."

She takes in a deep breath, eyes lapping around the parking lot a few times before coming back to mine. "It didn't seem like it when you left me in your room…" Her voice drops to a whisper. "After you took my virginity."

Elodie's never admitted out loud she was a virgin, but I knew all along. Maybe that's why I feel connected to her all of a sudden. Because she gave me something that she can't give to anyone else. That has to be it. That has to be the reason for all these fucked-up emotions I'm feeling.

"I know," I say apologetically. "I...I didn't know what to say. I got freaked out and I was scared I'd say something I'd regret. So...I just left the room. I figured you would want space."

I see the tears build in her eyes, but she won't let them fall around me. She rarely does. "Do you have any idea how that made me feel?"

"No," I tell her honestly. "Because you never tell me how you feel."

She rolls her eyes, wiping just under them. "Why should I? We're not dating, Rome." She laughs, but the sound is empty of any humor as she points between the two of us. "We're not even friends."

She's right. We're not dating, and we're not friends. I don't know what the fuck Elodie is to me. All I know is I can't quit her.

My hands go to my hair, pulling because I'm not sure what to say right now. I don't know what to do to get her to see that things have changed. I planned to show her later, but it's clear she needs assurances now. "Can we just get in my car and talk about this? Please."

"Since when does Rome Cromwell use words like 'please' and 'sorry'?" Elodie holds her bag to her chest like armor, and it pains me to see her build up these walls right before my eyes. "I have no idea what's gotten into you, but forgive me for not trusting this side of you."

I nod, clicking my tongue on the roof of my mouth. "I deserve that. You shouldn't trust me. I guess...forget it. This was a bad idea. I'll just go to practice."

There's a sharp pain in my chest that tells me to just walk away before I say too much. I can't explain what the hell is going on because I don't know this side of myself. With a heavy sigh, I shuffle my feet back toward the school, head hung low. This is for the best. She's too good for me, anyways.

No!

Fuck that!

She needs to know why I was such an ass the other night, and the days after. I need her to know it wasn't about her; it was about me.

I spin back around, ready to go after her, just as she calls out, "Rome! Wait!"

The parking lot is nearly empty now, and we're the only ones standing out here.

Quickly, we close the space between us. I narrow my eyes, hands at my sides. "I fucked up, Freckles. Your first time should have been special and I made it all about me."

She shakes her head. "I'm not mad at you for that. I don't want to be your enemy anymore, Rome. I want us to work together and figure out who's behind all this creepy stuff that keeps happening."

I nod. "I see." Elodie wants us to work together. That's why she called me back over. I shouldn't be disappointed because I'm not sure what I expected, but it wasn't that. "I've got you." I pull her in for a hug. "We'll get to the bottom of it." My fingers stroke through her soft hair as her head rests on my chest. I don't wanna let her go because I might not ever get her back.

Elodie takes a step back and I let go of her. "Still wanna drive me home?"

"Yeah." I swipe my thumb across my chin, fighting hard not to kiss her right here and now. "Yeah. Let's go."

I grab her hand and lead her to the passenger side of my car, then I open the door and wait for her to get in before closing it. Suddenly my little toy has made me her bitch. It's ironic as fuck.

Once I'm in the driver's seat, I start the engine, but pause before shifting into drive. "I need to say something before we go, Freckles."

I'm not good at talking about feelings and shit, but I have to try. I reach over and grab her hand, watching as I trace the lines on her palm. "My anger was never about you. It was about me. I fucked up and I just needed someone to blame. You were just a casualty in my own healing and I'm sorry for that."

"Rome—"

"Let me finish." My eyes shoot to hers. "When I looked down at you after our first time together, I realized I could never hate you the way I wanted to. In fact, I don't hate you at all."

I've never in my life felt this vulnerable. Even after I lost my mom, I didn't open up to anyone. When I got benched, I held in all my anger and frustration. So much was building inside me and I made horrible decisions that made everything worse for myself.

"I don't hate you either, Rome," she whispers, yet it feels like a shout in the small space because they are the words I desperately needed to hear. "And I noticed the sudden change in the way you were acting. I'm not going to lie, I assumed you had regrets. You've distanced yourself from me. You've been quiet when I'm around. I could tell something was heavy on your mind."

I nod in agreement because she's right. "It's been you, Freckles. I can't get you out of my fucking head. It's making me crazy." I drop her hand and grip the sides of my head, feeling manic. "I've never felt this way before and it's scaring the shit out of me."

Her head drops down and she looks at her open palm as if she can see the invisible lines I just drew before her gaze settles on mine. "What are you saying?"

I take a deep breath, gripping the steering wheel while searching for the words to explain, but I can't find them. "I don't know what I'm saying, to be honest."

Elodie reaches her hand over and pats my leg. "It's okay, Rome. When you figure it out and you want to talk about it, I'll be here."

Why is she so perfect? Why can't she be the horrible bitch I made her out to be in my head?

I drop my head, staring into my lap. "I'm a fucking mess, Freckles."

"Rome," she says with sentiment, and I turn to look at her. "You're not crazy and you're not a mess. I knew you before our first time, and I know you after. And I have to say, this version of you is my favorite."

I hum softly. "Is that so?"

"Yeah." She smiles. "You're being real and I kinda dig real."

I chuckle. "Still wanna run away and move back to Bakersfield?" I tease, hoping like hell she doesn't say yes.

"I haven't decided yet." And there goes all of the joy my heart was finally beginning to feel. But I made it about me for too long, this is Elodie's decision to make. "I guess it depends on how all this pans out."

"This, as in...?"

She sighs, leaning her head back on the seat. "Everything, I suppose. If this person who's tormenting me gets caught and arrested before they kill me." She shrugs. "I might consider staying."

"No one's gonna lay a finger on you, Freckles. I promise you that." I reach my hand out and turn her face to me, stroking my thumb over her soft cheek.

"How can you be so sure?" Her eyes search mine for answers she desperately needs.

"Because I plan to get to them before they even have a chance to try." I think back to how easy it was for me to crack that pipe against Winton's head. I don't think Elodie realizes just how much I mean it when I say I will kill to save her.

"Ya know, at some point we have to involve the police."

"Let's find out who it is and gimme five minutes with 'em first, then we'll call the police."

"Always trying to be the tough guy." She chuckles as I pull out of the parking lot.

I place my hand on her leg before slamming on the gas.

"Trying has nothing to do with it," I roar over the sound of my engine as I accelerate.

Elodie presses her back firmly against the seat. "Slow down, Rome!"

"Why?" I laugh. "You scared, Freckles?" I glance back and forth between her and the road, pausing for a moment when I look into her eyes. Her expression goes stoic, but her eyes are wide with wonder.

She swallows hard, her chest rising and falling rapidly. "Terrified."

Me, too, Freckles. Me, too.

I slow down as we approach a main road. It's quiet for a minute when I hear Elodie's stomach growl. She grabs her waist and coughs, likely trying to drown out the sound.

On a whim, I whip the steering wheel to the right and turn down the main street where a slew of restaurants are.

"Where are we going?" she asks, still holding her stomach.

"To get you some food."

She adjusts in her seat, trying to pretend like I didn't just hear her stomach grumble. "Don't go out of your way for me. I'm fine."

"Your stomach's growling," I deadpan, looking over at her. "You're eating, dammit."

She steels her back against the seat, smirking. "Yes, boss."

I know burgers are her favorite, so I drive through The Burger Den to get her anything her heart desires. I watch from the driver's seat as this girl inhales a double cheeseburger while I eat some fries. With my first game next Friday, I've been trying to stay in shape so I don't totally blow it, but a few carbs won't hurt.

"Where are we going?" Elodie asks with a mouthful of food when she notices I'm heading away from home.

I glance over at her and wink. "You'll see."

CHAPTER 27
ROME

A FEW MINUTES LATER, I pull down the two-track dirt road and Elodie quirks a brow, her body bouncing around as we travel up the bumpy terrain to the small mountaintop. "You're not driving me back here to have your way with me then murder me, are you?"

"It didn't cross my mind." I laugh. "But now that you mention it, I'm not opposed to having my way with you." She slaps my chest playfully. "As for murdering you? Nah. I think I'd like you to stick around a while longer."

Elodie takes the last bite of her burger then balls up the wrapper and tosses it in the bag on the floorboard.

The narrow trail lined with trees opens up to a clearing and I can't help but steal a glance at her, curious what she's thinking. Her eyes widen in awe as she takes in the view. "Wow. It's beautiful back here."

I bring the car to a stop, staring out into the abyss. "It's been a while since I've been here, but I used to come almost every day."

I grip the steering wheel, rolling my fingers around it as I think back to those early days after my mom passed. I was so lost, but this place helped me find myself again.

"Let's get out," I tell her as I kill the engine and reach into the back seat to grab a blanket. "The view is amazing once you get higher up."

I swing open my door and get out to meet her at the passenger side. As soon as she steps onto the path, I notice her skepticism. Chuckling, I take her hand. "I'm not gonna murder you, Freckles."

"I'm sure that's what all serial killers say." She squeezes my hand and I pull her close, wrapping my arms around her.

"You've got nothing to worry about with me, I promise."

"I know," she says softly. "But remember how I told you I'm afraid of needles and blood? Well, I'm also afraid of heights."

I crane my neck. "Damn, girl. For someone who went to a party with a bunch of strangers and pushed the star quarterback in a pool, you sure are afraid of a lot."

She shrugs. "We all have fears, right?"

"That we do." I take her hand in mine again as we start to walk, my way of assuring her she's safe. "And the only way to overcome them is to face them head-on. You got that blood draw and now we're going to walk up this baby hill."

"Baby hill?" She laughs. "This is a mountain."

"Nah. It's just a baby. The smallest one in the county." I pull her along with me, checking on her every couple steps to make sure she's all right.

Once we're at the top of the mountain, I notice the tension leave her body. Her shoulders visibly relax and she takes a deep breath, eyes wide with wonder. "Wow." She glances over at me. "This view is stunning."

I release her hand from mine, and with a flick of the wrist, I toss the blanket in the air and let it flutter to the ground.

Dropping to the ground, I bend my legs with my hands resting on my knees as I gesture for her to join me.

"So, Rome Cromwell..." She smacks her lips, putting extra emphasis on my name as she gets comfortable on the blanket beside me, legs crossed like a pretzel. "How many girls have you brought up here?"

I look out at the sky and the now setting sun, letting the peace this place brings sink into my bones.

"Honestly? None."

"Interesting." She taps her finger on her chin as I fight to hold back a smile. The way the light hits her face is mesmerizing. "I guess I should consider myself special for being the first."

I stare out at the town below. Everything looks so small. It's how I imagine my mom feels when she watches over us.

"My mom brought me and my brothers up here when I was, like, eight or nine. She said it was her special place, where she'd come to clear her head." Elodie's face quickly goes from joking to serious as I open up for the first time about my mother. "After she passed away, I came here every day for weeks. As time went on, I started coming less often. This is my first time here since summer."

I reflect on the anger I felt the last time I was here. How I yelled about the world not being fair. The way I kicked dirt off the side of the mountain and debated jumping off just so I didn't have to feel the weight of everything on my shoulders.

Elodie puts a hand on my back, moving her fingers slowly and making me realize just how much things have changed since then. "What was she like?"

A smile tugs at my mouth as the memory of her face comes into focus. "She was beautiful—inside and out. She had this way about her of making the whole room smile just by walking in. Her laugh was contagious. Everyone loved her."

Man, I miss her.

I probably shouldn't allow myself to be vulnerable with Elodie, given our past as enemies and our present as stepsiblings, but there's just something inside me that says I can trust her. I've held in a lot of shit over the last year, and I've desperately needed to get some of it out.

"I have no doubt she loved you more than anything in this

world." Elodie takes my hand, squeezing it. "She'd be proud of you, Rome."

An airy breath escapes me. "Yeah, right."

"Hey," Elodie huffs, straightening her back. "Don't think like that. She would be proud. We all make mistakes, Rome. But you've learned from them and that's the most important part. I've seen the change in you over the last few days, and I know it's just the beginning. You're going to do big things."

I turn and look at her, seeing the sincerity on her face, loving the way she believes in me. "Why are you being so nice to me after everything I've done to you?"

She moves her hand from mine and starts picking at the fuzz on the blanket. "Everyone deserves a second chance."

Celia said the same thing to me. It must be some motto for their family or something.

"I've never been good at giving second chances," I admit, "and I have a hard time forgiving people, but I'm learning… because of you."

I place my hand on hers and she turns her palm up. Our fingers intertwine—a perfect fit—sending a surge of warmth through my entire body.

Staring down at our hands, emotions surface again. There's this feeling inside me and I'm not sure what to make of it. No matter how much time I spend with Elodie, it's never enough. Every time I touch her, I crave more. This has never happened to me before. I was starting to think it wasn't possible for me to have feelings for a girl. But being with her is proof that I'm not completely broken.

"Rome," she whispers, and my eyes shoot to hers. "I really should get home. I've got a lot of homework."

I gulp, not wanting this to end. *Not yet.*

"Is there ever a time you don't think about school? It's okay to let loose and have fun once in a while."

She chuckles. "I tried that last weekend and look what happened. Besides, studying is fun for me. You know that feeling when you throw a winning pass? That's what it's like for me when I see a big A on my tests. Or when my GPA goes up a point."

"I guess I can understand the feeling, because you're right, nothing compares to the feeling of being on the field and passing the ball for that winning touchdown." I look down, my head hung low as I admit this next part. "As for school and grades, I'm not sure I'll ever understand that. In fact, my grades are going to shit right now."

She jolts, straightening her back like a rush of adrenaline just shot through her. "Let me help you."

"Help me with school?" My brows pinch. No one has ever helped me with studying before, I'm not even sure it would work.

"Yes!" Her excitement is enough to make me want to try though. "I live for this stuff, Rome. I've tutored students in the past. I was class president at my old school. I was even a mathlete."

"*You* were a mathlete?" I laugh. "Why am I not surprised?"

She dusts her shoulders off with her fingers, grinning from ear to ear. "Best in three counties."

I shake my head, unable to hold back the smile that her excitement brings to my face. "You're something else, Freckles."

Folding her hands in prayer, she leans closer. "Please let me help you."

I said I couldn't get enough of her, and now's my chance to have her all to myself for a while. So of course I say, "Fine. Teach, Ms. Astor."

Her hands fly up and I shake my head in disbelief at her excitement. I've never seen someone so giddy about school in my life. "Tell me something, Freckles. When did you realize you wanted to go to law school?"

Biting the inside of her cheek, she taps her chin. "Hmm. I can't really pinpoint a time, but I do remember when I was in eighth grade and I did a debate in front of the class on why homework should not be abolished and that was the first time I really thought about my future."

Uncontrollable laughter erupts from my chest "You fucking would." My head falls back and I clutch my stomach. "I bet every student in that class wanted to kill you."

"Hey. Don't poke fun." She swats my arm. "I got an A on that debate."

"I'm sorry." I try to control my outburst, but it's too damn funny. She's the most predictable girl I've ever met, but in the best way. "I wish I could have met eighth grade Elodie."

"No, you don't." She shakes her head. "You would've hated me more than you do now."

I stop laughing and get serious for a second. Grabbing her chin, I turn her face to meet mine. "I don't hate you, Freckles."

"Okay." She nods carefully. "Hate's a strong word. Let's go with 'loathe.'"

"I don't loathe you either." My thumb strokes over her lips. "Believe me, I wanted to. But no matter how hard I tried, I realized I never could."

I watch as she swallows hard and I get lost in her inviting eyes. "Does that mean the war between us is over?"

I nod. "I don't wanna hurt you anymore."

"I don't want you to hurt me, either."

We sit there, staring at each other in an unspoken battle as I dare her to make a move, and she dares me to do the same. I wanna kiss her so fucking bad, but I don't wanna fuck this up with her by going too fast.

What the hell am I thinking? We hit the ground running. I've already buried myself between her legs, touched her, kissed her, fallen for her. This girl is killing me. Since when am I such a damn pussy?

Fuck it. I'm going for it.

Just when I'm about to make my move, Elodie clears her throat and sits back, breaking our connection. "We really should go."

"Yeah," I quip, feeling the loss of her heat on my fingers instantly. "We should." I push myself off the ground then reach my hand out to her. She grabs hold of me and I pull her to her feet. The tension between us is so thick it's damn near insufferable.

"Thanks for this, Rome." I grab the blanket and lace our fingers together again. "It means a lot that you brought me to your special spot."

I sweep the air with my hand as we walk to my car. "Don't mention it."

After spending the entire ride home debating with Elodie why homework *should* be abolished, I'm already making notes to hire her when I need a good lawyer in the future. I've also promised to spend every evening the rest of this week studying with her so I can pass my history test this Friday.

Once we're parked, with the car off and the garage door closed, I get out and she does the same.

Caged between my car and my dad's truck, I look at her one last time before we walk in. I let the peace I found on that mountain flow between us so that hopefully she can feel just how much I mean it when I say I don't hate her.

"Well…" She smacks her palms to her thighs. "Thanks for the ride home."

"No problem. I'd give you a ride tomorrow, but Coach will kill me if I miss practice again."

I'm still not sure if Luke, or any of the guys, told Coach about me punching him in the face, but I haven't got a call, so I'm guessing he kept his mouth shut like I told him to. At some point, Luke and I will make up. This isn't the first time we've fought like this. He's stubborn and so am I. It's just the first time it was over a girl. Luke has to know this one is different. He's my best friend. How can he not?

I look at Elodie again, noticing the way she nibbles on her bottom lip. My cock twitches in reaction because she looks so fucking sexy.

Once again, we're stuck in that challenging gaze. And just like last time, Elodie breaks it.

"Hey, Rome. Remember how you said you fucked up after our first time together? Well, you did fuck up. But so did I."

I tip my head to the side. "You did?"

"Yeah, I did. I let you walk out of that room when I should have just done this." She puts a hand on my cheek and leans over, guiding my mouth to hers.

A low rumble climbs up my throat as I move my hand to her waist. When she moans, I have no choice but to pull her body flush to mine.

This kiss consumes me. I've been with a lot of girls, but none of them has breathed life into me with just a kiss.

Elodie slowly drops her hand from my face then takes a step back while biting the corner of her lip. "Too forward?"

I shake my head. "Not forward enough." Then I reach out and grab her again, pulling her body flush with mine. I kiss her harder, every emotion in existence poured into this kiss.

My mouth trails downward to the nape of her neck and she tilts her head slightly. I drag one hand up, cupping her breast in my palm as I peel back her sweater and kiss her shoulder.

She reaches down between us, rubbing her hand against my erection that's threatening to burst through the seams of my jeans.

"Mmm," I hum. "You're teasing me, Freckles."

She doesn't stop. Her hand moves relentlessly, massaging my cock. I can't take it anymore, the moment she pulls back, I lose all self-control.

In a swift motion, I pick her up, wrapping her legs around me while my mouth devours her. I don't want to get caught by our parents out in the open, so I make my way to the workshop area and kick open the door.

Elodie pulls back, breaking the kiss, only to trail her hot mouth down my neck in a move that makes me feral.

I quickly check that the lock is secure, then move her until she's sitting on the bench my dad once used for woodworking.

We take turns being in control. Her hands go into my hair, pulling me closer, and I let her take the lead. Just as she lets me when I bend down and strip off her leggings. She kicks them across the room and I spread her knees as I bring her ass to the end of the bench.

I lick my lips, hungry for another taste of my delicious step-sister. Her hooded eyes watch me as I spread her open and lick her from ass to clit.

"Rome!" She gasps, her hand instantly tangling in my hair.

More than determined to get all of those sexy moans from her since this room is soundproof, I keep going. I swear she tastes like nectar, like one of the gods talked about in Greek history. Addicting and all-consuming.

Just as she's about to come undone, I pull back.

"What the fuck, Rome?"

Her pissed-off face makes me grin. "You want to come?" I ask.

"Yes." She bites her lip as her cheeks flush.

"Then you can come on my cock." I turn her around and push her against the bench. Her chest flat on the cool surface.

Stretching my fingers, I grab a handful of her perfectly round ass. My hand draws back then moves forward as I slap her pale skin, leaving a bright red outline of my handprint.

Elodie winces on impact before a subtle moan slips out of her mouth. As the mark reddens, something inside me snaps. I want to claim every fucking inch of this girl.

In a frenzy, I quickly unbutton my jeans and yank the zipper down before dropping my pants and boxers to my ankles.

Leaning forward, I blanket Elodie's back with my chest, drawing in a deep breath of her lilac-scented hair. "You want this, Freckles?" I tease her entrance with the head of my swollen dick.

She nods. "Mmhmm. Please." Her begging leaves me help-less, wanting to give her what she needs.

With her permission, I shove my hard cock right into her tight pussy, relishing the way her walls clench around me.

My fingertips dig into her hips as I glide in and out, already on the verge of combustion.

Elodie drops her head forward, pressing it against the bench while panting and moaning with each thrust I give her.

I watch as her fingertips curl, her body winding tight and her cunt gripping me like a fucking vise.

I fuck her harder and faster, thrusting sounds of pleasure out of her until all I hear is my name, over and over and over.

"That's it, tell me who owns this pussy."

Consumed with an insatiable need to explode, I pause for a second.

"Don't stop," Elodie begs, but I only give her tiny pulses because I don't want this to end so soon. Her back arches and she sways her hips back and forth, milking me.

"Tell me this is mine." I smack her ass again, leaving a mirroring mark on the other side.

"It's yours." She pants as she rides me as best she can, pushing back until I'm fully seated inside her. I reward her by wrapping an arm around her front and playing with her clit. She clenches in response and I hiss.

"You're gonna make me come, baby," I warn in a raspy tone.

"I'm already there," she cries out. Her legs begin to shake as I keep up my pace on her clit. Her head falls back and I wrap my other hand around her throat, holding her there as I force her to take every fucking inch of me.

Every muscle in my body strains as I resume slamming into her, feeling her come on my cock. Waves of pleasure rip through me while the satisfying sounds of her moans ring in my ears and I come undone for her, pumping my cum so deep in her she will never be able to be rid of me.

Just as I'm pulling out, watching as Elodie's cunt drips with a mixture of both our arousals, I hear the automatic garage door slowly begin to open.

"Fuck!" I quickly pull up my pants while Elodie frantically grabs hers and does the same.

Once we're decent, I put a hand on her waist and guide her toward the door, unlocking it as we dart inside the house before the garage is fully opened. Thankfully it's the far door that is lifting, so no one can see as we run like our lives depend on it. "Go, go, go."

Once we're inside, we both curl over laughing. We pull ourselves together, and standing only inches apart, I stroke her cheek with the back of my hand. "Worth it?" I ask her.

"So worth it."

Elodie smiles back at me, the softness in her eyes piercing through me. I look around, making sure no one's in the hallway before leaning forward and pressing a soft kiss to her cheek.

Just as I'm about to tell her good night, the door to the garage comes flying open. Elodie books it down the hall, giggling as she rounds the corner.

Wilder steps in, shooting a thumb out the door. "Were you just in the garage?"

"Yeah. Just got home. How was practice?"

He drops his bag on the floor and it lands with a thud. "Fucking torture. Coach asked where you were. I covered for your ass and told him you had a doctor's appointment."

I slap a hand to his shoulder. "Thanks, man. Did he happen to mention anything about me and Luke?"

"You mean that shiner Luke's sporting. You fucked him up, dude." Wilder shakes his head in disapproval.

"He deserved it."

"He didn't tell Coach, but he did say this was all because he wanted to get with Elodie and you freaked out." Wilder turns, leaning against the counter and gripping the edge, seemingly as enraged as I was over the idea of Luke and Elodie.

"Then what?" I ask.

Wilder scoffs. "I flat out told him there was no fucking chance. She's our stepsister. That falls somewhere in bro code."

His comment is a reality check that smacks me hard in the face. Elodie *is* our stepsister. And I'm the dumbass who's falling for her.

CHAPTER 28
ELODIE

THE LAST COUPLE evenings were spent at the library with Rome in an attempt to lure out the mystery guy. At least, that's what I told Rome we were doing. We didn't see anything unusual during our time there, and I haven't received any more threats, but that doesn't mean I'm not still being watched. It was a disappointment for Rome, but my mini mission was accomplished.

In reality, Rome needed to study. He mentioned his grades not being up to par—particularly history—and if he doesn't get them up soon, he might not be able to play next Friday. This is his last week on the bench, and with a big test coming, he needs to pass so he's not out of the games longer.

Needless to say, I have no doubt he's acing his test right now. I'm on pins and needles waiting for the final bell to ring so I can find him and see how he did. Normally I'd be engaged in the lecture being given by my own teacher right now, but I can't focus. I've already got my books stacked and ready to grab as soon as it's time.

The second we're dismissed, I'm on my feet and out the classroom door.

"Elodie," I hear Brady holler from behind me. "Wait up."

I spin around to face him, tapping the toe of my shoe to the floor. "Hey. What's up?" I look around, searching from Rome.

"Someone's in a hurry," he jokes as Julia approaches us.

"Sorry," I tell him. "I just need to talk to someone."

"Is that someone Rome?" Julia asks, her eyebrows dancing on her forehead. "I notice you two have been hanging out together, and actually getting along."

I'm surprised Julia has noticed. It's only been a couple days since Rome and I even acknowledged that we don't hate one other, and we've been pretty secretive about our newfound friendship—if that's what you call it.

"It is Rome," I say truthfully. "I've been helping him study for his history test and I'm anxious to find out how he did."

"Oh," Julia deadpans. "He passed."

"What?" I beam all too enthusiastically. "How do you know?"

"Because I'm in that class with him." She laughs. "After Mr. Price gave back our graded tests, Rome was hooting and hollering, giving everyone high fives."

I clap my hands over my heart. "That's the best news."

Rome put up a fight when we first started studying for this test, but in the end, he was giving it all he's got. I made him do two practice tests and he passed both of them with flying colors. He deserves this. He really does.

I spot him coming down the hall, his hand raised holding his test. "I did it!" he roars over the noisy students. "I passed, Freckles."

Brady pinches his brows tightly. "Freckles? That's original."

"Shut up." I chuckle, my face blushing as I punch him teasingly in the chest.

Rome and I eat up the space between us and when I think he's just going to reach out and give me a high five like he supposedly did with everyone else, he throws his test, and it falls like a feather to the ground.

The next thing I know, I'm being lifted up and twirled

around in circles. "We did it. B-fucking-plus!" he sings before setting me back down on my feet. He peers down at me, a wide grin on his face. "I couldn't have done it without you."

My hand glides over his upper arm. "It was all you, Rome. I'm really proud of you."

"Thanks for your help." He moves his hands from my waist. "It means more than you'll ever know."

"It was no problem at all. So, it sounds like tonight's game will be your last one on the bench."

"Finally. I can't wait to be back out there next Friday." He shoots a thumb over his shoulder, then says, "I've gotta catch the bus for tonight's away game. You going now that you've got your car back?"

I've been around people all day, every day for more days than I can count, and I'm really looking forward to a quiet night home while the rest of our family is there.

"I didn't plan on going," I tell him. "I really should get a jump start on next week's assignments."

"Nerd alert," Julia intervenes with her hands cupped around her mouth. She throws an arm around my shoulders and pulls me close. "There's no way you're spending your Friday night doing schoolwork that hasn't even been assigned yet. It's just one town over in Ravencrest. You're going with me and Brady."

It's unnerving even considering going to Ravencrest, but I know there are more people there than the three I encountered last year. I can't blame the whole town for their asshole ways.

I sigh, shoulders stooped. "You're all bad influences, you know that?"

"It's settled then," Rome says. "I'll see you at the game." He cocks a brow, waiting impatiently for my response.

My backbone fails me when I say, "I guess so."

"Sweet." Rome flashes a smile before he turns and heads toward the gym.

Abby and a swarm of senior cheerleaders come down the hall

wearing their uniforms, looking all cute and confident. I feel like a gray house mouse compared to them.

Abby cups her hands around her mouth and shouts down the hall. "Rome!" Her eyes shoot to mine and she smirks like a little devil. "Wait up, babe. I wanna sit with you on the bus."

"Bitch," I mutter under my breath. A pang of jealousy slices through me, cutting me to the core. I bite the inside of my cheek, trying not to show an ounce of emotion.

Rome shoots a look over his shoulder then quickly pulls open the gym door and goes inside, completely ignoring her and calming my nerves slightly.

"What was that all about?" Brady asks.

I shrug my shoulders. "I don't know what you mean."

I can feel Julia and Brady watching me quietly. Like they want to say something, or want me to say something. I try to erase the grin on my face, but it won't go away. "What?" I finally blurt out. "Why are you two looking at me like that?"

Julia's shoulders do a little dance. "I sense some juicy secrets that need to be spilled."

I rub the back of my neck, averting my gaze. "You're both crazy. There is nothing juicy about my life and definitely no secrets to spill."

Julia narrows her eyes. "She's holding out on us, Brady."

Brady puts his hands on his hips and steps closer, examining me like I'm an art piece on display. "I think you're right, Julia."

"Oh my God, you guys!" I shake my head, laughing. "I'm going home."

I head down the hall toward the exit doors as Julia hollers, "We'll pick you up at five. Prepare to be drilled."

Then I hear Brady. "But not in the same way we think Rome has drilled you."

Unbelievable. All Rome and I did publicly is speak to one another and it's already raising suspicions. It won't be long until everyone is talking and it gets back to Brogan and Wilder, if it hasn't already. I need to talk to Brogan before she hears rumors from anyone else, but she's on her way to the away game as well, so it's going to have to wait until tonight.

As much as I know I need to stay away from Rome and end whatever is happening between us before it goes any further, I can't. My heart is too invested.

Walking out the doors into the parking lot, I see a few students are still lingering. Bypassing them, I head for my car. Not having my own wheels for a few days really made me appreciate getting it back. The seat is good as new with no evidence of the assault on it. Let's just hope it stays that way.

CHAPTER 29
ELODIE

"Lake," I holler from my bedroom. "Can you come here?"

Standing in the middle of my room, I look down at the pile of clothes surrounding me. I exhale a frustrated breath and fall backward onto my bed.

"What's up?"

I lift my head to see Lake standing at the door with a bowl of cereal in her hand.

"Are you going to the game tonight?" I ask, frustration boiling in my veins.

"Yeah. I'm riding with Mom and Grant when they get home. Why?" She walks in to stand by the side of the bed.

"I need help," I grumble, arms spread at my sides. "I have nothing to wear that has the school colors on it."

I learned my lesson about wearing anything that has the "Cromwell" name on it and I still haven't had a chance to buy any Misfits apparel.

"Go get something from Brogan's room." She scoops a spoonful of cereal and sticks it in her mouth. "That's what I plan on doing."

My eyes widen, and in a split second, I jump to my feet,

running toward the door. The next thing I know, Lake and I are in a race as we sprint to Brogan's room.

I shove Lake aside, giggling, and milk topples over the bowl, spilling down the side, but I'm the first one in her closet so I win.

"You suck," Lake scoffs as she rummages through the sweatshirts hanging on one end of the closet, while I work my way toward her at the other end.

Snatching a black hoodie off the hanger, I hold it up with both hands. It's not a Misfit hoodie, but it's got a teal lightning bolt across the chest that matches the school colors. I tip my head back and forth, contemplating the option. "Hmm. I think this'll do."

Lake stretches her neck out to look at it. "Nice." Then she holds up one she found. A Misfits crewneck. A bratty chuckle climbs up her throat. "Mine's better."

I hiss at her. "Now you suck."

We leave the closet and I kick through the mess on Brogan's floor. She has to be the biggest slob I've ever met in my life. And if you asked her, she would tell you I'm the biggest neat freak. Although, I think Rome might be a close second because his room is spotless, too.

Lake sits down on Brogan's bed and pulls her phone out of her bra before grabbing her bowl of cereal off the nightstand. "Have you seen Wilder's latest SnapTok video?" She laughs. "The guy is such a tool. How in the world does he have over a hundred thousand followers?"

"All girls," I tell her. "Girls love good-looking guys who do dumb shit."

And don't I know it.

I sit down beside Lake while she scrolls through her phone, stopping every couple seconds to take a bite of her cereal. With the sweatshirt balled in my lap, I peer over at her. Lake and I haven't talked much lately. My sisters and I were always so close, but lately it seems like none of us have time for one another.

"How's school been going for you?" I ask her, opening up the conversation.

"Eh." She shrugs. "It's school. They're all the same. Willow Creek is pretty much Bakersfield with more people."

"Do you miss your old friends?" She puts her phone down to look at me.

"Sometimes. But I still talk to them." She lifts her head momentarily. "How about you? Are you and Maggie still close?"

I think about my friend who I haven't talked to in well over a week. Life gets busy with school and drama so easily. "We text once in a while, and she's planning to come visit soon. But we've both just been super busy with the new school year."

Lake lifts her eyebrows. "And Ethan?"

I laugh. "Hell no. Ethan can drop off the face of the earth for all I care."

Ethan is my ex who dumped me right before I moved. He never actually said the words, but he didn't have to. We haven't spoken since and I have no desire to ever speak to him again. There was a time I thought I loved him, but after everything I've been feeling these last few days, I know I didn't.

"Holy shit!" Lake blurts out, her eyes nearly popping out of their sockets as she picks her phone back up. "El!" She turns her phone around, showing me her SnapTok account and a video playing on her feed. "Is that you?" She gushes. "Oh my God! Eleven thousand views already!"

I gulp, grabbing the phone out of her hand. It feels like all the blood has left my body as I watch the video of me dancing at the party.

My hands shake uncontrollably and I open my mouth to speak, but nothing comes out.

I hear my phone buzzing from my room next door, over and over again as I sit there watching myself acting like a fool on repeat. I've seen the video all of two times and every time it feels worse, and even more so now that I know I was drugged.

A call comes through on Lake's phone from Brogan, then a few text messages pop up from random people. The phone slips out of my hand, landing on the bed. I shake my head and try to get to my feet, but trip over something on the floor. Steadying myself, I press my hands to the mattress. "This can't be happening," I say to Lake. "Why would he do this to me?"

Nothing makes sense, but at the same time, everything does. Rome played me. He fucking played me just like he said he would.

None of this was real. It was all just a sick joke to him.

I straighten my back, pulling myself together, then rush out of Brogan's room. Before I even make it in mine, Lake is by my side. "It's just a dance, El. No one cares. It'll blow over."

Tears stream down my face. "No, Lake." I drop my head to my hands. "It's so much more than that. It's more than you'll ever understand." I go into my room and slam the door shut, making sure to click the lock.

This isn't even about the video, or the fact that the admissions office at Stanford might get it. Who knows, Rome might have sent it to them already. After all, he threatened to. This is about Rome and how he pulled my heart out of my chest and crushed it in the palm of his hand.

This is what he wanted all along.

I want it to hurt. Your cries are a sweet symphony to my ears. I want to be the reason for every tear that falls down your pretty little face. You fucked my life up, and now I plan to return the favor.

That's exactly what he said to me. And now he's won. He returned the favor and he's destroyed *my* life—my reputation, and my faith that people can change.

Rome hasn't changed. He just wanted me to think he did.

Lake pounds on my door, shouting for me to let her in so we can talk, but I don't want to talk. Instead, I shoot a quick text to Maggie.

Me: Up for a visitor this weekend?

I need to get the hell out of Willow Creek for a while, maybe even forever.

As I wait for Maggie to respond, I pack a bag with enough clothes and toiletries to last me a couple days. If she's busy, I'll just go to my dad's. He might not be there, but I'd rather be alone anyways.

Just when I fling my backpack over my shoulder, my phone pings.

Maggie: Hell yes! When are you coming?

Me: Leaving now. It'll take me about four hours. See you soon.

I pull open my door and Lake is still standing there. Her concern is evident, but I shrug it off, holding my head high. "El, it's okay. It's not like you stripped or anything."

I swipe the tears from my cheeks and sniffle. "You don't understand, Lake. Tell Mom I'm going to Bakersfield for the weekend to stay with Maggie."

Lake tries to grab my arm, but I shrug her off, trying not to fall apart completely. "Leaving won't make this go away, El. Just stay here and deal with it."

I step past her, eyes downcast. "I can't stay here anymore."

As I'm jogging down the stairs to get out of here before my mom gets home, I get another text message, this one from Gage.

I stop at the bottom of the steps and read it quickly.

Gage: Can we meet and talk? There's something you need to know.

Me: If this is about the video, don't bother. I've seen it.

Gage: It's not about that. I need to talk to you about Winton Brooks.

Reading his name on the screen of my phone sends my heart into my throat. I'm not sure what Gage knows about Winton, but it could be something that helps Rome's case, so I reply.

Me: It has to be quick. I'm leaving town.

Gage: Perfect. Can you meet me at Ravencrest Park?

Anxiety ripples through me. Just the thought of going to that park has me on edge. I'm not sure I'm strong enough to go there again. But I did it once with Wilder and I survived, so I can do it again.

Me: When?

His response is immediate.

Gage: Now.

Gage should be on his way to the game with the rest of the team, and the fact that he isn't tells me this must be important.

Me: I'm on my way.

I try not to let my anxiety over everything get the best of me, but my heart feels like it weighs a thousand pounds in my chest. Rome hurt me once when he ignored me and kissed Abby, but this is different. This was malicious and intentional.

I might have ruined his life, but I have been doing everything I can to make up for that. This video is unforgivable, though. Fool me once, shame on you. Fool me twice, shame on me.

And that's what I am, a damn fool who fell for her fucking stepbrother.

The second I pull into the parking lot at the park, my hands start shaking. I hold tight to the steering wheel, reminding myself that I don't have to get out. If Gage wants to talk, he can come to my window. He's not here yet, but I'm hoping he gets here soon because the sun is starting to set and I need to get on the road if I want to make it to Bakersfield at a decent time.

While I'm waiting, I torture myself by watching the video Rome texted me last week, just so I can see how bad it really is. I watched the whole thing on Lake's phone, but it was a much shorter version. At some point I'm going to have to explain myself, whether it's to my parents or my peers. I need to analyze this so I know what it is I'm defending.

I tap play, holding my breath as it begins.

It's obvious I'm fucked up beyond recognition. My eyes are slitted and glossed over, and I'm unsteady as hell on my feet. Anyone who watches this is going to assume I was drunk off my ass, when really, I was drugged by one of the people who might very well be in this video.

I'm dancing, waving my hands in the air while singing "Wild Ones" by Jessie Murph and Jelly Roll out of tune. It's humiliating to watch, but also sort of captivating. The girl on this screen doesn't have a care in the world. She's not stressed about high school, or Stanford. Her mind isn't focused on studying or getting good grades. She's living for the moment, and loving every second of it.

I wish I could be more like her.

As the clip nears the end, I hear Rome's voice. "What the hell are you doing?" I hear him say before there's some shuffling and static noise. Then it stops.

I don't know what to make of that. This part wasn't on the clip that went viral. Was Rome recording, or was someone else?

Once the two-minute clip finishes, I watch it again. This time I pay attention to the reactions of everyone around me, wondering if one of them could be the reason I was so intoxicated.

I see Luke and Aiden talking, but nothing out of the ordinary. There's about a dozen people I don't know, most of whom are just laughing and drinking.

A couple guys shout up to me, but I pay them no attention.

Gage comes on the screen by the French doors to the deck, which I expected, considering I kicked him in the face for touching me. I straighten in my seat and scroll back when I see him pull open one of the doors to talk to someone.

I pause the video and stretch my fingers on the screen to zoom in.

My heart stills as I stare into the demonic green eyes of Winton Brooks. I'd remember those eyes anywhere. Not to mention that face. It's him. It's most definitely him.

But why would Gage be talking to Winton when he plays for their rival team? From what I've gathered, none of those guys can stand one another.

I let the video play again, watching intently as Gage bumps knuckles with Winton like they're friends, just before he disappears out the door.

Could this be what Gage wanted me to come here to talk about? Did he see the video that went viral and noticed this part of the clip, too, and now he wants to explain himself? Or does he know Winton? Are they friends?

A sudden knock on my window has me fumbling my phone in my hands as I try not to drop it. I look out and see Gage standing there with his hands stuffed in the front pockets of his jeans.

My heart is beating so damn fast. I hesitate to roll my window down to talk to him, or just shift in reverse and leave.

Gage pulls one of his hands out of his pocket and motions for me to roll down the window. I panic, and do as I'm asked.

"Hey," I say with a shaky breath. "This needs to be fast. I really should get going."

Gage nods, his lips pressed into a white line. "It won't take long. So, I know I said this wasn't about the video, but it sort of is."

"I figured." I raise my eyebrows.

The look on his face speaks volumes. It's a mixture of guilt and trepidation. A chill runs down my spine. Rome was right—Gage is not a good guy.

He drags his tongue over his teeth, smirking devilishly. Red flags are raised and I slowly move my hand to the door, ready to roll up the window. But just as it starts to go up, Gage places his hands over it, holding it down. I keep slamming my finger into it, hoping the motor is stronger than him. "Please stop. I have to go, Gage."

"Get out of the car, Elodie."

I crane my neck in confusion. "Excuse me?"

"You heard me." He reaches his hand through the window and I gasp, grabbing him by the arm and squeezing with everything I've got.

"Stop!" I shout. "Just stop and let me go. Please." I drag my nails down the skin of his bare arm, leaving a trail of marks.

Gage grabs the keys from the ignition and I pull his arm, trying like hell to pry my keys from his grip, but it's useless.

"Please don't do this," I beg of him. "I won't tell anyone you drugged me. I promise."

"I didn't drug you." He scoffs as he jerks his arm back out with my keys in his hand. There's this deranged look in his eyes I've never seen before.

I have to get out of here. Somehow, I need to get away from Gage.

Turning to face my window, I stretch my arms behind me and attempt to crawl in the passenger seat, but the door comes open and Gage grabs my legs.

I kick and squirm, trying to break his hold on me, but I'm not strong enough.

Gage jerks my legs toward him and I fly out of the car, my back crashing hard against the ground.

"It didn't have to be like this, Elodie. You should have just gone back to where you came from. You're not wanted here."

I lie there staring up at him as his face lingers over mine, remembering a note I found in my locker. *Go back to wherever you came from. You're not wanted here.*

Naturally, I assumed Rome left the note, but now I'm positive it was Gage.

I try to hit him, slap him for all of the shit that's been happening because it was him. I went on a date with the guy who had me drugged.

Oh my gosh, if Rome hadn't shown up, I could quite literally have been a victim then. Like I am about to be now.

I try to wiggle free, using all of my strength to pull myself out from under him. Maybe I could run. I know those woods. If I could just run fast enough then get to a road.

"Bitch," he yells as I attempt to knee him in the balls.

His hand comes down in a hard slap, knocking my face to the side while I lie there in stunned silence. Before I can even move, Gage reaches into his pocket and pulls something out. Tears burn my eyes as I try to fight, but it's no use. A sharp pain slices through my upper arm, and then everything fades to black.

CHAPTER 30
ROME

"Damn," Aiden drawls from the bench in the locker room. It's halftime and we're getting our fucking asses kicked, so everyone's in a pissy mood. When Aiden passes me his phone, I realize he's not going off about the game. "Is that Elodie?" he asks while I watch the video play on his SnapTok account.

Squeezing the phone in the palm of my hand, my wide eyes move around and I notice the whole team whispering and laughing.

How the hell did this happen? I'm the only one who had this fucking video. I deleted it from Abby's phone.

"Fuck, man." Luke comes up beside me "That's at Newton's party. She looks as shit-faced as I was."

I grab Luke's phone, now holding his and Aiden's. "Who else is watching it?" I step out in the open, eyes darting from one person to the next. "Who else?" I scream as I slam both phones down on the bench, baring my teeth. "If I see any one of you watching or talking about that damn video, I'll beat all your asses."

I storm out of the locker room, heading back to the Bulldog field. On my way, I try to call Elodie. It doesn't even ring before going to voicemail, so I try texting her.

Me: Please call me ASAP. It wasn't me. I swear I wouldn't do that to you. I never planned to share that video. It was Abby. She did this.

Going straight to where the cheerleaders are huddled, I keep my eyes on one in particular.

Pushing my way through the crowd, I stare straight ahead as I grab Abby by the arm and walk her with me as I go around the visitors' bleachers.

"Geez, Rome." she cackles. "If you wanted to get me alone, all you had to do was ask."

"Shut the fuck up," I snarl, spit flying from my mouth as I squeeze her arm so damn tight, I'm surprised she isn't screaming in pain.

I sense some resistance, but Abby knows better than to defy me.

Once we're out of eyesight, I jerk her close, seething. "Did you share the video?"

Abby swallows hard, an expression of worry on her face. "She deserved it, Rome. Look at how she was acting. She's not the good girl she pretends to be."

My fingers dig into her skin as my heart begins to break. There is no way Elodie is going to believe I had nothing to do with this. "Who gave you the fucking right!?"

She scoffs. "I don't need permission, Rome. I'm a big girl." I let go of her and she crosses her arms tightly over her uniform top.

"You drugged her, didn't you?" I point my finger to her chest, pushing hard as she winces. "You got petty and jealous and you drugged her."

Her eyes pop wide open. "What?"

"It was you, wasn't it?" I keep my eyes focused on hers and she gives me exactly what I expected.

She tries to laugh it off, but if I've learned one thing about

Abby, it's that she laughs when she's nervous. "Why would I drug your stepsister?"

"You tell me." I cage her in between the bleachers, fear shining in her eyes.

She goes to walk around me, but I snare her arm. This time I squeeze so tight my knuckles turn white. "Admit it was you or I'm going straight to the cops. How will your father feel once he learns what you've done?"

Tears well in the corners of Abby's eyes. The girl is a fucking bitch, but she's usually a fairly decent human being. What she did is really bad, even for her.

Blinking away the tears, she looks down at the space between us. "I did it for us."

"Us?" I huff. "There is no *us.*" *When will she get it?*

"Not now." She lifts her head. "Not since she moved to town. Come on, Rome. I've seen the way you look at her. She might be your new stepsister, but you caught feelings for her, didn't you?"

"That's none of your damn business." She pulls her arm free as a tear falls.

"It is, though. Because I love you. I love you so much, Rome." She runs her hand down my arm. "I want us to be together."

I really pity this girl. I've told her a thousand times I am not interested. Even when we hooked up last summer, I was very clear that this was not a relationship and that I had no feelings for her.

"And you thought drugging Elodie," I raise my phone in my hand and shout, "and recording a stupid fucking video would bring us together?" She flinches.

"I didn't do it so I could record the video. That was just a bonus." She tries to rub my arm again, but I slap her hand away. "I did it to get her away from you. But their plan failed when you stepped in and rescued her. Just like you always do."

"Who?" I snap. Things are starting to make more sense. This behavior isn't like Abby, so my guess is someone manipulated her. But who would want to drug Elodie to get her away from me?

Abby covers her mouth, shaking her head like she's been caught.

"You said *their* plan failed. Whose plan?" I shake her body back and forth, yelling, "Whose fucking plan?"

She licks a tear off her lips and frowns before saying, "Gage and his cousin, Winton."

I let go of her, gripping the sides of my head as I try to figure out what the fuck is going on. *Gage and Winton are fucking cousins?*

That's why he was so invested in Elodie. He never wanted her. He's working with Winton fucking Brooks to hurt her the same way I planned to.

I ball my fists, the veins in my arms ready to jump out of my skin. Then I'm right back in her face. "You helped the asshole who got me arrested?"

She sobs harder as she tries to grab my hand, but I jerk away. "I just want us to be together, Rome."

I scream in her face. "We're never going to be together, Abby."

The waterworks just keep coming as she continues trying to reach for me, failing every time.

I shake my head, ignoring her outburst. "Tell me everything. Every sordid fucking detail. I want to hear it all, or so help me God, Abby. I will go straight to the cops and tell them everything."

When she stands there, allowing time to pass while picking at her nail polish, I snap, "Fuck this. I'll just call them now." As I swipe the screen on my phone, she grabs my wrist.

"Wait. I'll tell you everything."

I stick my phone back in my pocket, leaving my hand in there. "Let's hear it. Now!"

"Gage approached me a couple days after Elodie moved here. He said he had reason to believe Elodie had a thing for you. He manipulated me into thinking you were falling for her, too. I told him that was crazy because…well, she's Elodie." She chuckles. "I mean, come on now."

I roll my hand in the air. "Get on with the fucking story, Abby."

"Anyways, he asked if I wanted to work with him and his cousin to get Elodie to leave town. At that time, I had no idea Winton was his cousin. In fact, I didn't know until I found the video in my trash and saw them talking."

"Goddammit," I blurt out. "I didn't delete the video from your trash folder. Of fucking course." I slap myself on the head because this one's on me.

"I was actually surprised myself. But when I opened it up, there it was. So, after that, I asked Gage what his connection to Winton was, because I saw them talking. That's when he told me Winton was the one who wanted Elodie to go down because she's the one you saved the night you got arrested." The stupid bitch reaches for me again and it takes every ounce of willpower I have not to slap her across the face. "Why didn't you tell me that, Rome? I thought we told each other everything."

She's delusional. She doesn't know a damn thing about me, and everything she does know, she heard through the grapevine.

"So you slipped something in her drink, but you said you didn't plan to record the video and that it was a bonus. What was the original plan after the drugs took effect?"

The announcer comes through the speakers as the third quarter begins. It grabs Abby's attention and she looks at the scoreboard. "Can we finish this later? I need to get back to my squad."

She tries to leave, but I grab her shoulder, pushing her back. "Hell no, we're not finishing it later. Just hurry your ass up and tell me. Why did Gage and Winton want you to drug Elodie?"

"Okay. Here's the thing. I did it for you, Rome. But Gage did it because Winton promised him he could have Elodie when he was done with her."

"Done what?" I stammer out each word.

"I don't know. I guess Gage was going to take her from the party and bring her to Winton. They never told me why and I really didn't ask because that's their business." She steps closer to me and puts her hands on my shoulders. "I just want you, babe."

Okay, delusional and stupid. No blow job could have ever been worth this mess.

Shoving her hands down, I pull my phone back to call Brady. "Get your ass back to your squad. And stay the fuck away from me. For good."

"Rome!" She stomps her tennis shoe to the ground. "Don't do this."

I jab a finger in the air with my phone to my ear. "Go!"

Pouting, she just stands there, and I'm given no choice but to let her listen when Brady picks up.

"Hey, man," I say into the phone. "Is Elodie here with you and Julia? She's not answering my calls."

"No. She wasn't home when we went to pick her up. Her little sister said she was going to stay with a friend of hers in Bakersfield. I tried to call her but got her voicemail."

"Fuck!" I stomp my foot to the ground. "I need a ride home. Right now."

"But the game…"

There has been a nagging feeling in my mind saying something was wrong and I need to see her, and now that I know I was right, I no longer give a shit about this fucking game.

"Screw the game! Meet me at the entrance now."

I end the call and grab Abby by the shoulders aggressively. "If there is anything you're not telling me, Abby, you better tell me now."

Abby chuckles, another telltale sign that she's nervous. "What more is there to tell?"

"For your sake, you better hope there's nothing more. This is your last chance and if you miss one bit of information, I'll make sure you're arrested for drugging Elodie."

When she doesn't say anything, I give her a gentle push back and head toward the gate behind the bleachers.

"Rome, wait," Abby says with no enthusiasm in her tone. I turn around, and for the first time, I see sincerity in her eyes. "Gage skipped the game and he's supposed to meet up with her tonight while you're distracted. He's taking her to Winton at the old jail on I-96."

I don't even lash out or say another word as I run like hell, jumping over the gate and heading straight for the entrance to meet Brady. I know what Winton plans to do, even if Abby wants to pretend to be clueless.

I just hope we're not too late.

CHAPTER 31
ELODIE

Where am I?

My eyes flutter open and panic settles in. I can tell I'm in a chair, and when I wiggle my arms, I notice they are trapped behind me, bound tightly. Part of my body feels numb, like everything isn't online.

It's so dark—pitch black, and I can't see a thing.

How did I get here?

The last thing I remember is Gage. We were talking and then…fuck, those eyes. My legs start to regain feeling just as I remember him pulling me out of my car. He must have knocked me out and brought me here.

I frantically tug and pull, trying to break free, but this rope is tied so damn tight, it's cutting into my wrists.

"Help!" I shout at the top of my lungs. My throat feels dry as the words scratch their way out. "Someone, help me!"

A door opens and I expect to see Gage, but when the light comes on, I quickly realize it's not. I jolt, pinning my back to the chair as Winton takes slow strides toward me in what appears to be an old jail cell.

"So, we meet again, Elodie." His smirk sends shivers down my spine.

I open my mouth to speak, but everything gets caught in my throat as he gets closer and closer.

"Ya know, when I learned your name, it made me smile. You look like an Elodie. All innocent and pure." He crouches down in front of me and I notice the scar that runs from the middle of his forehead into his hairline. "But you're not innocent, are you?"

"Get away from me!" I hiss as I try to stretch my legs out to kick him, but those are also tied to the chair.

"That's what you said that night." He chuckles, as if this is all some game. "You told me to get away from you. But what did I say in response?"

The way he cocks his head to the side, searching for a response from me is unnerving. I swear my insides tremble from just that one look.

I don't answer him because I'm not wasting my breath on this deranged asshole.

"I told you, you weren't going anywhere until I got an apology. An apology you never gave. So now you owe me two." He holds up a finger. "One for being a nosey little bitch and coming into *my* park." He adds another finger. "Another for what your pussy-ass stepbrother did to me."

He stands, his posture rigid as he balls his hands into fists. "Did you know I was in the hospital for two weeks and I can never play ball again because of that fucker?"

"I...I didn't sic Rome on you." My chest heaves as I struggle to breathe. "I didn't even know who he was then."

"I don't fucking care!" Winton screams, rattling my bones. "It was all your fault! Everything that happened this past year was because of you!" He jabs a finger into my chest. "And now you're gonna pay for your sins."

I wish I had a dime for every time I heard that all of this was my fault. I'd be able to pay for Stanford all on my own. It was not my fault Winton had the urge to sexually assault me. It was not my fault Rome came to save me. And everything from then on out was sure as fuck not my fault, and I am done letting anyone make me feel like it is.

"It was you this whole time, wasn't it?" I cry out. "You drugged me. You left the notes, put the pipe in my car, and killed that poor rabbit?" I jerk on my hands. "But you couldn't have been at the library, could you?"

"Of course it was me, with help from a couple friends, of course." He looks over his shoulder as if someone else is here too. "One person can't be in two places at once."

Gage. Gage is the one who was at the library while Winton was at Big John's Pizza. He said friends, so that must mean there is someone else, but I can't even begin to guess who. It has to be either Damon or Miles, the two guys from my first night in Willow Creek last year.

How did I not see any of this? How could I be so naive? To think I went on a date with Gage. I trusted him. I even defended him to Rome.

"I never wanted anyone to get hurt that night. If you would have just let me go, none of this would have happened." I refuse to be weak in front of this man, even if I know it will cost me something great. I have no doubt Winton wants to kill me, so I might as well go down swinging.

"It doesn't matter if you meant it or not, it happened. You hurt a lot of fucking people that night, and you're still hurting them now." He ignores the part he played completely, making my nerves burn in anger.

"But you're healed…"

"I can't play football anymore!" His voice rises so loud, it echoes in my ears even after the words have been said. "Now you went and gave a statement and your bitch of a mom is getting the case overturned so Rome gets off scot-free!" Spit flies out of his mouth and I turn my head, pinching my eyes shut. "He still gets to play after what he did to me!"

Maybe if I just keep my eyes closed, he'll go away. Maybe I'll wake up from this nightmare and it won't be my reality. Maybe I can go back to that night and change the path I took so that none of this ever happens.

I squeeze them shut so hard, wishing with all of my might that I could just get a do-over. A reset. Anything. But it never comes.

"Look at me," he screeches, grabbing me by the throat until I'm forced to open my eyes and give him what he wants.

Ironically, my vision blurs as hot tears stream down my face, fear coursing through my veins.

Winton grins ominously, making me shiver in terror. At this point, he could do whatever he wants to me and no one would know. No one is coming to save me this time.

Chest heaving, I stare into his menacing eyes, feeling like I'd rather he squeeze the life out of me than face what he has planned.

"Do it," I choke out. "Kill me."

"Kill you?" He laughs grimly. "Now, why would I do that? I need you alive so I can fuck those apologies out of you. After that, I promised you to my cousin."

I swallow hard against his palm as he lowers the back of the chair to the floor, with me attached to it. Winton steps his feet out on either side of me, then lets go of my throat and straightens his back as I stare straight up at him.

"After we are done with you, you'll be begging for death."

He grips the button of his jeans and pops it open before dragging his zipper down. The sound is deafening. My fate has been sealed.

"Why are you doing this?" I ask as tears spring free. "Do you want me to recant my statement, have it erased?"

Winton tilts his head down, pointing to his scar. "Do you see this? This cannot be erased. The scars inside me cannot be erased. I can't play ball, I'm addicted to the pain meds I started when this shit happened, and now I am stuck selling everything I own to get more of them. I can't even walk a straight line because my coordination has been fucked. My life is hell all because you stumbled into that goddamn park."

If he were able to rationalize, he would realize that me stumbling into that park had nothing to do with what happened. It was his actions that caused this. It was Rome's actions that brought on his problems. I can't control what these guys do. I didn't do this, and I'll be damned if I'm going to keep being punished for it.

Winton pushes his pants down and I use the opportunity while they're around his ankles to jerk to the left, catching him off-balance. He stumbles to his knees, cursing and growling.

"You fucking bitch!"

He can call me all the names he wants, but he shouldn't have given this bitch the ammo she needed to take him down. *Fucking idiot.*

I keep rolling, trying to bide my time as I scream, "Help! Someone, help me!"

Winton gets back on his feet as I squirm and wiggle, desperately trying to break free. The coarse fibers of the rope cut into my skin, but the pain is nothing compared to what I know I'm about to feel.

Standing over me, he clicks his tongue on the roof of his mouth. "You've been a very bad girl, Elodie." He reaches down and flips the chair back over until I'm face up again.

Winton pulls a knife out of his back pocket, flicking it open and causing me to freeze. He leans forward, dragging it down my cheek before getting to my shirt. I don't even breathe as he cuts the fabric open, shredding any hope I had left in my veins.

My breaths come in short pants, and I know I'm hyperventilating. Maybe if I can force myself to pass out, it will give me more time to come up with a plan. Either way, I don't think I want to be awake for what's next.

He crouches down with his dick only inches from my face, my torn clothing hanging from me as everything is exposed to him.

Reaching out, he pinches my cheeks, forcing my mouth open on a gasp. "I want that apology around my cock."

A sudden knock at the door sends my heart into my throat while an ounce of hope returns.

Winton grinds his teeth and the thick vein in his neck pulsates noticeably. "What the fuck do you want?"

"We've got a problem, cuz." It's Gage's voice coming from the other side of the door. "I need you out here."

On his feet again, Winton pulls up his pants and heads to the door, stopping to flash me a devious smirk. "This isn't over."

Once he's out, I exhale a heavy sigh of relief, knowing I have a little more time to try and break free.

Using one of the spindles on the chair for friction, I glide my hands up and down, feeling the bones in my hand gyrate against the wooden chair.

I keep going, ignoring the pain but feeling hopeless when the rope doesn't loosen at all. Winton could come back any minute and force himself on me and there will be nothing I can do to stop him. Pushing the thoughts aside, I don't give up. I have to at least try.

I pull and tug until I feel blood dripping down my hand and my shoulder starts to feel like it might snap out of the socket.

The sound of voices on the other side of the door hits my ears and I work faster, ignoring the excruciating pain shooting down my arm. With any luck, the rope will snag on a piece of the wood and it will rip the fibers one by one.

When the door opens again, my stomach drops, and I start to hyperventilate again. That is, until I see who enters.

"Brady!" I cry out. "Brady!" I'm a blubbering mess as he hurries to where I'm tied to the chair and pulls it up.

"Jesus, Elodie. What the hell did he do to you?" He grabs my shirt and pulls it together to help cover me.

I'm too shaken up to speak, so I just cry while he pulls out a knife and works tirelessly to free me from this chair.

"You're safe now," he assures me. "The cops are on their way."

"G-Gage and Winton," I manage to choke out so he knows who is behind this before they manage to get away.

"We know." He places a calm hand on my arm. "Rome is handling them until the cops get here. Abby will be dealt with too."

I cry harder knowing Rome is here. He came to my rescue, once again. I don't know what Abby has to do with any of this, but once my head isn't spinning, I intend to find out.

As soon as my hands are freed, Brady moves to my ankles while I hold my shirt together and inspect the bleeding cuts around my wrists. Pieces of the rope seem to be clinging to my flesh and I have to hold back from vomiting as I try to get one loose.

The adrenaline starts to fade quickly. I keep still as he cuts through the thick rope, and a minute later, he's lifting me to my feet. My legs tremble, hardly able to hold me up.

I stumble and I'm not sure if it's because I'm in shock, or if it's from whatever Gage used to knock me out. My arms still shoot with pain from all of the jerking and twisting.

Brady steadies me with an arm around my waist as he leads me out the door of, what I can now clearly see, *is* an old jail cell.

A startled breath leaves me as I see Winton swing at Rome, just as we round the corner. I want to run to him, but Brady holds me back.

Rome dodges the hit easily and Winton stumbles. Gage tries to jump Rome from behind, but I scream to warn him.

Rome turns and pulls a gun out from his waistband, aiming it right at Gage's chest, and I gasp. Gage immediately holds his hands up in surrender. A choked sob escapes me as Winton and Gage keep their hands in the air and I run to Rome as fast as I can. One of my legs still feels numb and the other is sore from the position it was tied in, but I ignore that as Brady assists me.

"Elodie." Rome visibly relaxes. "Thank God you're okay!"

Now that Gage and Winton can't hurt us, I fall apart the second his arms are around me.

Rome holds me closely, stroking the back of my head. "I didn't do it, Freckles. I didn't send the video. I swear—"

"I know." I cry into his shoulder. "I'm sorry I doubted you."

"I'm so fucking sorry I didn't see this coming. I'm sorry I didn't get to you in time." He takes a step back, looking me up and down. "Did they hurt you? I swear, Elodie. If they laid a finger on you." He raises the gun in his hand, but I lower it slowly to his side, even though it hurts like a bitch to move my arms like that.

"They didn't hurt me," I assure him, knowing he isn't talking about the pain from being tied up. "Because you *did* get to me in time. You saved me. Just like you always do."

Brady comes up and gently takes the gun from Rome. "I've got them. You just take care of Elodie."

I glance over Rome's shoulder to see Brady getting tough, and I can't help the laugh that slips out of me. "Not so big and bad now, are we, boys." He throws his hands in the air. "Let's fucking go. Tell me to do your homework one more fucking time. I dare you."

Rome notices my shirt and pulls it together tightly, making me feel safe again. Then he shakes his head. "Brady's having too much fun with this."

I smile, even as the trail of tears continues. "Way too much fun."

"Let him have his moment." He cups my cheeks in his hand. "Because I need to do this."

His lips press to mine. It's soft and comforting and everything I never knew I wanted. I feel protected and adored as the pieces of my heart slowly come back together.

The sound of sirens has us stepping out of the kiss. Relief floods through me.

"Are you ready to do this?" Rome asks, his fingers grazing over the tearstains on my cheeks.

I take a deep breath and grab his hand. "With you by my side, yes."

Rome instructs Brady to keep Winton and Gage there while we go out and tell the cops where to find them.

After I give a quick rundown of what happened to the cops, Rome heads back in with two officers while I'm checked out by paramedics.

They advise me to go to the hospital overnight, but I don't want to be separated from Rome. Besides, we both still have to tell our parents what happened and I don't want to do that in a hospital room.

They bandage me up, and a few minutes later, Rome and Brady come back out.

An officer gathers us all together. "We're going to need all three of you to come down to headquarters to give official statements of what took place tonight."

I nod, feeling immense gratitude that this is almost over.

The officer heads back toward the jail where Gage and Winton are being cuffed inside, but Rome stops him. "One more thing," he hollers "There's another person who played a huge part in all this—Abby Bower."

My jaw nearly hits the floor. "Abby?"

Rome looks at me, nodding. "She's the one who drugged you at the party and also the one who told me I'd find you here tonight."

The officer radios something in before instructing us to mention that when we give our report, and he lets us know they'll get her in for questioning.

After all the noise has settled, and it's just us three left, I take a step back and look at the jailhouse in front of us. It's not a modern-day jail. Just a flat brick building about the size of a large house. But it's timeless and I find myself wondering what the walls inside would say if they could speak. Fortunately they can't, because I want the memories of what happened there tonight to stay locked inside forever.

With my fingers laced through Rome's, we make our way to Brady's car. The dirt beneath my feet crumbles with each step and in a way, it's symbolic. I'm leaving the past behind me where it belongs and heading toward a bright future. I make a silent vow to walk, not run. To no longer worry about what other people think because their opinions of me don't matter. And if they don't want to stand by my side, they can walk behind me.

CHAPTER 32

ROME

THESE LAST FEW days have been a fucking whirlwind. Giving statements, bandaging new wounds, and reopening old ones to start the process of healing. Now we're about to lay it all out there for our parents. The good, the bad, and the ugly.

The only thing that has been consistent and unwavering during this time are my feelings for Elodie. If anything, they've multiplied times ten.

"Thanks for taking the time to meet with us," Dad says as he unbuttons his suit jacket and sits down on the living room sofa. *Always so professional.*

Celia steps behind him and puts her hands on his shoulders, the look on her face is hard to read. I can't tell if it's good news or bad news. This could be about the case, or mine and Elodie's budding relationship. Either way, I'm on the edge of my fucking seat.

At least Elodie is here beside me. We're about an inch apart sitting on the couch diagonal to Dad and Celia. We decided together that it's best to keep the affection to a minimum when we're around our families, just so we don't make things awkward. At least, for now.

"Well," Elodie says impatiently. "What's the news?"

Grant looks up at Celia, grinning. "News? Do we have news, honey?"

Finally, a smile grows on Celia's face. "We do have news. Great news, in fact."

I scoot forward on the couch, clutching my hands together. Sweat pools in my palms as I anxiously wait for her to spit out this *great news*.

Celia and Dad share a look of adoration, making us wait even longer.

"For the love of God, Mom!" Elodie blurts out with a chuckle. "Will you just spit it out?"

"I suppose." Her tone shifts to one more professional and it has me wondering if this is how she speaks in the courtroom. "After reviewing the corroborating evidence with the defense attorney, I requested to file a motion for a new trial."

I take a deep breath, nodding as she speaks. "A new trial," I say. "This is good. It's fine. With the new evidence, we can win this, right?"

Celia's smile grows broader. "Actually, there won't be a new trial. As the district attorney, I decided not to pursue the charges in the interest of justice. Therefore, the case has been overturned."

My fingers curl around Elodie's leg, my grip tight with anticipation while she looks like she's ready to jump to her feet. "What's that mean?"

"That means the charges have been dropped," Celia says. Elodie and I both spring up and I throw my arms around her, lifting her in the air. "Effective immediately, you're no longer on probation. I'll just need you to come down to the courthouse to sign some documents, then it's over."

"Holy shit," I mumble to Elodie. "I can't believe you did this for me."

I set her down, gazing into her eyes, not caring that our parents are watching. "All I did was tell the truth. You saved me, Rome. You never should have been punished in the first place."

She leans closer, her breath a whisper in my ear. "Does that mean you no longer own me and I'm off the hook?"

"You put up a good fight, Freckles. But now that I've caught you…" I pull her closer as I whisper in her ear, "I don't think I'm ever letting go."

Dad clears his throat and Elodie and I take a step back from one another. "There are still a few things we need to discuss, kids."

Elodie bites her lip nervously because we both know what this is about. When our parents met us at the police station a couple days ago, after Elodie was kidnapped by Gage and Winton, they saw us together—the way I held and comforted Elodie, and the way she responded to me. They didn't ask questions then, but we knew they were coming.

"So," Dad says with a serious tone as he waves his hands between me and Elodie. "What is this? Did you two just get caught up in the moment for a little while, or is it something more?"

Elodie and I talked a little bit about what's happening between us and the consensus was, we've both fallen for each other. She said she doesn't want to be with anyone else, and obviously, I feel the same. Every inch of my soul is consumed by this girl. My heart feels complete and without her, I have no doubt I'd go back to being the heartless monster I used to be. She makes me want to be a better person, and I make her put down the books for a while. We fit, and that's all that matters.

I put an arm around her waist and pull her side to mine. "It's the real deal," I tell them point-blankly.

Elodie wraps an arm around me and rests her head against my chest, grinning from ear to ear. "I know it's not conventional, but I love him, Mom."

Surprised by her words, I look down at her with wide eyes. She's never told me she loves me before. But I've been dying to tell her. With no thought behind it, but meaning every word, I say, "I love you, too, Freckles." My forehead touches hers as I breathe her in, feeling the words deep in my soul.

My legs are literally shaking and I can feel Elodie tremble, too. Bracing myself, I look at my dad because he's one stubborn son of a bitch. There's a good chance he's going to tell us we need to end this relationship now. In which case, I'll tell him to fuck off, he'll kick me out, and I'll get my own place. I'm getting a little ahead of myself, but I'd do it if it comes to that.

"In that case," Dad says. "We need to set some ground rules."

Celia nods in response. "I agree. If you two are going to be dating, there has to be rules in place."

My shoulders relax and I exhale a sigh of relief, fighting hard to erase the smile on my face so they know I'm taking this seriously, but I can't help it. I haven't stopped smiling for days and I don't plan to anytime soon.

Dad continues, "No sneaking into each other's bedrooms at night."

"Absolutely not." Celia shakes her head. "And no late nights in the basement together."

"Be mindful of Sayer and Lake," Dad says. "They're young teens. You both need to be good role models for them."

Elodie and I nod along, giving a few *okays* and *you got its* as they keep going with the list of rules.

"If something happens and you two end this relationship, we're still a family, first and foremost." Celia puts an arm around my dad, and for the first time, I can see it—the sheer happiness on my dad's face. The zest for life that was missing for so long has finally returned.

Dad peers up at Celia, a sparkle in his eye. "And family is everything."

"I agree," Elodie says. "Now, if we can just get this all in writing later, I have some news to share as well."

I crane my neck, narrowing my eyes. "You do?" Elodie never

told me about any news. It seems she's been holding out on me. "What is it?"

Reaching into the back pocket of her jeans, she pulls out a folded envelope. "I got this a while ago." She passes the note to her mom. "Along with a few other acceptance letters. But this is the one. This is where I want to go."

Celia cocks a brow, smiling as she unfolds the envelope and pulls out the paper inside. "Stanford?" she gushes as she hurries to her daughter. "You got into Stanford?" She throws her arms around her. "I'm so happy for you, honey. I had no doubt you'd get in."

I step back, allowing them to have their moment. After the video of Elodie went viral, she wanted to issue a cease and desist to every person who shared it. However, since the majority were students at Willow Creek High, I told her I'd handle it and I sent them all a personal message telling them if they didn't take the fucking video down, I'd make their lives hell. Needless to say, the video stopped surfacing and people stopped talking. Instead, we've given them something else to talk about—us.

For the most part, people have been accepting, but there are a few naysayers I've had to put in their place. It really doesn't bother either of us, though. So what if our parents are married and we live together? If anything, it's just easy access and convenient. We also don't have to deal with the awkwardness of meeting each other's parents—aside from Elodie's dad, which has me nervous as fuck.

In the end, we're happy, and if that's not enough for everyone, then I suggest they fuck off.

CHAPTER 33

ELODIE

THE STADIUM LIGHTS GLARE DOWN, illuminating the turf and giving us those good ol' Friday night football vibes. There's a sea of teal and black in the stands while everyone waits anxiously to cheer on the Willow Creek Misfits.

Standing beside the bleachers, I wait impatiently for my guy to run out with his team so he can play in his first game this season. To say I'm excited for him is an understatement. Rome has done all the work, and then some. His grades are up, he's doing well at practice, and he's mending friendships that were on the verge of breaking.

Apparently Luke gave him some shit, but in the end, he told Rome it was all because he was trying to get him to admit his feelings for me. We can't fault him for that. I'm still not his biggest fan, but I tolerate him for Rome.

Rome and Brady have actually become good friends, too, since Brady assisted him in rescuing me. Last night I told Rome he needs to stop blackmailing Brady with whatever he's holding over his head, and Rome agreed that he's officially off the hook, too.

I still don't know what he has on him, and I don't need to. That's Brady's business and no one else should be involved, including Rome. He did say it was some juicy shit that would wreak havoc if it got out. Sure, I'm curious, but when, and if, the time is right and Brady wants to tell me, I'll be all ears.

The guys come out of the gym doors roaring as they hustle to the field. "Go, Misfits!" I rave with my hands in the air.

Rome passes by, flashing a wink as he keeps running with his team.

They tear through the banner the cheerleaders are holding and the crowd goes wild. One cheerleader in particular is missing, and I can't say I'm sad about it. Abby was kicked off the team and is currently out on bail pending her sentencing. I'm sure she'll just get a slap on the wrist, but as long as she stays far away from me, I'm okay with that.

Winton and Gage are also out, but according to my mom, they're looking at jail time—which they both deserve.

When it all comes down to it, no court sentence will ever be enough in my eyes. The emotional scars I've gained over the last year because of Winton will likely last me a lifetime. I jump at random sounds, sleep with my closet light on, and I still get nervous walking through the book aisles at the library. The only thing that has kept me sane through all of this is Rome.

The players huddle together and the scoreboard flickers to life. Wilder is back to his former position now that Rome has returned as quarterback. Rome was worried his brother would be disappointed and it would cause a rift between them, but Wilder assured him he was excited to take on his position as running back. He said there's nothing quite like scoring that winning touchdown that was passed to you by your own brother.

I'm just anxious to watch them both play together for the first time. From what I've heard, they're the dream duo on the field.

Julia walks toward me, her hand in the air. "Hey, girl." She's bundled in what appears to be multiple layers with a stocking cap on her head.

It's the coldest night so far this season, so I'm also decked out in a down winter coat and a pair of mittens. No need to sport that Misfits apparel when it's going to be hidden anyway. Although, I did finally get myself my own hoodie to wear in the future and Rome may or may not have gotten me a jersey with his number on it.

"Where's Brady?" I ask her, my eyes dancing around the accumulating crowd.

"I don't know. He said he had to do some work with his dad's campaign manager after school and he'd meet me by the concession stand, but he wasn't there." She shrugs and I glance back toward the stand.

"Should we go find a spot to sit in the student section, or wait for him?"

Julia glances at her phone in her hand, then says, "He's not coming. Said they'll likely be working on this non-profit thing late into the night."

"That's a bummer," I say as we climb the bleacher stairs to the student section. Each step has the roar of the crowd growing louder. It's crowded as hell as we make our way through the tightly pressed bodies. We find a clearing beside Jenna and slide in, and Julia wastes no time partaking in the antics of jumping up and down and shouting along with everyone else.

"Good evening, Misfits fans." The announcer's voice booms through the speakers. "Who's ready for some Friday night football?"

The crowd goes wild, and I step out of my comfort zone and join in. "Go, Misfits!" I shout at the top of my lungs.

"It's my honor to announce that Misfits' quarterback, Rome Cromwell, is back on the field. He's coming in hot and ready to carry the team to the big W."

Everyone goes wild, including me, as the bleachers vibrate beneath my feet.

"If I can draw everyone's attention to our American flag, sophomore Macie Gray will be singing our national anthem."

I place my hand over my heart, watching the flag sway in the wind under the lights as the chorus begins. Once she's finished, the chatter and cheering resume, and the game begins.

The clock ticks away and the first quarter comes to an end, and while the Misfits brought their A game, neither team scored.

Then, just before the timer runs out during the second quarter, the Jets break through the defense and score a touchdown.

Defeated voices rumble through Misfits fans, a feeling of helplessness as halftime rolls around. But the game isn't over yet.

By the end of the third, we're tied 7-7.

"Come on, Misfits. You've got this," I howl through the noisy bleachers.

As we near the final seconds of the fourth, I'm getting really nervous, right along with everyone else. With my hands on my cheeks, I watch intently, my sole focus on the field.

With my eyes trained on the field, I listen to the announcer. "Quarterback Rome Cromwell pitches a snap to his brother, Wilder Cromwell. It's good to see these boys on the field together again.

"It's a sweep to the left...hold up, Rome is streaking down the sideline." The announcer continues, "Wilder stops, he's gonna pass it back to his brother. Rome is wide open."

"What's he doing?" Julia asks, and I shrug because I have no idea. I don't know much about football, but it looks like Wilder is going to throw the ball to Rome.

A gasp comes through the speaker. "The ball's in the air. He's under it, there's no one in front of him. He's going. He's gonna make it all the way."

Everyone grows quiet as we stand on pins and needles, watching nervously as Rome runs with the ball.

Six seconds left on the clock. Come on, Rome. You've got this, baby.

I grab Julia's arm, squeezing as Rome dodges a couple Jets players. "He's in!" I shout victoriously. "He's in!"

"Touchdown, Misfits! By none other than Rome Cromwell.

And the dream duo does it again. Those Cromwell boys are unstoppable. Misfits win the game!" The clock runs out and everyone loses their minds, me included. Wilder and Rome embrace each other and I melt watching them.

I can't help myself as I run to the sideline to meet Rome. His eyes find me immediately and we eat up the space between us. The second I'm in his arms, he twirls me around. "I'm so proud of you, Rome!"

"You know what this means?" He sets me down on my feet, his hands cemented to my waist. "You can't miss a single game at this point. You're my new good luck charm."

I laugh, wrapping my arms around his neck. "I wouldn't miss any of your games for the world."

Everyone leaves the field, and Wilder passes by us. "Hey, Wilder," I holler as Rome sets me back on my feet. "Good job out there."

He tips his chin. "Thanks, El." I watch as he walks away, meeting someone by the bleachers.

"Is that Ms. Jenkins?" I ask Rome, and he shoots a look over his shoulder.

"Oh yeah," he quips. "She's been helping Wilder with his 'Future Business Leaders of America' essay. He must be thanking her."

"That's nice of her." I kiss Rome on the lips, and suddenly it's just us out here tonight. Even as people pass us by and pat Rome on the back, all we see is each other. "Go celebrate your victory with the guys in the locker room. I'll meet you at your car when you're done."

"All right, baby. It won't take long." He kisses me again, then slips away. My body immediately notices his absence and I shiver.

Last year a heartless monster stepped out of the dark and rescued me.

Now, he forever has my heart in the palm of his hand.

EPILOGUE

ELODIE

"Mmm. Everything looks delicious, Mom." I pull out my chair beside Rome at the dining room table, a smorgasbord of food on display in front of us.

"It sure does," Brogan chirps. "But this is a lot, even for you."

Lake grabs a roll and sinks her teeth into it. "What's the occasion?"

Sayer and Callan finally join us, dripping with sweat since they've been working out in the basement. "Boys," Grant snaps. "You smell like a damn locker room. Go clean yourselves up then get back down here."

The boys grumble then leave the dining room. After Mom says grace, we dig in while Sayer and Callan are still upstairs.

Once they come back and have their plates ready, Grant stands. His hands press firmly to the table and he clears his throat. "First of all, I'd like to thank my beautiful wife for this meal she's prepared for us. We all know how hard she works day in and day out, so this is much appreciated."

My mom blushes as she sweeps her hand through the air. "It was nothing, but thank you, Grant."

All I can think is that Grant is going to say something about

Rome and me, and I really do not want to live through that. The whole family knows about us, but we've been trying not to make a big deal of it. It's just a normal relationship that's happened under the least conventional circumstances.

"I've decided to run for mayor," Grant blurts out like it's no big deal, just a casual statement during dinner.

"Are you serious?" Wilder exclaims. "Dad, that's amazing."

Mom claps her hands together gleefully. "I'm so proud of you, honey. I have no doubt you'll win next year's election."

We all congratulate Grant, and Rome even gets up and gives his dad a hug.

"There's one more thing," Grant says, his tone more serious now. The corners of his mouth crinkle. "Once my candidacy is announced, we will be under the public eye. Mayor Jenkins is known to be a very competitive man, so he will dig deep to find anything he can use against me, and our family. Let's *not* give him anything to find."

"Is that Ms. Jenkins's husband?" I ask out of curiosity.

"Yeah," Wilder grumbles as he shifts in his chair, his face seemingly red. "And the guy's a fucking tool."

Grant's eyes snap to Wilder. "Watch your language, young man. But yes, the guy is…intense."

"We'll do whatever we can to help," Brogan says, speaking for all of us. "We're very excited for you, Grant."

"Thank you, Brogan. Your support means a lot."

When we finish eating, the guys clear the table while us girls work on the dishes.

As I scrub at a stubborn stain in a pan, Rome enters with a large casserole dish. Setting it down beside me, he leans in from behind and plants a soft kiss on my cheek. "Have I told you how cute you look washing those dishes?"

I smile, shaking my head. "No, you haven't, but you're welcome to."

"You look cute as fuck. In fact, you look so cute, I'm going to need to see you in my room. I've got news to share, too."

My eyes snap to his. "Good news?"

"You'll just have to wait and see." He taps my ass while no one is looking and my cheeks redden.

I chuckle. "Rules, Rome. We can't break them."

"Fuck the rules." He bites his lip and I nearly drop the damn dish, he's so fucking hot. "I need you so damn bad."

I clench my thighs at his words, washing the dishes faster just so I can escape and hide away with him. I used to be a rule follower without question, but nowadays, Rome has me questioning a lot of things about myself.

My patience gets the best of me and I'm anxious as hell to feel Rome's body against mine. Not to mention, he said he has news. While everyone is occupied, I slip out of the kitchen.

Moving quickly, I make my way to Rome's room, and without knocking, I go in.

He's on his back on the bed with his arms folded under his pillow. "Took you long enough."

I crawl up the bed, wrapping my legs around his torso as I lean into him. "Did you miss me?" My lips press to his in a soft, tantalizing kiss.

Grabbing my ass with both hands, he squeezes. "So fucking much. I missed you, and this ass." He smacks it lightly, careful not to be too loud.

"Mmm," I hum, peppering his neck with kisses. "Care to show me just how much?"

"Take these jeans off and I'd be happy to," he says as he pulls at the button.

I pull both of his wrists, planting them on either side of his waist. He bucks his hips in anticipation. My gaze meets his as he allows me to hold him down. "First, what's this news you have to share?"

Rome clicks his tongue on the roof of his mouth, testing my patience. I slap his chest playfully, deciding two can play at that game. I lift my shirt just enough for him to see the lace underneath before I let it fall back down again.

"You're such a tease," he says as his thumbs brush the skin just above my jeans.

"Out with it, dammit!" I nearly yell.

He laughs. "All right, all right. I planned to share at dinner, but when my dad made his announcement, I decided to let him have that moment. I'll tell them later."

I exhale a pent-up breath. "Tell them what?" I'm on pins and needles here waiting for Rome to just spit it out.

"Last night I got an email from UCLA."

My jaw drops open, heart racing. "And?"

"They issued an apology and wanna recruit me to play again. Said they'd like to come for a visit next week to negotiate a contract." I squeal in excitement as Rome pulls my mouth down to his. "They still want me, baby." His voice cracks with emotion and I swallow it down.

"I'm so damn happy for you, Rome." I kiss him again. "This definitely needs to be celebrated."

"Fucking right it does." He grazes my skin with his fingertips, gently lifting my shirt up and revealing my stomach. I lift my arms in compliance as he carefully removes it, exposing my lacy black bra. Stretching my arms behind me, I unclasp the back and slide it down my arms before tossing it carelessly to the floor.

Rome's hand slides up my body, making goosebumps erupt in their wake. One hand kneads my breast while the other pinches my nipple. Electricity shoots to my core as he sits forward to suck one into his mouth.

I hold his head close, not wanting him to pull away as my hips grind into his hardness. He groans as he pulls back, watching me carefully.

Dragging his fingers down my waist, my skin heats under his touch. He moves to my jeans and pops the button. I bite my lip, arching my back as he drags my zipper down.

Leaning forward, I kiss his hot mouth before flinging my legs over the side of the bed. I strip down until I'm completely naked.

"Goddamn, Freckles." He pushes down his gym shorts then fists his hard cock, stroking it as I climb back on him. "You are too sexy for your own good, baby. I might need to lock you up because all the guys are gonna want a piece of this."

I blush. "Yeah, right."

"Are you kidding me?" His eyebrows lift. "Elodie, you are fucking hot and the fact that you don't realize it makes you that much hotter." He grabs my hips and squeezes as if to make a point.

"As long as you think so." I kiss his chest, working my way down. "Then that's all that matters to me."

He grabs a fistful of my hair as I wrap my hand around his girth and suck the head of his cock into my mouth.

Swirling my tongue around his head, I sweep up a bead of precum, the salty taste awakening something inside me. My pussy pulses of its own accord, desperately wanting to be touched.

"God, Elodie." Rome's deep voice rumbles as I take him deep in my mouth.

"Shh," I hum around him as I lick him from base to head. "We don't want the future mayor to hear his son crying out his stepsister's name."

His nostrils flare, eyes hooded. Some people think the stepsiblings thing is gross, but Rome thinks it's hot as fuck, and I'm starting to feel the same.

I take his cock back in my hand, watching as I stroke him, the blue veins in his engorged cock bulging.

"Turn around, baby." I lift my head, eyes wide as he repeats himself, "Turn around and sit on my face."

He doesn't have to tell me three times.

Swinging my legs around, he gets a firm grip on my hips and guides me backward. I sit down gently, feeling the tip of his tongue circle my entrance.

A moan of pleasure slips through my lips as I wrap them back around his cock, bobbing my head up and down his length.

My hips roll against his face, seeking friction as two fingers dip inside my sopping cunt. "Ugh. Fuck, Rome." I pull him out of my mouth, stroking him with my hand as my breaths become labored.

"That feel good, baby?" he asks, his voice lustful and thick.

"So good," I whimper before taking him back between my lips.

His tongue does laps around my clit, his fingers digging deep inside me.

My back arches, fingers wrapped tightly around him as waves of pleasure radiate from my core. Gasps and moans escape my lips as I suck him feverishly.

I cry out in ecstasy, stopping my sucking motions as I come hard around his fingers. In an instant, Rome grabs my hips and lifts me up, then slithers out from underneath me.

The next thing I know, his cock is plunging relentlessly into my pussy from behind. Still at the height of my orgasm, it intensifies as he fucks me hard.

My body lunges forward and backward as his pelvis slaps against my ass. I fist the sheets, crying out into the comforter as I clench him tightly and come again.

Rome pants and moans, thrusting deep in my core. "Fuck," he growls headily, his cock swelling against the tight grip of my walls.

Driving into me with urgency, I feel the slickness of my arousal slopping his cock. His movements slow as he nears the edge of his orgasm, and I hear the heavy pants of his breath.

When he pauses inside me, pulsing in subtle movements, I bridge my back and rest my forehead on the bed.

A second later, he slips out, and I collapse just before he blankets my body with his. Warmth radiates through me.

We lie there still and quiet for a minute before Rome sweeps my hair out of my face. Leaning into me, he presses a kiss to my cheek. "I love you so damn much, Freckles."

I shift beneath him and he lifts up until I'm on my back. Then he lies back down and our mouths meet, a wave of emotions flooding through me. "I love you, too, baby."

The End.

Thank you so much for reading Heartless Monster. Another character has a book coming very soon, and I can't wait for you to read it!
Preorder Wicked Scandal Now!
http://mybook.to/wickedscandal

ALSO BY RACHEL LEIGH

Bastards of Boulder Cove

Book One: <u>Savage Games</u>

Book Two: <u>Vicious Lies</u>

Book Three: <u>Twisted Secrets</u>

Wicked Boys of BCU (Coming March 2023)

Book One: <u>We Will Reign</u>

Book Two: <u>You Will Bow</u>

Book Three: <u>They Will Fall</u>

Misfits

Heartless Monster

Wicked Scandal

Redwood Rebels Series

Book One: <u>Striker</u>

Book Two: <u>Heathen</u>

Book Three: <u>Vandal</u>

Book Four: <u>Reaper</u>

Redwood High Series

Book One: <u>Like Gravity</u>

Book Two: <u>Like You</u>

Book Three: <u>Like Hate</u>

Fallen Kingdom Duet

<u>His Hollow Heart</u> & <u>Her Broken Pieces</u>

Black Heart Duet

<u>Four</u> & <u>Five</u>

Standalones

Forget Me Not

Ruthless Rookie

Devil Heir

All The Little Things

Claim your FREE copy of Her Undoing!

ACKNOWLEDGMENTS

Thank you so much for reading Heartless Monster. I hope you enjoyed it!

A special thanks to my wonderful team for all the hard work you put into helping me create this book: My dedicated PA, Carolina Leon. All my girls for your support, friendship, and advice. My Street Team, the Rebel Readers for your help in getting the word out.

A an extra special thanks to…

My amazing alpha reader, Taylor for all your help and patience along the way! You helped shape this story into exactly what it was meant to be. Thank you to Amanda for beta reading! Your help means the world to me.

Lori Jackson for the stunning cover!

Fairest Reviews Editing Service for the beautiful edit!

Rumi Khan for proofreading and being so flexible!.

Valentine PR for spectacular PR Services.

XOXO Rachel

ABOUT THE AUTHOR

Rachel Leigh is a USA Today and International bestselling author of new adult and contemporary romances. She loves to write—and read—flawed bad-boys and strong heroines. You can expect dark elements, a dash of suspense, and a lot of steam.

Her goal is to take readers on an adventure with her words, while showing them that even on the darkest days, love conquers all.

Rachel lives in Michigan with her husband, three little monsters (who aren't so little anymore) and a couple fur babies. When she's not writing or reading, she's likely lounging in leggings, with coffee in her hand, while binge watching her favorite reality tv shows.

Join My Reader's Group: Rachel's Ramblers

facebook.com/rachelleighauthor

instagram.com/rachelleighauthor

bookbub.com/profile/rachel-leigh

goodreads.com/rachelleigh

amazon.com/author/rachelleighauthor

pinterest.com/rachelleighauthor

www.ingramcontent.com/pod-product-compliance
Lightning Source LLC
Chambersburg PA
CBHW060653190726
48289CB00002B/392